The Blue Sapphire Amulet

The Blue Sapphire Amulet

A Novel

HARALD LUTZ
BRUCKNER

The Blue Sapphire Amulet

Published by Hideaway Park Press
Green Valley, AZ

ISBN: 978-0-692-16077-0 (paperback)
ISBN: 978-0-692-16078-7 (ebook)
LCCN: 2018952423

To Ruth

Chapter 1

PERHAPS demonstrating his sadistic streak, or thinking that if he was up, everyone else should be, the postal clerk seemed to revel in the idea of waking Rachel and Otto in the early hours. It seemed as if his finger was glued to the doorbell of their dorm at Ludwig Maximilian University in Munich until Otto answered his incessant ringing.

"All right, all right," Otto shouted as he reached for the latch. "I'm not deaf!"

"Just doing my job," complained the postal clerk, as if he was the one who'd been dragged from his bed. "I have a telegram for a Rachel Adina Salm from an Ariana in Essen. There's no last name for the sender. Is this Salm person here?"

"Yes, she is," replied Otto, holding out a hand for the telegram.

"Oh, so you're fucking around with some Jewish bitch? I could report you to the authorities!" announced the clerk, suddenly full of self-importance.

Otto was speechless. He simply ripped the telegram out of the guy's hand and slammed the door in his face. A tip was the last thing on Otto's mind; his preference would have been to give the guy a fat lip. When he returned to the bedroom, Rachel knew from one quick glance at his face that he was enraged. She had heard mention of Ariana's name, and her expression was one of worry as she fastened her robe over her now huge stomach. Otto handed her the telegram from the woman who was the long-time maid living with Rachel's grandmother.

GRANDMA SALM IN FINAL STAGES OF LIFE. SHE WANTS TO SEE YOU BEFORE SHE DIES. URGE IMMEDIATE DEPAR-TURE FOR ESSEN. ARIANA.

Rachel seemed in a stupor when Otto gently touched her shoulder. Without a word, she passed him the slip of paper to read.

"Damn," he muttered before he put his arms around her, knowing how sad she was to receive the bad news. As she recovered from the initial shock, she slumped against his body.

"She can't be leaving me, Otto," she mumbled as the tears began to fall and wet his pajamas. "I don't know what I will do without her."

Her beloved grandmother was Rachel's closest and dearest family member, the one who had raised her and loved her all her life. Otto knew what losing her would mean to Rachel, and he had to take charge.

"We can get the ten o'clock train for Essen."

"But what about my finals?" she asked as she took a step back and looked up at him.

"Oh, don't worry about your finals; your profs will understand. A couple of them are Jewish and will know why you have to be with your grandmother at this time."

"Are you sure?" she asked, and Otto thought she looked like the little girl her grandmother brought up. He gently wiped her tears with his thumbs and gave her a reassuring nod.

"Just pack a couple of your more flattering maternity frocks," he told her. "Even if she's very ill, I'm sure she'll expect you to look presentable!"

Rachel managed a smile as she nodded her head, knowing that Otto read her grandmother perfectly.

"I'd better take the Varanasi silk scarf as well," she said, turning toward the closet, "because she's certain to want to know its whereabouts."

They both dressed and packed, and Otto had some breakfast. Eating was the last thing on Rachel's mind despite his urging that she needed to feed the baby. Their cab ride to the Munich station took longer than usual. The traffic was heavier than was the rule since two trucks collided at a red light. They barely made it onto the train in time. Running along the platform nine months pregnant was hard.

In contrast to the drive, the train was quiet, and they were pleased to have the compartment to themselves. The train's hiss of steam as it lurched into motion matched Rachel's deep exhalation as she fought to get her breath back. Otto stored their cheap suitcase on the rack and then encouraged Rachel to lie down. She didn't think she'd be able to sleep, but she was exhausted and lay still, breathing gently, for much of the almost four-hundred-mile journey.

Otto simply sat and stared out the window, not really seeing the passing towns and countryside as he wondered what the future might hold for him and Rachel and the baby, with pigs like the postal clerk growing in number every day. He knew there was not much he could do to fight the rising tide of hatred that was consuming the country, and it was certainly not a good time to bring a half-Jewish baby into the world.

They finally walked into the Salm house a little after eight in the evening to hear from the long-time family physician, Dr. Blumenstrauss, that Rachel's grandmother had just been heavily sedated. He gave Rachel a quick hug before he answered her question about the situation.

"I'm afraid she doesn't have long to live. The cancer has invaded all her vital organs, her brain, and her bones. You'd better stay nearby through the night. She desperately wants to talk to you. Please do so as soon as she becomes lucid. It might be your last chance to speak with her. She is in terrible pain and cannot be without heavy sedation for any length of time."

Otto finally found a chair that would be somewhat comfortable for Rachel. In her advanced stage of pregnancy, she found it difficult to sit for long stretches of time. When she was seated, Rachel reached out for her grandmother's left hand. She held it gently in her own. Rachel sensed a certain chilled dampness to the touch. Adina Daniella Salm woke at four o'clock in the morning. When she opened her eyes at last, a broad smile flashed across her face. She squeezed Rachel's hands as tears streamed down her face. Otto helped Rachel out of her chair. She wanted to bend down and put her arms around her dying grandmother, who spoke very softly. "I'm so happy to know you are here, my child. Without my glasses, I'm not sure what I'm seeing. Is that Otto standing behind you?"

"Yes, Grandma, it's Otto. Can you see my fat tummy? I'm about to deliver our first child." Rachel gently tapped her very pregnant abdomen. "Please, don't get upset; Otto and I are not married yet. We couldn't take a chance in Munich. Too many officials are Nazis. Otto didn't want to endanger me and our unborn child. He loves me very much." Grandma looked at Rachel with a questioning frown on her face. "There, there; stop your worrying, Grandma." Rachel gently patted her grandmother's hand and lovingly looked into her eyes.

Some of her grandma's old spunk momentarily found its voice. "I'm glad you found yourself a nice goy. I wish he'd waited to get you pregnant. When is he planning to marry you anyway?"

"Grandma, don't call him that. He isn't a 'goy.' He is a Christian and a gentleman, and he is planning to marry me." She kept looking at her grandmother's pain-stricken face. Rachel tried hard to appear positive in view of the devastating prognosis Doc Blumenstrauss had shared with her. "Now, what was the great hurry to see me?" Rachel feared she didn't sound convincing.

Rachel could tell by her grandmother's pained facial expression she had not succeeded in fooling the old woman. "Didn't the doctor speak to you? I have only hours to live." Grandma Adina Daniella reached up to her neck and removed the heirloom amulet she always wore. It bore a three-carat teardrop blue sapphire surrounded by small diamonds. The entire piece was set in platinum. It was worth a small fortune.

Her voice began to falter. "Rachel Adina, there is something I must tell you. You probably should have been told many years ago. You were the second of identical twins when you were born. Your sister, Juliana Daniella, was born ten minutes before you saw the light of the world. She was abducted at the hospital and never found. Your grandfather and I and the police gave up searching for her after seven years. Thus, you are my one and only granddaughter."

Rachel nearly tumbled off the chair at her grandmother's revelation. She knew she couldn't press her grandmother any further. It was evident that the old woman did not have long to live; this was obviously a deathbed confession.

Rachel's grandmother could hardly get out the words she wanted to say. "You have seen me wear this amulet for as long as you can recall. It has been in our family for generations. I was supposed to bestow it on your mother after she gave birth to you in 1913. Sadly, your mother did not survive the delivery of you two girls. I had to keep it for all these years. Since you are now the remaining and rightful heir, it is your turn to inherit this special family heirloom. Bend down, child. I can hardly move my arms."

Rachel could read the suffering on her grandmother's face. The beauty of her countenance had become a mask wracked with pain. "Come near, Rachel. I want to place the amulet on your lovely neck." Her voice was raspy. She spoke close to her granddaughter's ear. "Rachel Adina Salm, I hereby make you the keeper of the Blue Sapphire Amulet. It is yours to have until you pass it on to your own daughter. I am hoping the child you are bearing is a girl. You will give it to her when she reaches maturity. You will know exactly when to bestow that honor on her. Now, kiss me, my child. Mazel tov. Happy New Year, dearest. Go and get Otto. I must speak to him—*now!*"

Rachel grabbed Otto's arm and pushed him toward her grandmother. "You must look into her eyes. She needs to know that you are sincere. Grandma has always been my staunchest defender."

Otto took Rachel's place by her grandmother's bedside. He laid his warm hands on those of the dying woman. Her fingers felt like ice. He had never known his own parents or grandparents. He looked at her with kind eyes. "Hello, Mrs. Salm. I'm so sorry to see you in so much pain. Do you want me to summon the doctor? Do you need another injection?"

There was that flare-up of the old spirit one more time: "Never mind the doctor; never mind another injection. There are more important matters tearing my heart apart. I don't have much time. Listen to this dying woman. You are involved with my most beloved granddaughter. She is with your child. I expect you to do the honorable thing and marry her. And I mean marry her—*now!* You must promise me you will be good to my Rachel. She is a jewel." Her voice gave out. She had lost all color in her face. It had turned ghostly white.

Otto leaned down to her. He spoke softly. His eyes couldn't betray his feelings for the dying matriarch. His tears covered her pained face. "I make you my solemn promise. I will marry your granddaughter. I love her with all my heart."

Adina Daniella Salm sunk back in her down pillows. Surrounded by Rachel, Otto, and her faithful servant, Ariana, Grandma Salm took her last breath. Rachel turned her eyes in a heavenly direction and was thankful that God was kind to her grandmother. Adina Daniella Salm was spared much heartache. It was six o'clock in the morning, September 5, 1937. Rachel's grandmother did not live to celebrate Rosh Hashanah with her family. Grandma Salm was buried within twenty-four hours in the family plot at the *Parkfriedhof* (cemetery) in Essen.

At last Rachel and Otto were alone. All other mourners had left.

Rachel and Otto stood in front of the grave for a long time. Otto finally spoke up. "You were so fortunate to have your grandparents. I envy you that part of your life, especially the time you were allowed with your grandfather. We never took the chance to share some of our childhood experiences; we were always too busy with our studies. What do you remember about your grandfather?"

Rachel reached out to touch the gravestone; it was almost like she was trying to connect with the man who had loved her so dearly. "As you can see, I was twenty when my grandfather, Adam Jethro Salm, died in 1933. Thank God he didn't have to suffer the humiliations visited upon my people."

"Oh, yes! He was spared a lot of heartache, and it doesn't look like it's going to get better anytime soon. Did he ever tell you what made him pursue the business interests at which he was so successful?"

"He was born into a middle-class Jewish family in 1867. As a young man, he always admired the elegant silk dresses worn by my great-grandmother. Often, he would let me touch colorful pieces of silk in his store and tell me how much he loved the feel of silk as he grew into manhood. In 1893, he opened the Salm House of Silk in downtown Essen. The place isn't far from the Münster."

"Were you able to see the new synagogue from his office? I always thought that was such an imposing structure in the cityscape of downtown Essen."

"Yes, Otto. In the early 1900s, he watched the construction from his second-story office. *Zayde*, that's what Jewish children call their grandfathers endearingly, made it a point to remind me the new edifice opened the year I was born and only a year before World War One began."

"Did your grandfather have to serve in the army?"

"No, he was fortunate. He didn't, but the war brought an end to his extensive travels. He was often gone. His journeys frequently took him along the silk road, where he purchased many exquisite fabrics throughout the years. None were more exciting than the acquisitions he made at Mehta International in Varanasi, India. I can still envision the scenes he described, such as watching the smoke and flames rising from the funeral pyres bringing closure to the lives of hundreds of Hindus everyday and seeing the multitudes of bathers in the Ganges with the rising sun in the background. His retelling of his experiences was so vivid, I used to sit at his knee spellbound. I loved learning of his adventures and absolutely adored Zayde. When I wear this scarf, I feel like his arms are wrapped around me."

Otto held her tightly. "It looks so beautiful on you. I hope you will have it for the rest of your days. It's a strong connection to your ancestors."

"He told me years ago that the sapphire amulet came from India as well. Grandfather's great-great-grandfather brought it back from a visit to Jaipur. It's been passed down from mother to eldest daughter for all those generations. If our baby is a girl, she will receive the amulet from me in good time. You didn't hear what Grandma told me when she graced me with the jewel, did you?"

"No. She spoke so softly and directly into your ear. I was wondering what happened when I thought you were about to faint and fall off your chair."

"You're not kidding. I did come close to passing out. Grandma informed me that I'm the younger of identical twins and that my twin, Juliana Daniella, was abducted at the hospital, never to be heard from again. I still cannot believe my grandparents never shared this with me. Apparently, they and the police gave up searching for my sister after seven years. According to family rule, Juliana Daniella would have been the rightful heir to the amulet. Would she be alive, Grandma would have bestowed it on her rather than me. Because of our mother's death, Grandma held onto the amulet for all these years. It nearly broke my heart when she placed the precious jewel around my neck yesterday."

Rachel looked pensive when she finally continued to speak.

"That certainly was a shocker Grandma let loose on her deathbed. I wasn't prepared for that at all."

Otto couldn't take his eyes off Rachel; she looked so lost and forlorn. "Did you ever figure out who those people were who pulled up in that fancy black limousine just before the rabbi started the Mourner's Kaddish?"

"I almost didn't recognize him when he stepped out of the car. It was Uncle Avraham Adam Salm and his second wife. I hadn't seen them in years. He is my mother's only brother."

"They must have remembered you. Why didn't they at least speak to you and express their condolences? Weird family!"

"He and the family have been estranged for many years. Grandma told me once that she never liked either of the wives of Uncle Avraham. When Grandpa died, she was tempted to sell the business rather than let her only son carry on the tradition. I never knew what happened. It's too late to ask her. Well, my dear, let's forget the ghosts of the past. We do need to face the present. I'm not sure if I want to deal with another shock today."

They turned to leave the Parkfriedhof. Rachel grabbed Otto's arm with desperation in her voice. "Otto, something strange is happening to me. We better walk a bit faster."

"Are you telling me the baby might be on its way?"

Chapter 2

OTTO looked frightened. He held Rachel closely. "What is wrong, Rachel?"

She supported the bottom of her enormous belly with both hands. Rachel stood in a sizable puddle of fluid. She was terrified looking at her feet, what she could see of them. The stain of fluid was growing moment by moment. She didn't speak; she screamed, "Get me to the cemetery office right away! See if you can get ahold of a cab. My water just broke. I'm about to deliver our first child." She was concerned, and yet she smiled at Otto.

"Never mind the cemetery office." Otto put two fingers between his teeth and whistled. He caught the first cabby's attention. "Take us to the closest hospital. I don't care which one. We're about to have a baby." Rachel was breathing hard. It was obvious she had gone into labor. She lunged for the back of the front passenger seat. Rachel squeezed the seat mercilessly. With the next surge of pain, she longed for Otto's touch and reached out for his hands. Her face was contorted with every wave of labor pains surging through her body. The cabby realized the seriousness of the situation and drove as fast as he could. They got there in a hurry.

Otto ran into the hospital. He had heard unbelievable stories about current hospital admission policies. Looking over his shoulder, he yelled "Don't drive off; my girl is still in the backseat. I want to make sure they will admit her."

Otto faced the receptionist. "My beloved is about to deliver our child. For your record, her name is Rachel Adina Salm." He sensed immediately what went through the woman's mind. The Salms were a well-known Jewish family. He could tell by her posture what he was about to be told.

She just glared at him. "Sorry, we don't accept Jews at this hospital."

His face turned beet red. "Lady, you must be kidding. What kind of a hospital is this? I doubt you would have worked for the founders of this institution. They were decent people. How can you be so heartless? Who the hell will accept her?"

"Try the Franz Sales House. They might take her. It's the institute for the mentally infirm."

"I can't believe what I'm hearing."

He stormed out of the hospital. Getting into the cab, he slammed the door. "Take us to the nut house. I'm sure you know where it is."

א

Miriam Daniella Salm was born shortly after noon at the Franz Sales House. Rachel had no difficulties with the delivery. The nurse placed the baby in her arms. Rachel smiled and lovingly counted ten tiny fingers. She couldn't wait to do the same with those cute little toes. She looked up at Otto. "Isn't she just the most precious little girl? I wish Grandma had lived to meet her. Lying on that delivery table, I couldn't help thinking about the terrible pain she was suffering in her last hours. Her reward was death; mine was her first great-grandchild, Miriam Daniella."

They held each other. Tears escaped their eyes. They mourned the loss of Rachel's grandmother and were momentarily overjoyed with the birth of Miriam. "May I hold the baby for a spell, Rachel? I love her as much as you do."

Otto looked tenderly at their beautiful creation. "I'm glad she's a girl. Your grandma would be so pleased. Most guys would like their first-born to be a boy. Not me. I'm thrilled to have a daughter, especially in our present environment where mothers are constantly encouraged and rewarded for producing sons. Hitler is looking for all the cannon fodder he can find. I hate to even think what I'm about to say to you. We need to be concerned about what might happen to our child." When Rachel looked up to him, she saw that the joy of beholding his baby girl had vanished from Otto's face. Instead, fright and anxiety were written all over him.

He kept cradling Miriam in his arms as he continued. "I have never said this before, but I've carried this fear in my heart for as long as we have lived together and especially since you were pregnant. We have seen what's happening with our Jewish friends in Munich. No one seems to know where they are sent after they are hauled away by the Nazis. This could happen to us and especially to you and Miriam. I'm sorry to put fear into your heart at this joyous moment, but it's a reality you and I need to face."

Rachel's arms reached up to Miriam. She began to sob. "You can't be serious. Are you asking me to desert our just-born child? Please let me hold her, Otto. I can't believe what you are suggesting we do. I cannot give up Miriam. She was just given to us. What kind of unfeeling woman do you believe I am?" Her eyes were flooded in tears. Rachel could tell the baby was wanting to be fed. She placed Miriam on her left breast and held her tightly. She couldn't stop sobbing. Her hot tears fell onto the baby's face. Otto stood ever so close to Miriam and her. He didn't attempt to hide his own sadness.

Rachel looked up at Otto, her eyes imploring him. "I need to think about this. Let's talk about it after I'm discharged from this place." Otto decided it was best not to discuss his concerns any further while Rachel was still confined to the hospital. He was fully aware of the possible insults to her general well-being resulting from psychological trauma. Rachel had a difficult-enough time dealing with the place where she was forced to have their baby.

Whenever her thoughts were not dwelling on Otto's plan to shelter their precious Miriam with strangers, she would cry out uncontrollably. "I still cannot believe I gave birth to our beautiful baby in an insane asylum. I am outraged by what my countrymen are doing to my people and to us. If I wouldn't shake the rafters in this damnable place, I would scream."

Mother and child were discharged from the facility ten days later, and they arrived at the home of Rachel's grandmother. The aura of death was pervasive throughout the apartment. Ariana had not yet removed all the black cloth covering the mirrors throughout the place. The air smelled stale. They sensed a certain pungency. In Grandma's bedroom, the odor was intolerable. Rachel pinched her nose and holding her breath, quickly left the room and closed the door tightly behind her. Rachel called Ariana. "We have to open the curtains and windows. We need to get some fresh air into this house. Otherwise, I might get sick."

After Ariana retired, Otto and his little family sat down in Grandma Salm's living room. The plush chairs and love seats spoke of faded elegance. Rachel had always admired Grandma's richly carved ebony furniture and adored her grandparents' many paintings artfully collected throughout their lives. A few serving pieces belonging to Grandma's favorite Hutschenreuther china graced the large sideboard.

Otto sat down with Rachel. He cradled Miriam Daniella in his arms. His hand gently touched the cap of dark hair covering her scalp. He looked down on his daughter and smiled through his tears. Rachel was touched. She had only seen him showing such gentleness when he made love to her. "I hate to bring up the matter of seeking a safe haven for our child. You must know by now how difficult such a decision will be for me. My mind tells me, we need to give her up for adoption. Neither you nor I are in a position to leave the country. First of all, we don't have the means and, without our degrees, who would consider employing us? The biggest thing is, we haven't got big bank accounts. More importantly, who would give us a visa allowing us entry into neighboring countries? Every time I give thought to abandoning our child, I don't know if I can do it. My heart cries out at the thought of it. The present circumstances demand that we make every effort to shield our beautiful baby. Can you find it in your heart and soul to give away this precious child God has entrusted to us? What are we going to do, Rachel? Speak to me! I need to hear your thoughts; I need your help in making this awful decision." He bawled without restraint.

Rachel shook almost convulsively. "It's bad enough for us to deal with what might happen to either of us. I don't want our child to be sent to some camp or, worse, to be killed by these hoodlums. I can't rationalize what you are asking me to do. How can I give up Miriam to strangers? The thought of giving away the child I just brought into this world is unbearable. And yet, when I listen to the hateful speeches, watch the disgusting attitudes of fellow Germans toward my people, and imagine what might happen to my first-born, I am compelled to put my feelings aside and reluctantly go along with your idea of shielding her." Rachel sobbed openly and could not stop crying.

She took Miriam from Otto and hugged her tightly against her full breasts. She wanted Miriam touched by the sapphire amulet. She began to whimper and wondered what Grandma would say. "What would she decide to do with her first great-granddaughter?"

Rachel sputtered, "I won't give her up for adoption. I want to speak to the nuns at the cloister. It isn't very far from here. Perhaps they'll agree to accept her and shield her from evil. What's on your mind?" Rachel turned to Otto. Her face was marked by rage. "You weren't thinking of leaving her on some doorstep by a hospital, fire station, or police department were you?" She spat out her words with vengeance, not hiding her disgust toward the demands of their predicament.

Otto had never even thought of the cloister. The idea of leaving Miriam in the care of loving nuns appeared to be less threatening than giving the child up for adoption or perhaps to caretakers of whom they knew nothing. "Let's do some investigating."

Three days later, they bundled up Miriam Daniella and took a cab to the cloister. A young postulant opened the door and was startled when she saw the child in their arms. They walked up many stone steps to the second floor of the building. There was no elevator. There was a chill in the air, and they could feel the dampness on their exposed skin. The presence of incense was overpowering. The walls were stark, very plain, and without evidence of art of any kind. They followed the young woman to the office of the mother superior. In response to their knocking, the door opened to them. "Please come in. I am Sister Maria-Angelika. Please have a seat." Mother Superior appeared to be cool and apprehensive. Otto looked around the room and believed it to be totally lacking in warmth. Everything was neat and tidy. The starkness was overwhelming. A large statue of Mother Mary dominated the scene in the back of Mother Superior's desk.

Otto wanted to speak first. "I'm Otto von Graben. Rachel Adina Salm is the mother of our child."

Mother Superior nodded, making a mental note of their names. Rachel rocked Miriam in her arms. The baby started to cry. It was time for her to be fed. Rachel laid the baby on one of her breasts, draping the Varanasi scarf over her. Mother Superior wasn't bothered by the suckling sound made by the contented infant.

Otto continued. His voice was shaky and almost guttural. Mother Superior realized immediately the difficulty Otto experienced in explaining the situation. His words became almost unintelligible when he began to speak slowly. "My girl is Jewish; I am Christian. We aren't even married yet. We didn't dare get married in Munich, where both of us are in the throes of finishing our doctorates in dental medicine. We would never be granted a marriage license at the registry office. Seeing how we are treated, we are fearful for our lives."

Otto stopped momentarily to clear his voice. He reached for his handkerchief and wiped tears from his face. His bloodshot eyes stared back at Sister Maria-Angelika. "We are even more worried and concerned about the life of our infant daughter. Miriam Daniella was born a few weeks ago in an insane asylum. Staff at the regular hospital refused admission to Rachel. We are fully aware of the hateful attitudes by many Germans toward Jewish people. Neither Rachel nor I want to give our child up for adoption. We are imploring you to hide and shield her from the evil that's enveloping us."

Sister Maria-Angelika was stunned. Seeing their emotional turmoil, she felt terribly sorry for Otto and Rachel. "You realize we are not an orphanage but a school. We serve hundreds of students of all faiths—not only Catholics. This is a relatively new and large facility. Our order has been in education since the seventeenth century.

"You can see my dilemma, and I'm fully aware of yours. I must confess I don't walk through this world with my eyes closed. I see and hear every day what is happening all around us." She stepped closer to Rachel holding the baby. She laid her left hand on Rachel's dark crown of hair and likewise blessed Miriam Daniella with her right hand. Her eyes brimmed with tears. Rachel and Otto knew she had made her decision. "Our Lord is a forgiving God. He would not want me to act in any other way. I am willing to bend the rules.

"My youngest sister just died in childbirth. God forgive me! These are terrible times. In view of what is happening, I will proclaim that Miriam Daniella is my niece. Henceforth, Miriam will be known as Marika Leander, the name my real niece shall bear in East Prussia. No one will ever question it; she will be raised by my parents there. As you know, it is hundreds of miles from Essen. No one will ever be the wiser. Desperate times require desperate measures. As far as my sisters in the cloister are concerned, you are close friends of my deceased sister and were willing to bring the infant to me. It was my sister's dying wish for you to do so. She wanted her child to be protected and raised by me. I will note your full names on separate pages in my prayer book. No one but the three of us will ever know that I was aware of your identities.

"None of us know how and when this nightmare shall end. I will do everything in my power to shield your daughter as long as the situation demands. If you discover each other later in life, let serendipity determine the outcome. Are you planning to return to Essen after obtaining your degrees?" She added up quickly the number of lies she had just proposed. Sister Maria-Angelika shrugged and then let her shoulders sag. She would deal with God and Mother Mary later.

Otto responded, "At this point, we are not sure. More likely than not, we will open a practice in our hometown, Essen. We feel more comfortable in the environment we shared as we grew up."

"If you do return to Essen, I would like to know where you are located. There is a tiny mailbox mounted on the large steel gate. I am the only one with a key to that box. Drop me an innocuous note informing me of your location. If need be, I will always let you know in extremely subtle ways that Miriam is well and safe. You must wonder about me. I never thought I would commit such acts of violating my vows, but my Prussian parents raised me to be much too much of a pragmatist. They instilled in me the desire to always do the right thing. I will have to live with my conscience and make peace with God, Mother Mary, and myself." She made the sign of the cross and continued.

"You must understand you may never return to the school. You cannot see Miriam, contact her, or attempt to retrieve her; certainly not as long as she is a young child and as long as she must remain in my protective custody."

Otto replied. "Never is a very long time. Are you suggesting that we may never see Miriam, even if this regime might end in disaster?"

"Of course, that would be a different story. If there would no longer be any danger to your wife and Miriam, I would expect you to resume your parental rights and duties. No question about that.

"You brought your precious baby girl to us in an act of desperation. You are not abandoning her. You are seeking our protection. I will see to it that Miriam Daniella will always be granted shelter to the best of my abilities. She will grow up with my sisters and me. I will raise her and love her as if she were my very own. I never thought I would have such a privilege."

Rachel and Otto stared at each other. They embraced and began to sob. Sister Maria-Angelika left them in her office. She knew they needed to be alone. They hugged Miriam Daniella fiercely and kissed her cheeks and forehead. "I don't know if I can do this, Otto." She took the baby in her arms. Rachel wanted to speak but couldn't. Her body shook convulsively as she wrapped her hands around her child. Finally, she controlled herself and spoke softly into Miriam's ear. "I gave you life. You were part of me for nine months. I felt your very first heart beat and the first movements of your limbs." Miriam Daniella's face was flooded in Rachel's tears. The baby began to cry.

Otto raised his fist to the heavens. He spoke in anger. "Why do we have to live at this terrible moment in time in this hateful country?" Just for a split second, he conceived of the idea of seeking freedom in death for the three of them. He didn't want to confuse Rachel, but he wondered if they were doing the right thing by abandoning their child.

He asked Rachel to kneel with him, facing the statue of the Madonna so prominently featured in Mother Superior's office. Miriam Daniella was sound asleep in the crook of Rachel's left arm.

Otto enfolded Rachel's right hand in his left and gently touched the baby's head with his right palm as he looked up to the benevolent face. "Holy Mother and Almighty God, protect our child and protect us from all evil. Grant us forgiveness in the act of deserting Miriam Daniella, and forgive Mother Superior's transgressions in committing herself to saving our child." They beheld each other and said "amen" in one utterance.

Still weeping, they rose to their feet. Otto opened the door slowly. "Please come back and speak with us. We have decided to leave Miriam Daniella in your kind care. We have no other choice. Otherwise, she might become another victim of the evils of Nazism. We don't want to see her taken away in some cattle car to an unknown destination or, God forbid, struck on her head with a billy club. We have seen firsthand what the Nazis are doing to innocent people—Jewish or otherwise. Rachel and I love each other very much. We'll find a way to get married; we just don't know yet how and when. The laws of the land are not in our favor. We pray that perhaps somewhere in time, there will be a way for us to be reunited with Miriam."

"I understand what you are saying. I feel sorry for you. Are you absolutely sure you want to leave your child with me? It's a terrible decision you have to make. Be assured Marika will be much loved and protected to the best of my and my sisters' abilities."

Rachel finally found her voice. "We sensed since the first moment we spoke to you about entrusting you with our child that she will be cared for by loving hands. On another matter, we must ask for your help and understanding. The day before Miriam Daniella was born, my grandmother passed away. Minutes before the Almighty took her, she gave me this family heirloom." Rachel reached for the sapphire amulet and removed it from her neck. "It's been in our family for many generations and was always passed on from mother to first-born daughter. I received it from my grandmother because my mother died when she gave me life. My grandmother kept and wore it until just before she died. I want Miriam to have it at the right point in time. I don't want it to fall into the hands of the Nazis should the time come when I'm arrested. Would you be willing to wear and protect it until Miriam is grown?"

"I'm touched by your trust. I can tell it's a very valuable piece of jewelry. By doing this, do you realize I'm committing another sinful act? I'm not to wear any adornments other than this large cross. 'Lord, forgive your sinful servant.'" She turned her face in a heavenly direction. Rachel hung the sapphire amulet around Sister Maria-Angelika's neck. Sister tucked it in under her habit never to be seen again by anyone who could condemn her.

Sister Maria-Angelika picked up the baby and hugged her intensely. She wondered, "What am I doing with a baby?" and shuddered in fear. Mother Superior cradled "Marika" in her folded arms and held her out for Rachel and Otto to kiss her farewell. They looked at each other and burst into tears. Otto thought for a moment of Wotan kissing Brünhilde farewell in *Die Walküre*, one of the most moving scenes in all of opera. He could hear the phrase in his tortured mind. "Farewell you spirited, wonderful child." They held each other, trying to be one another's support. Finally, they walked hesitantly out of Mother Superior's office. Rachel and Otto could not bring themselves to look back at their child cradled lovingly in the arms of Sister Maria-Angelika. Rachel looked into Otto's eyes. "Are you sure we made the right choice?"

He responded, "It's now all in God's hands."

Chapter 3

RACHEL and Otto took the express train back to Munich. They hardly talked. They were lost in thought. Rachel stared at Otto. "I cannot even begin to think about that damn dissertation. All I come back to is that moment of walking away from Miriam. I hate this world for making me do such a dastardly thing. Why can't these damn Nazis just leave us alone?" She whispered into Otto's ear. She had no idea who was listening to them in adjacent compartments.

Otto reached out and enfolded her in his arms. "I feel the same way. I wake up in a sweat in the middle of the night and wonder if we abandoned our child. I know we promised the good sister that we would never return to the cloister to reclaim our daughter."

He leaned over to Rachel. "I'm glad I raised the question about a total change in the scenario that made us do what we did. I'm confident Mother Superior will only do what is best for Miriam. I trust her completely. Some of those older nuns might believe that story about the orphaned niece. I'm not so sure about that one younger, kind of feisty nun. Did you hear her tell me that she will be a full-fledged nun in a couple of months?"

"No, I heard little of what she was telling you as we were walking along those long, stark corridors. I thought her name, Irmgard-Dolcinea, was unusual. She seems to be full of it from what I could detect just watching her as she walked us to the offices of Mother Superior. I know I'm a worry worm. I'm praying every night that we made the right decision."

The next day, Rachel had an appointment with her doctoral advisor, Herr Professor Doctor Abraham Weiss. Rachel often wondered why the Germans always insisted on all those damn titles. Dr. Weiss was good enough for her. He had lived in the States from 1924 until 1935. He had become an American citizen and taught at Colombia University. Weiss was a good-looking man. He had an impressive handle-bar mustache. There were touches of gray on his temples. His suit was the latest in style. He looked distinguished with the darkness of his jacket contrasted by a bright-red tie and a sparkling white shirt. Dr. Weiss had much appeal to most of his female students. He was a bachelor in his mid thirties. He was a Jew.

Rachel was respectably dressed for the meeting with her mentor. She wore her stunning brunette hair in a fashionable chignon that was held in place by an amber clip she received from her grandmother. Her eyes reflected the state of her heart and mind. As much as she had been looking forward to working on her dissertation, it had lost its priority status. All she could dwell on was Miriam being raised in a cloister by a bunch of nuns—caring nuns for sure—but nuns nevertheless. Miriam's mother and father weren't there for her.

"Come in, young lady. How is your grandmother?" Rachel looked puzzled. "I thought you might have learned from the note I sent you that she passed away the night we arrived in Essen."

"I'm so sorry; I just got back from a lecture series and haven't looked at much of my mail. Accept my sincere condolences on the loss."

Rachel nodded acceptance. Looking at his deep tan, she was wondering what kind of a lecture series he attended.

"When did you have the baby?" Weiss wanted to know.

"Miriam, a beautiful and healthy girl, was born on the day of Grandma's interment."

While chitchatting with Rachel, he walked over to close his office door. "Have a seat. I want to hear all about it. How are you planning on finishing your studies while needing to take care of an infant?"

"For now, a maiden aunt of mine, who lives in the Münsterland, is taking care of her. I hope Otto and I will finish our dissertations at the same time and get married one of these days. We'll be ready to live as a family." She didn't blink an eye telling the blatant lie.

Dr. Weiss stared at Rachel. "I have to tell you, you remind me so much of Gypsy Rose Lee."

"Who the heck is Gypsy Rose Lee?"

"That's exactly how she would have phrased that question. There was never anything ordinaire about her. She was a neat lady. Gypsy was a high-class burlesque queen. She truly believed in less being more and never revealed any part of her body other than her midriff, arms, shoulders, and gorgeous legs. She knew how to tease with wonderful ostrich feathers and fans. I saw her whenever she was in New York."

He got out of his chair and walked over to Rachel. He stood behind her and touched her hair. Rachel's perfume intoxicated him. His hand slid down inside the shawl collar of her dress. His hand sought to reach and touch her firm young breasts. Rachel jumped out of her chair and faced her advisor. Dr. Weiss interpreted her move as wanting more of him. He moved close to her and began to kiss her. "I have been wanting to make love to you from the moment I first met you. I need you to lie down with me on my sofa. Come,

come now. I know you are hot for me. Let me ravish you right this minute, my gorgeous one. I have double-locked the door. No one can surprise us."

Rachel backed away from her abuser. He let go of her arm. She hauled off with her right knee, striking his groin in total surprise and vengeance. There was murder in her eyes. He fell to the unforgiving floor. Dr. Weiss was in complete shock. He held his exposed prick and screamed in utter pain. As she picked up her papers, she stepped over his convulsing body. Rachel was all business. "Give me a call for another appointment when you have recovered. I like you very much as my professor and advisor—not as my secret lover. Remember, I would be married to the father of my child if it wasn't for this damn Nazi regime." She could talk that way to a fellow Jew. She walked away from the bastard, proud to have stood her ground.

Chapter 4

THEY were still in Munich during Kristallnacht, the night of November 9, 1938. Most Jewish businesses were attacked by the Nazi hoodlums all over Germany. Rachel and Otto could not believe what they saw as they carefully stalked around their neighborhood. They didn't know what happened to Uncle Avraham Adam and his wife in Essen. Seidenhaus Salm was among many Jewish businesses that became targets for total destruction that night. What the Nazis didn't steal, they burned in the streets in front of many onlookers. Their aggressors arrested the Salms and hauled them off on one of their ugly trucks packed with people. No one had any idea where they were taken. Women and children were crying; babies were screaming. The hoodlums used their billy clubs and beat the hell out of them, leaving many with severe head injuries. The more blood they saw, the more sadistic and aggressive the attackers became.

As time moved on, Rachel wondered what Miriam might be doing. Could she be walking and making her earliest attempts at communicating? Many precocious children did by the time they were twenty-one months old. She had worked with enough very young children during her medical training to see it for herself. At the end of the day, Rachel fell into bed in a state of exhaustion. She'd wake from nightmares, at times screaming and shaking Otto merci-lessly. "I keep seeing Miriam in my dreams from hell. I don't know how much longer I can deal with the deprivation we've laid upon ourselves. How will Miriam react to us, should that day come? And now all this damn talk about war. It's bad enough what they are doing to us in Germany; now they want to erase my people from the earth. Adolf is a total madman." After consoling Rachel, Otto would get up and pour himself a stiff drink. It was his way of dealing with his depression and nightmares. All Rachel was interested in at this point was to have them finish school and get out of the Nazi hotbed called Munich.

Rachel and Otto finished their dissertations in April 1939. She couldn't wait to leave. Six years of living in Munich had been too long. She wanted to be closer to her family. She was not aware they no longer existed. What Rachel really wanted was to be closer to Miriam. There had to be ways for her to steal glimpses of her now and then. Otto's entire family had fallen victim to the horrible influ-enza epidemic that claimed millions in 1918. He was raised in an orphanage from the time he was eight years old. While he didn't broach the subject of their abandoned child with Rachel, deep down in his heart, he shared her need for seeing Miriam even if it was just from a distance. As he closed his prayers for Miriam each night before he finally dozed off, he would whisper into space, "Always remember I love you!"

The long train ride to Essen was welcome. Otto held Rachel close to him and finally rocked her to sleep. For once, Rachel had pleasant dreams of Miriam. Miriam appeared to her as Rachel imagined her to look at this stage. She woke up as the train was leaving the Düs-seldorf train station. Essen was the next stop. Otto was reaching for their suitcases in the racks above their seats. Rachel looked up at him. "I've had the most wonderful dream. I saw Miriam walking around the playground with Mother Superior. She was such a pretty little girl. They were holding hands, and Miriam was talking and laughing. I loved listening to her sweet and innocent voice." Tears were coming to her eyes. She stared at Otto. "I must see my child." That was all she could say.

They took a cab to Rachel's grandmother's house. Ariana answered the door. She began to cry immediately. "There is plenty of room in this place but nothing else. The only thing they didn't steal was my little mattress. Everything else, they pissed on, stole, or burned. I was the only one here. They hadn't realized your grandmother was dead and buried. In my heart, I was glad she didn't have to experience such terror and humiliation. I cannot believe my people are doing these things. You are my friends, not murderers and thieves. That's what they are."

Rachel put her arms around Ariana and hugged their family friend; she didn't treat her like an employee. "You've been in my family and with Grandma since before I was born. When my father was killed during the waning months of World War One, you couldn't leave Grandma alone with a young child. Thank you, Ariana, for always staying with my family and me.

"I need to ask you something. Why didn't you or my grandmother ever tell me about my twin sister? I'm sure you knew."

"I had to swear on the Bible that I would never tell you. Nothing about Juliana Daniella was ever discovered in the seven years of investigating the case. In time, all who knew forgot about her and thought it was best to do so. I'm so sorry you had to find out. It must have really disturbed your grandmother for all these years. She must have felt she couldn't take the secret to her grave."

"I'm sure you are right. It troubles me deeply, but there is nothing I can do about it now. It seems they are all gone."

Rachel walked from room to room. Ariana hadn't exaggerated. There was nothing left in the apartment. Only dark shadows scarred the wallpaper where once paintings and mirrors had hung. She finally caught the strength to speak. "We'll just stay for a few nights until we can find a place to rent and open our dental office. We know there is need for good dentists in this town. Maybe we can pile up some of our clothing and create a pad to sleep on. It will do in a pinch," she told Ariana.

They went to a neighborhood restaurant and picked up the local newspaper off the rack. Reading the ads carefully, they saw one offering as a possibility and decided to check it out the next day.

Otto turned to Rachel. "I intensely disliked deceiving Ariana, but I believe we did the right thing by telling her we left Miriam in the care of a Christian orphanage without letting her know exactly where. Not having that information is for her own, Miriam's, and our protection. I was glad to learn that Ariana is leaving next week for Dresden to live with her younger sister."

Rachel just nodded, staring absentmindedly into space. "You were wise not to share with her where we chose to leave Miriam. Were Ariana ever to be questioned by the Nazis as to Miriam's whereabouts, she would have nothing to tell them." At last Rachel surrendered and escaped into the world of Morpheus, seeking much-needed sleep.

The next morning they got off the tram at Breslauerstrasse. The office had been the dental practice of a Jewish dentist who closed his business in 1937. The family escaped to Lisbon. The owner of the building was not able to find suitable tenants. Otto did all the negotiating. He never let on he and Rachel were not married and that she was Jewish. Apparently, the landlord was very anxious to have income from the property that stood vacant for so long. He didn't question them closely. Otto and Rachel opened their practice in August 1939.

Chapter 5

RACHEL turned to Otto. "How did you sign the contract with that obnoxious man? I was ready to hit him over the head the way he talked about the previous tenant. God forbid if he discovered that I'm Jewish as well."

"I signed the lease in my name only. You will be listed as 'and Associates' on the shingle. I hate all this cloak-and-dagger business, but it's for your protection. Lord knows, you are as qualified a DDS as am I.

"By the way, I didn't tell you. I met the neighbor who has the apartment across from ours. She is a single lady and operates the vegetable kiosk at the corner of the street. Her name is Mimi Foster. You can't really miss her. She is a very large presence. I was impressed by her friendly smile and demeanor. She told me she leaves most days very early in the morning to shop the wholesale market and spends her days at the kiosk on the corner. I think you will like her when you meet her. Mimi is a jolly soul." Otto reached out to Rachel. He held her closely as he began to speak. "There's an even more important issue. I believe we need to take care of becoming legal as husband and wife. This coming weekend, I want us to head for this little town called Telgte in the Münsterland. I called about the appointment a couple of weeks ago. I don't care about a church wedding. All we need is this piece of paper issued in a civil service."

When they walked into the registry office, they looked like a couple of students. Rachel had barely tucked up her hair in a bun. She was trying to appear youthful and ready to tie the knot quickly. The registrar looked at them. "I see you contacted our office a couple of weeks ago arranging for today's service. Are you both German citizens?" They answered in the affirmative and were holding their breath for the next question. It didn't come.

The official looked sort of puzzled peering around them to see if anyone had shown up with them to be their witnesses. "Looks like another case of the young and foolish never even giving thought to needing a couple of witnesses to get married. Not to fear. You're not the first young folks to appear before me." He swiveled around in his chair, waving at a young man and woman seated behind a glass wall in the next room. They got the message. Rachel and Otto signed the prepared document. Their signatures were duly attested to by the handy instant witnesses. The final touch, the all-important stamp, was affixed with a flourish by the registrar himself. He beamed from ear to ear making the statement they had sought for years. "I pronounce you husband and wife."

Rachel smiled at Otto. He hugged and kissed her lovingly. They were walking out of the "promised land" holding hands. Otto spoke close to Rachel's left ear. "Thank God he forgot to ask us what our religion is. Do we care? We are married at last. We are legal in the eyes of man and certainly in the eyes of God. I'm glad we have overcome that hurdle. Let's go home and celebrate."

Rachel concurred. "But let's not think about making more babies right away. We have no idea what the future holds, especially now that it looks like we may go to war with the world. On Saturday, I would like to go into the city and buy some furniture, especially good beds."

With their savings, they were able to furnish the apartment

adjacent to the practice. They were pleased to have a place to call their own. It was a marked improvement sleeping in halfway decent beds rather than on top of their clothes piled on the floor. "This feels a lot better, but I didn't expect a new bed to be squeaking so much. That was one thing the pile of clothes didn't do. Never mind the sounds of the bed." Rachel liked the new and improved love-making.

Once they started seeing their first patients, they didn't have that much time on their hands. Rachel remembered Sister Maria-Angelika's request to share their whereabouts with her should they return to Essen. She wrote on a plain piece of paper. "The infidels have landed at Breslauerstrasse 6." She slipped the sealed envelope into the tiny metal mailbox by the steel gate.

Rachel would always wear her hair down and sport very large sunglasses trying to disguise herself. Stalking the playground of the cloister school, Rachel was hoping to catch sight of Miriam outside with Sister Maria-Angelika. Sometimes she'd be talking to herself. "I can't believe that you are two-and-a-half-years old. Are you a happy child? Are the nuns loving you the way your father and I want to love you?" There never were any answers to her many questions. She would go home and cry her eyes out; no matter how hard Otto tried to console her, she couldn't stop being totally distraught. Rachel didn't give up on Miriam but learned to accept their fate. She did not want to get caught in the process of violating the conditions spelled out by Mother Superior. Every chance she had, Rachel walked by the school's playground in hopes of spotting her child.

Sister Maria-Angelika was thrilled to discover the note in her secret mailbox. She burned the note as soon as she read it. Knowing Otto and Rachel were safe and nearby gave her peace. She prayed to give thanks and asked, as she did daily, for forgiveness.

X

On March 22, 1940, Good Friday, a convoy of military vehicles moved into the plaza in front of the cloister school. Several uniformed men jumped out of their cars and banged on what appeared to be the main entrance to the school. The youngest of the nuns, Sister Irmgard-Dolcinea, rushed down the stairs responding to the yelling by one of the intruders. The men kept rapping on the cloister door. When she opened it, the man in front pushed her aside. "Who the hell is in charge of this damn school?"

"Allow me to take you to Mother Superior's office."

"Who the fuck are you to allow me to do anything? Keep moving and take us to the bitch in charge. I have some important words for all of you in this place."

Sister Irmgard-Dolcinea led the way up the many slick steps to the second floor. She was several steps ahead of the soldiers. The clanging of the boots on the tiled flooring echoed throughout the building. The fat, short soldier, the loudest of them all, had a hard time breathing and keeping up with the nun's swift movements. As they approached the office door, the leader vehemently pushed the young nun aside. She almost tripped over her habit which had caught on her left shoe. The men entered the room without knocking.

The harsh noises caught Mother Superior off guard. She stood tall in front of her desk. Marika was seated at her school desk and was coloring pictures. The corpulent officer approached Mother Superior. From all the ribbons and medallions decorating the left side of his uniform, she assumed he was the man in charge of the hoodlums who had invaded her sanctuary. The nasty man walked right up to the nun and was practically in her face. Mother Superior backed away from him. With her imposing headpiece, she appeared to be almost two feet taller than the "little man." She just stared into his eyes. She could tell he hated having to look up at her as he finally opened his big mouth flashing numerous gold crowns. "What do you say now, you papal bitch? What's your name?"

"I am Sister Maria-Angelika, the mother superior."

"Say it more loudly! I cannot understand you. And who the hell is that kid sitting over there? Have you been fucking one of the priests?"

"I beg your pardon? I forbid you to use such language in our presence. That child is my niece; her mother died in childbirth. Her father could not take care of her; he has been serving your cause since 1936." She had no idea where her brother-in-law was or whether he was alive.

The fat pig continued his tirade. "We want you and your ilk and all of your pious students out of this place. We are in need of office space for various important projects. This space has been requisitioned by the German government and will remain under our jurisdiction for as long as necessary—certainly until the end of our victorious war effort. We expect most of these classrooms and offices to be empty and cleared of all papal frocks in short order. Do you understand me? What did you say your name is? Would you mind speaking more slowly and clearly?"

"I am Sister Maria-Angelika, the mother superior."

She glared at the Nazi, making sure he understood her. She wondered how someone that hard of hearing could be an officer in the German army. "I resent your tone of voice and your implications. Are you quite finished with me? It's time for our midday prayers." She turned her back to the intruder and was ready to walk away. In her anger, she almost knocked her headpiece to the ground.

He grabbed her shoulder, tearing away at her habit. "Get off that pious high horse of yours. If you were a bit younger and without the kid hanging around, I'd give you a good fuck—one you wouldn't forget so quickly. Have you ever done it, you dumb bitch? Let's get the hell out of here before I get tangled up in all that frockery!"

They "Heil-Hitlered" and walked out of the room, slamming the door behind them. Sister Maria-Angelika momentarily was in shock. She had lost all color in her face. She was soaked in perspiration.

Never had she been spoken to in that kind of language by anyone—even before she entered the cloister. Then she remembered who she was. She stood tall and proud as she faced the other nuns and Miriam, who had been privy to the entire event. Sister Maria-Angelika was a born leader.

Mother Superior called a general meeting of students and staff two days later. Nuns, secular teachers, and students met in the large chapel. "Our school has been taken over by the government. I have spoken to the superintendent of schools in Essen. All sisters other than Sister Irmgard-Dolcinea and the five oldest sisters on staff need to return to the Mother House in the Münsterland. Secular teachers will be absorbed in city schools. All children, other than my niece and the six students who lost their parents, will need to attend regular city schools. I regret closing the school but must follow the orders imposed on us."

A hush had fallen over all who attended the meeting. One of the secular teachers spoke up. "Isn't there anything that can be done to stop these actions? Did the superintendent give you any idea which schools will accommodate the teachers and our students?"

Mother Superior was prepared to answer some of the questions. "I believe there is nothing we can do to stop the government from requisitioning our property under the War Act. The superintendent assured me that all teachers and students will be assigned to schools relatively close to their residential addresses. That should help a little. I realize this is a great hardship for all of you. Considering the insults to which I was subjected, I believe there is no other way out of this situation. I feel sorry for us all."

Leaving the cloister school would be traumatic for both teachers and students. They realized to what degree the environment of the cloister sheltered them from the harsh realities of working and teaching in Nazi-dominated schools. All the secular teachers had a meeting immediately after Mother Superior's announcement. Harriet Eigensinnig became their spokesperson. "We cannot let all our educational efforts go down the sewer. What do you think of this plan? Each of us will accept the responsibility for six to eight students. Let's approach the parents and offer lessons at no charge. Each of the parents must take a turn at providing the temporary 'classroom space.' It's just a plan. Shall we take a vote?" The majority of teachers present liked Harriet's approach. While not truly private lessons, the students would experience some meaningful continuity in their education.

Back in their living quarters, Mother Superior turned to her strongest supporters. "We cannot leave the cloister, especially not I. I have the responsibility for my niece. We all have prayed for the child and me. I hope God has forgiven me for taking on the responsibility of caring for Marika. She is an innocent child and needs our protection. I won't be bullied by any Nazis. I have pretty broad Prussian shoulders. None of their threats and insults shall deter me from taking care of my flock."

Chapter 6

MOTHER Superior believed she was all through with Nazi invasions of the school. Not so. It happened again two years after the initial closing of the school. Sister Maria-Angelika and her charges had reluctantly adjusted to having all sorts of uniformed and undercover men invade the privacy of the school. No one ever spoke at normal loudness levels.

Once again, a truck with dozens of brownshirts on board pulled into the courtyard of the cloister school. Mother Superior gasped at the sight of the vehicle. She caught herself saying a nasty word in front of the others. The door to their humble quarters flew open. The invaders confronted Sister Maria-Angelika and the other nuns who were instructing five-year-old Marika and the six other children in their care.

The apparent leader of the intruders screamed at Mother Superior. "Have you not gotten word that your teaching methods and subjects are no longer permitted in the Third Reich? We are not interested in the hogwash your ilk dispenses to these kids. German children need to be taught allegiance to the Führer and conform to the ideals of the Nazi Party. They need to be taught to hate all Jews and other riffraff that poison the Aryan lifestyle and ideals."

His eyes searched the room and fell on little Marika. "Come here, child. Do you know how to salute the Führer—and us, for that matter?"

"What did he say?" was little Marika's reply.

"Let me show you, you little wench! You raise your right arm as high as you can and shout 'Heil Hitler'. You do that whenever you enter or leave a room. Take a look at this uniform. Do you know what the Führer looks like?"

Marika hesitated. "Is that the man with the funny hair on his lip? It's so small. It looks goofy."

The brownshirt stared in disbelief at Mother Superior. "Is this how you teach these children? It's downright disrespectful what this child just said about the appearance of our venerated leader."

"Sir, I must apologize for the child. You must remember, she isn't quite five years old. I personally will make sure that she will recognize and respect your uniform and the images of Herr Hitler in the future."

He turned back to Marika. "Did you understand me? Look at us and do it."

Marika looked back and forth between the brownshirts and Sister Maria-Angelika and the other nuns who taught her. The child was red-faced, perspiring, and looking confused. The leader who gave the instructions moved right in front of the child. He jerked up her right arm, demanding she repeat after him, "Heil Hitler."

He faced the nuns and yelled at them. "You better start teaching these kids how to properly conduct themselves in our presence. Forget all about this genuflecting and crossing shit you taught in the past. In a few years, these kids will need to be ready to join the BDM and the Hitlerjugend when they attain age ten." He clicked his heels and raised his arm in salute before he and his troop marched out. They slammed the door shut. The ugly sound of their stomping boots faded away. The nuns and their charges had watched the disgusting maneuver with their mouths wide open, not saying a word.

Mother Superior made the sign of the cross and quietly asked for forgiveness for the thoughts that had crossed her offended mind.

Sister Maria-Angelika took a deep breath before she spoke quietly. "Let us continue with our readings this morning. I really did not appreciate this rude interruption of our class. Sisters, you and I will need to confer regarding the matter at hand later this afternoon when our students are resting. The other issue we must discuss is where we will seek shelter in the event of more bomb attacks. We are fortunate that the cloister's substantial underground vaults are intact and there for us to use. When we are finished with our classes this morning, I would like us to start with a fire drill. I want everyone to know where to run in case the warning alarm is sounded." The other nuns and the children were all ears. Until now, none of the cloister property was damaged by the incidental bombings that occurred earlier.

Sister Irmgard-Dolcinea came up with a brilliant idea. "Come here, children. I have a wonderful job for all of us. As soon as we are done with learning our ten new words for the day, we'll have a coloring session. We'll make paper signs with arrows. Then we will place our pretty drawings where they are easily seen; they will lead us to the right places in the vaults. Don't you think this will be fun, children?"

"Good idea," echoed Sister Maria-Angelika. The children and their guiding teacher had their work cut out for them. All enjoyed making colorful arrows and placing them. At three o'clock, after everyone's naps, they had their first fire drill. It was easy to follow the signs and get to the vault quickly. Sister Maria-Angelika timed the whole operation. It had taken them less than three minutes to reach the safety of the cellar. "Very good, everyone. We'll do this at least three times a week to keep in shape and improve our timing. It's a lot easier for you kids to make it than for us with our voluminous habits. This headgear can really get in the way on those narrow, steep steps. But we did OK, don't you think, children?"

"Yes, Mother Superior" was the chorus of the kids. They were all pleased with their very first fire drill. It was that evening, mother superior conferred with the other nuns. "After our exercises earlier today, I realize the importance of timing in the event of future attacks. We and the children no longer can afford to be wearing night clothes. Preparedness is of the utmost importance. I believe it best if we and the children sleep in our habits, clothing, and shoes and merely dispense with wearing our headpieces. That will save us much time in reaching the safety of our vault." There was discussion and some initial objection by her cohorts. Ultimately, everyone agreed with mother superior's recommendation.

Chapter 7

THE dental practice of Otto von Graben and Associates was doing well. Most of their patients lived in the immediate neighborhood. The adult population consisted largely of women of all ages whereas most of their male patients were older. All young men were serving in the military and fighting Hitler's battles on many fronts. Otto truly enjoyed treating his older patients. He was especially drawn to and loved the relationships he built with some of the older men. It was an aspect of life that completely passed him by having grown up in an orphanage. He couldn't recall his parents or any grandparents.

Although Rachel never knew her parents, she could draw emotional sustenance from recalling her loving relationship with her maternal grandparents. She was always immensely grateful for the love and care she was given by them. Sometimes she would wonder about the lost twin sister Grandma had spoken of on her deathbed. Did Juliana Daniella live, or was she perhaps murdered? Why wasn't she ever told about her before? Rachel felt guilty about the privileges bestowed upon her for all these years. She didn't dare share her questions with Otto.

Early in her training, she discovered that she truly enjoyed working with children. Thus, her primary professional focus became the care of children and young adults. Taking care of her young charges and succeeding at putting their frightened minds at ease gave Rachel much pleasure in her work.

Looking at a five-year-old girl in the dental chair wasn't always easy for Rachel. "Who does Miriam resemble? Does she have normal and pretty teeth? Is her hair dark like mine or ash blond like Otto's? Is she well-adjusted and happy, or is she sad?" She was often tempted to get answers to all the questions that haunted her mind during the day as well as in her dreams. Otto didn't own up to similar experiences. He would be her rock in such moments of utter recrimination and regret for having abandoned their baby.

Letting her cry on his shoulder, Otto would try to ease Rachel's guilt. "Just look around and see what's happening. I hate reading the paper and listening to the news on the radio. Things are going from bad to worse. I truly believe we made the right choice by leaving Miriam in the care of Sister Maria-Angelika. It's for her protection from the evils of this world that we made this ultimate sacrifice of separating ourselves from our child. We were fortunate enough to encounter the sisters and especially Mother Superior, who accepted the responsibility of raising Miriam, even violating her religious vows in coming to our aid." Looking up at Otto with her bloodshot eyes, she had to agree with what he told her. And yet, it was all so cold, calculated, and pragmatic. He would try to bring peace to her troubled soul in such moments.

Rachel raised her eyes to Otto. "It's all true, and in my brain, I can accept all your concrete rationales; in my heart and soul, it's a different picture. I feel we deserted our child. We cheated ourselves of experiencing with her the most wonderful years. I lie in bed at night and wonder how Miriam will view us if and when there should ever be the opportunity to discover our connections in years to come. I try to put myself in that little girl's mind and know how I would feel were I to learn that I was left in the care of total strangers a few weeks after I was born. We deliberately made Miriam an orphan. Can we ever forgive ourselves for what we did?"

X

Two boys and their mother were sitting in the waiting room to be seen by Rachel. This gave Otto a break. He wasn't certain how to help Rachel in her latest state of depression. As hard as he tried, his attempts at consoling his troubled wife often ended in failure. "Let me say hello to the Birken boys and their mother while you splash some cold water on your eyes. You don't want them to see you like that. They might get frightened."

Otto walked into the waiting room. He smiled at Helena Birken. "How are you boys today? My wife will be right with you. Why don't both of you come with me to her examining room? Who wants to go first? Hektor or Albert?"

Just then, Rachel walked in. Her white coat was spotless. She had fixed her hair and the cold water had done wonders for her bloodshot eyes. A couple of eye drops did the rest.

Albert greeted Rachel. "Hello, Dr. von Graben. Are you going to hurt me today?"

Rachel smiled. "Albert, you know better than that. I never hurt you. With the Novocain, there is just a little pressure."

Rachel made eye contact with Albert's brother and spoke warmly. "Come on, Hektor. I know you always want to go first. Hop up into the chair. Please, open your mouth wide." With the bright light behind her shining into Hektor's mouth, Rachel could quickly see that his teeth were in perfect shape. "You are lucky again - no cavities today." Hektor was pleased and gave Rachel the biggest smile.

"What about you, Albert? Are you ready for your checkup? I know it's not one of your favorite activities. Let's take a look. Open your mouth. Much wider, please! Sorry to say, you are not as fortunate as Hektor. I see a couple of spots that need filling."

Albert winced. "I knew you were going to torture me again. Do you have to use that noisy machine? I hate the way it feels when you dig around in my mouth."

Rachel had the syringe in her hand. "You know the drill. It's not the first time I had to do this. Come on, Albert. There is just a little prick. Your mouth will go numb. You won't feel the drilling at all." She distracted him by running her index finger across the lower gums. He had closed his eyes in anticipation of the perceived pain. Rachel took advantage of the shuttered eyes and injected the Novocain quickly where needed. "You see, that wasn't so bad, or was it? I'll have you sit in the waiting room for a few minutes. It won't take me long to get the job done. Remember, there won't be any hard candy for the rest of the day. Get into the habit of sucking those bonbons instead of chewing them." Albert still looked utterly frightened and didn't say a word.

Rachel made some notes in the boys' files and checked her watch. It was time to get started on Albert's two fillings. She was grateful for the pleasant distraction. "Let's finish this little job, Albert. Get up into the chair and open your mouth wide." She set the drill on the first tooth. Rachel knew it couldn't hurt. Albert kept pulling away from her. "Albert, stop moving your head. The more you fight me, the longer it will take." He finally realized he was just feeling a bit of pressure and had to listen to the sound of the drilling. A half hour later, both teeth were finally filled. Both Albert and Rachel could breathe more easily. "I will see you in six months, young man. And remember what I told you about sucking the candy." She walked Albert out to the waiting room. "Here we are. All done. It was nice seeing you and the boys again, Mrs. Birken. We'll chat some other time. This young lady is waiting for me. Come in, Erika. You are next." Rachel loved the work with her young patients.

Chapter 8

ON March 15, 1944, Otto looked through the morning mail. One letter had that official appearance. He tore it open. Rachel was aware of the tearing sound as Otto ripped the envelope in his examining room. She excused herself from the young girl sitting in the dental chair. Pushing away the protective glasses from her face, she dropped the stainless-steel tool on the floor. "Damn it" escaped her lips. When she faced Otto, she could tell he was breathing heavily. She didn't want to hear what Otto needed to share with her.

"Rachel, I got my draft notice. We knew this was going to happen one of these days. I have to report for basic training in Krefeld in three days."

"Oh my God. What will I do without you being here with me? You are my rock. You are my protector during this horrible time." She was hoping the child wouldn't hear what she was saying. "Isn't there a way for you to get out of serving? Perhaps the need for your professional services might be a good excuse. Do you have any idea how long you will need to serve?" Rachel had moved close to Otto; she was within reach of his arms. He knew she needed to be held by him.

Otto embraced her firmly and looked into her beautiful but very sad eyes. "Rachel, there are no excuses that would keep me from serving. They are so desperate for men in the military. Perhaps being on one's deathbed might be a reason to be excused. I have no idea how long I will have to serve. My assumption is until the end of this war, if I survive it. It's a reality you and I need to face. When I leave here in three days, we may never see each other again." Rachel clung fiercely to Otto and sobbed deeply. The top of his lab coat clearly was spotted by makeup and tears and Rachel slobbering all over him. She didn't want to let go of Otto. She finally remembered her young patient. Rachel was still crying when she walked away from Otto.

She looked at her patient and excused herself. "My husband just had some very upsetting news. I'm sorry for keeping you waiting this long. I'm almost finished with you for today."

"What was the bad news, if I may ask?"

"Dr. von Graben has been drafted into the military. He is leaving me in three days."

"Then why are you crying? Aren't you happy that he will be serving our Führer in the fight against our enemies?" Rachel knew immediately how guarded she needed to be. She couldn't resist responding sarcastically.

"Spoken like a good German girl. But still, I will miss my husband very much. And so will his many patients. There are so few doctors and dentists left to serve all of you." Rachel decided to say no more. She was glad when they saw their last patients for the day.

After they had their quiet moments together, Otto reread the letter that had created their emotional turmoil earlier. "Just listen to these instructions. They are telling me not to bring anything other than two complete sets of underwear and socks and to just wear a pair of pants with a good belt and a short-sleeved shirt. Uniforms and boots and everything else will be provided to me at the basic training camp, compliments of the German government."

Rachel started to bawl again. He held out his open arms to her. Otto knew what this separation would do to them, especially to

Rachel. Yes, they would miss each other's presence in their respective lives. Emotionally and physically they had become soul mates since they first met in medical school. They shared the sadness of being separated from their child. Rachel felt that she was losing the safety net Otto had always provided for her. All along, his presence shielded her from the Nazis. She rushed into Otto's arms, needing to feel his strength and love. Rachel looked into his eyes. "I can't believe it. They are taking you away from me. What will happen after you are gone? It makes me feel so vulnerable. Actually, I'm scared to death what they might do to me. I may not even know where you are and what is happening to you. Likewise, you may have no idea what's happening to me. Deep in my gut, I knew this day would come, but I'm not ready to face it. I feel completely alone and utterly frightened." She was shaken to the core. Her face was flooded in tears. She didn't know how much more she could cry. Rachel didn't dare look into a mirror. Her face had to be a mess.

Otto believed they needed a distraction. He offered to prepare dinner. Food was the last thing on Rachel's mind. They sat down on their comfortable sofa in the living room. "I would like some wine. I need something to relax me." He poured each of them a healthy glass of red wine.

"I expected this to happen before. At my club, I heard some of the older men talk about the desperate need for younger, educated, healthy guys to join the fighting forces. There is no way that I would get any kind of deferment. They have lost a lot of good men by now. One of our patients talked with me the other day. Every chance she gets, she listens to the BBC on her short-wave radio. Things aren't as rosy as we are told by Dr. Goebbels. I can't stand that Liszt 'Les preludes' thing anymore. It's like getting an aural whipping."

Otto couldn't stop. "Yes, I can't deny it. I'm very worried about leaving you alone. You're not safe any longer, even with me around. They don't give a rat's ass that you are a much-needed professional person and married to a Christian. That's all just icing on their narrow-minded and vindictive cakes. All they want is to annihilate and erase your people from this earth. I'm totally alarmed about your safety. I'm also worried about Miriam Daniella. How safe is she with Sister Maria-Angelika? I understand they go to the vaults under the cloister when the alarm goes off. I have honored her request of not seeing our child, but I try to keep tabs on Marika, as she's known at the cloister. I have never confessed this to you before. I hated what we did but still believe we did the right thing under the circumstances. Miriam is as much my flesh and blood as she is yours. She seems to be safe with the sisters, and the shelter at the cloister is quite substantial and deep underground.

"I never said anything, but I was fully aware of your stalking activities around the cloister during the first year we were in this office. I couldn't really blame you. Often, I was tempted to join you just to get a peek at our little girl."

Rachel confessed. "I never did tell you. Right after we opened our practice, I let Mother Superior know where we are. I stuck a one-line note into the metal box she spoke of the day we left Miriam in her trust."

Otto seemed to be pleased. "Thanks for letting me know. That makes me feel a little better. But now I have to leave you alone here. What choice do I have? I must follow orders and appear in Krefeld for basic training—whatever that means. I suppose they'll teach me how to fire a gun, use a bayonet, and kill innocent people. In my mind, all soldiers are innocent; they just do the job they are told to do. And for what? To keep this glorious asshole and his hoodlums in power? I better watch what I'm saying and how loudly I say it. This apartment is not as tight as it was before the last bomb attack."

Rachel took him by his strong hands and pulled him to her, letting him feel how much she wanted to be held in his arms and loved. They needed to savor the two nights left to them before Otto left to "serve the country." Neither one saw it that way. He was forced into a situation for which life had not prepared him; however, declaring himself a pacifist would have cost him his life. Rachel and Otto were fully aware that the arrival of the notice had changed their lives forever.

Tears flooded their eyes as they beheld their nakedness. Rachel drew Otto onto their bed. "Come, lie with me and hold me tight. Lord knows how long it will be before we'll be together again. It's all in the hands of the Almighty or maybe even the devil himself."

Otto enjoyed their physical togetherness. Their sexual feelings had always been reciprocal. They rested for a while and talked. "I wonder what it will be like sleeping in sweaty-smelling barracks with a bunch of horny guys?"

"Just lie there quietly and think of me being alone in this bed. It won't be any different than before you met me at LMU."

Neither was willing to waste any time on sleep. Yes, they had patients to see for the next couple of days, but they needed this time together, and they needed it now. They made passionate love to each other and finally fell asleep exhausted from lust. The odor of sweat and spent semen was pervasive in their bedroom. They acted like it might be their last time together for a long time, perhaps for forever. There might never be another tomorrow. Neither of them knew what the fates held in store.

Rachel accompanied Otto on the tram that took them to the *Hauptbahnhof* in Essen. Lots of young couples were standing on the platform waiting for the train to Krefeld. They were not alone holding hands and taking every opportunity for another stolen kiss. Rachel was sweating like a pig. She was glad she had laid on another coat of deodorant before they left the house. She certainly didn't want to stink on this last day of being together with Otto. They were thankful for having taken their last shower together before getting dressed.

The train pulled into the station. Otto hugged Rachel fiercely, and she clung to him, feeling almost weak in her knees. "I don't want to let you go. You are my everything. What will I do without you? I need you so much."

"I need you too. But I have to get on this train. Did you hear them blow the whistle? I love you forever!" He jumped on the train as it began to move. Beautiful Rachel just stood there with tears streaming down her face. She lifted her eyes to the heavens after she couldn't see Otto any longer.

"Almighty God, protect us all." She almost stumbled on the steep stairway taking her out of the train station. She got on the number 18 tram and nearly missed the stop where she needed to get off. Her neighbor, Mimi Foster, was waiting for her; she enfolded the bawling Rachel in her massive arms.

Chapter 9

OTTO arrived at the camp in just over two hours. Lots of young men got off at the station. They were transported by a huge open truck to the camp. *Feldwebel* (Sergeant) Schnabel greeted the guys as they hopped off the vehicle. "Boy, you guys stink. Head straight for the showers. There are wire baskets on the wooden benches. Put the clean stuff you brought with you in one basket and the stuff you take off in another. Take a hot shower and towel yourself off. There are dry, clean towels hanging from nails above the baskets. Do not put on any clothes. Did you hear me? Do not put on any underwear or clothes. I need to inspect your naked bodies. Just carry the baskets with your stuff in front of you."

The guys, probably fifty or sixty of them, headed for the showers. Schnabel was right. The showers were hot and the pressure great. Just the way most men like their showers. Some guys acted like they had never experienced a good shower. After ten minutes or so, Otto thought he was clean enough and turned off the spigot. The guys sharing the shower with him gave him dirty looks. "Sorry, you've got hands. Turn the damn thing back on if you haven't had enough." Just for a second he touched his dick. The *Glockenspiel* was still intact after all the sex he and Rachel enjoyed during their last night together.

He walked away and grabbed a towel. It wasn't exactly fluffy, but at least it was dry and clean. He toweled himself dry and ran his hands through his hair; he didn't have a comb handy. He picked up his baskets and followed some of the younger guys exiting the shower for Schnabel's inspection. "I wonder what he is looking for? Gonorrhea, syphilis, genital herpes?" He didn't have to wonder for long.

"Hey, buddy, what's your name?"

"I'm Otto von Graben."

"My God, I thought you were about to say Otto von Bismarck. That's quite a dick you have there. How come you are circumcised? Are you a Jid?"

"No, I'm not a Jew, but I dated a beautiful Jewish woman while I was a student. I had myself circumcised to please her. Hygienically, a circumcised penis is easier to keep clean. The Jews know what they are talking about."

"That must have been some broad for a big guy like you to get his dick mutilated to please a Jewish bitch. Sounds to me like you are really taken with fucking Jews. Speaking of fucking, I'll talk to you about that later when I'm not this busy inspecting sixty new cocks. Move on, buddy. Make sure you put on the clean underwear and march to the next room. The corporals will fit you with boots and uniforms. Next!" Schnabel yelled.

Otto got into his underwear quickly before there would be further inquisitions regarding his circumcised dick. The young man in the next room looked him up and down and decided Otto needed a size 48 uniform and a size 12 in his boots. "What sizes do you wear in suits and shoes?"

"Forty-eight and twelve."

"Right on; that's exactly what I predicted. It's those broad shoulders that require the 48. And broad men like you stand on big feet. Welcome to our world. I couldn't help overhearing that little discussion you had with Schnabel." He bent over and spoke right into

Otto's ear. "Be watchful of him. He's *schwul*. Next thing, he'll proposition you to fuck him with that circumcised dick of yours. Watch your back at all times with that guy around. Believe me, I'm speaking from personal experience."

"What's your name?"

"Bodo; Corporal Bodo!" He clicked his heels. "Heil Hitler; you might as well get used to it!" he winked at Otto.

"Thanks, Bodo, for the good tip. Whereto next?"

"Stop in the next hall; they'll assign you a bunk and tell you where you eat and where you need to show up tomorrow at five o'clock for your first drill. Welcome to the German Army. Next!" Bodo didn't yell as loudly as Sergeant Schnabel.

Otto got all the information and went on the discovery trip for his sleeping bunk. His was a lower one at the very end of the long hall and right next to an emergency exit. "That's a pretty good location. I'm glad not to be assigned an upper bunk," thought Otto. He was thirty-four; he was three years older than Rachel. Otto was in great physical shape. For years, he belonged to an exercise club and did a lot of walking and hiking when time permitted. He could have handled an upper one but preferred to be closer to the ground. Those bunks didn't look all that sturdy and obviously had had a good workout for the last four years. He questioned how many men had been processed through this place. He wondered how many men had satisfied themselves lying in those bunks. Rachel's words rang true in his ears.

At six o'clock in the evening, he went to the chow hall. The food wasn't too bad although nothing like what he would have fixed at home for Rachel and himself. He loved to cook their dinners. Rachel handled breakfast and lunch. After chow, he tried finding a public phone. He wanted to hear Rachel's voice while he had the chance.

"Hi, love. I have safely landed in Krefeld. I have showered; had my circumcised dick admired and questioned; have found my bunk; eaten my chow, such as it was; and love talking to you."

"That's quite a day and quite a mouthful. What's the bit with your circumcised dick? What's so unusual about that?"

"Well, Feldwebel Schnabel wanted to know if I was a Jew. I told him I wasn't but that I knew a beautiful Jewish woman while I was a student at the university and did it to please her. I purposely didn't say it was you for whom I suffered the pain. The next guy I talked to told me that Schnabel is queer and to watch out for him. If he as much as touches me, I'll report him to the next higher officer. Supposedly, Hitler 'loves' homosexuals almost as much as Jews. That should take care of Herr Schnabel in a hurry. Now that we have discussed my adventurous day, how did yours go?"

"I cried all the way home on the tram. Fortunately, Mimi was there to hug me to her ample bosom. She is such a warm and friendly person. I don't know what I would do without her now that you are gone. She and Helena are coming over later to have a glass of wine with me and discuss things. Helena misses her boys; they have been in Baden for more than a year. Next time you call, give me the number from the public phone you are using, and I'll call you back from the phone on the corner. Mimi always warns me what to say and not to say on our private phone. She may have a point. After the last three nights, I will be terribly lonely tonight. Think of me and have sweet dreams. I love you!"

"I love you too! Sleep well! God bless you!"

Rachel sobbed. She hung up. The connection was gone.

They called reveille punctually at nine o'clock. Most guys were already snoring in their bunks. They knew the next time they heard that damn horn was much too early. There was still a bit of daylight when he turned in. Otto stripped down to his skivvies and slipped under the blanket. It was much too warm for wearing pjs. He finally got rid of everything. It felt good to be naked. He was out within seconds.

Sometime later, he felt uncomfortable; actually, he felt chilly. The hall was pitch dark. A strong draft seemed to come from the direction of the emergency door. All he could hear was the snoring of dozens of men. He turned to lie on his stomach. He was ready to pull up the blanket and cover his back. He felt someone standing next to him. He could almost feel the hot breath on his neck. Then he felt a hand touching his backside. It was Feldwebel Schnabel keeping his promise.

Otto was fully awake now. He turned over and sat up straight. He found his skivvies in one move. They were tucked under his pillow. He slipped into them easily. He grabbed the attacker's penis, twisting it mercilessly until Schnabel stifled his screams by burying his face in Otto's blanket. "Let go of my prick. I thought you were lonely and wanted some good sex with a man. I won't do it again!"

"You are goddamn right, you won't do it again. Not to me or some other poor sucker. You and I are marching right out of this hall to your commanding officer. We'll go just the way we are; you with your sorry prick hanging out of your pants and I in my skivvies. And then we will tell the man what you tried to offer me. That is, you will tell the man in your own sweet voice. Got that, buster? March, you lousy prick. You won't be fucking any of these men anymore. With a bit of luck, the officer on duty isn't a queer too and will send you where Herr Hitler would like you to be. You know where that might be, don't you? You'll be where you can keep company with the poor Jews you like so well. Keep your ass moving before I kick your butt."

"Please, please, don't do this to me. I'm so sorry. You are right. The officer on duty hates homosexuals. No one has ever objected to my overtures. Most guys are horny enough and open to any kind of sex. This guy will send me to a KZ camp for sure. He adores Adolf. Nothing would please him more."

"Why should I worry about your miserable prick? You are talking to the wrong guy. Come on, Schnabel. Try to talk yourself out of this one. Here we are. Speak up loudly, as you did when I first encountered you upon my arrival earlier.

"Sir, excuse my appearance. Officer Schnabel has something he wants to share with you. Don't be shy, Schnabel. Open up!"

"Sir, I am a homosexual and tried to accost Private von Graben. I'm sorry I did that. Please forgive me one more time."

"Oh no! This time you've done it. Before, it always was hearsay since none of the guys you attacked were willing to fess up. You finally picked the wrong guy. I have no choice but to report you. I'll make sure you wind up in Dachau, where your kind belongs." He looked Otto straight in the eye. "Thanks for turning this bastard in. I wanted him sitting and suffering in a camp for a long time. What's your name again, young man?"

"Private Otto von Graben. I just arrived today."

"You will hear from us; there will be an inquiry. Your testimony will be pertinent."

"Yes, sir. I will be there." Otto said, with pleasure. He thought of Rachel and smiled.

"You, over there. Lock up Feldwebel Schnabel. I hope the rest of the night will be more pleasant."

Otto walked back to his bunk. "What an introduction to my new life" ran through his mind.

Chapter 10

OUTSIDE the cloister school, the world had fallen apart. The living quarters had seen many changes since the beginning of the war. None for the better, but Marika felt cared for and deeply loved. It had never occurred to the child to question her relationship to the mother superior. Marika was content with her life in the abbey. Out of necessity for warmth and comfort, Marika had been sharing a bed for the last two years with her gentle caretaker. Sister Maria-Angelika always gave her a motherly hug before kissing her good night. And, of course, there always were prayers. The good nun had been her mother for all intents and purposes. The other nuns, the children still at the school, and Marika herself believed that she was Mother Superior's niece.

Sister Maria-Angelika had always been circumspect when getting ready for bed. She undressed in a dressing room and switched from her habit to nightclothes. In the beginning, she apparently had slept in her habit and just put on a fresh one in the morning. All this had been so new to the nun who had never dreamt of taking care of a baby. She even had to learn how to prepare a baby bottle and how to feed a baby. While she had generous breasts, they had never been "programmed" by Mother Nature to nurse an infant. Clearly, the bottle had to do it in those early days of 1937. Where had the seven years gone?

It was unusually warm during the month of February 1944, almost unheard of in that part of the world. Mother Superior quietly spoke to herself. "I need to take a bath before I put on a clean habit and go to bed. I'm so hot and sweaty. I cannot lie down next to Marika as hot as I am." Maria-Angelika did something she had never done since Marika was with her. She completely undressed and slipped into the cooling waters of the tub. She pledged to the heavens, lifting her eyes, "Forgive me, Holy Mother!" All she was wearing was the Blue Sapphire Amulet. No one had ever seen her wearing it since Rachel Salm had placed it around her neck all those years ago. She did some gentle splashing in the water and felt so much better. As she stood up in the tub to dry herself, Marika awoke and had a straight-on view of Mother Superior standing before her in the nude. Before Sister Maria-Angelika could cover herself, Marika spotted the amulet.

"That is beautiful. Why did you never wear it before? Can I touch it?"

"Marika, this amulet is very dear to me. It was given to me by a special person. I have been wearing it as long as I have known you without ever taking it off. This will have to be our deep, dark secret, just between the two of us. We can't share this with anyone else. If you want to, you may look at it now and then, just to refresh your memory. You cannot tell the other sisters or anyone that you saw me wearing it. You weren't even supposed to see me without any clothes."

"I didn't know you had such big boobs. You always look so flat under that habit."

"Marika, you are too observant for someone so young."

"What's that supposed to mean?"

"You are too smart for your own good. To answer your question, I have to wear a special plate across my breasts. With a harness, my breasts are flattened out. Geishas in Japan do it all the time."

"What's Japan? What's a geisha?"

"One of these days you will learn all about it in geography. For now, let me get into a clean habit before I lie down next to you. Then you can touch the sapphire amulet one more time. I promise you will learn all about it when you are a bit older. Close your eyes now and sleep. God bless you. And, Holy Mother, forgive me."

Chapter 11

RACHEL was thrilled to see Otto's handwriting as she sorted through the mail. He let her know that he was not allowed to leave the barracks and make phone calls. She was appalled to learn what had transpired during his first night in boot camp. Among other things, Rachel learned that Otto was by far the oldest among the men being trained. He gave Rachel to understand there were some fourteen-year-old boys among the men being trained with him. Things had obviously become desperate. Tears were falling on Otto's letter as she read what might happen six weeks hence. She couldn't face the possibility of not having any kind of communication with her beloved husband. Neither could he imagine such a situation. She kept reading the last lines of his letter over and over again. "I miss you, miss you – very much! Wish I could hold you in my arms and kiss you. For now, only my words will have to do. Always, Otto."

Rachel had checked her appointment book and thought she was done for the day. As she walked into the reception area, she nearly fainted when she saw a man in uniform sitting there. It was clearly one of the brownshirts. He heard her approach and looked up from the magazine he was holding in his hands. "I presume you are still open for business since it is only three o'clock in the afternoon. Most practices are open until five in the evening, right?"

"You are correct. How may I be of help to you?"

"I've been dealing with a severe pain caused by a tooth in the back of my left lower jaw. It might be the last of my wisdom teeth that is giving me trouble."

"How did you get to my office?"

"A neighbor of mine, Herr Mutig, is a regular patient of your husband's. He recommended your practice to me. Where is your husband? I had actually anticipated being treated by a man. I've never dealt with women before; that is, in any sort of medical or dental capacity. Are you qualified to deal with my problem?"

"I certainly am. By the way, I'm Frau Doctor von Graben. Both my husband and I are graduates of the dental program at LMU in Munich. May I ask you your name?"

"Oh, sorry. I'm Fritz Lustig."

"Why don't you follow me to the examining room, Herr Lustig. I would like to look at your teeth before we proceed." Lustig followed her and took a seat in the dental chair. Before Rachel could ask him to open his mouth, he began to speak. "I remember coming to this office several years before the outbreak of the war. It was some Jid that was practicing in this place. I can't even remember his name. Did you take over from him? You have any idea what happened to the guy? I'm sure glad Hitler is getting rid of all this Jewish scum."

Rachel had to catch her breath. She felt like telling him to take his pain elsewhere. She remained professional. "My husband and I opened this practice in 1939. We never knew our predecessor." She pulled down the floodlight and turned it on. "Please open your mouth wide, allowing me to examine all your teeth." Within seconds, she had to concur with Mr. Lustig's assessment of his situation. Gums and tissue around the last lower-left molar, a wisdom tooth, were red and very sensitive to her gentle touches.

"I believe you are facing some serious discomfort for a couple of days after I extract the tooth. She swiped his lower left gum with disinfectant and prepared Mr. Lustig for the Novocain injection. "This will take a few minutes before you will feel the desired effect. I had to give you a considerable dose since it may involve a protracted extraction. Please relax if that is possible. I will try to make this as painless as I can. Wisdom teeth often present with complications." Rachel was glad that Mr. Lustig chose not to ask any more questions about the former dentist.

She noticed that Mr. Lustig's brow had broken out with perspiration. There were huge stains from sweat on his uniform in the regions of his armpits. After twenty minutes, he appeared to be completely numb, and Rachel proceeded with the extraction. She had carefully selected the appropriate extraction tool based on the size of the tooth and the man's jaw. While it took all of her strength, she managed to remove the tooth and all roots during her first attempt. After frequent rinsing of the patient's mouth, she packed the giant socket with ample gauze and instructed Mr. Lustig regarding post extraction care.

"When you get home, place an ice bag externally to reduce any swelling. Bite gently but firmly repeatedly on the gauze pad until a clot is formed. The bleeding should stop after an hour or so. If you do feel like eating, make it soup. If you need to chew, do so on the right side. I'm giving you some Bayer aspirin. Take two of these every four hours for the first two days. You should be OK after that. I would like to see you back here in a week." Mr. Lustig gave her a crooked smile. Rachel didn't reciprocate. She was glad to see him leave. When he finally was gone, she realized that she had experienced her own kind of anxiety attack. It wasn't the extraction procedure that caused her to be drenched in perspiration but the initial view of the brownshirt sitting in her reception area. For a moment she had envisioned he was there to arrest her. After taking a shower and having a bowl of soup for her simple meal, Rachel responded to Otto's note. She let him know how pleased she had been to recognize his handwriting when sorting through the mail. Rachel shared with him that she was thankful for the friendship of Mimi and Helena.

Otto liked hearing she had expanded her services to include many of his former patients. As he read about her encounter with Herr Lustig, Otto began having his own anxiety attack. He was glad that Rachel had not reacted to the nasty insinuations and had kept her professional dignity intact. He liked knowing that he was dearly missed as he slumped under his stinking blanket all alone. He reread her note before he finally fell into a sound sleep. Just a few written lines from Rachel was all he had of her.

Chapter 12

MARCH 26, 1944. Shortly after dark, all the alarms went off in the city. Marika and Mother Superior jumped out of bed and rapped on the doors of the other nuns and the room where the other six students were sleeping. Mother Superior got everyone's attention with the big brass bell she was swinging as she ran down the hall. "Be sure to check the laces on your shoes and put on a warm coat. Follow the signs that will take you down to the vault. Follow Marika. She knows where we need to be. I will be the sweep and make sure everyone makes it to safety. That alarm is pretty persistent. The bombers must be close to Essen." She had to set down the weighty bell; it was straining her arm.

Within less than three minutes, all were huddled in the vault. Fright was written over everyone's faces, children and adults alike. Mother Superior could tell by Marika's eyes how scared she was. Some of the other children were covering their ears with their hands. "Listen to me, and do as I say. Kids, each of you grab one of those large down pillows. Sister Irmgard-Dolcinea, help me with getting these children covered. Marika, show them once again what we have practiced. Hurry up. I can already hear the first bombs falling. They are not very far away from us."

Marika took one of the other kids by her hand and marched her over to one of the older nuns. She encouraged the nun to spread her legs and create an opening in her habit. "Kneel in front of Sister and put your head down in her lap. Grab this pillow and cover your head. You won't hear as much of what's happening out there." Marika was the last to get into position. She had her head buried in Mother Superior's lap. The naked light bulbs went dim. Then they were out. All were sitting in total darkness. The cacophony of the falling bombs was only interrupted by the sounds of rosary beads moving in the hands of the nuns saying their prayers. "Hail Mary, full of grace. The Lord is with thee. Blessed art thou among women, and blessed is the fruit of thy womb, Jesus. Holy Mary, Mother of God, pray for us sinners, now and at the hour of our death." Marika could barely hear Mother Superior's voice. She wasn't saying the repetitious prayers of the other nuns. "Holy Mother, dear God, protect these children and us. Spare our church and the chapel. Let us keep our humble home left to us in the cloister. Bring an end to this madness that engulfs our daily existence. How much longer do we need to suffer the injustices and cruelties of this world?" Marika could feel tears falling on her hands.

A bomb struck the cloister school or nearby. And then another hit was close at hand. The nuns and some of the children screamed in fear. They felt the vibrations in the floor of the vault that sheltered them. Sister Irmgard-Dolcinea smelled smoke. "This place must be on fire. I can smell it. Thank God we are deep underground and the steps leading us out of here are not made of perishable wood."

Sitting next to Mother Superior, Irmgard-Dolcinea received an elbow in her ribs. "Stop frightening all of us with that kind of talk. It's bad enough we cannot see anything. Now we have to listen to your frightful observations."

A third bomb hit the school. Plaster was falling off the ceiling. They could feel water under their feet. A water main must have been struck. Even Mother Superior became frightened momentarily. Sister

Irmgard-Dolcinea held her hands. The prayer beads of the other nuns were noticeably at work. Mother Superior spoke. "I hate to admit it, but I'm frightened to death. We have had some attacks before, but nothing like this. Now I can hear water running down the steps. My feet are really getting wet. You children better get off the floor. Sit next to us on these benches. If it helps, stick your little fingers in your ears." Time stood still. At last, there appeared to be a lull in the air. Sister Maria-Angelika took charge. "I have not heard any bombs falling for ten minutes. Let's all just be very still and listen for the all-clear. As soon as we hear it, we will make our way out of the vault." She looked toward heaven. "Dear Lord, let this thing be over soon." Sister Irmgard-Dolcinea could see Mother Superior's anxiety written all over her face when she could hear her say, "There, there, I hear the all-clear. Let's go."

Their eyes had adjusted to the darkness. There seemed to be a reddish glow at the top of the steps as Sister Irmgard-Dolcinea slowly made her way out of the vault. "Why didn't we think of the lights going out? We better have some flashlights down here in the future," she tossed over her shoulders. Marika and the others were following her carefully. Mother Superior brought up the tail end. She had never been as frightened as during this bomb attack. No longer did she just fear for her own life; she feared for the lives of all who were with her and especially the life of Marika. As she forced her body up all those steps, she realized the top of her habit was soaked in perspiration. It matched the bottom that was dripping from the water that had invaded the vault. She couldn't wait to get out of the place.

Mother Superior was afraid of what she might see when she got to the top of those endless stairs. The higher they climbed, the stronger the smell of smoke hung in the air. Not only could they smell it, they felt the acrid substance in their eyes. It got worse by the minute. Irmgard-Dolcinea screamed, "It's our building that's on fire. I can see the flames. Hurry up while all of us still can get out.

The stone steps will hold and get us to the main entrance. Rip off those habits, sisters, before you turn into walking torches. These fabrics will instantly catch fire. I don't care who sees me; I refuse to set myself aflame."

Sister Maria-Angelika couldn't agree more and started peeling off her habit as well. The other nuns followed their example. Their undergarments were quite substantial, and no parts of their bodies were revealed. "Let's run directly to the large fountain in the plaza. If worse comes to worse, we'll jump into the waters." All of them made it to the exit and ran straight for the cooling fountain. Neither the children nor their caretakers turned into torches. Mother Superior held tightly onto Marika; her knuckles were white.

They leaned with their backs against the pools of water and, for the first time, really saw what was happening. Most of the cloister was destroyed by bombs; the free-standing structures of the church and chapel were engulfed by fire. The flames reaching up the walls were licking at the heavy wooden beams supporting the ceilings. They could hear the popping and crackling of the wood being consumed by the flames. In horror, they witnessed the buttresses of their beloved church cave in. The roof crashed to the ground.

Earlier in the evening before the attack started, a chill was in the air. Now, no one would talk about a chill in the air but rather a heat wave. The entire neighborhood had gone up in flames. Mother Superior asked everyone to get down on their knees. "Holy Mother, we give thanks for sparing our lives. We pray for all souls who have perished in our troubled city. Be with us all in this hour of despair."

They could hear sirens, perhaps from fire trucks or police. Periodically, there would be massive explosions close by and in the distance. "Those must be gas lines exploding," said Sister Irmgard-Dolcinea. She was the most vocal of all the nuns still on the premises, but Marika's "aunt" was clearly the leader.

Mother Superior took charge. "We must float an extra prayer to the Almighty. What the Nazis took away from us fell victim to this attack. Our halls of prayer are being decimated by fire as I speak. I give thanks for what is left of this once proud institution. It will shelter us in the days to come. No matter how humble, we still have a place to be. After all the destruction, the wing where we have been living is still habitable. God must have a purpose for us. He does not want us to leave the cloister yet. The fires engulfing church and chapel will just have to burn themselves out; there will be no firemen coming to our rescue. Tomorrow morning, I will post a notice on the gate that is still standing." She felt compelled to do so. It said, "All souls on the premises are safe and sound." Mother Superior thought a certain person might wonder about the survival of the cloister's inhabitants. There was nothing left of the church or chapel before the night was over. The destruction of most of the cloister school struck fear into their hearts.

Chapter 13

RACHEL wrote to Otto. Not knowing whether he received any current news, she needed to let him know she and their home had miraculously survived the latest severe attacks on the city. The cloister school hadn't fared that well; much of it had fallen victim to bombs and incendiary devices. Thanks to Mother Superior's note, she knew that all had survived the terror of the night and could remain on the premises for the time being, be it ever so humble.

Otto was relieved to hear from Rachel. He had not been aware of the terrible destruction visited upon his hometown. Their ears were constantly exposed to the blaring announcements of "war victories" but nothing else. His mind was eased by Rachel's good news that Marika, her classmates, and the nuns were safe. He promised Rachel to keep all of his loved ones in his nightly prayers. Otto commented on his training procedures and expressed his doubts about being ready for combat. He mentioned his mental stress. He saw bayoneting a dummy different from killing another human and questioned if he could do it when called upon. Rachel treasured his final words: "I miss you too as I am slumping down under my flimsy blanket; I miss you and our feather bed. Be safe! Always, Otto."

Mimi became Rachel's confidant. She knew she was safe in

saying to her almost anything that was troubling her soul. After Otto's departure for boot camp, she felt utterly lost and alone. Her life had become totally disjointed. Rachel was desperate to share with Mimi what was happening in Otto's and her own life. She was often tempted to let her closest friends know about Miriam's existence and her whereabouts but couldn't bring herself to do so. Otto and her decision to leave Miriam with the nuns at the cloister more than seven years ago still haunted her daily.

The last patient left. Rachel stood in the examining room, committing the last of the used tools to the autoclave for sterilization. Her eyes glazed over with tears as she envisioned Otto lying in his bunk at the barracks. She was collecting her thoughts; she wished she could speak with him and tell him what was on her mind. She finally sat down and shared her feelings and thoughts on paper. "I can't believe you've been gone from me for three weeks. Things are still pretty rough in the neighborhood after that last devastating bomb attack. I feel so badly for many of our patients who lost everything. In some cases, not just things but family members as well. It's all so senseless.

"I think about you being trained to kill people. It just isn't in your nature to commit such horrible acts. I know men are supposed to protect their country, protect their families, and be strong. You are strong in many ways and have always shielded me as much as humanly possible. Now that you are gone, I feel terribly vulnerable and subject to persecution.

"Every time I hear some strange vehicle pull up in front of our building, I wonder if they have come to take me away. It's happened to so many dear friends and much of my family. Many believe the only reason I am still around is my profession and the fact that I am married to you.

"Although we made a terrible sacrifice, I am thankful that you insisted on sheltering Miriam Daniella. I believe she is in a safe place. Sometimes I wish we had tried for one more child, a boy to carry on your name. Perhaps we will have that chance after we wake up from this nightmare?

"You must sense by my very sentimental and philosophical thoughts, I am not a very happy person. I suffer terribly being alone and miss you day and night. I realize in three weeks you will be transported to some front and may not even be allowed to write at all for fear I might learn where you are. Knowing we will not be able to stay in touch gives me chills. For now, let me take you in my arms and hold you ever so close to me. I send you a kiss good night and all my love. Forever, Rachel."

A few days later, the mail brought Otto's reply. She needed to share it with her trusted friend. Rachel wrapped on Mimi's door. "I just heard from Otto. He's as down in the dumps as am I. Sorry to bend your ear. I just cannot be alone right now."

Mimi's arms embraced her crying friend. "Come in, my dear. You know I'm always here to listen. What does dear Otto have to say?"

"Otto is responding to the depressing output I mailed to him a few days ago. Boy, did I have the blues. That explains his response."

She read Otto's note. "Never apologize about being sentimental or philosophical. I feel the same way. We might have been raised with different religious backgrounds. Yet, intellectually, you and I are cut from the same cloth. Your grandparents raised you to be a law-abiding, decent human being. Even growing up in an orphanage, the nuns instilled good habits and behavior in me. We were privy to a good education and were endowed with the desire to help our fellow man.

"What we were not given was the desire to hate others and to harm them. I have always believed in a God for all mankind and not a God who would speak to us according to our blood type, religion, or whatever.

"I hurt to think that I will not be able to stay in touch with you after my last two weeks in this hellhole. Pardon my ungentle-man-like language. I'm tired of being called a useless asshole, being someone that needs to be fucked, and other endearing terms. These people are brutal. No wonder Schnabel tried doing to me what he heard others threatening to do. Now, I feel almost sorry for the poor bastard being tortured in Dachau or wherever they send people.

"My days are filled with misery being brainwashed and prodded into believing that it will be a marvelous experience to kill anyone who doesn't believe in German supremacy. My nights are torture in loneliness and longing to hold you and touch you. I miss you terribly. Not just for the good sex but for our ability to speak to each other, for the chance to recall and relive the events of the day, and just be close. Yes, I am horny. I better learn to live with it until this goddamn war is finally over. I take you in my arms and hold you firmly; I kiss you good night. Always, Otto."

Mimi held Rachel firmly in her arms as she placed Otto's note on the coffee table. "Have you eaten anything yet? You are wasting away. Every time I look at you, it seems you have shrunk another size."

"I have lost my appetite completely. Don't even mention food to me. I seek to lose myself with a snifter of stiff brandy. It works most nights. Dead tired from standing on my feet all day in the busy practice, it doesn't take too much to knock me out at first. It's when I awaken after a few hours of restless sleep that my wheels begin to turn and don't let me have the sleep I so desperately need. I worry what might happen to Otto and to me. There are still so many unanswered questions."

Mimi got the hint and stopped pushing food. "Have some of my treasured cognac. It will do in a pinch!" She lifted her glass. "Here's to you and Otto!" Rachel took a healthy sip and smiled through her tears at Mimi.

When Rachel got back to her apartment, she was exhausted—more mentally than physically. She fell into bed. She couldn't face writing a response to Otto. That would have to wait until the next day.

Rachel awoke with a terrible headache. Looking out the window, she saw it was raining buckets. A strong northeast wind was blowing the torrents in every direction. Rachel began to wonder if her early-morning patients would even show. She knew her first one lived about thirty minutes away and had to walk. This patient couldn't afford a cab even if one had been available. Rachel sat down at her desk and penned a note to Otto. "Oh my, we are in emotional trouble. It's kind of sad needing to express our feelings on paper. I'd much rather hold you and be your mother confessor. We are living in terrible and frightening times. I can hardly stand to turn on my radio. Every time I learn of another German victory, I ponder where and how it all shall end.

"I wonder how long this misery may continue. What shall happen to us after a victorious outcome of this war? Will we ever be able to claim our child as our own? How will she feel when she learns that we abandoned her? In my mind, I know we did the right thing; in my heart, I'm not so sure any longer. Now that they took you away from me, I would at least have my own child to care for. Of course, what would happen to her if they incarcerated me? Never mind me, what if they put Miriam and me into one of those camps?

"I shouldn't burden you with the tortures of my mind. You have your own hell to live in every day. That place sounds awful. I had no idea men in the military, German or otherwise, conducted themselves in such a deplorable manner. That would be tough to take for a gentleman such as yourself.

"My days are long. I continue to be thankful for all our faithful patients. I cherish the few friends I have. I was so upset reading your last letter, I had to read it to Mimi last night. She softened my emotional blows with some of her very best cognac. Although she offered to feed me, I had to decline. I can't even stand to look at food, never mind cooking it. My friends keep me in the know and try to cheer me up as well as is possible under the circumstances. I don't know what I would do if I were all alone. My first patient just walked in. My arms enfold you with all my love. I return your kisses. Forever, Rachel Adina."

April rains gave way to sunny days in May. Rachel couldn't wait to hear from Otto. She was fully aware of the completion date of training at the boot camp. If his previous concerns were well founded, his next letter might possibly be the last for her to receive for a long time. She would always treasure it.

On April 29, 1944, Otto wrote to her.

My Dearest Rachel Adina,

I love the sound of your name; whisper it into your beautiful ears and touch your stunning hair and then draw you tight against my body. I need you so much. Just imagining it, I'm becoming aroused. Forgive me.

This is my last chance to write to you and share with you how I feel. I have absolutely no idea where I will be sent. It's all a deep, dark secret. I don't even dare speculate. Since our mail is censored, whatever I might hint at would be blackened out. That is the rule. Some say that we might be able to call once we are away from the basic training camp. However, if we are in some foreign country, I cannot imagine that to be a possibility.

I have not often said this, but I do pray for you and our child every night. I pray for an end to this nightmare, and I pray for all of us to be reunited and alive when it is all over.

Now, I do know how to hold and fire a gun, affix a bayonet, and hit a target. I have learned to properly salute and how to click my heels and shout Heil Hitler. What I have not grasped is the idea of shooting at an enemy or ramming my bayonet through his body. I almost hope they get me first before I have to do it to them.

With a little bit of luck, you will get this letter in an unedited version. I just don't know. Since you have never commented on this since we have been writing, I presume we are OK. Perhaps whoever is doing the "reading" feels the way we do or has lifted a couple too many beers before taking on the task of reading his comrades' most private thoughts. One just never knows.

I am thinking of Wotan and kiss you farewell, my stoic, beautiful bride. I realize how well both of us know that most wonderful scene between father and daughter. The words and the music are in my head, and the tears are streaming down my face as I am writing to you. I kiss your eyes, and I kiss you farewell. With all my love forever, Otto.

Rachel clutched the letter to her heart. She wished she could read it to her friends. But she couldn't. Its content would've revealed Miriam's existence. At this point, she was not willing to risk Miriam's or her own safety. For now, her and Otto's secret was safe with her.

Chapter 14

ON the morning of August 10, 1944, it happened. Otto and Rachel had feared the moment for years. Rachel was with her second patient of the morning. A large, canvas-covered military truck pulled up in front of her building. Three brownshirts jumped out of the cab of the vehicle. Two headed straight for the door leading to Rachel's practice. She could hear the clanking of boots on the tiled floor as they approached her office. They didn't even ring a door bell and easily forced their way into the examining room. Her patient's and Rachel's eyes stared at them in total disbelief. "Are you Rachel von Graben?"

"Yes, I am. How may I be of service to you?" Rachel tried to be polite. She could tell by the tone of voice and their demeanor that they were there to take her away. Her hands began to shake. She felt like calling for help and knew instantly, no one would be able to stand by her. Her eyes swept around the room; she was hoping to see Otto, but Otto wasn't there. She had to face her situation alone.

"Don't try being polite. It won't help you. You are under arrest." One of them grabbed Rachel's patient by her arm and yanked her out of the dental chair. "Lady, get your coat and purse, and leave these premises immediately. You better find yourself another dentist, preferably one who isn't Jewish. Get out of here before we throw you out." He gave the poor woman a shove; she almost fell down four steps.

They turned back to Rachel. "Guess you thought we'd never catch up to you. How dumb do you think we are? How long did you think you could hide behind that von Graben name? No wonder it never said Rachel von Graben. Some of your patients suspected that you were a Jew and let us know of your existence. You have about three minutes to grab whatever you care to take with you. You won't need much where you are headed. They'll provide you with a free uniform. Hope you like stripes, not that you need anything to slenderize your appearance."

Rachel's mind was racing as she crossed the hallway into her apartment. "Who was the Judas who betrayed me? How could any patient of ours be that mean?" She grabbed a hand towel as she passed the bathroom. She needed to stifle her screams. She was utterly frightened. She looked at a photo of Otto and snatched it. She longed for his protective arms around her. Rachel ran to her bedroom and grabbed her purse and the Varanasi scarf. She was wearing a comfortable dress under her lab coat. What should she take? There was no time to think. She had no idea where she was being taken. All she knew at that very moment was that she was probably seeing the end of her life near. One of the brownshirts latched onto Rachel's right arm and pushed her toward the front door.

"Come on, bitch. Your three minutes were up a long time ago. How much time do you think we have every time we pick up one of you miserable scum?" He decided that wasn't humiliating enough. He pulled the amber clasp out of Rachel's chignon and threw it on the sidewalk. It broke into many pieces. He switched his grasp from her arm to her beautiful hair and yanked her literally out of the house. Mimi looked on from her window totally aghast. Rachel's face was stark white against the darkness of her hair. Her facial expression was that often seen on insane people—wild and totally disconnected from the world.

Being dragged to the truck, Rachel could hear women and children crying. The third brownshirt on hand had flipped down the lid in the back of the truck. He jumped onto the truck; his boots hitting the flatbed in a single try. His agility was impressive. What came out of his mouth was not. "You filthy Jewish bitches better shut up before I give you another workout with my billy club. Did you understand me? I don't want to hear another fucking peep out of you!" The sounds from the truck became muffled.

Rachel felt manhandled—and she was. One of the guys had slipped the "Jewish badge" onto her left sleeve as they were pushing her toward the back of the truck. She tightly clung to her Varanasi scarf. "Get moving, you dumb bitch. We'll let you take that useless rag. It might keep your tits warm where we'll send you. Who knows, they might even let you wear it with nothing else. We understand the new commander at Theresienstadt has some weird peccadilloes. He has some of the inmates dance for him to the 'Seven Veils' from *Salome*. Rost is known to like fucking the prettier Jews in all sorts of positions. Some say he even likes men now and then. We hope you enjoy your visit to Theresienstadt." With that, they threw Rachel onto the back of the truck.

Rachel cast a last glance at her friend. They were both stunned. Tears were streaming down their faces as the truck pulled away from the curb.

X

As soon as the three hoodlums had closed the back of the truck and put the vehicle into motion, Rachel stood up. She could not sit down with the others who were crammed sitting on hay and straw saturated with vomit, urine, and human feces. The smell was unbearable. Rachel kept pulling her lab coat and the scarf tightly around her. She was afraid some vermin might latch onto her and crawl all over her body. The filth surrounding her made her sick to her stomach. Rachel was fearful she might vomit.

On their way to the railway station, their captors picked up three more women. The truck was jammed full of human bodies, full of human misery. Eventually, the truck pulled up to a distant and isolated track in the railway station. No observers could be seen. The selection of the barren location for the train to hell aided their captors in the act of hiding their dreadful deeds.

The truck stopped; the doors on the last of the cattle cars were pushed open. More brownshirts and some uniformed military came on the scene. "Get your dirty asses moving, you fucking Jewish vermin. Get in that cattle car!" He swung his billy club and struck a young boy across his face. The child screamed in pain. His mother tried to stop the bleeding of his nose with her dirty skirt. The brownshirt just stood there and laughed; he was ready to strike the next helpless victim. The prisoners in this wagon were all women and children. If they thought the stench was bad on the truck, it was far worse in the cattle car. One of the guards yelled at Rachel. "Hey you, while you are still standing, make yourself useful; empty that shit and piss out of those pots. Perhaps your Jewish honker isn't offended by the odoriferous treat in the wagon." Rachel did as she was told. She almost gagged as she was emptying the vessels that were filled to the brim. They realized theirs was the last cattle car to be packed with Jews being shipped to some camp.

Packed was the operative word. Rachel decided it was best not to sit down. Others were too weak to do so. She would only look for a spot to sit when she no longer had the stamina to remain on her feet. The train started to move at about nine o'clock that evening. While the outside temperatures became slightly more tolerable, inside the wagons, they stayed unbearable. There was a bit more air entering the cattle car when the train was in motion. Most of them had no idea where they were going; Rachel knew they were being shipped to Theresienstadt; she had heard what her abductors said when they arrested her.

Rachel looked at the misery surrounding her. One of the women took a handful of the drinking water and tasted it before giving some to her screaming baby. She tossed it onto the filthy straw. The drinking water was spoiled. Other mothers sifted through the straw in hopes of finding anything that might be edible. Those sitting at Rachel's feet were coughing, sneezing, and vomiting. Modesty had been left somewhere along the wayside. Those who needed to relieve themselves initially used one of the pots Rachel was forced to empty. Once they were filled again, everyone simply urinated and defecated wherever they were standing, lying, or sitting. Children were crying to be fed. Mothers held them to ease their discomfort. A couple of women were trying to nurse their babies. The starving infants kept sucking on sore nipples that had gone dry and were incapable of providing the needed nourishment. The mothers beheld their screaming babies with expressions of horror on their faces. One mother actually choked her starving baby to death to put him out of his misery.

Their captors didn't care about how anyone died or the lack of food; the less food, the less production of excrement. No one cared if some Jews starved to death in transport. The fewer they delivered alive, the fewer they needed to gas and cremate.

This was August. The temperatures inside the freight car became unbearable. The almost airtight wagon caused some to suffocate from the stench in the overheated car. Every so often, she would cover her face with the scarf. It didn't help. There was no getting away from the foul odors. Periodically, Rachel would try to stand near the few slits in the door, which allowed a bit of fresh air into the stifling conveyance. Most were willing to share except one of the women who was determined not to relinquish the spot promising momentary relief. Rachel pushed against the woman who had garnered the desired position. "Move over; you can't hog it all. I need some of that air before I pass out!"

"Who the hell do you think you are? I was here first. I feel just as sick as you, bitch."

Rachel became incensed. She hauled out at her nemesis and hit her so hard, the woman toppled over and landed on her back in the straw. After a few minutes, Rachel allowed another woman to take her place. Listening to the terrible cries and moaning of those suffering with her, Rachel had to cover her ears for temporary relief. She kept hearing the mantra by one of her fellow prisoners. "Please, dear God, let me die. I can't take it anymore." Rachel understood that death would be a welcome escape. But what kept Rachel from wishing to die was her strong desire to be reunited with Otto and Miriam somewhere in time.

Chapter 15

PEERING out of one of the vents from the slowly moving train, Rachel could barely see the new moon rising. Days had gone by when their journey came to a jerky stop. The vision of the moon was replaced by glaring spot lights. Billy-club-swinging female guards pushed the doors open with a vengeance. The burst of fresh air spelled temporary relief. Earlier in the day, Rachel and her fellow prisoners discovered that three women and two children within their wagon had died. "Are you all alive?" demanded the uniformed woman standing by their door. The guard was rather short and stocky. Her hair was cut in a mannish style barely covered by a Garrison cap. Her voice was harsh and loud. One of the other guards called her Olga.

One of the prisoners spoke up. "Three women and two children died during the transport."

Guard Olga demanded, "One of you other bitches help her. Pull out anyone who didn't make it. You can dump them right into these wheelbarrows. One of you stronger ones can move the corpses to the mass grave site once you are off the train. Get moving. We don't have a lot of time to be dillydallying around. Get those Jewish asses going! It's already way past my bedtime."

The site was extremely well lit. In the distance they could spot watchtowers manned by machine-gun-carrying guards. No one would dream of attempting an escape. Women and mothers holding onto their small children leaped from the cattle car. Had they looked to their left, they would have seen hundreds of people jumping out of their wagons to be processed by camp personnel. Some of the older children were afraid to jump. Olga demanded, "Hurry, hurry. If you can't hold onto those brats, push them off the wagon before you jump. We don't have time to lift these kids off the train." As the kids hit the ground, they screamed in pain. Their attending guard struck them fiercely with her club. Mothers and children were crying in pain all around. Rachel couldn't deal with what she saw. She closed her eyes or tried looking away from the scenes of horror surrounding her. Rachel heard the guard yelling, "Before the last woman jumps off the car, take this shovel and push out all that dirty straw and hay. We'll add clean for the next transport later. Don't ever say we don't do anything nice for you people. That's using the term loosely. You ain't people. You're all nothing but worthless shit."

Olga grabbed the arms of two of the younger women. "You two look strong enough. Get these wheelbarrows out of here. Take a look at those deep depressions on your right. Those are mass graves. Get moving and push these dead bodies to their final destination. There are piles of lime and shovels on site. After you dump your loads, cover the corpses with the white stuff. It helps with the decomposing and cuts down the stink."

Rachel just stood still as if she was nailed to the ground. Guards up the line gave other commands. "Line up in three columns. Men to the left, children who can walk in the middle, and women to the right." Rachel observed the guards using their clubs and stocks of their shotguns to prod their victims in line. Women screamed when their children were taken away from them. The guards were ruthless. Anyone who objected was beaten with their clubs or threatened with pistols and shotguns. One woman refused to let her child go. Both she and the child were shot and killed by a guard. Other prisoners were ordered to carry their bodies to one of the mass graves. Total silence fell over the adults who saw what happened. Eventually, the columns were ordered to move briskly. They entered the camp under the arch marked with the slogan *"Arbeit macht frei!"* (Work makes you free!).

Olga, who handled the last wagon of the train, brought up the rear. "Don't stop walking until you are told to do so. When we pass the Marktplatz, it's not very far. You can't miss the place. You will be instructed how to proceed."

The first of the new prisoners had reached the Podmokly Barracks. Olga's cohorts close to the front of the columns of marchers started yelling, "Stop; all of you stop." They had learned to obey; they had observed the consequences of not following orders only minutes earlier. Using megaphones, the guards blared again and again, "Men enter through the left, children through the middle, and women through the right door." Bringing up the rear, Rachel and her fellow prisoners from the last wagon took a long time before reaching the point of entry.

As they were marching toward their check-in point, Rachel noticed three uniformed men practically walking next to her. One appeared to be in his thirties. The other two were considerably younger and of lower rank. Rachel was aware she was being looked over, especially by the older of the three.

Like all prisoners, Rachel was registered. A six-digit number was written with indelible ink above the inside of her left wrist. If time allowed, the number would later be permanently tattooed. She was about to be transferred to the next station for hair cutting or shaving, delousing, and a shower when Major Johann von Rond-stett intervened. "Release her into my care. I'll see to it that she will be properly taken care of." His demand was instantly acted upon. Major von Rondstett was second in command at Theresienstadt. The current camp leader, Klemens Rost, liked the young man who had recently been transferred from a post he held in Paris for more than three years. His reputation as a ladies' man preceded him. He lived up to that reputation since his arrival at Theresienstadt earlier in the year. Johann von Rondstett made a striking figure in his black full-length leather coat. Under his officer's cap, he hid a full crop of blond hair. Just looking at his appearance, he represented Hitler's ideal of Aryan manhood. He pointed to his two sidekicks as he spoke to Rachel. "These are my adjutants, Kern and Adel. They will take you to my private quarters where you can shower and discard all the trash you are wearing.

"Kern, on the way, stop at the collection center and pick up some clean things for the lady. I know I can trust both of you to select the best possible. You have such exquisite taste in ladies' undergarments." He looked back at Rachel. She could read between the lines.

"By the way, what's your name?"

"My name is Rachel Adina von Graben."

"Pleasure to meet you, Frau von Graben." Rachel detected the sardonic tone in his voice. Why was she being singled out by this man? Why did he order his underlings to get clean clothes for her? She felt ashamed and cheap being treated preferentially by a captor. She certainly wasn't seeking any favors.

"Are you alone among these visitors?"

"What do you mean by visitors? We are prisoners. Let's call the child by its proper name." She didn't know what made her so brazen in her response. It was more than clear to her that she was at this man's mercy. He could shoot her on the spot and no questions would be asked. She might find herself in one of those mass graves if she didn't keep her mouth shut.

"Is there a Mr. von Graben? And if there is, why isn't he with you? Were you separated in transport?"

"My husband was drafted last March. I have no idea where he is. And he doesn't know that I have been incarcerated."

"Don't use that word. You are staying for a while at Theresienstadt. There are far worse places. We are in the process of making this center into a showplace. We want the world to realize that no one is mistreated in our camps. I'll talk with you later. First, I need to finish supervising the registration process of the new visitors." He clicked his official heels, Heil-Hitlered those standing near him, and caught Olga's eye. Since his arrival from Paris, she always cooperated with him in finding new sex partners to satisfy his insatiable appetite for pretty women.

Kern hooked his right arm around Rachel and guided her toward the collection center. Clothing, shoes, and other items on hand were confiscated from the luggage of many of the prisoners. Most had no need for the items after they were issued their striped prisoner uniforms. Adel looked at Kern with disgust. "How can you touch that filthy bitch? Just look at that once-upon-a-time-white coat. She must be some kind of doctor. That thing is covered with dried shit and stains from piss and vomit. I wouldn't go near her. Can you understand what von Rondstett sees in her? I think he was taken in by her hair and her sharp figure. He probably got a hard-on just envisioning her cavorting in front of him with nothing but that damn thing draped over her breasts and cunt." He opened the door and pushed her in disgust. "Here we are. Let's see if we can find the right thing von Rondstett might like." Rachel was beginning to wonder if these two guys were gay. When she was arrested in Essen, some of the brownshirts talked about the commandant having strange peccadilloes. She hadn't realized von Rondstett was not the commandant but his right-hand man.

Kern and Adel knew exactly who to speak to at the center. Adel approached the woman in charge. "How come you are working this late?"

"We are always open when we have an incoming train. Commandant Rost insists on cataloging all the stuff taken from the new arrivals. We don't launder anything this late. But other things are all recorded and put into proper places."

Adel was impressed by the thoroughness of the center. "Therese, we need some sexy underwear, a couple of blouses, and a pretty skirt or two for von Rondstett's latest paramour. I think he would bust his balls if he saw her in red and black underwear. Let me check out your breasts, bitch." Adel cupped her breasts with his large hands and pronounced her tits to be a good-sized C.

"Von Rondstett will like these knockers; he's a breast and leg man."

"What do you think of these two blouses, Kern? I like these black skirts, particularly this one with that long slit up the left side. That ought to get his pecker going." Adel turned toward the woman behind the counter. "I think that just about does it, Therese. Put the stuff in a bag and put the charges on von Rondstett's account. He's good for the money."

The way these guys treated her and acted in her presence made her feel like a whore. Rachel let her imagination run wild. *How would she act with a man who had sought her out from among hundreds of other Jewish women delivered to the camp this day? Why me? What does he want from me?* For now she just let herself be dragged and pushed by Kern and Adel.

Von Rondstett's executive housing was on the second floor of an old building. It might have been a villa in olden days. The walls in the stairwell could've used a coat of fresh paint. Rachel was pushed through the large, ornate, and heavily carved door. Adel flicked on all the lights. She was surprised by the size of the living room. It also could have been improved easily. There were only minor cracks in the plaster. The décor looked old world but appeared to be clean and featured well-worn leather furniture. Large curtained windows allowed plenty of sunshine into the living room. The large sofa looked comfortable. She walked through the place in a trance. The sofa was facing the door that led to the bedroom and a large bath. She was aghast looking at the wallpaper in the bath and bedroom depicting sex orgies. There were huge mirrors hanging above the sofa as well as over the headboard of the bed. The few pieces of art gracing the other walls were in pretty good taste. They were copies or prints for sure.

Rachel's thoughts were totally off track. Why did she care what this place looked like? Was it because of her recent inhumane experiences that she was searching for a touch of civility somewhere? She and her fellow prisoners had been treated worse than animals. And, of course, she was imagining what would happen once her captor arrived on the scene. She shivered and shook from head to toe as she faced Adel and Kern.

Adel spoke first. "Here you are, Ra-chel," giving her name the Yiddish pronunciation. "Or should I have said Frau von Graben? Either way works for us. Get out of those rags and dump them in this drum. The maid will get rid of all that trash when she comes in tomorrow. She knows the drill. Get going! Make sure you close the bedroom door and turn on the fan in the bathroom. Von Rondstett doesn't like it when his walls get all wet. He prides himself on that fancy wallpaper they put up for him. He's kind of into decorating and design. He enjoys all those depictions of naked men and women screwing each other. By the way, von Rondstett is not the big wheel around here. That is Klemens Rost, the commandant. You'll hear all about their big project after he's fucked you a couple of times."

Rachel had heard enough. At least now she knew with whom she was dealing. She headed for the bedroom and the shower. She did with her filthy clothes as Adel had said. Rachel couldn't help seeing her naked body in the giant mirror over the headboard. Never mind over the bed; there was another one mounted on the ceiling. She was shocked to see how emaciated her body appeared. Her breasts were still firm, but she could see every rib on her torso. Otto would be shocked to see her like this, especially naked in the bedroom of a total stranger. She already could feel von Rondstett's hands all over her body. Rachel shuddered at the thought of being raped by the Nazi. What could she do to protect herself? She might be exposed to venereal diseases. She was thankful Otto had insisted she have an intrauterine device after they were married; they didn't want to create another child during war times.

For the moment she couldn't think of any answers to the many questions that tortured her. She needed to wash off the filth on her body. She scrubbed and scrubbed, especially her hair. She had visions of fleas and lice crawling all over her. The hot water felt good on her skin. She sat down on the floor of the shower and sobbed. When the temperature of the water became uncomfortable, she finally turned off the water and dried herself. She couldn't decide what to select from the garments the guys had picked out for her. She really didn't care what she looked like. Her scarf was filthy. She decided to wash it in the sink. She grabbed two clean towels and rolled out the scarf until it was just damp. Holding it up to the light of the bathroom, it looked much improved. It was clean and the colors were completely restored. All that remained in her small satchel was Otto's photo.

Approaching the living room door, she thought she heard some strange sounds. Rachel opened the door and held her breath. Adel and Kern were were standing on the sofa and facing her, stark naked and engaged in sex. She hadn't realized they were both blond and quite Scandinavian looking when not wearing their officers' caps. Kern smiled at Rachel. "Don't mind us; we like to take advantage of coming to von Rondstett's place and his shower. He knows all about us. I see you washed that rag of yours. Hang it over that curtain rod. It will be dry by the time he gets here. Go sit down somewhere. It's very late, and you must be exhausted from that long train ride." She did as told and caught herself in the last second; Rachel couldn't afford to blunder by telling them what her experiences were on the train.

She hung up her treasure and found a chair. She spotted a small desk near the balcony. When Kern and Adel were too busy enjoying themselves, she slipped the little satchel into a top drawer of the desk. "Phew! That was a relief." With another deep sigh, she collapsed and realized she hadn't sat anywhere for days except for a few moments on that filthy hay and straw while in transport to Theresienstadt. She reached up and touched her hair. Thank God, it felt good to have it there, clean, and not crawling with lice. The horror of it all passed in front of her eyes. Had it not been for her captor, she probably wouldn't have hair any longer. While standing in line, she had seen hundreds of shorn heads heading for the showers.

Chapter 16

RACHEL finally succumbed to sleep. Her body and mind were exhausted. Scenes of the last few days even haunted her in her sleep. She heard the screams of the hungry babies and was horrified once again as she witnessed a desperate mother murdering her own starving child. When she got out of the shower, she was stunned to see the blue and black marks on her buttocks and thighs where the guards had struck her with billy clubs and shotguns. Her own mistreatment by her captors, the sights of death and pain inflicted by humans on their fellow man, and the misery witnessed after her arrival at Theresienstadt weighed heavily on her.

Kern stood next to her chair. Rachel was mumbling in her sleep. Her body moved frantically. He touched her shoulder. "You were having a nightmare. You are safe for the moment. We are leaving now. It's already long after midnight. Major von Rondstett will be here soon. You may want to take a look at those magazines. He picked them up at a bordello he frequented during his stay in Paris."

Rachel's eyes popped wide open. "What the hell are you talking about?" She had no idea how long she had slept. She was still half in a stupor. Rachel thought about Otto and Miriam before she dozed off; even in her sleep she was haunted by the tortures she had witnessed. Her beloved Otto and Miriam were all she truly cared for and worried about. All she could fathom at this very moment was her desire to survive.

Kern and Adel left quickly. Against her better judgment, she picked up one of the magazines. She was stunned and threw down the trashy magazine. She assumed that all of them depicted lurid sex flagrantly and openly displayed in keeping with the bathroom's wallpaper. It brought to mind the experiences Grandfather Adam Jethro shared after visiting the temples in Khajuraho, India, while he was on one of his buying trips. He always said, "The Taj Mahal is about love; the temples of Khajuraho are all about sex." She couldn't help thinking about Otto and the last time they made love. How she missed him. Where was he? Thinking about their last night together made her close her eyes. She was trying to relive those moments.

The apartment door was pushed open with anger. It caught Rachel by surprise. She turned to face von Rondstett. He smiled. "I'm glad you had a chance to clean up and rest for a while. I see you revived that beautiful trapping of yours. I want you to tell me its story. I'm sure there is one. Let me open a bottle of this fine Bordeaux to let it breathe while I get into the shower. I'd ask you to join me, but I prefer your beautiful hair to be dry while I have you. It's been a very full day at the camp, and I do need a shower badly. Come to my bedroom. I want you close to me. Tell me your full name; I'm not about to call you Frau von Graben in my moments of ecstasy."

"My full name is Rachel Adina Salm von Graben."

"I like that!"

Rachel began to feel lie a cheap whore in some French bordello. She wasn't sure how she would handle the seduction scene that awaited her. She had read about illicit affairs and seen movies dealing with the subject, but she had never been with anyone but Otto. He was her first and only love. For a moment she recalled that scene in her advisor's office. "You better forget about that way of dealing with the major. Your hair will be shorn for sure if you hurt him" ran through her mind.

As commanded by von Rondstett, Rachel followed him to his bedroom. He started stripping off his uniform while he was still talking to her. She was astounded by the color of his hair as he tossed his military cap. It landed perfectly on the top of his coat rack. Within seconds von Rondstett stood split naked in front of her. He was tall and broad but not quite like Otto. And, of course, Otto wasn't blond. She turned her head, trying to look away from Johann. The last thing she wanted to convey to him was any sexual interest or desire. It had been five months since she had last been with Otto, but she found this situation abhorrent. She knew she was about to be ravished. Should she expect to be raped? He kept talking about making love to her. As soon as he got into the shower, she walked out of the bedroom.

Rachel could hear him talking. With the water running hard, she had to strain to understand what he was saying. "I won't be long. Come back to my passion pit and get out of those damn clothes. I want you waiting for me when I get out of the shower, Rachel Adina. I like that sound. It's so exotic. You won't be sorry I picked you from among all the other prisoners that arrived today. You're stunning. I can't wait to have you." Rachel wasn't sure about having been saved from whatever. As so often during the last weeks, she was wishing she was dead rather than alive. And then she would return to her need to fight for her life at all cost; she had to be there for Miriam and Otto whenever this nightmare ended.

Von Rondstett stepped out of the shower. He saw Rachel standing in the living room looking away from him. She was still fully dressed. "Didn't you hear me? Why are you still dressed? I asked you nicely to be ready for some action. Did you think I was joking? Come here; let me help you get out of these rags. I want to see you naked, Rachel Adina. I want to hold you and touch you."

Rachel didn't move. She wasn't ready to be raped. She was

utterly frightened. The scene of praying with Otto in Mother Superior's office flashed in front of her eyes. She felt like praying for her own soul. She knelt and just closed her eyes. "Dear God, shield me from this evil; guide me in all that I must do to survive the horrors in the days and weeks to come. Protect my Miriam and Otto. Let them be waiting for me when I am finally free."

Johann couldn't believe his eyes. He could hear her mumbling. He finally realized she was praying. He became infuriated. "What the fuck are you doing? Don't tell me you are one of those fucking converted Jews who believe in all that praying shit?"

He stormed into the living room and grabbed Rachel by her hair. She couldn't stand to look at him. "I'll give you something to pray to as long as you are on your knees. How about wrapping your praying lips around my dick and giving me a blow job I won't forget?"

He reached for her chin with his left hand, putting so much pressure on her jawbone that Rachel began to scream in pain. When she opened her mouth, he forced his prick down her throat. Rachel nearly choked as he fired away with rapid movement. He pushed her to the floor, anticipating his first ejaculation. Rachel knew the strength of her teeth. She was tempted to decapitate his dick. She knew it would be her death sentence had she done so. When he finally let go of her, she thought she was going to gag. She spat his semen into his face and shuddered in disgust realizing to what she had been subjected.

"Come here, bitch. I'm not done with you." He yanked her to her feet and ripped off every last piece of clothing she was wearing. Walking by the window, he tore the scarf off the curtain rod. He tied it around Rachel's neck, yanking her like a dog on its leash in the direction of his bedroom. Rachel was whimpering; she draped her right arm across her eyes, not wanting to look at her attacker. "Well, Rachel Adina, now for my real treat. I want to fuck you until you beg me for more. It must be some time since you have been with a man. I'll take care of that little matter right now."

Johann pushed her off the bed; she nearly fell onto the floor. "Get up, bitch; I want to see all of you." He stared at her body, particularly her taut breasts. He turned around and reached for a button on a record player. She hadn't even noticed it before. As the record began to play, she knew immediately what was to come next. "Are you familiar with *Salome*, the Richard Strauss opera? I am playing the 'Dance of the Seven Veils' for you. Go put that rag of yours to good use. Pretend I'm King Herod and dance for me. It will drive me absolutely mad watching you perform."

Rachel did it to appease him. She knew every note of the music and danced accordingly. In her mind, she pretended to be dancing for Otto. She wasn't sure how she would handle what was certain to happen. As the music came to its concluding fever pitch, she shed the "last" veil in front of her captor. The Varanasi scarf fell to the floor. He was leering at her and sensed her total rejection. Rachel was longing for him to be Jochanaan and asking for his bloody head served to her on a silver platter instead of being raped by Herod.

Johann reached for her hair. "Get back here. I want to ride you like a stallion. Make it fast before I have to drag you into my arms." When she reached his bed, he pulled her down to his chest and then forced her into the large down pillows. The coolness of the silky covers was relief to her heated body. Once again she resorted to covering her eyes with her right arm. He glared at her as he pulled her arm away from her face. Rachel kept her eyes closed, almost pinching them shut. She couldn't stand to look at the disgusting man.

"Oh no, you are doing this all wrong. We can make this a good or a bad experience for both of us. Try to remember what I prevented from happening to you just a few hours ago. Had I not fallen for you on first sight and claimed you for myself, your beautiful hair would be shaved off by now. You would be wearing an ugly gray-and-black-striped uniform and lying with the rest of the prisoners in some lice-infected bunk. Is that what you would prefer? You can have it, if that's what you really want. I'm sure I will find another bed partner in no time flat. Perhaps, without your beautiful hair, but stuck in one of those horrible uniforms, no one would desire you as much as I desire you. As you can tell, I'm very much aroused by the way you looked during your performance. I have found lots of paramours in my life who satisfied my sexual needs."

Rachel stared at him while he painted this devastating picture for her. She viewed herself shorn and in that ugly uniform lying in a lice-covered bunk. What would Otto have her do? She wasn't sure. There was no question about it. She was at von Rondstett's mercy. He pulled her close to him. He got on top of her. As he inserted his distinctly strong tongue into her mouth, she almost choked. For the first time, she noticed the size of the hands stroking her all over, starting with her breasts. She closed her eyes. She tried to pretend she was with Otto. It was von Rondstett attempting to make love to her. He became angry at the lack of her responsiveness. He wanted to look into her eyes and have her look into his. The total lack of eye contact enraged him. Without another word, he mounted her and forced himself mercilessly into her. He rammed her with a fury that made Rachel scream in pain. "I know you were pretending to be with that man of yours instead of with me. It was so blatantly obvious. It could have been so much better for both of us if you just gave me half a chance at pleasing you. I could toss you into the midst of all that evil right now. I won't. For some idiotic reason, I feel differently about you than any other bitch I've fucked in the past." He pulled away from her and got in the shower. Rachel covered her violated body with the silky sheet and sobbed bitterly. She wanted Otto's arms around her, but he wasn't there to help her. She was utterly alone and devastated.

Johann got out of the shower and suggested Rachel get herself cleaned up as well. "Use the hand-held shower; you won't get that beautiful hair of yours all wet. Make it quick; I don't like my fancy wallpaper all steamed up!" She could tell his enormous anger had abated. He put on a pair of attractive pjs and tossed a beautiful silk kimono in her direction. "When you feel like it, join me in the living room. We need to talk."

Rachel couldn't wait to get into the shower and wash herself thoroughly after being raped by her captor. She cried softly, not wanting to engender further anger in von Rondstett. She also found herself in a quandary. She saw first hand what was being done to the women who were ahead in line when Major von Rondstett had interceded on her behalf. She cried into her towel as she was drying herself. "Otto, Otto, where are you to help me make an acceptable decision? I cannot let myself be killed. I must survive this nightmare. I don't even know if you are still alive. Who will be there for Miriam if I don't get out of this hellhole alive? If it takes being von Rondstett's whore, I'll do it. I must be there for our child."

The major was waiting for her in the living room. She declined drinking the wine he offered. Rachel needed to remain sober if she wanted to face the reality of her dilemma. Johann spoke first. "I have been with many women since I turned sixteen. I can't believe it's twenty-one years since I lost my virginity. I always liked sex; all kinds of sex. You are different. There was something about you when I first spotted you in that line of miserable prisoners getting off the train. Even my queer adjutants were taken by you. There was something about the way you carried yourself. Underneath all that dirt and grime, I could see a woman of elegance, class, flair, style, and grace. Call it what you will. I didn't want to rape you; I wanted to make love to you. I presume you understand what I am trying to tell you. It was your reaction to my love-making that enraged me. It was your unwillingness to love me in return that made me hurt you. It wasn't what I wanted."

Rachel wasn't sure she was hearing correctly. Was he trying to win her over with a torrent of insincere words? What was he attempting to tell her?

He continued talking. "This is a terrible place, where terrible things are done to all who are sent here. I'm not proud of what's going on. I do not condone the treatment of your people by Commander Rost and his ilk. For me, it's a job, and I try to do it with as much civility as I can without putting myself in harm's way. Yes, I am wearing the SS uniform. It was forced on me. It opened doors for me while I was in Paris. I didn't want to come to this house of horrors. I was transferred here against my wishes. You could report me, and I would be shot as a traitor to Germany.

"Never speak to anyone about my feelings concerning Theresienstadt. I don't even understand why I am sharing my innermost thoughts with you. Forgive me. I must warn you. If you divulge any part of what I just said to the wrong people, it will mean execution on the spot for both of us. Do you understand me, Rachel Adina? Don't trust anyone!"

Rachel decided to take advantage of Johann's confession. "I have good reasons for wanting to survive this nightmare. I'm ready to do almost anything to escape from this place of evil. I'm willing to make a pact with the devil. Never will I speak to anyone of what you just revealed to me, since I cannot afford to get myself killed. I shall stay with you and take advantage of your protection. I will even go so far as pandering to your needs in public. Let the outside world believe that I am your whore indeed, but you will never again do as much as lay a hand on me. If you are really as honorable as you are trying to make me believe, you will accept my conditions." Rachel took a deep breath before she shared with von Rondstett a bit of her background as far as her family and Otto were concerned. She never mentioned the existence of Miriam. He was stunned. "You drive a tough bargain. As I said earlier, I knew there was something extraordinary about you. I will find it difficult to have you so close to me and yet so far and untouchable. It will be good to come home at night from a day of horror and have someone decent and pleasant to talk to. I'll find some other ways of satisfying my sexual needs. No one shall ever be the wiser. I will do nothing but brag about my nightly conquests of beautiful Rachel Adina. Let's be sure to make this convincing to the maid who cleans the place daily. I suggest we sleep in my bed without ever crossing the line. If that works for you, it will work for me. I promise you, I will never betray you."

Rachel wasn't sure she could trust him, but she was willing to take the chance. She believed Otto would forgive her the pact she just made with the devil. When Johann left the room to use the WC, she retrieved Otto's photo from the drawer and kissed it.

Chapter 17

JOHANN had gotten out of bed long before Rachel finally wakened. She hadn't realized what that traumatic train ride from Essen to Theresienstadt had done to her body. He looked at the clothes Kern and Adel had selected for her and decided there was a definite need for more practical things. "After breakfast at the canteen, I will introduce you to Klemens Rost, the commandant of the KZ.

"Your background in the world of silk and your profession may come in handy. I'm going to play up your artistic side first. I won't even mention your DDS degree. He might have some horrible way of channeling your professional skills. What's foremost in Rost's mind right now is to make this place into a showcase. He wants the world to believe that those who come here live a life of luxury and class. For the last few weeks, hundreds of your fellow prisoners have cleaned up the place. Plantings and beautiful flowers are everywhere. Some of the barracks have seen major improvements. There are stages and theaters where talented Jewish musicians are encouraged to perform. Others are allowed to put on famous plays. There are libraries and reading rooms. Everything is done to convey the idea that being in a concentration camp is not such a bad experience. He hired Kurt Gerron to direct a propaganda movie. Filming is supposed to start close to September first. Just let me do all the initial talking. I know how to schmooze with that asshole."

They walked into the canteen. The walls looked like they saw a fresh coat of paint recently, all in keeping with the beautification efforts. There were hardly any soft surfaces. The noise from silverware striking china plates was annoying. One could hardly hear what someone said who was seated across the large round tables. Commander Rost was sitting at his regular place surrounded by some of his yes men as Johann approached with Rachel. Rost was in uniform flashing numerous decorations on his left chest. Rachel spotted a large medallion surrounding the SS symbol hanging from his neck. The top of his shirt was not buttoned, showing off some of his hairy chest. She found his appearance unbecoming for a leading officer, and thought, "What do I care how this guy shows up in public? He doesn't give a damn about any of us, including some on his side of the fence." His hair, styled in a typical, short military cut, was dark brown and looked greasy. He looked like he could have used a better shave that morning. Much to Rachel's surprise, he rose from his chair. She noted that he was just of medium height. He didn't particularly impress her. Rost looked her up and down. "Who is the young woman, von Rondstett?"

"I'd like you to meet Rachel Adina von Graben."

The commander reached for Rachel's hand. He planted a wet kiss on the back of her right hand. Rachel felt like slapping him. He introduced himself. "Commandant Klemens Rost; welcome to Theresienstadt." He clicked his heels before reclaiming his seat.

Johann von Rondstett swallowed and coughed lightly. "I confess I spotted her yesterday when she arrived on the evening train. I claim her for myself. Besides, last I knew, you are happily married."

"Do I dare ask if she delivered as good in the sack as she appears to promise?"

"I vouch for that. Olga sanctioned my latest 'acquisition.' She has done an excellent job of finding me suitable bed partners since I landed here. Paris was definitely easier in that respect. The reason I didn't hide Mrs. von Graben in my apartment was that I wanted you to meet her. I believe she could be helpful with the beautification act."

Rachel decided to speak on her own behalf. "I understand you are presently working intensely at sprucing up the institution. Johann spoke to me this morning about the upcoming production of a film showing off Theresienstadt in its best light. I have always been very much interested in theater, especially opera. I'm particularly fond of staging and costume design that involves the use of silk. It is such a versatile, durable, forgiving, and luscious fabric."

Rost was all ears. "We are only a couple weeks from starting to shoot the film with Gerron. Of course, he has his own ideas as to what he wants to feature. I'd like you to work up some designs, Rachel, and share them with me and Kurt Gerron. Would tomorrow be too soon?"

"Would it be OK for Major von Rondstett to give me a tour of the camp? I would like to see the venues under consideration for artistic rejuvenation."

"Excellent idea. I'm too busy with so many new 'visitors' to Theresienstadt. He'll make an outstanding consultant on the matters in question. He's been working closely with me on this project. Thanks for making yourself useful. We'll talk a lot more in the weeks to come." He stood up and gave her the once-over again. It was obvious he was interested in her for matters other than her artistic bent. He clicked his heels, Heil-Hitlered her, and walked out of the canteen. As he passed von Rondstett, he spoke directly into his left ear. "I want to fuck her, and I mean very soon. Don't wear her out in a couple of nights!"

Johann stood there with his mouth wide open. "Looks like you made quite the impression on Commandant Rost. Let's go someplace where we can talk in private. Let's have a cup of coffee at my place. The walls and doors are thick; I feel pretty safe talking there.

I doubt they have thought of bugging my apartment. Before we go any further, let's stop and find you some other things to wear." He allowed Rachel to select a few items to her liking and then headed for his place.

They walked into the building. He slammed the front door by giving it a quick kick with his right foot. He stormed up the stairs ahead of her. He got the key out of his pocket and unlocked the door. Inside, he kicked the door shut, again with his foot. For a moment Rachel thought he was going to rape her again.

It was hard for von Rondstett to break certain patterns. So often his arms were heavy with a hot number he couldn't wait to get into his bed. He had learned to open and close doors with quick maneuvers from his feet.

Rachel watched the strange behavior with some amusement. "Didn't your parents ever teach you how to open and close doors? You act like a monkey, not a grown man. And an officer to boot. Let's talk about this project Commandant Rost has in mind."

"Let me call Kern and Adel. They are both into that sort of thing and love the theater. I know Kern adores opera."

Kern and Adel were there promptly. They had closed the bedroom door. No need for the "boys" to view the terribly rumpled bed. "Guys, here is the problem. Frau von Graben has been invited by Rost to participate in enhancing some of the theatrical venues. She wants to use silks to create backgrounds and sets. Any idea where we might find silk in this god-forsaken place?"

"Not here, but what about Prague or Dresden? You have a car at your disposal. All of us could go together. Who couldn't stand a day of being away from this damnable place? What do you say?"

"I'll call Rost and present your suggestion. Personally, I believe it's a winner. Prague, I haven't been there in years. What a treat!"

He got Rost on the line. "Kern and Adel think we might have a chance of finding silk in Prague. If not there, perhaps in Dresden. You have a problem with the four of us doing a foray to those two places? We'll be gone for just the day. No need to stay overnight. Do I hear a yes?"

"As a matter of fact, you do. Just be back before reveille. And no hanky-panky along the way. Just stick to business. Before you leave, pick up a couple of thousand Reichsmark at my office. That should allow you to buy the silk Frau von Graben needs." As usual, he was short and to the point. Sometimes he could be a real bastard. He was known for having a short fuse and a terrible temper. No one wanted to be on his shit list.

They left in von Rondstett's Mercedes the next morning and arrived in Prague shortly after eight o'clock. The silk store wasn't open until nine thirty. With the guys all being in dress uniform, they had no difficulty finding entry to a nice café. Everyone ordered what they wanted. Johann paid the bill. They were ready to leave shortly after nine o'clock.

"Finish your coffee. Remember Rost's words: No hanky-panky! Let's get in the car and tend to our mission. Some of the locals told me that this is the best place for us to find bales of silk. Let's hope they were right." When they got to the store, a sign in the window stated that the shop was closed. Adel wrapped hard on the wooden door. They saw a man approaching. It was obvious the storekeeper was hesitant to open the store when he saw the three guys in their SS uniforms. Rachel's smile made him change his mind. "Come in, please. How can I help you? What exactly are you looking for?"

"We want the biggest bales of silk that you have on hand. Preferably solid colors: Red, white, and black. Might that be possible?"

"I have lots of black and bright red, as in Swastika. The white is a bit skimpy. But let me check in the stock room." It gave them a chance to look around the store. The ceilings appeared to be ancient. The white wash had grayed over four centuries. The sign on the outside stated that the board and batten structure was erected in 1510. Ceiling beams were coal black, adding to the drama of the room. Colorful silks were arranged on countless tables in chromatic order. The visitors were duly impressed with the beauty of the fabrics on display. None could resist touching the various bolts of smooth material. The old man came back smiling. "I guess we are OK on the white as well."

Rachel stepped up to the counter. She wanted to feel the weight of the silk under consideration. If it was too light in weight, she couldn't use it for her backdrops. She grinned. "Just what I had in mind. While I take a look around for some accent pieces, find out what he wants for the three bales. I'd say they are worth about eight hundred Reichsmark."

Johann inquired. "Kind sir, how much do you want for the three bales?"

"For you, gentlemen, and the lovely lady, five hundred Reichsmark it is." Rachel couldn't help overhearing the price quote. "We'll take it," she said without hesitating. "I also would like to have these couple of remnants."

"Ma'am, they are yours for the taking."

"My zayde would have said you are a real *Mensch*." He knew she was Jewish. None of the guys realized she had mentioned her grandfather. They packed the silk carefully in the trunk and were wondering why they would want to drive to Dresden.

"It's only a good hour driving straight north of here and only one hour from there back to Theresienstadt. My tank was full when we left. We'll be just fine. Let's do it as long as we get back before nine o'clock this evening. Supposedly, there is a fabulous silk store between the Frauenkirche and the Semper Opera House."

They were in Dresden for lunch. It was one of the few cities in Germany that was not bombed by August 1944. Kern had attended several operas in Dresden; the others had never been at the famous opera house or any place in Dresden. He played tour guide and showed them the highlights. Although not his home, he was in love with the ever present graciousness of the old town. He showed it off with great pride. When they at last discovered the silk store, Rachel knew immediately she was dealing with another *"Landsmann."* She looked around the place with great care. She was looking for some striking silk prints that could enhance the starkness of the black, red, and white theme she had in mind. They were not necessarily colors she would have chosen. But she planned to appeal to Klemens Rost's nationalistic taste. She selected three prints to her liking; a remnant of one of them would probably make a nice dress for her. Rachel inquired about the price of the pieces she had selected. The handsome, old man looked her straight in the eyes. "How about two hundred Reichsmark. Is that fair enough?"

"Thank you, sir. That's just fine. Johann, please pay the man the two hundred marks. It's a bargain." Kern and Adel picked up the pieces of silk and took them out to the car. Rachel took the man's hand. "I know it's a few days early. Mazel tov, mazel tov! May it be a good year for us all." With tears running down her face, she gave the man a big smile. Rachel wanted to put her arms around him. He looked like he could use a hug. She blew him a kiss instead and walked out behind Johann.

Johann's Mercedes pulled into the ghetto of Theresienstadt at seven o'clock. The guys helped empty the car and took off for their quarters. Rachel and Johann went to his apartment. Rost had tentatively agreed to allow Rachel to stay with Johann in his place. Secretly, he was pleased that she had not been subjected to routine treatment upon her arrival, thanks to von Ronstett's interest in her. Rost had his own ideas as to what he wanted to do with her. Sitting in his office and thinking of Rachel, he let his sexual fantasies run rampant.

Back in his villa, von Rondstett called Rost. "Commandant, we just got back. Mission accomplished. Rachel found beautiful silk in both cities. The roads were not the best; nevertheless, we made pretty good time. Glad we were able to make this trip worthwhile."

Rost's mind was in the gutter. All he could see in front of his eyes was Rachel getting laid by von Rondstett. He responded, "I'm looking forward to Rachel's treatment of the three venues involved. Relax, and you and Rachel have a good evening. I know it will be a very good night." He hung up, not wanting to give Johann a chance to respond.

Johann commented on his conversation with Rost. "He was pleased with our accomplishments and looks forward to seeing your work in the next week or so. He expects everything in place in time for Gerron's filming."

He was ready to pour Rachel a glass of wine. "Don't bother with wine for me. I need some sleep; I'm exhausted. If you don't mind, I'd like to retire. I need to catch up on some much-needed rest. I need to clear my mind and come up with some crazy schemes to please that boss of yours. I hope you don't mind sleeping on the sofa in the living room tonight. After tomorrow, I would prefer the living room for myself. That arrangement of yours didn't work for me last night. You got just a bit too friendly." She turned away from him before he could respond and closed the bedroom door firmly behind her.

Chapter 18

JOHANN was studying the morning papers as Rachel opened the bedroom door. He pointed at the headline of the paper. "Don't look at the morning paper. The news is not great. They have apprehended a lot more people who are related to the perpetrators of the Hitler assassination attempt. Those they caught were either shot or hung!

"I shouldn't even comment on German troop movements relative to the invasion in Normandy and the advancing Russian army. It doesn't look good for us. Whatever you do, don't ask Klemens Rost any questions pertaining to the news or give any answers should he ask you. Pretend like you know absolutely nothing. Act dumb! You and I never talk about anything of importance. We just fuck."

Rachel shook her head and rolled her eyes. "How dumb do you think I am? I'm getting the picture. I wasn't exactly born yesterday. You made what's at stake perfectly clear to me just a few hours ago."

"You can be bitchy. I'm not so sure I want to put up with you indefinitely, especially with the arrangement you managed to connive."

Rachel thought better of responding in like tone and changed the subject. "As I told you last night, in the future, I'll sleep in the living room unless you want me out of here. I did get up after a few hours of sleep and worked on the plans for Rost."

"Let me see. Did you make some sketches for him?"

"Yes. Here they are. Let me explain. This is for the Terrine Town Hall, the most widely used performance venue. The solid background will be in that Swastika red, beautifully draped. Off-center, I envision a huge peony-like flower shaped out of black silk with touches of the white for highlights. I will have some colorful umbrellas made with the accent silks we bought in Dresden. They will be artistically staggered and suspended in midair with silk strands and the ropes almost invisible from the audience. It should give the whole thing that *Madame Butterfly* impression. What do you think?"

"Wonderful. What a stroke of genius. I'm sure Rost will be impressed. Those colors should tickle his Nazi fancy. What else do you have up that artsy sleeve of yours?"

"Won't you be surprised? I believe in repetition to make an impact. At the Music Pavilion, we will use the same draping idea but will use black as the main color in the background. A different kind of huge, off-centered flower will be in white with touches of the Nazi red. The accents will be suspended shapes of colorful hot-air balloons. The kids performing there will love it.

"The café they opened in 1942 has a more intimate stage. There, I will use the white silk background with a red flower with touches of black. Of course, it must be placed off-center to appeal to my artistic flair. The suspended colorful silk touches will be triangles and balloons to convey a geometric feel. Look at my sketches. You think Commandant Rost will like my designs?"

"No question about it. I'm impressed! Let's walk over to town hall and meet Kern and Adel. I asked them to bring all the silk with them. You did want to actually do some on-site experimentation, didn't you?"

"Right you are. Tell the guys to fetch a heavy rope from one of the workshops. It should be at least seventy-five meters in length. I'll need that to stage the whole thing for Rost."

They walked up Lange Straße. Just past the Marktplatz, they turned right on Rathausstraße and faced the town hall. Kern and Adel had arrived with all Rachel needed to stage the planned designs. She tried to be respectful to her gay princes.

"Gentlemen, I would like you to string that heavy rope clear across the back of the whole stage. Do it about one to two meters away from the back wall. Make sure the rope is taut and firmly affixed. First, take that bolt of red silk and continuously drape it over the rope. Don't cut the fabric, but arrange the strands of red silk artistically, creating that elegant look across the expanse of the stage. That's the idea. Keep going, you two.

"Adel, you are the taller. Come over here to the right of center. Extend your arms. Pretend you are suspending Kern in midair. I'm sure you have experience in doing this with Kern in some of your more inventive acrobatics. That's the idea. Kern, please help me with these bolts of black and white silk."

Rachel proceeded to create a large black peony by arranging the elegant fabric around the "statue" of Adel. The last thing she did was arrange a ruffle of white around his long but slender neck. All that wasn't covered was his blond mane and his face. He looked like a Swedish god in drag. Rachel tossed over her shoulder, "Don't you think he makes a lovely peony?"

Just then Rost strolled onto the stage. Kern addressed him. "What do you think of Rachel's design ideas? We think the major discovered quite a talent. What you need to envision yet, are seven to nine colorful accent silk umbrellas suspended from very thin white silk ropes—almost mysteriously hanging in midair off-center to the left. She wants the scene to have that *Madame Butterfly* look. You should be impressed by the colors she selected. Don't they tie in with Hitler's and your preferred color scheme?"

Rost strutted around like a peacock. "Absolutely! It's making my

Nazi heart burst with pride." They all knew they had pushed the right buttons. "Give me a call when you're done with staging the other two venues. I can't wait to see how you trump this layout." Von Rondstett took several photos with his trusted Leica. He thought the Adel statue needed to be preserved for Director Gerron to see.

Rachel Adina and her male entourage strolled over to the music pavilion. Since the stage wasn't as big as that at the town hall, the creative process was not as lengthy. This time Rachel had chosen Kern to be her floral piece de resistance. Von Rondstett immortalized him in a series of images captured by the Leica before they moved their equipment to the final venue.

The new café had a most-intimate feel to it. Rachel staged the white background with Adel posing as the red flower with black accents. The intimacy of the space was perfect for performances by the beloved quartet of well-known musicians who had lost their way in life; that is, whose lives had been short circuited by the inhumanity of the Third Reich. The symbolism of the geometric shapes complimented the world of classical music. Rachel Adina, the newly born star in the world of creativity and design, was pleased with what she had delivered.

Johann and Rachel were on the way to their meeting with Commandant Rost and director Gerron. Rachel felt confident enough in her ability to bamboozle Rost; she wasn't so sure about the world-famous actor and movie director Kurt Gerron. Convincing him of her hair-brained schemes was another matter. They picked up the photos at the lab before meeting with Commandant Rost and director Gerron.

Gerron checked out the photos of the staged venues. "Very impressive! I like your ideas! Very impressive indeed. My crew will have no difficulty realizing your designs, especially the idea of the different flower shapes and the respective colorful inventions and floating accents. Just wonderful and extremely creative." He muttered under his breath, "Too fucking bad. This travesty can't be shown in anything but black and white!"

Gerron smiled at Rachel and continued. "I love that superb soft look of silk. These venues will do exactly what Commandant Rost has in mind. They will certainly convey to the beholders of the film that Theresienstadt has a distinct flair for elegance. It won't be the color but the designs that will convey the idea."

Rachel wasn't looking for accolades from Klemens Rost when she saw him open his large mouth; all of his gold work was exposed. "Great job, Rachel. I agree with Kurt. Your designs and concepts are exactly what I was hoping for. These wonderful touches of silk will decidedly add to the picture of Theresienstadt I want to convey. Herr Hitler and Herr Dr. Goebbels will be proud of me. I want the entire world to see us in the best light. Roosevelt, Stalin, Churchill, and de Gaulle have no idea how well we treat and accommodate these misfits of society." Kurt Gerron had to swallow hard, as did the others. Kurt was a prominent Jew himself. He had acted in and directed some of the greatest films in German cinematography, including the first German talkie, *Der Blaue Engel (The Blue Angel)*, with Marlene Dietrich.

"Let's call it a wrap!" intoned Kurt Gerron, in his inimitable booming voice as a movie director. He couldn't wait to get out of sight of that vermin called Commandant Klemens Rost. He knew he had secret friends in Rachel, Johann, and his adjutants Kern and Adel. He despised Rost and the idea of creating this monstrous propaganda film ordered by Dr. Joseph Goebbels. He was hoping by doing their bidding, he would save his crew and himself from the worst.

Klemens Rost added, "I concur. Everyone, relax and enjoy your days until we start filming on September first—such a special day in the history of Germany. It's the glorious beginning of freeing the world through German power. It's the start of eradicating the scum of this earth! I will order a crew of Jews to implement your designs, Rachel."

Kurt Gerron thought, "He's got chutzpah to voice his horrible ideas in front of us." Rachel just closed her eyes; she couldn't face the man who had just insulted her and any Jew under his rule of command. Rost saluted them and walked away. Having his back to them, Rost didn't see Kurt's gesture, calling him an asshole. All of them walked out without saying another word.

Johann longed for a long nap in his bed. He hadn't slept well on the sofa. His legs were much too long for stretching out in the living room, and he accepted Rachel's offer to let him return to his bedroom. He headed straight to his place, not even waiting for Rachel to walk with him. He knew he had evening duty that night.

Rachel took a circuitous route back to the villa. Some of the guards and many of the prisoners viewed her with a jaundiced eye. Everyone knew by now that she was Johann von Rondstett's whore. The word had gotten around quickly after Johann yanked her out of the lineup of newly arrived prisoners. Rachel looked at the prisoners clinging to their raggedy and filthy uniforms. Some of their scalps were bleeding from their incessant scratching to find temporary relief from the itching induced by fleas and lice covering their exposed skin. Rachel shuddered to think she might wind up among these unfortunates.

She thought about the preposterous attempt at conveying a false picture to the world by making the propaganda film. Rachel hated to be part of the horrendous betrayal. Tears were flooding Rachel's eyes as she beheld a very old woman who was literally just skin and bones. Her abdomen was hugely distended, a clear sign of starvation experienced in the camp. When Rachel walked close to her, the woman spat in her face. "Goddamn whore. Get the hell out of here before we kill and then roast you. You'd taste better than rats!" Rachel suppressed her scream in her handkerchief and quickly walked away from her attacker. She went straight to von Rondstett's place. As soon as she entered the apartment, she sobbed uncontrollably. Johann was sound asleep; he didn't hear her.

She took off her clothes and slipped into the kimono Johann had left lying on the sofa. Rachel felt chilled and closed the balcony door before she drew the drapes. The closed curtains not only gave her more privacy but also protection, at least in her mind. She took one of the books from the shelf and began to read. It had been forever since she had taken the time to look at a book. This was a first edition of Daphne du Maurier's *Rebecca*. It wasn't very long before she was totally engrossed in the story.

She looked up when she saw Johann step out of his bedroom. He was in full official dress, including his long black leather coat and military cap. He walked over to her and stood right next to the sofa where she was lying. "It's time for me to go down to the railway track. The evening train with the next bunch of prisoners is to arrive any minute. I probably won't be back much before one in the morning. It's supposed to be a very long train tonight. If you get hungry, there is some good bread and cheese in the kitchen area." Without another word he simply walked out and closed the door quietly but firmly behind him. She heard the lock snap into place. Rachel was not afraid to be alone.

Fifteen minutes later she heard the train whistle blow and heard the movement as the wheels squealed, bringing the train to a stop. Rachel couldn't help recalling her own arrival and what she had experienced just a few nights earlier. There was sorrow and pity in her heart. She was staring into space; the book was lying in her lap. Suddenly, she was aware of footsteps coming up the steep stairway. These were not military boots calling attention to themselves. A key was being turned in the lock. Was Johann coming home early and didn't want to disturb her? Perhaps he had taken his boots off not wanting to wake her had she fallen asleep on the sofa. Rachel suddenly was frightened. She stared at the door. When the door handle was pushed down and the door opened slowly, she gasped. It was Klemens Rost. He held his boots in his left hand, standing there in stockinged feet. He held a whip in his right. Rachel knew she was in trouble. All the windows were closed, and there wasn't another soul in the building.

Rost kicked the door shut with the heel of his right foot. He dropped the boots on the floor but held on to the whip. "Come here, you bitch. I've been fantasizing about this moment since I first laid eyes on you. And you thought you were safe in von Rondstett's castle? Well, let me tell you. I have keys to every damn place in Theresienstadt. No place is off limits to the commander." Rachel looked at Rost wide-eyed and absolutely terrified. He walked toward her and tore the book out of her lap. He tossed it in the direction of the balcony, making it slide away on the smooth hardwood floor.

Commander Rost reached for Rachel's hair and pulled her face right in front of his own. She saw his tongue emerge and felt the vicious insertion into her mouth. With his left hand, he ripped off the kimono. Within seconds he had stripped Rachel naked. "If you make just one unwanted sound, you'll regret it. You see this pistol in my holster? It would silence you forever." He unbuckled the holster and laid the weapon on a side table. He tore off his uniform and unbuttoned his pants; they dropped easily to the floor and puddled around his feet. He was not wearing anything under his military pride. He stood in front of her wearing nothing but a neckband with an SS medallion and his gartered stockings. "Get up, bitch. Bend over." He stood back and struck her buttocks ferociously several times with his whip until he drew blood. Rachel stifled her screams by shoving a fist into her mouth. She knew he would kill her if she yelled loud enough to be heard on the outside. He was totally out of control when he entered her, alternating between shoving himself into her vagina and rectum. His fingernails tore into her breasts as he ejaculated into her rectum. He made her turn around and tore her fist from her mouth. "I heard from Johann you like sucking his dick. Well, you stinking Jew, now it's my turn. Go, suck that hot cock."

He grabbed her hard and forced his instrument of torture into her throat. When he found his relief, Rachel nearly choked on his cum. She fainted and fell onto the floor.

When she came to, Commander Rost was gone. The door was closed. There was blood all over the smooth leather sofa and the floor. Rachel glanced up at the living room clock. It was just after eleven o'clock. Johann wouldn't be home for at least two hours. She made up her mind not to share with him what had happened.

Rachel didn't know where she found the strength. "It must be adrenaline," she rationalized as she hurried to get the sofa and floor cleaned, making sure all evidence of the rape scene had been erased before she stepped into the shower to clean herself. Rachel knew she had to control her convulsive gasps and crying; her eyes would be a dead giveaway to anyone looking at her. The pain in her violated body was unbearable, but she was determined not to reveal the event to Johann. In his medicine cabinet, she saw a bottle of Bayer aspirin and decided to take four of them before she got under the shower. She disposed of her torn undergarments in the trash by putting them on the bottom of the barrel. Kitchen trash concealed the evidence of the violent attack by Rost.

She felt some relief after the hot shower and put on clean undergarments and the kimono. She reached into the desk drawer and hugged Otto's photo before she hid it again in its safe place. Rachel covered herself with a blanket. The book, open to page fifty-eight, was lying on top of her stomach. She pretended to be asleep when Johann walked in shortly after one o'clock in the morning. He didn't disturb her. He just picked up the book, inserted a bookmark, and laid *Rebecca* on the coffee table in front of the sofa. He turned off all the lights and went to his room. Johann showered and went to bed. Within minutes, all Rachel could hear was his snoring. He had no idea what had transpired in his apartment three hours earlier.

It was daylight when Johann walked out of his bedroom. He was wearing his pajamas. Rachel was still lying on the sofa; she was hurting all over. She wasn't certain how she would conceal her pain. She gritted her teeth as she rose to her feet. She needed to use the toilet in Johann's bathroom. Walking in the direction of the urgently needed throne, he noticed that she was limping. "What happened to you? Why are you walking like that?"

"I have no idea. It might be lumbago. I had problems with it years ago when I was standing for prolonged periods in our dental practice." She was glad to reach his bedroom and close the door behind her. She didn't want him to watch her having difficulty seating herself on the stool. Pulling down her panties, she couldn't help seeing herself in all the mirrors surrounding her. She closed her eyes when she saw the red streaks from the whipping she had received. God forbid, if Johann saw them, he would know immediately that she had been abused. She feared Johann might kill her abuser no matter who he turned out to be. She shuddered thinking of what the outcome might be. Rachel was certain it would spell the end of Johann and herself.

Rachel cried her tears without shedding them. Rost's hateful words and actions not only hurt her to the core but caused her great physical pain at the moment. She knew in her heart last night's episode would not be the only encounter with Klemens Rost. It was difficult enough for her to pretend to be Johann's whore; she hadn't banked on being a sex slave to his superior. She felt utterly hopeless and dirty. Rachel couldn't even begin to envision how she would act in Rost's presence during their meetings in days to come.

She couldn't come to terms with the fact that she was living a lie since her arrival in Theresienstadt. Rachel was wondering how she could ever defend her experiences to someone like Sister Maria-Angelika should the opportunity arise. She turned red with shame when she recalled the first night with Johann, but even more so, after the abuse suffered by his commander. She had discovered only the day before how she was viewed by her fellow inmates.

Johann met her when she emerged from his bedroom. She

seemed rather unsteady on her feet. "Please, let me hold on to you. I don't want you to fall. Are you sure you can attend any meetings later today? Would you want me to give you a massage or apply some ointment to your back? I'm pretty good at it."

"Oh no, no! No massages or applications to my back. I'll be fine."

"Why are you acting so standoffish? I won't hurt you. No one in their right mind will probably believe this. I know you are Jewish and you are a prisoner under my control. I am second in command at this place and could do anything I choose to do with you. When I strut around Theresienstadt, I'm a Nazi because that is what I am forced to do. I never wanted to be a soldier and certainly not one put into a position of exterminating my fellow man. I was drafted into the army and sent to France after the occupation. I never fired a gun, and I never had to kill an enemy. I loved being in Paris. I hated it when I was transferred to this hellhole. My misfortune is that I fell in love with you at first sight. It doesn't just happen in the movies.

"Second thoughts about our relationship? Regrets to have made a pact with the devil? Wondering what's right and what's not? Sorry about your pretense to be the artist and designer you are not? Sorry to have me present you to others as my whore? Rachel, don't do this to yourself. You are a good and decent human being. Your misfortune is that you are living in a terrible world at an unfortunate time. Both you and I are victims of circumstance. And at this moment, we need to use each other to survive what is threatening our very existence outside these walls. I realize your decency plagues your mind. I know you see yourself through your husband's eyes. For all we know, the sight of his eyes may already be dimmed. He may be part of your past. You and I are here and now confronting an ugly reality. I love you and want to shelter you from the hurt that is trying to engulf both of us."

"I'm sorry, Johann. I cannot love you. I hate what you stand for. I believe I don't hate you, but I hate what you are doing to my people." She was hurting so badly, she began to cry. Johann thought she was decrying their situation. Rachel barely could get up from the sofa and limped back to his bedroom. She had to get to those aspirins. Rachel slammed the bedroom door shut with a vengeance and reached for the pills. She nearly dropped the bottle on the floor. She swallowed a handful, hoping she would never wake up. Johann walked in. He reached out to her. She thought he was going to embrace her.

"I can't. I love my husband. I can't wait for this nightmare to end. I hope to be reunited with my love. I look forward to that day. That's what keeps me going. I am human and do have feelings for you, but they are not feelings of love. I don't crave your body the way you obviously desire mine. Let's make the best of this miserable existence that has been created for us by an unfortunate situation. You have to accept that I'm married to another who is pining for my love while tolerating the miseries of an ugly war in a distant place. You may very well be right; he might already be dead. He never even knew that I was so brutally torn out of my life by Nazi forces. Neither of us has any idea what happened to the other since our lives were ripped apart. I love Otto too much to sacrifice him on the altar of uncertainty.

"I face the reality that you could drag me out of here this very moment and turn me over to Olga or any of the other guards and have me join my fellow Jewish inmates. You have the right and the power to do that. Perhaps you will; perhaps you won't. All I'm telling you is that I cannot have you seduce me and make me a willing sex object. You could rape me day and night, and I could do nothing about it. Right now, I have a good idea what would be happening to me had it not been for you. I have eyes to see what is going on in this damnable place. If pretending to be your whore is what keeps me alive, I will do it. I must survive. I have to survive no matter what the cost." She slumped down on the sofa and sobbed bitterly. Johann wanted to help her but refrained from doing so.

He poured himself a large snifter of cognac and headed for his bedroom. His shoulders sagged. He felt utterly rejected. Deep down in his heart, he knew he truly loved Rachel. He found it difficult to accept the rejection. He could have forced her into submission but found it distasteful. In his thirty-seven years of living, he had never loved another woman the way he had fallen for Rachel.

Chapter 19

EARLIER in the year, the number of prisoners was drastically reduced by shipping many off to be exterminated in other camps. This was done to show a pleasant environment to visitors from neutral countries. Barracks were spruced up and beautified. Artists were allowed to perform in their respective fields of endeavor. The documentary to be filmed under the direction of Kurt Gerron was designed to reinforce the image of Theresienstadt previously conveyed to certain visitors.

The staging for the propaganda production was completed. Rachel and minions of slave laborers had done all that was needed for creating a false impression to the world. Kurt Gerron and his crew were ready to commence with the production of the black-and-white documentary simply entitled *Theresienstadt*. He thought Rachel's efforts at creating the colorful, stunning settings fashioned from the beautiful silks she had chosen were a waste of time and money. Filming started on September 1, 1944, as projected, and was completed in eleven days. There was minimal need for editing. In Commandant Rost's opinion, Gerron had delivered what they had hoped for. The film met with the approval of those in power. Even Der Führer and Dr. Goebbels liked what they saw.

On the morning of October 25, Kurt Gerron, his wife, and anyone involved in the filming of *Theresienstadt* were rounded up. There was a rap at the door of Kern and Adel's apartment. Their door wasn't locked. It was pushed open with force. Two armed guards marched in and headed straight for the bedroom. They found the two lovers naked in an embrace. "Get out of bed, you damn queers. It's high time you get what you deserve. Put on some pants and a shirt. Nothing fancy. You won't need much where you're going. It's not that long a train ride to Auschwitz."

Adel pulled away from Kern. They jumped out of bed as they were prodded by billy clubs and guns. One of the guards actually aimed his gun at Kern's naked butt. "I could be kind and let you off easy by accidentally firing this thing up your ass. You might just like it. Sure would be quicker than taking that last shower together in Auschwitz-Birkenau." They weren't sure how to interpret that last quip.

The guys slipped on their clothes, realizing their fate. They had often talked about what might happen after they were discovered to be gay lovers. Both knew their time had come to face the Almighty.

"Come on, you sick bastards. Get moving. The train heading to Auschwitz is waiting with all that other Jewish vermin we had to round up this morning." They kept punching and prodding both young men with the butts of their guns. There were no attempts at hiding what they were doing with Kern and Adel. Everyone watching knew they were being herded toward the train station. When they got there, they yelled at the guard minding the designated cattle car. "Open up that fucking gate to heaven. These two queer bastards are joining Gerron and his Jewish scum on their last journey. They are firing up the ovens already in Auschwitz-Birkenau. They can't wait to return your ashes to ashes. What a bunch of sorry pricks. Get your asses up into that wagon before I beat and kick the shit out of you."

Adel jumped up first; he extended his right arm to Kern to give him a lift. As they looked around the stinking conveyance, they spotted Kurt Gerron and his wife. He was a very large presence. "Large presence" actually euphemised his size. He was immense. His head and face were huge. Gerron looked like he weighed at least one-hundred-fifty kilos. He was dealing with advanced frontal baldness. His big brown eyes were staring at the world from his jowly face. Tears were running down his bulging cheeks. Most of his film crew and the wives of those who were married were there. He and all surrounding him knew what was in store for them. They had been told making the propaganda film would guard and protect them from harm. It was a horrendous lie.

The guards slammed the door. All were sitting or lying on soiled straw. As always, in these horrible conveyances, the smell of sweat, piss, vomit, and human excrement was pervasive. There was hardly any ventilation in the wagon. There were no stops along the seventy-two-hour train ride. It was much further than implied by the guards who arrested Kern and Adel. The train ride was traumatic. Hardly anyone spoke. They were all lost in their thoughts, each dealing in his or her own way with his or her mortality and impending execution. Now and then, they heard the heavy breathing and weeping of their travel companions.

The train came to a halt in Auschwitz on the morning of October 28. The doors were ripped open. The burst of air was welcome. "Out, out, get out! Get your asses moving," the guards yelled at them. Two younger men of the film crew jumped first from the wagon, wanting to give Kurt Gerron a helping hand with his exit. "Look at that fat Jewish pig. He can't even move his huge ass off the car by himself." One of the bigger male guards grabbed Gerron and literally yanked him down to the ground. As soon as Kurt Gerron was upright, he gave him a mean kick in his rear. "March, you fat swine. We'll teach you how to move around at this place. Welcome to Auschwitz. We hope you'll enjoy your short stay!" None of them realized what was meant by "short stay." Was there a possibility of being liberated?

They had heard rumors of the Allied troops and the Russians making significant inroads and devastating the German defense lines.

"Leave whatever you brought with you on the train. I repeat, leave all luggage or whatever you had in your possession on the train! Form two lines. Men go left; women line up to the right. March in single file and follow the uniformed leader. There is no talking allowed. Concentrate on walking and moving swiftly. There is another, much longer train pulling in shortly. We are very busy at this premier installation. Move your asses until you are told to stop at a certain point. You then will be given further instructions."

After a considerable walk, they had reached the registration table. With German mentality, even their prisoners had to be processed precisely. The guard yelled, "Empty all your pockets. What's your name? Is that your family name?" Kurt Gerron owned up to the fact that he changed his name from "Gerson" to "Gerron" when he switched from medicine to acting/directing in the movies. "Where were you born?" Gerron was born to a wealthy family in Berlin. They were all asked the same questions, and their answers duly recorded by efficient clerks. "Step through those doors for further processing!" So far their captors had been polite.

Their greeting was not quite that friendly in the next hall. "Step over there, and take off everything you have on, even your socks and shoes. Hang your clothes on those nails. You won't have any more use for them. We want you buck naked. Get a move on.

"Go to that woman over there. She is waiting for you with a sharp barber's razor. Your heads, face, and your entire body will be shaved, including your genitalia. Did you get that guys? She'll shave you from head to toe, including your prick and balls. You'll feel like the day you were born with not a hair on your bodies."

The woman shaving Kurt Gerron was challenged. The others were asked to proceed to the next shaver waiting to do her job. When they were shaved, their heads were checked for lice and advised to move on to the next station. "Open your mouth; I want to see your teeth. You are lucky; you have healthy teeth. I see neither fillings, bridges, nor crowns. You can move to the showers. If you had any gold fillings, crowns, or bridges, we would have yanked them out on the spot. We have neither the means nor the intention of using any form of anesthesia." Adel counted his blessings. Kern was not so lucky. He had two crowns and a bridge that involved dental gold. They pulled them without benefit of Novocain. He screamed in agony. The guard slapped his face hard and pushed him toward the shower, hitting him with the butt stock of his rifle.

They joined hundreds of naked men in the shower. The water was ice cold. The soap was the most awful smelling stuff. Most men, when they emerged from the showers, were allowed to pick up one set of underwear and a striped prison uniform. They were lucky if they found a pair of shoes or sandals that might fit them.

Not so for Kern and Adel. A guard grabbed them as they were trying to dry themselves off. "Don't bother with underwear or footwear. You won't need anything where you are going next." He struck Adel with his club across his buttocks.

"You queers are on your last leg." Next, he struck his billy club across their heads. Kern showed signs of fainting. Adel caught him before he went down. They stumbled to the gas chamber. As they entered the hall, mostly naked male bodies were writhing in agony on the floor. Others were grabbing their bare chests fighting for air. Adel held Kern's hand firmly. He looked at him. "I'm listening to the very end of *Andrea Chenier*. The score and the words are floating in my head. I know you are with me. Like Maddalena and Chenier, we are walking in triumph to face our guillotine." Adel embraced Kern and kissed him farewell. They collapsed in unity to the floor. Their bodies twitched for a moment as in an epileptic fit. Their eyes wide open, they beheld each other.

There was a strange odor in the air. Kurt Gerron had finally survived the shaving and removal of his teeth. He dared to inquire as to the odor. "That comes from the bakery," he was advised. What it really was turned out to be the stench generated by the crematoria, operated twenty-four seven.

Kurt Gerron, his wife, and all but two of the film crew met their deaths in the Auschwitz-Birkenau gas chambers on October 28. Most succumbed to Zyklon B mercifully and quickly. The terrible burning sensation in their chests preceded heart failure and then death.

Chapter 20

IT was December 10, a gray-on-gray day in dismal Theresienstadt. Commandant Rost had ordered Johann and Rachel to meet with him in the canteen. Rachel barely could stand to look at the man. She was there, and yet she was not. She felt his hot, sweaty hands grabbing and digging into her breasts. She could feel the pain of his invading manhood. She hardly nodded in response to his greeting.

Rost kept blabbering about the successful completion of the propaganda film. "Thank you again, Rachel, for your part in making this production as successful as it turned out to be. It was too bad that Gerron didn't have the means to produce the film in color. He strongly believed film noir was the only desirable métier in which to produce the work; he was adamant about filming the subject in black and white. Well, we are done with that. Sorry to say, Gerron and his crew, as well as Kern and Adel, were reassigned at the direction of headquarters in Berlin.

"There are other matters I need to call to your attention. All of us know that your living arrangements are not exactly in keeping with the rules of a concentration camp. Since you are discrete in your conduct, I continue to look the other way."

Rachel thought, "You bastard!"

Johann responded. "No problem. We like our shared quarters."

Rost smiled in a sardonic way and raised his left eyebrow. "I hope you have done better than just sharing living quarters with this beautiful creature I have sanctioned to get into bed with you?"

Johann was getting irritated. "Come, come now. You know what I mean. Naturally, Rachel and I have enjoyed each other's company." Johann chose not to divulge the details of their arrangement. It was none of Rost's business what he and Rachel did or did not do behind closed doors.

Rost went on looking at her smugly. "I'm sure, Rachel, you have observed the massive daily transfers of inmates to other venues. I dislike losing so many of our most talented inmates. They made such great contributions to the quality of life enjoyed by all who were assigned to us here in Theresienstadt."

Rost continued. "I have done a little digging into your past, Rachel. It took just one phone call to Essen, and I discovered what a multi-talented lady you are." She could tell by his facial expression what he was thinking about. She felt undressed and naked.

"I learned of your academic background, and that you and your husband had a successful dental practice in Essen until his induction into service to his country."

"Actually, I didn't stop working when my husband was taken into military service. I needed to be busy, and our patients relied on me. My routine was interrupted when I was selected to appear in Theresienstadt." What she said and what she thought were two different things. She felt like screaming at him, "Until you bastards decided to incarcerate me and ship me off into this den of iniquity!"

He could read the sarcasm between her lines. "You realize, now that I'm aware of your other talents, I must utilize your skills in a productive manner. All of us here must function under our leader's motto: Arbeit macht frei! You may continue to stay with Major von Rondstett, but you will need to assume certain other responsibilities too. I will introduce you to Elsa Brand, a dental technician. Elsa was born in 1915 to German Jews who lived in Dachelhofen, Bavaria. She never finished high school and was eventually apprenticed to a local dentist. That's where she learned the skills she brings to her trade today. She is small in stature but very strong. She pretty much has run our dental extraction program for a considerable time. It's not one of our most pleasant jobs."

"What do you mean by extraction program?"

"Anyone who dies in this camp is subject to visual inspection prior to cremation. Any gold fillings, bridges, or crowns need to be extracted prior to cremation. Reichsführer Himmler believes it's a waste of resources not to recover such elements prior to completing the final solution. He regrets not having implemented the action for prisoners who are dead on arrival. Digging up corpses from the mass graves was viewed as simply too challenging." Rachel covered her mouth. She reached for a napkin as she began to vomit.

"The latest edict from Himmler is that we execute extractions immediately as our visitors arrive. Preferably, the extractions are to be performed without the benefit of anesthesia to save time and money. It's your choice. You may work with Elsa Brand or head the new program. You think about it; just report to the station where you want to function. You know where the work is done. I expect you on the job Monday morning."

He stood up and slipped on his leather coat. It was a chilly morning. "I have to get back to my office. By the way, do you have any idea what's happened to your husband?"

"I haven't heard anything from him since he left the basic training camp in Krefeld many months ago. How could I? I was not allowed to communicate with him; neither was he allowed to get in touch with me. It's the price we had to pay."

"Let me see what I can do. Do you have any idea if he was sent to the eastern or western front of engagement?"

"I wish I did. I'm totally in the dark."

"I'll let you know if I learn something." He was hoping the poor sucker was dead and buried. Rost was already speculating when he might get back in the sack with Rachel. He couldn't remember when he had enjoyed himself as much as he did when he surprised her in von Rondstett's apartment. Just thinking about whipping her buttocks caused him to be aroused. Having raped her did something for his ego. He walked away without his typical salutation. Rost scratched his ass; his hemorrhoids were obviously bothering him.

When she felt safe, Rachel turned toward Johann's ear. "I need to talk to you in private about this job assignment. Either job sounds nightmarish to me."

Johann rose from his chair to help Rachel. "Let's go back to my quarters. We won't have to whisper." He expressed his thoughts as soon as they were alone. "I don't know how you feel about pain. I couldn't do what he is suggesting be done to incoming prisoners. I think it's sadistic."

Rachel concurred. "I'm relieved to hear you say that. I have never extracted anything without the use of anesthesia. I just couldn't do it. I hate the thought of working with corpses, but I'd rather do that. I wondered how long it would take before my true profession would be discovered. Was Rost just making idle talk when he offered his wherewithal to locate Otto's location?"

"I'm not sure of his motivation, but if anyone can do it, he is the person. We'll see. You must know I really have little use for the man. He hates it when I look down on him. He doesn't like it when we stand next to each other. He's almost two heads shorter than I. He has a typical Napoleon complex."

Chapter 21

ON Monday morning, Rachel walked over to the dental compound. Johann had shown her the location on a map. It was less than five hundred meters from Johann's place. He would have gone with her, but he had to be at the track for the arrival of another train. He pointed her in the right direction when they emerged from the villa.

Rachel didn't listen to the nasty comments fellow prisoners made as she was passing by their quarters. Here and there she could hear men hissing, calling her a fucking whore. She kept her eyes down. The tumult of human bodies in striped uniforms nearly made her dizzy. As she was approaching the dental facilities, she could see the lineup of shivering men and women to be processed by dental clinicians. Pathology and mortuary science supposedly were practiced in the adjacent building.

There was no way around it; Rachel had to walk through the clinic where the live extractions were performed. She opened the door. There were at least a dozen dental chairs, all occupied by victims and attended by a clinician with extraction tools at the ready. The sound of screaming prisoners echoed through the glaring atmosphere in the hall. The lights were so bright, they nearly blinded Rachel. There was blood and vomit all over the floor. The technicians were wearing rubber galoshes. Their lab coats were covered in blood and slime. Walking by swiftly, Rachel saw boxes next to each dental chair that were filled with gold crowns and bridges. She didn't trust her eyes and began to run. Rachel wished she had thought of sticking cotton in her ears; the screaming of the miserable creatures became unbearable. The stench in the place was overpowering. The whole scene was beyond her imagination.

She didn't reach Elsa Brand's domain any too soon. There were corpses lying all over the floor or propped up against the wall. Elsa was already working away when Rachel approached her. "Hello, I'm Rachel."

"I'm Elsa. Commander Rost told me you might be working with me." They just nodded politely at each other. Rachel had lost all color in her face. Before Elsa could say another word, Rachel spoke with urgency in her voice. "Point me to a WC. I'm nauseous; I'll heave any second."

"It's right over there in the corner. I'm sorry you are not feeling well." Rachel barely made it to the WC. She knelt in front of the stool and threw up. The projectile vomit hit everything. When she finally got to her feet, she was facing a major clean up of the stall. Rachel needed to wash her face before she faced Elsa again.

Elsa looked at Rachel and realized the trauma she was experiencing. Rachel's eyes were beginning to tear. Elsa wanted to reach out to Rachel but didn't dare do so with her dirty hands. "When Rost assigned me this work, I had no idea what I was told to do. In the beginning, I felt just the way you must be feeling at this moment. When he talked about pathology and mortuary science, I thought I was examining and preparing corpses for funerals. Extracting gold crowns and bridges from corpses was not what I had envisioned."

Rachel nodded. "That's exactly what I thought. Talk about incorrect use of terminology."

Elsa pointed over her shoulders at the back wall. "Grab a clean lab coat over there, and help me with the extractions. We probably have a couple hundred to do before the day is over. Let me handle the corpses. You don't look strong enough to do the job. Let's use both of these dental chairs. While you do the extractions, I'll get the next corpse propped in place and force the jaws open. All you need to do is shine a light into their mouths and determine if extraction is indicated. Some have no gold in their mouths, others don't even have teeth. That's one thing that is easier and faster in the live clinic, but I couldn't handle the torture and the screaming of the poor suckers."

Rachel followed Elsa's instructions. She was thankful for Elsa's willingness and ability to handle the corpses and place them into position. She realized she could have never done what Elsa was able to do. It was almost noon, and they had processed more than one hundred corpses. As soon as Rachel was through checking and extracting a corpse, prisoners in their striped uniforms were at the ready to haul the bodies to the mass grave pits. Rachel was relieved that duty wasn't part of Elsa's and her job.

Rachel was stunned when she saw Rost enter the facility. He walked straight up to her. "Finish up that corpse and get rid of that filthy lab coat. I need to talk to you in my office. Just follow me." When he looked away, she shrugged her shoulders at Elsa. Neither knew what was up. Rachel began to tremble. She had a pretty good idea what was in store for her. "How brazen of him to make me come to his office in the middle of the day," she thought.

She had never been to Rost's office and was surprised that it wasn't all that distant from Johann's villa. As they walked in, staff in other offices were scurrying about. His secretary looked up from her desk. He demanded. "Have your lunch right now. I have some dictation for you when you get back in an hour or so. I do not wish to be disturbed while I'm dealing with the prisoner."

The secretary knew what that meant. She took her purse and left. Rachel could tell by the woman's face she was fully aware of what was about to happen to her. He opened the door and pushed her hard, forcing her into his office.

She was looking at a sizable room. A large handsome desk was the centerpiece. A leather chair stood behind the desk. On the wall was a huge photographic enlargement of a Hitler portrait flanked by the German and Nazi flags. His cap and the whip were hanging from a coat rack. Light through a large window flooded the room. The only thing in sight was the windowless side of one of the barracks giving Rost total privacy. In front of the window were two comfortable leather side chairs that flanked a low table. A huge ceramic ashtray was filled with cigar stubs and ashes. The smell of cigar smoke hung in the air. He faced her. "Get out of those fucking clothes. I want to enjoy looking at you in your full glory." He was running his tongue around his lips and was salivating as he contemplated his next actions. Rachel removed her garments quickly. She did not want to make him any angrier than he was already. She didn't cry, but she was shaking fiercely. "I like the markings I left on your cheeks." He ran his large hands across her exposed buttocks and pulled her closer to him.

"I don't have the time or the inclination to give you another whipping. I love doing it because it brings me to full arousal. I gather you've never had rough sex with any man? It's a major part of my enjoyment. That's why I love this job; I can degrade this scum all I want. You are too pretty to be called scum. Nevertheless, you are a Jewish bitch that needs to be fucked."

He unzipped his fly, yanking out his sizable manhood. He was in full uniform when he pushed her without warning against the front of his desk. He was too short to reach the object of his intentions. Rost bent down and reached for a footstool he kept under his desk. Standing on it he was just tall enough to make penetration possible. He reached up to his mouth and expelled a big glob of saliva and covered the entire length of his tool of torture. He rammed Rachel mercilessly and reached his climax within seconds. Rachel stifled her screams and moaned softly. "So you liked that? You want more?"

"Please don't hurt me again," Rachel pleaded. Against her better judgment, she began to sob.

He withdrew his deflated prick and tucked it away in his uniform. "Too bad, I don't have the time today. I'm expecting a visit from the high command this afternoon. I want you to report to my office every Monday from now on at lunch time. I'll make sure that useless broad sitting out there is gone for a couple of hours. If there is a change in plans, I'll give you warning and make other arrangements. If you ever breathe a word about our little tête-à-têtes to anyone, I'll shoot you with this pistol. You wouldn't be the first one to wind up covered with lime in those conveniently located mass graves. Do you understand me Dr. von Graben? And if you tell von Rondstett, he'll keep you company in the grave."

He looked at his neatly arranged desk and saw a note sitting next to his telephone. "Before you leave, I have some good news for you." She read his insincere smile. "I was able to learn where your husband was last seen. He's fighting on the western front in Belgium. He went MIA just a few days ago. Thousands of men have already been killed on both sides. It's our last stand in that area. It doesn't look good. He may very well have been killed. There's just a small window of hope. But don't be sad. It should make things easier for the three of us. You can fuck Johann and me all you want without worrying about Otto."

Rachel burst into tears as she beheld herself in the large mirror facing her. She had been totally unaware of its existence until this very moment. Strands of her dark hair were covering part of her face and her naked breasts. She felt utterly ashamed, although she had no control over her attacker. She was totally at his mercy.

As far as Rost was concerned, the discussion was over. "Dress yourself quickly before that nosy bitch has the nerve to knock on my door. Get back to work. I need more of that damn gold bullion for future plans." He slapped her hard on her naked buttock, leaving the shameful hand print of his right hand. She got dressed and stormed out of Rost's office. The secretary hadn't returned yet. She spotted a WC and wanted to use it. She peed quickly and took advantage of the availability of clean water to wash her face and eyes. The soft, clean towel felt good on her sensitive skin.

When she finally returned to her work with Elsa, no matter what she tried to hide, Elsa knew there was something wrong. "Mind telling me what happened?"

"No, not at all. You must forgive me, but I'm not quite myself." She told Elsa what she had learned about Otto.

"That's terrible news and certainly not something you needed to learn today. Today of all days. As if you didn't have enough of a nightmarish day already." Elsa wished for clean hands, allowing her to touch her new assistant. We are down to the last sixty corpses for the day. I'm glad you decided to come back and help me."

"There was no choice. Rost commanded me to return to work. There isn't an ounce of empathy in that man. He's absolutely ruthless."

Rachel and Elsa were making the last extraction when the whistle blew at five in the afternoon. Sounding the end of the workday was more for the benefit of their captors than for the working prisoners. Had they been trusted to work without being heavily guarded, the prisoners would have been made to work around the clock. There was never any concern for them. Rachel and Elsa tore off their filthy lab coats and dumped them in the designated hopper. A night crew in the laundry room made sure there would be clean coats for all medical personnel by the next morning. They walked out of the building together. Rachel learned of an obscure entrance to their place of work. She was grateful to discover that she didn't have to walk through the regular clinic. The two women walked quietly to their places of housing. Elsa had a tiny nook in a barrack practically adjacent to von Rondstett's villa. Rachel looked at Elsa, her face stained by her tears. "I'll be OK in the morning. I need the night to conceal my sorrow. I appreciate your understanding and compassion. Good night, I'll see you at eight in the morning.

Johann could tell she was terribly upset when she walked in. "I need to shower and change my clothes. I feel atrocious; I feel filthy. I didn't think I had studied mortuary science. But that is what I'm practicing these days. Elsa is great; she is most kind to me. She is willing to do her part. Elsa is able to handle the grossest aspects of the task. I couldn't prop up those corpses in a dental chair. I don't have the strength. Elsa does. But enough of my daily chores. That's the proper name for what is demanded of me." She headed for the shower.

Rachel's beautiful hair glistened in the late-afternoon sun. It was freshly washed and casually tucked up in her favorite style with an abstract chignon held with a new amber clip Johann had found in a shop in Prague, but it wasn't quite like Grandma's. She put on the kimono Johann had gotten for her in Dresden. She couldn't hold back any longer. "We need to talk."

"What about? If it's about Kern and Adel, as well as Kurt Gerron, his wife, and the entire crew, it won't be news. It's all over the camp. Rost shipped them off to Auschwitz-Birkenau. All of them were sent to the gas chambers the day they arrived. They were cremated before the sun set for a second time. Horrible! How can humans visit these actions on fellow man?"

"No, no, Johann. We need to talk about Otto and me. Rost had a talk with me in his office at lunchtime. He was able to locate my husband's regiment. He's in Belgium and involved in what they call 'The Battle of the Bulge.' Otto was listed as MIA a few days ago." She looked up at Johann. He thought she was going to faint in mid sentence. He caught Rachel as she was about to fall over. He held her close to his chest as she sobbed.

Rachel continued. "There were too many bodies left on the battle-field. Otto was not identified among those they were able to recover. There is a very slim chance for hope. But more likely than not, Otto perished in battle." She drew back from Johann, not wanting to be too close to him.

"Rachel Adina, that makes me very sad. If Otto indeed is gone, know that I will be there for you. You must believe that my love for you is sincere. These things happen, and we must be willing to accept the fact we were meant to meet under these circumstances. I will do anything to shield you from evil in Hades. I didn't want to be transferred to this damned place. When I first saw you getting off that fateful train and being pushed around by officer Olga, I instantly realized I was destined to be here. As if struck by lightning, I knew you had to be mine. I only hoped you wouldn't spurn my overtures. After all, I was one of your captors, and you're a much-hated Jew destined to die in hell. Give me a chance to create a new and happier life for us when all this is over. I have an inkling the time is closer than we think."

Rachel contemplated her captor. "Forgive me. I need time to sort all this out in my mind. I carry much guilt within me. I am still married to Otto, and I owe him my allegiance and my love. We had a very special relationship, which I can neither ignore nor simply dismiss. I hope you see the quandary in which I find myself. Grant me time to accept the sad news that Otto may have died. Allow me to distance myself from the past in order to face the future."

Johann's brow was wrinkled. "I respect you and the feelings you just shared with me again. Stay with me. I won't violate your privacy or personal space. Just know that I'm there for you when you need me." When Johann retired, Rachel reached for Otto's photo. She ran her hand gently across his image and then placed her lips on the glass. "Farewell, dearest," she cried softly, and almost dropped the frame to the floor.

Chapter 22

RACHEL subjected herself to Commandant Rost's prurient indulgences as commanded. She was relieved he never again resorted to the use of his whip; his weekly sexual deviances were bad enough. Christmas fell on a Monday and Tuesday in 1944. Rost arranged for Rachel's conjugal visit on the Wednesday between holidays. Had she gone on Christmas day, Johann might have questioned the purpose of a visit to Rost's office. She felt indeed like a whore. She began to view her submission to Rost's demands as a means to survival. She had to if she wanted to be alive when the trauma would finally end. And end it would, she was confident. She just wasn't certain when that day would be.

After Epiphany, Commandant Rost summoned Rachel and Elsa Brand to his office. Rachel knew this had nothing to do with sex. "We will have to make changes in your work schedule. While we continue to have people die in the complex who need to be checked and treated by you, the number of "healthy" transients has significantly increased. You have seen the hundreds of people get off the trains and even more leaving us by train for Auschwitz-Birkenau. I am interested in getting as many of these inmates processed by you as possible. The dozen technicians who have handled live patients up to this point need your assistance. They cannot cope with all the extractions that are necessary. Frankly, I'm unwilling to let all that gold slip through my fingers. I like counting the gold bars that have materialized in my safe. It's a nice stash for when I retire from this snake pit. You will start working with live patients immediately. It makes no sense for you two to stand around waiting for people to die. Go to work on some of these live ones. Your work will keep you awake."

Rachel shuddered as she and Elsa entered the dental clinic. "Torture chamber" would have been a better descriptor. Luckily, most of the victims were adults. There were very few children left in Theresienstadt at this point. As they entered the room, a dozen men and women were just undergoing extractions. Every chair was occupied. The technicians were deftly handling the extraction tools. As they yanked out their victims' appliances, screams echoed through the hall, greeting the new help. The technicians made sure they removed any crowns, fillings, and bridges that contained gold and handed their victims thick swabs of cotton on which to bite. "This will reduce the pain and stop the bleeding. Just eat soup for the next couple of days. You will get used to the sockets in your mouth. You won't need your teeth after you have met up with the greeting committee in Auschwitz, your final destination on this journey." The rumor mill saw to it that all inmates knew what that meant.

After a day of torturing countless fellow inmates, Rachel and Elsa left the place for their respective quarters. They had started out in white lab coats. Now they were covered in blood and vomit. Rachel grabbed Elsa's arm. "I'm sorry. I've been fighting this all day. I can't hold it back any longer. I'm about to throw up. I have never been so violated in my professional life." She heaved and hit the side of the building they were passing. Elsa steadied Rachel as another wave surged through her body. She couldn't believe what was happening to Rachel. When she finally stopped vomiting, she looked up at Elsa. "Not in my wildest dreams did I ever imagine myself doing such inhumane work. Rost is an animal having us do this to these people. I nearly passed out when he talked about his damn bars of gold. I felt like saying 'open your mouth wide' and giving him the treatment. I wonder how he would feel having his fancy crowns and bridges extracted without Novocain? And how about chipping out gold fillings with a hammer and chisel? No wonder these people scream to high heaven."

She walked into the apartment. Johann immediately could tell something dreadful had happened to her. She burst into tears. "You have no idea what Rost did to Elsa and me today. We were transferred to the 'live extraction' clinic and will be on indefinite duty. He needs to build up his stash of gold bullion bars."

"Is that what he said?"

"You better believe it. I have an idea he is envisioning the end of the war and the end of his military career. It wouldn't surprise me one bit were he to desert this place. In the meantime, Elsa, myself, and a dozen technicians are his executioners. I have never heard such screaming and wailing in my entire professional life. I can well imagine how these poor people are hurting without benefit of anesthesia."

Johann was stunned. "Perhaps you are onto something. The possibility of us losing the war is becoming a greater reality with each passing day. Winning the race to use the first atomic bomb is the only way Germany might save its hide."

"Elsa and I have no other choice. I don't dare confront or challenge Rost's decision to use my professional skills in this manner. If I did, it would be the end of my life. Rost doesn't like to be questioned or contradicted by anyone; he has made that quite clear. I'm thankful that you intervened on my behalf. You paved my way as the artistic consultant. Only you know what a stretch that was. I was lucky. He might have processed me to Auschwitz with Kurt Gerron and his crew. I guess my time isn't up yet."

"That makes two of us. If Otto didn't make it, I'd like to think that you will give us a chance. I would love to make babies with you. I've always wanted a family. I was an only and terribly indulged child. My mother doted on me. You would have loved her. She was an elegant and vivacious lady; she loved all the arts, and she loved life. I clearly take after her. I hardly knew my father; he was killed in Verdun in World War One. She was spared this horrendous experience. My mother died on December seventh, 1941, a day I shall never have difficulty recalling."

"Johann, you must be patient with me. My days are filled with nothing but horror. I'm not in any position to give myself to you. When I walk through this place, I question how anyone could call this a "model concentration camp." I really don't understand how Rost, or whoever came up with the idea, can view this as such a wonderful place. Just getting to work every day, I see the misery in people's eyes, hear their screams in my ears, and watch people being transported and treated worse than cattle. I suffer nightmares in broad daylight and at night."

Johann nodded his head in agreement. He wasn't willing to concede but felt like a little boy whose favorite toys had been taken from him. He was clearly disappointed that he had failed to convince Rachel he truly loved her and needed her.

Chapter 23

THE first months of 1945 at Theresienstadt dragged on one hand and became totally frenzied on the other. The leadership shipped tens of thousands of prisoners to Treblinka and Auschwitz during the final months of the war. Small and very select groups were released to neutral countries in exchange for exorbitant ransoms deposited in secure bank accounts. Inhumane treatment and executions further reduced the numbers of remaining prisoners. Many prisoners were outright murdered or died of starvation, mistreatment, or a rampant presence of typhoid.

In late February, Rachel complained of extreme abdominal pain. Taking heavy dosages of aspirin did not solve her problem. When Rost wanted his due, she had guts enough to refuse him.

"I'm in extreme abdominal pain. As much as I am willing to submit to your desires to use me, I can't. There is something seriously wrong with me. I don't believe it is my appendix. It involves my vagina. I would rather have you kill me than submit to having sex with you." Rost realized she meant business. He picked up his phone and called one of the ob-gyns on staff.

"This is Commandant Rost. I have a prisoner in my office who needs your attention. Send someone over to take her to your examining room. I have a special interest in this woman. Her services are highly needed in our dental clinic. Make it quick and see what's wrong with her. I want the bitch back at work ASAP."

Ten minutes later, Rachel found herself on the examining table, her feet suspended in stirrups. The doctor shined his light into her vagina and realized that Rachel's self diagnosis was correct. Her cervix was highly inflamed. He suspected an infection or inflammation involving Rachel's intrauterine device. "I will give you an injection to reduce the pain. I need to remove your birth control ring. I firmly believe it is the source of your extreme pain." Upon close inspection, he found the easiest way of removing the device. Rachel was numbed and didn't feel any discomfort. He irrigated the area thoroughly and noted there was minimal bleeding. He refrained from packing the vagina. "I want you to rest here for a good hour before I send you back to the dental clinic. Don't have anyone come near you for at least three days and take warm baths every day for the next week if that is possible where you are housed. Take two aspirin every four hours. I believe you will be just fine in a few days." He helped her off the examining table and steered her to a cot where she could rest. She was back working side by side with Elsa two hours later.

The next day, Rost called on her in the dental clinic. Hundreds of patients had to be processed by fourteen people. Rost could see that Rachel was terribly busy. The screams of tortured victims echoed through the facility. Rost walked her aside where no one could hear him. She could feel his hot breath as his words insulted her ear. "What did you find out? What's wrong with your cunt? I need a session with you. When can you come to my office?"

"The doctor told me not to have any sex for three days. It was a serious infection of my cervix. He had to perform surgery. You cannot come near me until Thursday."

"I don't give a fuck what he did and what he told you. I want you in my office at lunchtime. I can give you a rear treatment and get off a load or you have the choice of giving me a first-class blow job or both. I might even enjoy whipping your ass. I'm getting a hard-on just picturing you there. Be there at noon. I'll be ready for you!" He pushed her back toward a waiting victim. Rachel bit the fingers of her right hand, trying to stifle her outburst of total disgust. She had reached the limits of her degradation.

When she arrived at Rost's office, everyone had left for lunch. She knew she was in for a traumatic experience. She softly knocked three times on his office door as he had instructed her to do. This way he knew for sure it would be Rachel coming to see him. The door opened slowly. All she could see was his hairy right arm. He grabbed her hand and pulled her into the office. He kicked the door shut. He was stark naked and fully erect. She saw the whip still hanging on the coat rack and was hoping he had not forgotten about his promise of not using it again on her. He pushed her toward his desk. "Face Adolf and bend slightly over my desk." He grabbed the footstool, getting into position to sodomize her. He thought he would be kind and so lubricated his weapon with his own saliva. He entered her with fury. "You like that, don't you, fucking bitch? I want you to scream for more. I made sure there's no one out there to listen to us."

Rost withdrew from Rachel. He pulled her away from his desk and pushed her toward his chair. He leaned into the chair and forced Rachel to her knees facing him. "Go, suck my dick until I come. I hope you like the taste of your asshole." Rachel gagged as he unloaded his ejaculation into her throat. She spat at him. His face was covered in semen and spit. "You'll be sorry you did that." He reached for the whip and beat her mercilessly. No longer did she stifle her screams. She didn't care if anyone learned what was going on in the commandant's office. He yelled at her. "Get dressed, and get the fuck out of here. Be here promptly next Monday."

Rachel didn't know how she managed to get back to the clinic. Never mind getting back to the clinic. How could she work, and how could she face Elsa? Anyone looking at her knew she had been violated and traumatized. Elsa didn't ask any questions. She had figured out many Mondays ago what was going on. Whenever Rachel returned from her regular office visits with Commandant Rost, she acted distraught and often disturbed. Perhaps things were more painful on this given afternoon. Elsa just kept working and was hoping Rachel wouldn't collapse while she worked for hours even though she was obviously in great pain.

Chapter 24

RACHEL returned to Johann's apartment on the night of May 3. It was another traumatic day at the dental clinic. Extracted gold was melted as fast as possible and pressed into convenient bullion bars. At Rost's urging, the bars were taken promptly to his office.

Johann was waiting for Rachel. "I couldn't wait to tell you. We are getting the hell out of this place. I have made a flight plan. We cannot stay around here any longer. This nightmare is about to end. Perhaps it's leading us into another one, but we must get out of here. There is a slim chance we might make it. I don't want us to get caught in this place when the Russians overrun the camp. Tomorrow is your last day at the clinic, your last day at Theresienstadt. I have taken the liberty of packing the few things of yours worth taking. All are neatly contained in a light-weight satchel. I ran across a photo of me that Kern must have taken when I bought the kimono for you in Dresden. Was there any particular reason why it was in the drawer with your underwear? I was shocked to see it."

Rachel was caught off guard. She looked at the photo. "I don't know where all this shall end. I just felt like keeping it."

Johann took the photo from her. "I will slide it in this secret pocket on the bottom of the satchel. It ought to be pretty safe there unless someone conducts a serious search. The Varanasi scarf was cleaned and restored. It looks beautiful. I disguised it as a liner inside an old pair of pants that I've outgrown. I've put on a few pounds since I was twenty-five." Johann slapped his stomach with the flat of his hand. "My gut isn't too flabby for thirty-seven, but it could use a workout now and then." Rachel gave him a sideways look. He went on about the preparations he had made. "Unless someone is interested in old men's slacks, no one will ever discover your treasure. You came with little and will leave with little. I'm a bit disappointed in the story of the hidden photo. Here I thought you were carrying a secret torch for me." Johann smiled widely. He assumed the stance of a muscle man. Both he and Rachel laughed; it felt good to laugh.

Rachel decided she could not leave Otto's photo behind. "I have to confess to something that has sustained me here on many a night." She walked over to the desk and withdrew Otto's framed photo. "I took this and hid it when they arrested me last year. It found its resting and hiding place in your desk the night I arrived."

Johann took the photo gently out of her hand and looked at Otto's image. "I can see why you love him as much as you do. He's quite a handsome specimen. I'm not angry at you for having his photo. I'm glad to know what Otto looks like. Let me take it out of the frame and put it right next to the photo of me. We'll be two men in hiding." He smiled at her lovingly.

"I will travel almost as lightly. Nothing that speaks of my military life will be on me or in the Mercedes. We don't know who we might run into. Our breakout might be fraught with many challenges. I'm not worried about German interference. I'm much more afraid of running into Russian or Polish troops on the march to Berlin. I will stash our bags and whatever in my car tomorrow night after dark. I've given some thought to Elsa. You and she have become pretty close in that ghastly work you perform for Rost. How would you feel about asking her to make the getaway with us? I don't know what might happen along the escape route. If we are intercepted, they might arrest me. Elsa would be company and a help to you. It's all pure speculation on my part. I never had to flee from anywhere or envision a jailbreak, so to speak. If you agree with my assessment, go speak with Elsa right now. Lay the cards on the table, and tell her what needs to be done."

Rachel grabbed a black jacket and ran out the door. She was less likely to be seen in black, although she was aware that the curfew wasn't enforced as strictly as in the past. Several guards had disappeared overnight. No one seemed to know, and no one seemed to care any longer. Everyone was out for themselves. She heard the whispers expressing fear of retribution by those surviving the evil acts visited upon them. Her hair was a mess. She pounded on Elsa's hovel.

"My God. What are you doing out at this hour? Come in." Elsa closed the door behind Rachel. "My roommates have already crawled into their bunks. We were talking earlier. The atmosphere has changed. So many of the guards have left. Does Johann have any idea what's happening?"

Rachel grabbed Elsa by her left shoulder. She spoke very softly. "We need to talk right now. Johann is planning a getaway the day after tomorrow. He wants you to come with us. He knows how much we appreciate each other. That horrible job forced down our throats brought us together. I don't know how I ever would have survived without you. Johann is right; I cannot simply desert you."

"Are you sure von Rondstett wants me to come along? I might be just another burden for him and for you."

"No, you would never be a burden. You were my savior for the last few months. How would I ever think you were a burden? Please come with us. I need your help; I need to draw strength from all that you can give."

"How's he planning to escape? What's he taking with him? He's got so much stuff accumulated in his place. What about all those fancy uniforms, coats, and caps?"

Rachel raised her eyes. "Elsa, he's just taking a small valise with a few absolutely necessary things. Nothing else. He's driving his Mercedes. He wants you and me to take only a small bag each. Not knowing where and how far we may be able to drive, he believes we should be able to carry anything we take with us. It makes sense. God forbid, but we may have to walk for many kilometers. He packed a small satchel for me. I suggest you do the same. Take advantage of everyone soundly sleeping. I'll see you at the lab in the morning. Plan on being ready to cut from this place first thing on the fifth. Johann is anxious to leave this havoc behind. Personally, I'm sure he doesn't want to get caught by foreign troops. They are not too far away. The artillery fire has kept me awake for days. I was looking forward to being freed. Now, I'm not so sure. I might feel differently were our saviors coming out of the West instead of the East."

She gave Elsa a quick hug. "See you in the morning. Pack lightly. Glad you want to be part of our plan. I'll need you."

Elsa reciprocated the friendly hug. She had grown fond of Rachel. They were a team riding a roller coaster to hell. "Thanks for asking me. I'll do anything and everything to make this thing work. I'll be careful getting ready. No one will be the wiser." She closed the door quietly behind Rachel, who was already running toward von Rondstett's apartment.

Rachel rushed in. She almost slammed the door behind her. She had gotten chilled walking back from Elsa's barrack. She noticed her packed satchel standing next to Johann's valise as she glanced over to the open door of the large wardrobe. Every one of his uniforms was still neatly hung in his shrine of propriety. She caught his eyes. "Elsa was touched that you wanted her to join us in our getaway. She's bringing her small bag over tomorrow night. The night air really got to me. I know it's a travesty, but would you mind heating me some of that fancy Bordeaux of yours and put some honey and lemon in it? I feel like I need a hot toddy. I need something to settle me down. This whole affair has me scared out of my wits. I hope I didn't catch anything from some of our sick prisoners."

Johann reached out to her. He had taken a shower while Rachel went to talk to Elsa. He was wearing his favorite velour robe. She saw his bare chest peeking out from beneath the wide lapels. He heated the wine on the stove and handed her the concoction she had asked for. He thought it was a God-awful drink but made it for her anyway. These days, he did almost anything to please her. He was still very much in love with Rachel but didn't dare to be flagrant about his physical needs. He knew when he was rejected.

Rachel gulped the first two sips. "Perfect, perfect! Thanks, that's just what the doctor ordered."

"And who's the doctor? Is it Dr. Rachel Adina von Graben?" Her name just rolled off his tongue. She knew he had done it on purpose. He wanted to get the better of her. He had walked over to the sofa and stood in front of her as he was posing his questions. He stood there like a little boy lost in the woods. But he wasn't a little boy. He was a grown man who loved her and wanted her. He grinned at Rachel and then she saw tears in his eyes. She never knew what made her do it. She reached for his hand and pulled him toward her. The cup of hot wine sat on the table. Johann bent down to her and held her chin in his hand. He made her rise from the sofa. His eyes were no longer glistening; they were flooded with tears. He embraced Rachel and kissed her deeply. He took her breath away. Rachel responded to his caressing kisses.

"Rachel, look at me. I need to see your eyes. It's Jochanaan you're looking at, my beautiful Salome. It's not Otto. It's me. I'm here with you in this fucking nightmare of a world. I don't know if he is rotting in some hole in Belgium or if he is alive in some prison camp. But I'm here right now. I need you. I can feel it in my gut. We don't even know if we'll be alive in a couple of days. There are no certainties. Neither you nor I have the foggiest idea what is in store for us. All I know at this very moment is, I want to love you with all that is in me. And, I want you to love me. I don't want to rape you. I want you to accept my love and enjoy this night with me. I want you to love my body as much as I want to ravish and cherish yours. I want to have sex without abandon and without any regrets. Can you do this for me? I love you, Rachel Adina!"

Rachel leaned into Johann. He had left her speechless. She touched the hairs on his broad chest and ran a hand over his nipples. She could feel them harden under her touch. She loosened the belt on his plush robe. He was totally nude. There was no question in Rachel's mind that this man wanted her. She slipped off his robe. It was Rachel's turn to have tears in her eyes. Were they tears of regret? Was she feeling sorry for herself? The horrible scenes with Commandant Rost flashed in front of her eyes. Why did she never say anything to Johann about the horrors that she was subjected to for so many weeks? Was she crying for Otto? Was she feeling guilt about what was about to happen with her own consent? She felt like she was on a cheap, cranking carousel that was spinning her mind around in uncontrollable gyrations in all directions. She let herself be guided by Johann's strong grasp toward the inevitable celebration.

He undressed her completely. Johann couldn't wait to touch her nakedness with his hands and his tongue. He wanted to taste the woman for whom he had longed for months. He had honored her pact with the devil. It wasn't always easy for him. But not once did he satisfy his immense sexual drive after that day when Rachel Adina had come into his life and had thoroughly denied him the pleasures of their bodies. Yes, he had taken her forcefully and with uncontrollable passion and anger. He knew he had hurt her. He had behaved like an infuriated bull. His anger had been caused by Rachel's rejections of his romantic feelings for her. While he accepted her reasons for denying him and still loving Otto, he was hurt to the core. No woman had ever done that to him.

Johann carried Rachel Adina to his room. He ripped the fancy covers off the bed and tossed them on the floor. He picked up Rachel. Her skin was rippling with goose bumps. She was shivering. He laid her down on the silky sheets and immediately covered the entire length of her slender body with his broad existence and held her tightly against his hot body. She could feel his warmth radiating toward her. While she desired all of Johann, she wanted just to be held by him at this moment. She hadn't realized how much she had desired to be held by a loving man. Yes, it had been Otto she wanted all along. But he wasn't within her reach; for all she knew, Johann was right in his assumption that she was longing for a dead man.

Rachel realized she was human after all. How often had she fantasized about the great sex she had enjoyed with Otto for all the years they had lived together. And it wasn't always about the sex; it was the feel and the touch of another human's hand. She was hoping, should Otto be alive, he could forgive her the sin she was about to commit. She looked into Johann's eyes, letting him know she was willing to be loved by him. It felt all so different after the tortures she had suffered with Rost.

Johann realized what was happening as Rachel maneuvered him gently off her body. There still was a hint of her intoxicating perfume on her skin. She guided him firmly to lie down on his back. Rachel wanted to be in control. She could tell he was waiting for her. "Sit on top of my dick. Ride me like a bronco as hard as you can. Try hurting me the way I tried hurting you the first and last time we were together." Rachel kept hoping he would not look at her back and her buttocks; traces of Klemens Rost's whippings were still visible.

Rachel rode him with a fury. "I don't want to hurt you, but I want to gain total release from all the anger I have felt since I was torn out of my other life. I want to feel your life and your body merging with mine. I want you to fill me with your strength and energy. I will need it for the challenges of life in the days to come. Oh, oh, *yes, yes, yes,* Johann!" As she could feel the balm of his generous relief soothing her womb, she collapsed on top of him and experienced her own fulfilling moment.

He grinned from ear to ear. He was totally relaxed and satisfied.

He hadn't realized how much he had missed sex, especially the kind of sex he had just enjoyed with Rachel. "That was quite a ride. Give me a chance to recover. Then let me see how I can trump that." He almost asked her if she had practiced that position with Otto in their Munich days. He bit his lip before committing a major faux pas. "I want to look into your beautiful eyes while I make love to you. I want you to look into mine. Let's concentrate on that while we slip and slide slowly along easy street of blissfulness. Let's enjoy each other rather than closing our eyes, envisioning nirvana." When he finally pulled up the sheets to cover their satiated nakedness, they fell soundly asleep in each other's arms.

Chapter 25

IT was about eleven o'clock in the morning. Rachel was putting things in order in the apartment. She didn't know why she was doing what she was doing. None of it made any sense. Their escape was planned for the next day. Who would care what the apartment looked like? She mused about Johann's love-making during the previous night. She couldn't help smiling. Rachel would have been a liar had she denied the attention Johann had given her.

Johann left early in the morning. He was supposed to have a meeting with Rost and some of the other officers on the campus. After the meeting, he intended to get his car out of storage and have the tires checked and the tank filled. The Mercedes had not been used for many months. He wanted to make sure it was in good driving condition. He had no idea what the roads would be like.

Rachel heard boots coming up the stairs. She assumed Johann was returning faster than she had anticipated. The key was turned in the lock, and the door opened. It was Rost. He glared at her, holding his whip in his hand. "You thought you would get away with him, didn't you? I saw him futzing around with his Mercedes after he left my office. My car is packed to the hilt with heavy gold bullion. Wouldn't you like to be known as a rich Jew? I'm getting out of this fucking place tomorrow. How about joining me instead of running away with Johann? When this is all over, he'll be piss poor. More urgently, I missed you this Monday and am ready for a make-up session."

He got undressed except for his SS medallion hanging from his neck and his gartered stockings. "Get out of those damn rags. I want to see those streaks on your body. I'm getting aroused just thinking about giving your ass another whipping. But before our little farewell session, I need to take a crap badly." He strutted toward the bedroom and slammed the door hard as he sat down on the stool. She couldn't help hearing the loud noises as he was defecating. She chose not to heed his command. Rachel remained fully dressed. She never felt any surer of what she was about to do. She had dreamed of this moment for months.

She reached for Rost's holster on the side table and withdrew the Glock he always carried. She knew it was loaded. Rachel was thankful for the lessons Otto had given her during their college days in Munich. He wanted to make sure she knew how to handle a gun if there was ever a need for it. She spread her legs and had solid footing as she faced the bathroom door. She heard Rost get off the stool and flush the toilet. She knew he wouldn't wash his hands. Rachel was ready. She couldn't wait to glimpse the surprise and fear on the bastard's face as he opened the door and saw her.

Her voice was icy and dark. "Don't come any closer. You have three seconds to make the sign of the cross." He did. She aimed at his penis and fired. He screamed. Rachel laughed hysterically. Before he could fall to the floor, she hit his chest and his head. Her aim had been perfect. She finished the job when she blew out his brains at close range and turned his body right-side up by kicking it with her left foot. His dead eyes were staring back at her. He was lying at her feet in a pool of blood. She stepped on his gut and spat in his face. "And, yesterday, trembling Terezin lay prostate at his feet." For a moment, she was Floria Tosca having dealt Scarpia his losing hand.

Rachel rushed down the steep steps and ran to Elsa's barrack. "Elsa, Elsa, I need your help," she yelled as she walked in. "Come with me quickly. Take one of the wheelbarrows standing over there. We'll need it. Don't ask any questions. You'll see why I must have your help when you walk into Johann's apartment."

Elsa followed her, easily pushing the empty wheelbarrow. There was no one on the streets. Elsa stopped when she saw Rost lying dead in the pool of blood. "He came to rape me for a last time. That scumbag did it every week to me for months. You have no idea how often I dreamt of killing him. I'm thrilled I finally got my revenge. What do you think we should do? We need to get rid of him before Johann comes back."

Elsa looked around the room. "That water-resistant picnic tablecloth will do fine for the first wrap." Rachel took it off and spread it on the floor near the body without getting into the pool of blood. She grabbed him by his stockinged feet while Elsa held him by his arms. His body was still warm and pliable. They succeeded in getting him onto the cloth and wrapped him up tightly. Next came a couple of blankets that finished the mummy. They dragged him to the front door and pulled him down the steps, each holding onto one of his legs. A hollow sound echoed in the stairway every time his head struck one of the steps. Elsa had no trouble dumping the body into the wheelbarrow with Rachel's assistance. Elsa took charge of the conveyance. She headed to the mass gravesite. She dumped him on top of hundreds of bodies, all people Rost had condemned to death. She didn't even bother covering him with lime since he was well wrapped. She glared at his body. "Rot in hell!" She left the wheelbarrow and walked back to Johann's apartment.

Rachel had scooped up a lot of the blood into a bucket using a dustpan. She was mopping up the rest with Johann's thick bath towels. Elsa looked at Rost's garments lying on the floor. "What are you going to do with all his stuff?"

"Roll up everything in his uniform. There is an empty drawer at the bottom of the wardrobe. I want to mop this floor just one more time. It looks pretty normal to me, but I can still sense the smell of blood. Let's open all the windows in the living room. We need some fresh air." Both women sat down. The evidence of the murder had been erased. She couldn't help gloating. "I'll tell you all about what I suffered at that man's hands when we have left this place behind."

Elsa understood and decided to leave before Johann returned. The women hugged. Rachel stood back and looked at Elsa. "Thanks, my dear friend. We'll see you early in the morning. Are you all packed?"

"Yes, Rachel, I am, and I was glad to help you. There's no one more important in life than good and trusted friends." She quickly descended the steps. Half an hour later, Rachel could hear Johann trumping up the concrete steps. The sound of his boots was distinct. He walked in. "What's that strange smell? Why are all the windows open?" And then he spotted the Glock lying on the small table next to the sofa. He picked it up. "Mind telling me what happened here?"

Rachel told him the whole unbelievable story from start to finish. As she did, she undressed herself completely. He knew she wasn't telling lies when he saw the evidence on her back and buttocks. He reached out to Rachel and held her in his arms. She was sobbing against his shoulder.

"I had no idea this was happening. Why didn't you tell me?"

"Rost threatened me on day one. If I ever spoke to anyone about his actions, and especially to you, he would make sure I or we would wind up where he found his final resting place. I couldn't take that chance. I need to live. I have good reasons for wanting to survive this hell and all that it represents. Thank you for sheltering me from the evil surrounding these walls."

Chapter 26

THE Mercedes pulled away from Elsa's place at nine o'clock on the morning of May 5. The trunk held three small satchels. Johann was glad he had slipped on his favorite pair of unlined pigskin gloves. He could feel the tension in his body. The palms of his hands were uncharacteristically sweaty. He didn't want to alarm his companions. They were silently sitting in the vehicle. Rachel and Elsa were staring out of their respective windows as they passed the last vestiges of Theresienstadt. The two young women were hopeful they would never again have to lay eyes on the miserable place. Their hearts and minds were filled with nothing but memories of havoc, hate, and horror.

Rachel was sitting next to Johann in the front passenger seat. Elsa declined squeezing between them; she opted for sitting comfortably in the back of the car. None of them had any idea how far they would get. He steered the car carefully trying to avoid any deep potholes or shrapnel that could puncture or pop a tire. He headed ever so slightly northwest toward Dresden. The drive that took them less than an hour in September 1944 would last longer than four hours. The road conditions had taken a definite hit in the waning days of the war. Closer to Dresden, they became aware of artillery fire. Johann slowed down. So far they hadn't seen any action. When they entered the city, especially old town, they were astounded. The city had been totally destroyed during the attacks from February 13 to 15. The crown jewel of the East lay in total ruin.

They left what once had been one of the most beautiful cities in the world in a great hurry and were totally disillusioned. They were soon in the country. Johann hoped to find a little inn or café. They were near a farm. Whoever lived on the land had started to plow the fields.

Suddenly, they were surrounded by armed soldiers. They were not German military. Johann, Rachel, and Elsa tried to make out what they were yelling. Johann spoke quietly. "They are Polish and Russian." He could feel sweat running in rivulets down his chest. His pants were soaked in perspiration. What he really needed was to take a piss. He wished he had pulled off the road before they were cornered.

With their bayonets fixed, they motioned for Johann and his passengers to get out of the car. Four or five of the soldiers jumped Johann. He was clearly outnumbered. He tried to communicate with them. His efforts were in vain. A huge guy kicked Johann in the groin. He hit the ground hard, convulsing with pain as he grabbed his crotch. The uniformed men ripped off all of Johann's clothes. Rachel and Elsa screamed. They watched in horror as their protector was brutally sodomized. None understood a word the attackers were saying; the languages used were clearly Slavic. There was no question Johann had become a victim of revenge. No one needed to understand what they were yelling. All seven of the brutes had their turn at assaulting Johann. When the last of the Russians ejaculated with a vengeance, he tore at Johann's blond mane and screamed, *"Nemetskaya svin'ya!"* (German pig!) *"Idi k chertu!"* (Go to hell!). Johann lay on the ground like a rag doll. He was covered in blood and semen. Rachel stifled her screams by pressing her right palm over her mouth. Johann was staring at her with vacant eyes. He was in unbelievable agony.

One of the Russians looked for the car keys. The keys were in Johann's pant pocket, lying in a heap somewhere on the ground. Obviously, the brute had other ideas. He used his bayonet to break open the trunk. He yanked out the three satchels and walked away from the car. Without understanding a word, Rachel and Elsa knew he was bragging about the loot he had discovered. The first satchel was Rachel's. He turned it upside down and dumped everything on the ground. He gave the stuff a quick kick. Johann's old pants caught his eye. He held them up. Johann's waist was much too small for the fat slob. He tossed them away. Rachel held her breath. She knew what Johann had hidden in them.

Next, he emptied Elsa's satchel. Likewise, women's clothing was not what he was searching for. He tossed the bag away in disgust. Johann's piece of luggage was slightly larger and heavier. His pants and shirts weighed more than Elsa and Rachel's blouses and skirts. He realized Johann's pants wouldn't do. Rachel remembered his taut belly and slender waist. The shirts might fit since Johann had such broad shoulders. He gave the bag a final shake. A silver Swastika with the SS symbol encircled in its center fell to the ground.

Rachel blurted, "Oh my God! You promised me you wouldn't have anything incriminating with you!" The slob picked it up with glee in his eyes as he screamed "Nemetskaya svin' ya!" and flashed his discovery to the others. He tore at his fly, grabbed his prick, and pissed all over Johann. He gestured to the others to do the same. They obliged only too willingly. They were ready for another round of sexual assault.

Four of the brutes accosted the two women and tore their clothes off. They shed the tops of their uniforms. None wore any underwear. Rachel stood close enough. She almost choked on the stench coming from their bodies. They dropped their pants. Each woman was attacked by a pair of men. They raped and sodomized them in concert. The remaining three held up Johann's head, making sure he could watch the attack on Rachel and Elsa. Both were crying and screaming in agony. Rachel could feel the blood running down the inside of her legs. Johann closed his eyes and hung his head. No sooner had he done so than one of the brutes yanked his head back by his golden mane. Another was ready to sodomize Johann again. It was a scene of total debauchery.

Done with their deed of defiling Johann and the women, they threw Rachel and Elsa to the ground like garbage. The seven brutes got into a huddle. Within minutes, they stripped themselves naked and put their boots back on their feet. They encircled Johann, singing and dancing around his broken body. Passing his head, they yanked it up and dangled the silver Swastika in front of his eyes. In chorus, they repeated their terms of endearment: "Nemetskaya svin'ya!" and "Idi k chertu!" Completing their song and dance, those who could defecated and urinated all over Johann. It was the height of obscenity. One pulled his pistol, inserting it in Johann's rectum. Rachel fainted as he pulled the trigger. She did not see Johann writhe on the ground. He convulsed and screamed in utter torture. "Finish the job. Kill me!" The seven brutes didn't understand Johann's words. They were ready to finish their act of revenge. The guy with the pistol emptied the chamber into Johann's back. His bullet-riddled body lay still at last.

Elsa held her naked friend against her own bare breasts. Rachel opened her eyes. She couldn't fathom what had befallen Johann. Four of the guys picked up his body. Each held an arm and a leg. They threw his corpse inside the car. The silver Swastika was hanging around his neck. The man who had killed Johann reloaded his revolver. He stepped to the back of the car. He yelled to the others. They retrieved their uniforms and ran away from the car. At last, the gunman fired the entire chamber, hitting the gas tank of the Mercedes, and the car became an instant inferno. Johann's spirit escaped the flames. With one last glare at Rachel and Elsa, their attackers marched off.

Finally, the women got dressed in their torn rags. Both gathered their belongings off the ground. Rachel hugged Johann's old pants.

She shed bitter tears as she lifted her eyes to the heavens. Rachel mouthed the Mourner's Kaddish softly. Johann's car had become his funeral pyre. They decided to stay around until the remains of Johann's body could be touched. With their bare hands, they dug a shallow grave in the soft ground.

It took the strength of both women to lift the charred body out of the shell that had not long ago been Johann's pride. The blackened and deformed silver Swastika lay on the ground. Rachel laid it on Johann's chest. She kissed what had been his forehead. They gently covered his remains with the warm, soft soil of May. Rachel and Elsa knelt by Johann's humble grave. Each said a silent prayer. They picked up their satchels and slowly walked in a southwesterly direction.

Chapter 27

THEY made it to the next village. Elsa and Rachel were thankful for the warmth of the late-afternoon sun. They were walking barefoot. "I can't walk another kilometer," said Rachel. "We must rest and hopefully find a kind soul that will allow us to clean ourselves. Asking to be fed might be pushing it." Elsa agreed. They spotted several small farm houses and decided to take their chances. Rachel took heart. She knocked several times on the door. She finally picked up a rock, hoping to strengthen her effort. There was no answer. They weren't certain if they were purposefully ignored or if the place was deserted.

"What now?" asked Elsa. She grabbed her abdomen, feeling indescribable pain. She lifted her skirt and turned to Rachel. "Would you mind checking me out? It feels to me like I'm bleeding from my bottom."

Rachel took a look at Elsa's back. "You did bleed, but it looks like it has stopped. The back of your skirt is soaked in blood. There are all kinds of wounds and scratches. It looks like one of the guys who attacked you sunk his fingernails into you. The sides of your breasts show similar marks. Would you mind checking me out?"

Elsa carefully removed Rachel's blouse and skirt. She gasped.

"How did you get those streaks? These are not new. Don't tell me they stem from Rost's whippings?"

Rachel nodded affirmatively and gave Elsa a helping hand with getting dressed. "I feel sorry for you. What the Russians and Poles did to me was nothing new. I was initiated to those insults to my body by Klemens Rost. I still shudder to think that men can do such things to women and brag about their enjoyment of inflicting pain."

Elsa nodded. "I'm ready to collapse. I need to pee so badly. I cannot wait until we gain entry into one of these places." She pulled up her torn skirt; her panties had been ripped to shreds. Elsa crouched on the ground and just let go.

Rachel began to cry. "There's got to be someone in one of these godforsaken places." She thought she heard the cry of a rooster as she walked up to another farmhouse. She didn't knock on the door; she banged it with both of her fists as hard as she could. The door flew open. An angry-looking woman stared at her and Elsa. "Who the hell are you? What do you want from us? Whatever ya looking for, we ain't got it. Beat it off my property, you filthy-looking bitches." She slammed the door in Rachel and Elsa's faces. Rachel stumbled and fell on the ground. Elsa thought she had fainted.

"Let me help you up." She held Rachel in her short but strong arms. "Let it all out. Let's try that tiny little place over there. I don't know what it is, but I feel drawn to it." She had to drag Rachel up the narrow garden path and made her sit down on the front steps. She firmly knocked on the wooden door. The door was opened with care. They were facing a middle-aged man. He was shocked when he looked at them.

"Who are you? Where did you come from? What happened to you?"

Rachel couldn't speak; she was still clinging to the step where Elsa made her sit. She was using the tail end of her ripped blouse as a handkerchief. There was blood in her spittle. She tried to suppress her blubbering.

Elsa offered to answer the man who had just opened the door to his home. "The woman sitting down there is Rachel; my name is Elsa. We escaped from Theresienstadt early this morning."

"Then how did you get here? You couldn't have walked from Theresienstadt."

"One of the officers at the camp, Major Johann von Rondstett, made the breakaway possible. He drove his personal car. He offered to take us away from the camp."

"Well, where is the major? Did he dump and desert you?"

With great difficulty, Elsa choked back her tears and continued. "He drove for more than four hours and made it to the west side of Dresden. A few kilometers east of here, we were intercepted by a group of Russian and Polish soldiers." She broke down crying. When she caught her breath, she continued. "The soldiers sodomized and eventually killed Johann. They raped and sodomized us as well. Then they turned his Mercedes into his funeral pyre. After they vanished, Rachel and I scraped a shallow grave and buried Johann's remains in a field. All that is left of the scene is the burned-out shell of Johann's car."

The man listened intently. He wasn't sure he could believe what he heard Elsa tell. "Well, how did you wind up at my doorstep?"

"We gathered up what the vigilantes didn't abuse or burn and started walking. We were desperately looking for someone to help us. There wasn't an answer to our knocking at the first house. A woman came to the door of the second house. She acted like she was ready to attack us. We ran away from her. It's that farm house way over there."

The man looked in the direction Elsa was pointing. "I understand. She's a real bitch. Her husband was a big-time Nazi before Hitler was even elected. He was killed a few weeks ago on the Western Front.

"By the way, I'm Fritz Unrat. As you can tell by my yard, the troops have been through here. They drove their tanks right up to the front door and mowed down everything in their paths. They ransacked the inside of my house which wasn't of interest to them, but they stole all my livestock. I was glad they didn't molest or kill me. Come in, you two. Let me see what I can do to help. You look like you could use a caring hand."

Elsa more or less picked up Rachel. She spoke softly. "The man seems nice enough. He asked us to come in. He wants to ease our pain. I don't believe he will harm us. Were he to try anything untoward with us, I could handle him. He doesn't look all that strong to me. His name is Fritz. Looks like he's living here by himself. Have faith in me, Rachel. I'll make sure he won't harm us."

Looking worse than a couple of disheveled scarecrows, they stepped into Fritz's small house.

Elsa looked around wanting to check out the place. Two large photographs caught her eye as she walked through the kitchen. "Are you living by yourself?" she asked Fritz.

"Yes. I lost my wife in February. She was visiting our daughter and grandchildren in Dresden. None of them survived the bomb attacks. I never even saw their burned corpses. They were buried in one of the many mass graves." Unashamedly, tears stole down his cheeks. Rachel and Elsa felt for the man.

"This is not a fancy house, but I have a place where you might wash up. Let me show you where you can take a bath and change your clothes. You might consider washing them. We can hang things on a line. With the breeze we are enjoying, they will be dry in a hurry. I'll pull a couple of robes from the wardrobe. They'll do in the meantime."

He walked them to the back of the little house. Everything was surprisingly clean. The bed was made; there were no piles of dirty dishes as they passed through the little kitchen. "There is a hot water well in my gigantic stove in the kitchen. My wife used to like baking and cooking. You may help me carry a few buckets of hot water to this big, old bathtub. My arthritic shoulders are not what they used to be. It will be nicer to have warmed water instead of cold from the well. While you bathe and change, I'll rustle up some hot tea and whatever I can find that's edible."

Elsa schlepped several buckets of hot water from the kitchen stove to the wooden tub in the back room. When there was just enough, she almost collapsed from exhaustion. It would have to be enough. She bent down to Rachel, who was slumped against the wall, staring at some point on the ceiling.

"Do you want to go first?" she asked Rachel. "I don't mind using the same water."

Rachel shook her head and mumbled, "Can't allow that....Too much...." She waved a hand over all the blood that had dried on her legs. "You....g-go....first."

Elsa nodded and straightened her stiff back before she slipped off what was left of her clothes. Rachel watched as Elsa lowered herself into the tub, wincing as the water covered her wounds. As Elsa leaned back against the edge of the tub, Rachel closed her eyes and tried to think of Miriam.

Fritz had provided them with soap and a very bristly brush. She scrubbed herself as hard as she could. She was thankful for her short hair. She finally stood up in the tub and started to dry herself.

"Rachel, you cannot possibly take your bath in this water. It's too filthy. Let me slip on one of these robes Fritz laid on the bed. I'll drain the tub and fetch you clean water from the kitchen. He had a roaring fire in that stove; there'll be plenty of hot water again."

Elsa drained the tub and scrubbed it. Rachel sat on a hard wooden chair. She didn't want to soil anything with the filth clinging to her body. Her vacant eyes were staring into space. She hardly caught on to all Elsa tried to tell her. She couldn't stop her gasps of crying. Her mind was reliving the events that had taken place just hours ago. Her bath was finally waiting for her.

"Rachel, you will need some help with washing your hair. Please let me assist you with that. Why don't you kneel down in front of the tub? I'll wash and rinse your hair first. Then you can scrub your body. That soap looks terrible but actually does a pretty good job. You'll love the feel of the brush. It'll make you feel really clean."

Rachel acted like a zombie. She was only too willing to have Elsa help her with her hair. After the final rinse, Elsa wrapped Rachel's hair in one of the smaller towels Fritz had provided and encouraged her to slip down into the warmth of the tub. When she did, she almost went under. She looked up at Elsa and didn't say a word. Elsa became frightened.

"Oh no; we haven't come this far to do something as stupid as drowning ourselves. Remember, you have Miriam to think about and possibly even Otto. You don't know for sure if he is dead or alive. Sit up. Let me scrub you. I'm not letting you out of my sight. We have survived hell. We've survived those fucking Russians and Poles. We won't be done in by a tub full of soothing warm water." Elsa held Rachel firmly in one of her strong arms and ran the soap all over her body before she applied the pressure of the brush. Rachel felt like a baby receiving a much-needed bath. She was thankful to Elsa for attending to her needs.

Fritz had become curious. What was taking so long? He didn't dare invade their privacy. They might get the wrong idea after all that happened earlier in the day. He yelled from the kitchen. "Are you ladies all right? I'm getting worried about you two! Are you getting along with that old bathtub?"

Elsa had to come up with an answer. "We are just about done. It took a good while to get all that dirt and blood off our bodies. My friend is still in shock. She's still reliving the events of the last twenty-four hours. We'll be there in a few minutes. Be patient with us. Thanks for the robes. Maybe we'll do some washing later."

He was relieved. Their scrubbed appearance was a marked improvement over what he saw when they first knocked on his door. Elsa pulled Rachel by her right arm and pushed her gently into the seat of a slightly worn, overstuffed chair standing close to the tiled oven in the living quarters adjacent to the kitchen.

Fritz had set the table for three. The teakettle was whistling. When he looked over at Rachel, she was slumped down in the chair. She looked like she had passed out. He stared at Elsa. "Is she OK? She looks like death warmed over!"

Elsa could read the concern in his voice. "She's OK, Fritz, if I may call you that. Anyone who has been through what we experienced today has good reason to look that way. I'm just a bit tougher than Rachel. I was in that damn camp for more than three years. Warmth and sleep will do wonders."

Fritz was looking at Elsa and then at Rachel. He still couldn't fathom all they went through just hours ago. "How about some tea and cookies? I baked them myself." He didn't have to ask twice. Elsa felt she needed something in her stomach.

He poured her a cup of tea and put the plate of cookies in front of her. She hardly had bitten into the first cookie when she reached for another. She felt like a glutton, but her stomach was longing to be fed. Elsa nodded off still sitting at the kitchen table. Soothing sleep was a welcome friend.

Fritz decided to do the kind thing. As much as his shoulders were bothering him, he walked a few buckets of hot water to his washing machine. He gathered up Rachel and Elsa's dirty clothes and put most things in the washer. By the time his surprise visitors gradually returned to the living, their clothes were gently drying in the breeze that had become steady in the afternoon.

Elsa was the first to waken. At first, she was startled. For a moment, she couldn't recall where she was. When Fritz walked in, his arms holding the clean, dried clothes he had taken off the line, it dawned on her where she was. Rachel was still in a deep sleep.

Fritz poured Elsa another cup of tea. "Where are you planning to go when you leave here?"

"I'm not sure. The Nazis arrested my parents and me in Dachel-hofen, Bavaria, in 1942. I was kept in Theresienstadt. I never saw my parents again. I presume they were murdered like so many others." Fritz handed Elsa his handkerchief to wipe away the tears.

"Much depends on what Rachel wants to do. My fate seems to be linked to hers. From what she told me in Theresienstadt, she wants to get back to Essen. She and her husband had a dental practice there. More importantly, last Rachel knew, their daughter was still in the care of some nuns in the area."

"How are you planning to get there? You do realize there are no trains running, don't you?"

"I have no idea. I presume Rachel plans on walking. It seems almost an impossible task. I've stood on my feet a lot, but I've never walked any distance. This will be a challenge for me. She seems to be set on making it there. Rachel has good reasons for wanting to return to Essen. I will abide by her decisions."

Elsa and Fritz were studying his old maps of Germany when Rachel finally opened her eyes. She was totally disoriented. "Where am I?" She recognized Elsa but wasn't so sure about Fritz sitting next to her. It finally came to her who she was looking at when he spoke.

"Remember me? I'm Fritz, the man who let you take a bath in his house."

"Forgive me; I'm still in another world. I just relived this whole bloody day in my dreams, or should I say nightmares. I still cannot believe what happened to us this morning. I presume it still is today?"

Elsa spoke up. "Yes, Rachel. It's shortly after ten. Fritz washed and dried all our filthy clothes while we were asleep. Don't worry. He saw your scarf. It was still in good shape. That's the only thing he didn't put into his washing machine. It's safe."

Rachel released a stream of air from her lungs and finally became curious. "What are you doing?"

"Fritz is showing me on his map how far it is to Essen. I had no idea. Are you sure you want to walk six hundred kilometers?"

"I can't think about that right now. Could I have a piece of bread or something? I feel like throwing up. I need something to quiet down the pain in my stomach. I'm starved."

Fritz reached into his breadbox. "Are you sure you don't want to try one of my special cookies?"

"Just the thought of something sweet makes me want to vomit. No, thank you, a piece of dry bread is all I care about right now." Fritz got out his knife and cut her a thick slice of his hearty bread.

"You want some cheese on it?" He couldn't imagine eating just dry bread. There was no butter in the house, but he did have a hunk of cheese he could slice.

"No, thanks. The bread will be fine." Rachel grabbed the slice of bread out of Fritz's hand and took an unladylike big bite. She chewed slowly. The last thing she wanted was to vomit all over the kitchen table or on Fritz's floor.

At last, she glanced at the open map. Fritz was drawing an invisible line with his large index finger between Dresden and Essen. Rachel was fully awake now. "Looks to me like about six hundred kilometers in an almost straight line west. In our condition, we'll be lucky to manage thirty kilometers a day. On rainy days, it might be less. Elsa, are you up to walking for three weeks?"

"If that's what it takes, I'm willing to do it. I can't stay here, and I certainly won't let you do it on your own, Rachel. You and I are all we've got, for better or for worse. But we need to rest up for a day or two before we undertake this jaunt. It sounds scary to me. Lord knows the kinds of things that can happen. That's quite a distance to walk."

Rachel did a quick calculation. "If we leave early on Wednesday, we might be close to Essen on June first."

Elsa was more practical. "No one is waiting for us. We'll get there when we get there. I may need to rest up for a day here and there. I just cannot envision myself walking six hundred kilometers in one stretch.

"Speaking of rest; I need to lie down somewhere. I'm suddenly dead tired." Her yawning interrupted what she was trying to say. Fritz walked them back to his bedroom. "I put clean sheets on while you two were sleeping. I hope the bed is comfortable enough for the two of you. You don't mind sleeping together, do you? I'll sleep on the sofa in the living quarters. I don't mind. You need a couple of nights of halfway decent sleep." He wished them a restful night before he closed the bedroom door.

They were stretched out in seconds. "Forget about brushing hair or teeth; never mind putting on face cream," thought Rachel. Elsa fell asleep instantly. Her snoring kept Rachel awake. She tossed and turned before finally succumbing to fitful sleep. She almost hated to close her eyes, fearful of reliving the day in another nightmarish dream.

Over a simple breakfast, Elsa and Rachel discussed with Fritz the long trek across Germany. They believed his recommendations to be reasonable. Rachel commented, "You might be right about sticking to country and back roads rather than moving along major highways. There's a good chance they weren't bombed as heavily as the autobahns and major roads. Walking back roads, we'll have a better chance of meeting with rural rather than city folks. It will be easier to sleep in a barn than to seek shelter in someone's home." Fritz concurred with Rachel's assessment of the situation.

Elsa couldn't help seeing all sorts of women's clothing hanging in the wardrobe in Fritz's bedroom. She raised the question with Rachel. "All these things must have belonged to his wife and daughter. I wonder if he would mind letting us take a couple pieces. What's left of ours is mostly in tatters. I cannot imagine he'd be unwilling to help us."

Rachel chose to pursue Elsa's idea. "Fritz, we noticed a lot of women's clothing hanging in the wardrobe in your bedroom. Are these by any chance things that belonged to your wife and daughter? Would you let us have a few pieces since our garments were so badly damaged?"

"I'm glad you mentioned it. I didn't want to offer you used clothing that once belonged to my deceased wife and daughter. Take what you need. My wife was closer in size to Elsa. Our daughter, Trudi, was more your size, Rachel. Try on what you like. I'm not so sure about footwear. There are lots of shoes in the bottom of the wardrobe. See if you find any that fit you. You can't walk six hundred kilometers barefoot. Also, I suggest you each take a collapsible umbrella and a rain cape. It's May, and you might run into some rain along the way. These things don't do any good hanging in my wardrobe. It makes me happy that they will be put to good use."

Fritz was pleased to help his desperate visitors in any way he could. He was so glad to have someone to talk to. There were days when he talked to the walls. He was becoming a hermit. Fritz was taken by Rachel. "There's nothing here you cannot have. Just remember, you must schlepp the stuff for all that distance. Also, I want you to take some money. You may need to buy something to eat along the way." He reached into his pants and pulled out a few small wrinkled paper bills. "It's not much, but please take it. I don't want you wandering about without any money in your pockets."

Rachel looked at Elsa, and then both made eye contact with Fritz. They were in tears.

Rachel spoke. "We will never be able to thank you enough for your kindness. You are our Good Samaritan. Thank you! Thank you! Thank you, Fritz!" She reached for his shoulder and hugged him.

When the opportunity arose, Fritz guided Elsa to his desk. Rachel was dressing in the bedroom. "You are the stronger of the two of you. I want you to take this small pistol I've had for years. It was well hidden. I checked it last night and cleaned and oiled it.

I would feel so much better if you had it with you. I have no need for it, but it might protect you in an extreme confrontation. You are not afraid to have a weapon on you, are you? Have you ever used a pistol?"

Elsa wasn't sure she wanted to take it. "When I was a teenager, my father showed me how to use a gun, but I've never owned one myself. Are you sure you want us to have it? How would you protect yourself without it?"

"I'm staying right here in this godforsaken place. What would someone want to do to a poor man? I would feel much better if you and Rachel had it in your possession. Just put it in the bottom of your satchel, and keep it to yourself. I hear Rachel coming this way." He tapped his index finger on his lips.

On Wednesday morning, they started out on their long trek across the country. Fritz had packed a few sandwiches that would keep for a couple of days. There were good eating apples off his tree, and much-cherished chocolates. He was happy to share anything he had. Rachel and Elsa didn't have enough words to express their appreciation to Fritz for his compassion. He had helped them greatly and gladly.

Their unexpected visit had made him forget his loneliness in the empty house if just for a few hours. He hugged them intensely and wished them well on their journey. He sobbed when he finally had to let them go. They parted company with the promise to stay in touch.

Chapter 28

RACHEL and Elsa got an early start on the morning of May 9. Their first goal was Leipzig. It would take them four days to make it to the western outskirts of the city. They heeded Fritz's advice and avoided big cities. They lay largely in ruins; little villages had generally gone unscathed.

Sometimes, they walked for an hour without saying a word to each other. They were both off in their own personal worlds. Out of the blue, Rachel would burst into tears. "I cannot get Otto or Johann off my mind. I see both of them rotting away in their respective graves. I still can't believe I shot and killed a man, although I did it in self-defense. Rost deserved what he got. It was horrible what those beasts did to Johann. There were days when I envisioned all sorts of revengeful acts upon him after he raped me on that first night in Theresienstadt. But never in my wildest imagination did I wish for anything like what happened outside of Dresden. If it's true what I was told by Rost, Otto may very well be dead and buried somewhere out there. I must get to Essen. I must find out what happened to Miriam. She is my one link to reality and to life. I so want to live and share my life with her. She is the link to my past and to my future."

All of a sudden Rachel became frantic. She stopped and emptied her satchel. She touched the bottom where Johann had shown her he hid the photographs of Otto and himself. Rachel could feel them and pulled them out. She touched her lips to both and then hugged them for a split second. Elsa took a peek and smiled at her. Rachel put them back into the protective place and then continued walking.

Elsa would halt for a moment and grab Rachel's free hand. "You're absolutely right, Rachel. We must make it to the end of this frightful journey; we must find Miriam. She's all you might have left. If and when we make it to Essen and you discover that the practice was destroyed, there will be ways of starting somewhere else. What's most important is that we find Miriam, hopefully alive and well. That's all that matters.

"I'm beat. My feet are killing me. I told you those shoes of Fritz's wife were too small. But there was no other choice. I don't know how many pairs of her shoes I tried on. All of them struck my ankles the wrong way. I'm sure I have blisters on both feet. I can't walk one more kilometer in these instruments of torture!" She yanked both shoes off and threw them into her satchel. "Phew!" she exhaled. "Walking in Fritz's heavy wool socks feels better. Now I can keep going for a little while."

Most nights, they managed to find "lodging" in a farmer's barn. They got used to their bodies itching after a night on hay or straw. They rationed the treats Fritz had packed for them. Some farmers took pity on them and offered a bite to eat. They were thankful for what they got. Only at one house did they meet ugliness.

"Are you escapees from a concentration camp?" they were asked on the third night. They decided not to answer the questions. Who knew? They might be dealing with leftover Nazis. In this case they assumed correctly. The nasty woman screamed at them, "They didn't operate those gas chambers and ovens long enough. Get the hell off our property, you damn Jews." The heavy oaken door was slammed in their faces. They moved on to find friendlier souls.

The trek to Halle was shorter. It took only two days. They had a little rain. Rachel and Elsa were thankful for the rain gear and the umbrellas Fritz made them take. Bedding down on the hay felt great. Their legs were beginning to feel tight. Neither of them had ever walked that much on a given day, let alone for day after day. Elsa continued to limp along. When they found shelter in the evening, she asked the woman of the house for a favor. "Would you be kind enough to boil some water for me? I want to see if I can stretch my shoes. It's an old trick my shoemaker in Dachelhofen taught me many years ago."

Rachel and the kind woman stood there with their mouths wide open. A few minutes later, their hostess handed Elsa the teakettle with boiling water. Elsa stepped outside. She took off her shoes and filled them with the hot water. She counted to thirty and then emptied both shoes and stepped right into the still-hot footwear. She enlightened both women who were staring at her feet. "The boiling hot water allows for stretching the leather. I'll walk around in them for two hours or so and the shoes will conform to my feet. I don't know why I didn't think of this sooner." Elsa had solved her most imminent problem.

Rachel was delighted that Elsa finally had a pair of shoes that no longer plagued her. They had been able to buy a piece of cheese and some good bread at a local store. Fritz's gift of money came in handy. They had reached the end of a happier day.

They were grateful for every morning when they were greeted by sunshine. "I woke up again with terrible cramps in my legs," said Elsa. Rachel was wondering if they weren't drinking enough water. "I don't suggest we drink water from any rivers. Those little fountains we have seen in some of the villages might be safe enough. I still have that little bottle Fritz included with our sandwiches. The apple juice is long gone, but I kept the bottle. Let's use it to get water from one of those fountains. Also, the next time that happens, wake me and I'll massage your legs. I'll do anything to keep you going. We have the longest stretch between points still ahead of us. We can't give up at this stage."

Rachel's mind turned to Miriam. "I have no idea what happened in Essen. Rost and Johann mentioned a few times heavy bombing in the Ruhr district. That probably meant mostly, Duisburg, Essen, Dortmund, and neighboring cities. I keep praying every night that Miriam and the nuns are safe. When we finally get there, it's the first place I want to check out."

"Absolutely," agreed Elsa.

Rachel looked forlorn. "Miriam will be eight in September. I often wonder what she looks like and whether she is a happy child. I told you about Mother Superior; she was a godsend."

Their next leg of the long journey took them to the area near Kassel. It was by far the most challenging portion of their journey. Their walk took nine days. Most farm families continued to be willing to help a couple of stranded DPs (displaced persons) on their way home. The weather gods were largely inclined to be kind. A sprinkle here and there did not sideline the two travelers. Once they got closer to Kassel, they were told they had safely escaped Russian territory. They were now near the American zone. "I'm happy to learn that. At least I speak some English and will be able to communicate should it become necessary."

"I'm glad to know you speak English," Elsa confessed. "I don't speak anything but German. There was no fancy schooling for me. I grew up in that little town of Dachelhofen and was apprenticed to the local dentist. That's where I learned my skills. Not like you, dear Rachel, at LMU. That must have been some experience. It's one of Germany's finest universities."

"It was, but don't minimize your learning experience. What you learned you learned well. I don't know what I would have done without you at Theresienstadt. Depending on what we may find in Essen, we'll be able to open a dental practice again. I hope that you will be willing to work with me as a dental hygienist."

"That sounds pretty fancy. But if that is what you want me to do, I believe I'll be able to handle it. I look forward to working with you again, as long as I won't have to torture anyone."

On the eighth day and not too far from Kassel, a Jeep overtook them on the country road. Two MPs were occupying the strange-looking vehicle. One was white, the other very dark. He was a huge man. He was the driver. They pulled over and wanted to know where they were going. Rachel spoke.

"We are both DPs and escaped a hellhole called Theresienstadt. We have been on our journey for the last nineteen days. Our walk will take another nine days until we reach our destination, the city of Essen. We have stayed away from autobahns and big cities. The country roads and lodgings on little farmsteads have worked well for us."

"That's quite an undertaking. We are headed for Kassel. May we give you a lift? There is enough space for you and your things in the back seat."

"Thanks for your offer to take us. It will probably save us a day or two of walking. That is very kind of you."

"Some of the other officers and we occupy what used to be a little pension. Perhaps you can find a niche for the night in the place. We'll see what we can do for you. By the way, your English is excellent, young lady."

"Thanks for the compliment. Young lady? I will be thirty-three pretty soon. The bloom is off the vine."

"You better let us determine the bloom. You look pretty sharp in those slacks. My name is Heathrow; this great driver is Officer Maroon. We would like to be at your service."

"I'm Rachel; this is Elsa. We worked on the same projects in Theresienstadt. My husband and I practiced dentistry in Essen until he was drafted and I was sent to that concentration camp near Prague."

"Looks like you could use a bit of a respite. Put your bags in the back. Let us help you into your seats."

The women did as told. They put Rachel in the front passenger seat and Elsa behind the driver. Heathrow sat behind Rachel. They were off in a hurry. Officer Heathrow checked out Elsa. He looked at her as he put his left hand on her knee. "Nice and firm. You must have done a lot of exercising at that camp?" Elsa wasn't so sure about the attention she was receiving. Was this the service they had been talking about? She looked him straight in the eye as she smoothed out her slacks. She was hoping he got the message. "Either of you gals have a boyfriend or perhaps a husband waiting for you? Must be some time since you have been with a man."

They realized the trap they had gotten themselves into. A couple of miles down the road, Officer Maroon pulled off. He aimed the Jeep into a dense forest. He slammed on the brakes. Both jumped out. Maroon touched Rachel's hand, assisting her in getting out of the car; Heathrow grabbed Elsa, pulling her with him further into the woods. Apparently, he wanted his privacy. "Take off every stitch of clothes. I want you buck naked. I'm so horny, I'll probably come in ten seconds." Elsa didn't understand a word he said and she screamed. Heathrow pulled off his boots and socks. He was out of his uniform in no time. Elsa screamed as he forced himself into her. He raped her without mercy. When he finally emptied himself into her, she fainted. She was unaware that he took her for a second time before he left her lying on the hard ground. She was bleeding profusely. He was back in his uniform when he shook Elsa like a rag doll. "Wake up, you useless bitch. I thought you would like getting laid. You don't know what you missed." He tossed Elsa's clothes in her direction and helped her get dressed.

He was anxious to see how Maroon made out with Rachel. Elsa wished she had access to her satchel; she might have made use of Fritz's pistol. Heathrow tapped Maroon on his shoulders. "I hope you had more fun with her than I did with this one. She didn't want any part of it. I let her really have it; she fainted after I came the first time. I've had better in a whorehouse."

"That's your problem, Heathrow. You need to learn to treat women with a little respect. I'm not sure if Rachel enjoyed my love-making, but at least I didn't rape her. I learned a long time ago, one catches a lot more flies with honey than with vinegar." Rachel glared at both men as she threw on her clothes.

Heathrow and Maroon needed to return to their platoon before they got caught; they supposedly had been out on a routine patrol and not to amuse themselves. They had no intentions whatsoever of taking Rachel and Elsa to the officers' pension. They dropped them off on the west side of Kassel. Maroon stopped the Jeep near a few isolated farmhouses. He helped Rachel and Elsa down from the vehicle. He grabbed their satchels and handed them quickly over. They sped away.

Rachel could tell Elsa was in much pain. She stopped walking and set down whatever she was carrying. She took her friend in her arms and tried to console her. "I'm sorry. I had not expected this from a couple of nice American soldiers. We won't do that again. If anyone wants to give us a lift, we'll decline and keep on walking."

Elsa said nothing. She was still seething with anger, but even more so, she was suffering from the abuse and confessed to Rachel. "I've never been with a man before those Russians and Poles took my virginity. If that wasn't bad enough, to be raped again was more than I had bargained for when we escaped. I hope to God none of the dastardly men succeeded in getting me pregnant. I don't care if I ever feel the touch of another man. I've had it with them!" Rachel burst into tears. "My God, can you imagine me getting pregnant by a black man from Senegal."

The women held each other and cried. They started walking when Rachel spotted a large farm house in the distance. "Let's hope we'll be allowed to spend just one night at this place. Maybe there's a fountain where we can wash up a bit. I feel absolutely filthy and violated. I don't care how cold the water might be. I'll be happy with just a sponge bath. Fritz had foresight when he stuck soap and wash-cloths in our satchels. We have about eight more days of walking ahead of us."

Elsa spoke up. "You think you feel filthy? My whole lower body is covered in dried blood. If I don't get cleaned up soon, you may not want to walk very close to me. Between Heathrow's semen and my blood all over my body and legs, I'm a sight to behold."

"Elsa, again, I'm so sorry I got us into that situation."

"Don't do this to yourself, Rachel. You had nothing to do with it. Even if you hadn't been able to communicate with those bastards, they would have found a way of getting into our pants. We were at their mercy. As I told you before, I'm finished with men. They better stay away from me."

"I agree, Elsa. Otto was my first love. When Johann raped me that first night in Theresienstadt, I felt like you. Being raped every week by Rost confirmed my decision until Johann showed me that he truly cared for me. While Rost got what he had coming to him, Johann did not deserve to die the way he did. I'll never forget watching him being abused and senselessly murdered by those brutes."

They arrived at a cluster of barns. Elsa wanted to change the subject. "What do you think about stopping at this next farmhouse? Let me try negotiating for a change."

There was a large brass bell hanging by the door. Elsa decided it was there to get someone's attention. She rang it with vigor. A young girl answered the bell. She backed away when she saw Elsa with Rachel in tow. "Let me call my mother. Just wait out here for a moment." The girl turned her back and yelled, "Mother, there are two strange-looking women at our door. They look like they need some help."

"Got that right," thought Elsa. With that, the mother appeared behind the young girl. There were all sorts of questions written over her face. Then she fired away. "Who are you? What do you want? This isn't a home for wayward women." She was almost ready to slam the door in their faces.

Elsa decided to address the woman's questions. She was desperate. "Ma'am. My friend and I have been walking for days. We left Dresden on May ninth. We are trying to get home to Essen. Hopefully, we'll find our families still alive. Just this afternoon, we were both raped by a couple of soldiers. We need a place to clean ourselves. And yes, we could use a bite to eat. You don't need to put us up in your house; we'll be happy to sleep in the barn. Have a heart, lady." Tears were running down her face. She wasn't going away without trying her hardest.

"There's a bucket by the fountain. You can wash up in the barn. When you feel up to it, come back to the house. My daughter and I are having our evening vesper and a snack in a little while. You two are a sight to behold." She closed the door gently. Rachel and Elsa headed for the fountain and the barn. "You did OK, Elsa. We'll make it yet to Essen."

They washed themselves thoroughly and decided to put on the second sets of clothes from Fritz. They always included him in their prayers of thanks. They headed for the farmhouse, looking forward to talking with the woman and her daughter but even more to getting something between their teeth. Their stomachs were growling.

The woman came to the door and waved them in. "It ain't anything fancy," she said in her thick local dialect. Rachel didn't mind her speech. The woman tried her best. "Come sit down by the table. I bake our own bread. The liverwurst is some my husband canned before he was taken from me. He was killed in one of the last battles of the war. My daughter and I fend for ourselves. We get along with our neighbors. Not too many menfolk around these days. Adolf managed to get most of them killed." She looked quizzically at Rachel.

"Let's not talk about Adolf. He and his ilk were responsible for dragging the two of us off to a concentration camp in Theresienstadt. That's where we started out. We've seen it all in the last few years. My name is Rachel. My friend Elsa and I are thankful for your kindness of sheltering us for the night and giving us something to eat. Most country-folk have been willing to help us. God's grace does still seem to be alive and well."

The woman had tears in her eyes as she was listening to Rachel. "I'll have some hot porridge for you in the morning before you continue on your journey. It's time for us to retire as well. Our two cows want to be milked early."

The walk from Kassel to Dortmund took six days. Most of their "accommodations" were easy to take. A few shared meals with their hosts were also a welcome relief. Luckily, there were no more pick-up attempts by soldiers or creepy civilians. The last two days of their tour de force brought them to Essen. Being familiar with the city, Rachel held her breath. Outside of Dresden, they had avoided most large cities. The total destruction of Essen came as a shock.

When they reached Breslauerstrasse, Rachel broke down. She reached for Elsa's hand to steady herself. She couldn't hold back her tears. She pulled Elsa into her arms and sobbed on her shoulders. "I cannot believe it. With the destruction all around us, our house still stands."

Elsa noted all the shrapnel. "The building is literally polka dotted with holes. Be thankful it's still there. Was that shingle yours?" She read Otto von Graben, DDS, and Associates.

"Yes, Elsa; that was us, Otto and myself. I was the 'associates.'" She started bawling all over again. One second she could almost feel Otto's arms around her, the next she envisioned him rotting away in some shallow grave wherever.

"I wonder if Mimi Foster is alive and still living here. She was a tough cookie. If anyone could survive the war, it would be Mimi."

She tried the doorbell. There was no response. She pushed in the flimsy front door of the building and knocked on Mimi's apartment. After a couple of hefty tries, she heard someone stirring inside.

Mimi opened the door. "Oh my God, it's you, Rachel. Let me touch you. Are you for real? I never thought I would see you again. Come in, come in. She enfolded Rachel in her arms and held her close. Who is the woman with you?"

"Sorry, Mimi; sorry, Elsa. I'm overwhelmed by the moment. I still don't believe this is happening. This is Elsa Brand. We found each other thrown together in that horror called Theresienstadt. It's too long a story to share right now. Mimi, we are starved. We haven't had a thing to eat in more than two days. For the last two nights, we slept in some farmers' barns. They didn't mind putting us up; they didn't have enough to eat themselves, let alone to feed others."

Rachel looked around Mimi's living room and at Mimi. She still hadn't grasped the reality of being there. She thought she was experiencing a *fata morgana*. Rachel's sudden return got to Mimi.

"Whatever I have, I'll gladly share with you. It won't be fancy, but it will soothe your hungry stomachs. I cooked up a big pot of vegetable soup. This hearty bread will taste good too." Rachel and Elsa were already salivating at the thought of home-cooked soup. Vegetable soup and hearty bread sounded divine.

Rachel couldn't wait to ask about the cloister school, the practice, and their home. "Do you know what happened with the cloister school? What about our place after they hauled me away?"

"The cloister school was completely destroyed during the last bomb attack in March, but I understand all got out safely."

Rachel raised her eyes toward heaven. "Thank God, that's the best news you could have for me." Mimi wasn't sure why Rachel had such an interest in the cloister school. "As far as your place is concerned, you'll be surprised. Most things are there, especially in the professional realm. It's perhaps a bit dusty. Someone stole the large crystal chandelier from the dining room. They are all just things. Nothing that can't be replaced. When you feel up to it, you and Elsa should try to tackle cleaning the place. You might be open for business in no time flat."

Mimi kept staring at Rachel and Elsa. "I'm still in a twitter when I see you sitting there. Before I go on, let's sit down and have some of my soup. I want to hear all that happened since you were taken from us." Rachel wasn't so sure she wanted to share all.

Chapter 29

MIMI didn't think they could sleep in Rachel's place. Dust and dirt were everywhere. The beds had been stripped. They couldn't find any sheets. The duvets were gone. The whole apartment needed a major cleaning and restoration. "As much as you want to sleep in your own home, that just won't work tonight. You and Elsa stay with me for now, perhaps even a few nights. You can start with the cleanup of that place tomorrow morning.

"You are too kind. Elsa and I appreciate your helpfulness."

Mimi continued. "I want to hear the rest of this story when you are wide awake. I'm still dealing with your unexpected return. It's a miracle. Both of you look like you are about to pass out. You're falling asleep sitting there. Get yourselves ready for bed. I need to get to bed as well. It's up with the sun every morning during the week. Hope you sleep OK! I'm still in shock!" She kept looking at Rachel and Elsa, shaking her head.

Rachel was having her own shock in the morning. "I feel sick to my stomach. How are you feeling, Elsa? Is your stomach queasy? I wonder if I ate something along the way or last night that isn't agreeing with me. Clear the way. I'm about to heave." She barely made it to the toilet. On her knees, she proceeded to throw up, almost violently. Returning to bed, she stared at Elsa. "You don't think I got pregnant, do you? And if I am pregnant, who might be the father? Rost? God forbid. Johann? One of those damn Poles or Russians? The black guy, Maroon, couldn't possibly be the cause. It's too soon. Rost, Johann, and the others are a distinct possibility. Johann made love to me two nights before we left the camp. Today is the second of June."

Elsa went into her own kind of shock. "Almighty, what if I got pregnant? I'd find a way to have an abortion or kill myself. Would you consider having an abortion?"

"My God, Elsa. What a thought! Abortion has never crossed my mind at any time. I never would have aborted Miriam if Otto had asked me to in those dark days of 1937. He would have found a way of getting it done had he wanted me to have an abortion. But he didn't. He wanted our love child as much as I desired to have his baby. We paid a dear price, and I'm still paying it. I must find Miriam. Now that I'm no longer hunted, I want her in my life. It might be a challenge, but I'm willing to face it. I need to get up to that cloister and see what transpired there. Just thinking about going up there gives me the creeps after what Mimi told us last night. The uncertainty of what might have happened to Miriam or Otto weaves in and out of my nightmares about Johann and his devastating demise. My whole life has turned into a three-ring circus with bizarre and traumatic outcomes. I can't face another."

She looked up at Elsa. Her eyes were red from all her crying. "That brings my thoughts back to this pregnancy—if there is one. I couldn't abort this or any other child. I saw too many lives destroyed in Theresienstadt; I couldn't bring myself to aborting a new life. No matter who the father might be, I'll take my chances. Johann told me again and again that he loved me. While I succeeded in staying clear of any relations with him after he raped me on the first night in the camp, I finally succumbed to his pleas two nights before our escape. He told me he wanted to marry me and have children with me if Otto had not survived the war. All I ever saw him do was oversight of arrival of prisoners at the camp. By his own admission, he hated being assigned to the place; the system forced him to be where he never would have been could he have chosen. Elsa, you were in Theresienstadt much longer than I was. Are you aware of anything indecent Johann might have done before I arrived?"

"Not really, Rachel. Many of the prisoners took a liking to him. It was Rost who wanted to climb the ladder of success and ordered many of the inhumane actions degrading and hurting prisoners. Rost's meanness was widely known among all prisoners. The guards were executing Rost's and not von Rondstett's orders."

"Thanks for sharing your impressions of Johann with me. If he hadn't been decent, he never would have honored the pact I made with him after that first night. If this child is Johann's, I hope it will be a boy. Not knowing what happened to Otto, I'm desperate to learn if Miriam is alive and well. That's one of the first things I want to find out. No one other than you is aware of Miriam's existence. For now, let's keep it that way."

After breakfast, they dressed and went on that fateful walk. Rachel's feet didn't need a compass. They took her swiftly to the cloister. Rachel shuddered looking at the destruction. "Just look at this place, Elsa. This school was huge. There is nothing left of it. Let's walk over to the entrance gate. It looks to me like a notice is posted on the old steel gate." She stared at Sister Maria-Angelika's writing. "All of us are safe. No one was hurt. The underground bunker saved us. They dug us out in good time. We are about to start our march to a sister cloister near Münster. We'll be back when all of this is over." The note was dated March 11, 1945, and was signed by Mother Superior. Rachel turned to Elsa. Tears were streaming down her face. "My Miriam is safe! Thank God!" Totally uncharacteristically, Rachel sank to her knees. She didn't care that the ground was rocky and muddy. She made the sign of the cross and thanked God for all he had made possible since she and Elsa escaped from the KZ.

Elsa stared at Rachel. "Have you become a Catholic? I don't believe I'm seeing right."

"No, Elsa; I have not become a Catholic. You might as well get used to the idea. I might have to accept my child as a practicing Catholic. I put her into that environment. More likely than not, Miriam accepted Catholicism as her faith. And furthermore, I wouldn't dream of wanting to change her to suit my personal beliefs. That wouldn't be right for Miriam; that wouldn't be fair to Sister Maria-Angelika, who loved and cared for her for the last eight years."

Rachel picked herself up off the ground. "Are you feeling in the mood for a major cleanup? I am energized by the good news about Miriam. I'll make some subtle inquiries about this place in the Münsterland to which they fled after the attack in March. It will take a balancing act on my and Mother Superior's parts in this drama. Both she and I will have to do some fast explaining to Miriam and the remaining nuns. Mother Superior did some serious fibbing about Miriam's sudden appearance at the nunnery in 1937."

Elsa could see the pain on Rachel's face, reliving the scenes that took her back eight years. "Mother Superior chose a new name for Miriam. She called her Marika Leander, the name given to the baby of her younger sister. The sister died giving birth to the child. None of the other nuns knew where the younger sister of Mother Superior lived. Her orphaned niece was placed in the care of grandparents in East Prussia. Lord knows what happened to them during and after the war."

Elsa was looking straight into Rachel's eyes. Her mouth was wide open. "How awful, Rachel. I can't believe you and Otto did this to yourselves. To have to abandon your newborn."

Rachel looked devastated. "I gave birth to Miriam Daniella in a home for the insane. No other hospital would admit me, a condemned Jewess. It was Otto's idea to give up our child. I agreed to leave Miriam in the care of the nuns. I never offered her up for adoption. Sister Maria-Angelika felt safe doing what she did. She asked the Holy Mother for forgiveness. No one would ever be the wiser that Maria-Angelika committed multiple sins and lies to protect an innocent child whose mother was Jewish."

"I admire you and Otto for making the decision to protect your child. But what a price to pay! I cannot imagine myself doing it. You are a very strong person. I feel great admiration for the mother superior. I hope and pray you and Miriam Daniella will find each other one of these days now that this nightmare is finally over."

Elsa and Rachel left the site of the cloister school. They walked arm in arm back to Breslauerstrasse. Both felt safer that way. The sidewalks were still in deplorable condition. Neither said a word. They were lost in their respective private worlds and had no inkling what lay ahead of them.

Rachel said silent prayers. She was grateful knowing that Miriam was safe. Rachel also was thankful for her caring neighbor. He had bricked in all broken and lost windows and replaced the entry door to her quarters. Her home and practice weren't violated by intruders. All that was lost was the crystal chandelier. Elsa and she would enjoy future dinners by candlelight. She thought there was nothing wrong with the serendipitous ambiance. She thanked God for the restoration of electricity. Higher wattage would make it possible for Elsa and her to reopen the practice. She needed to find out if the man who made their original shingle in 1939 survived the war. No longer needing to hide her Jewish identity, she wanted the new shingle to reflect Otto's as well her credentials.

Rachel turned to Elsa. "Mimi showed me where she keeps cleaning materials. Let's get started this morning while she is gone. We probably won't get a thing done later when Mimi returns. Right now, all I want to do is work really hard at getting our own place in order. I feel the need to work. I have this urge to look to a future with Miriam, perhaps even with Otto. I need to force myself to forget the past."

Elsa could do nothing but agree. "Hard work sounds good to

me. After all that walking, I probably can stand all day without ever complaining. Like you, I need to forget the past. I hated what they made us do to all those innocent people. The degradation they and we suffered is indelibly impressed on my mind."

The practice was their first objective. Walls, floors, ceilings, and furniture were thoroughly scrubbed. The autoclave was kept busy for most of the day. All dental tools needed to be sterilized. Rachel thrived on getting their practice up to speed. "I'm proud of us, Elsa. Talk about a job well done." A sincere smile stole across her face. Just then a knock at the door interrupted them.

"Oh my God, it is you!" Rachel bent down to allow Mimi's friend to put her short arms around her neck. "How I have prayed for this moment. The Almighty must have listened to my fervent interces- sions. To be honest, sometimes I felt I was praying in vain. I still can't fathom the horror stories Mimi shared with me when we talked this morning. It all was so inhumane. To think that millions of innocent people were annihilated, a whole human race almost eradicated."

Rachel interrupted. "Mimi and Helena, I would like you to meet my fellow inmate, Elsa Brand. We met at the camp in Theresienstadt and were forced to participate in atrocious work assignments. We escaped together from the camp. Elsa will be working with me when I reopen the practice."

"Nice to meet you, Ms. Brand."

"Let's skip the formality; make it Elsa."

Rachel invited the others into the practice. "Elsa and I need to brag. Come, look and see what we accomplished this morning. For now, Elsa and I will share what used to be my examining room. We'll leave the other one for Otto, if and when he does return. I wouldn't want him to feel I usurped his working space. But before we go any further, I want us all to sit down. I have to share with you a bit of news that you should have been aware of for several years.

Mimi looked at her friend; she was dumbfounded. "While Otto and I studied in Munich, I became pregnant. We were not married.

Our daughter, Miriam, was born in September of 1937. Otto was utterly afraid of what might happen to our precious baby and felt we needed to shelter her in a relatively safe environment. We left Miriam in the care of the sisters at the cloister school less than a month after she was born. She has been in the care of the nuns for almost eight years. No one in Essen ever learned of the existence of our child. But the time has come for me to seek her. She is my responsibility. Right now, I don't know how all of this will play out. Hopefully, well in good time."

Mimi and her friend looked at Rachel in stunned silence. "You mean to say your child was at the cloister school all along? Why didn't you tell us about her? We might have been able to check on her and make sure she was properly taken care of."

"Sorry. That wasn't part of the deal. No one but Mother Superior knew our identity, not even Miriam as she grew older. It was only under those conditions that Sister Maria-Angelika agreed to keep Miriam at the school. The cloister is a school, not an orphanage. Furthermore, the nuns didn't adopt Miriam; they agreed to take care of her. Elsa and I walked up to the school this morning. We couldn't get over the total destruction of all the buildings. We discovered a note that was posted by the mother superior on March eleventh. We learned that everyone survived the last bombing and the nuns and children fled to another cloister in the Münsterland. I will make every possible effort to get in touch with the mother superior. I'm determined to be reunited with our child. Should Otto return, I want us to be waiting for him."

Mimi felt she needed to be part of this discussion. "Rachel, we'll do whatever we can to make a reunion with Miriam possible. It won't be easy, but I can see it happen. We will give you all the help we can muster. Wow! What a bombshell—but a good one."

Rachel faced the reality of things. There was no telephone, mail service, or public transportation available. No one was allowed to travel within or between zones of occupation. For now, she accepted her fate and put her trust in God. She would pray that Miriam survived the remains of the war in safety with the good sisters.

Mimi read the worry on Rachel's face. "It will turn out all right. Just trust in God. On a lighter note, we'll see to it that we get some bed linens for you. We don't have a lot, but what we can spare, we'll share with you."

Rachel changed the subject. "Do you know if the company that produced our shingle is still in business?"

Mimi was in the know. "I believe he survived. It's a much smaller business right now. He is still in the same location. What do you have in mind?"

"I don't know exactly what happened; however, I learned through a confidant at Theresienstadt that Otto went MIA on December sixth of last year. There is only a very slim window of hope that he survived the Battle of the Bulge. His body was not among those they were able to recover. For now, I want Elsa and my credentials added to the shingle. I want it to read: 'Otto von Graben, DDS; Rachel Adina Salm von Graben, DDS; Elsa Brand, Dental Hygienist.'"

"That sounds good."

Rachel and Elsa moved into the apartment and offices the middle of June. They officially opened the dental practice a few days later. The new shingle was hung days earlier.

Chapter 30

SISTER Maria-Angelika and her entourage returned to Essen in October 1945. The cloister school was slated to reopen, although, initially, only on a very limited basis. On one of her rare outings, Mother Superior rode her bicycle by Rachel's office. She was thrilled to see the new shingle. She decided to pull over and face the inevitable. Rachel had a right to know that Miriam was safe and close by. When she walked in, Elsa knew immediately at whose face she was looking.

"I'm Sister Maria-Angelika. I need to speak with Dr. von Graben. Is she in this morning?"

"Yes, she is. I'll take you to the waiting room. Her next patient isn't due for two hours. I'm sure she would want to see you."

Rachel, talking to her last patient as they were walking out of the examining room, spotted Mother Superior. She stopped talking in mid sentence. As she was rushing toward Sister Maria-Angelika, she advised her patient. "Mrs. Auer, please make an appointment for next week with Ms. Elsa. I'm sure you will be just fine with the medication I ordered."

A second later, Rachel was face-to-face with Mother Superior. For a moment, neither appeared to be able to speak. Rachel's eyes betrayed her; she began to cry as she reached out for the nun. Mother Superior opened her arms and enfolded Rachel. "There, there, my dear child. I have prayed for this day since I first laid eyes on you eight years ago. Let it all out. You have good reason to cry." She continued to hug Rachel, gently patting her back. "Let us sit down somewhere and talk. Miriam is doing just fine. She is a beautiful and very bright young girl. I love her as if she were my own. She gave me joy I never imagined I'd experience once I joined the order."

Rachel finally looked at the sister. Her face was marked by a radiant smile. "Thank you, thank you, dear Sister Maria-Angelika. You have no idea how I have longed for, as well as dreaded, this moment. I was hoping you wouldn't reject me. I still don't know if my husband, Otto, is alive or perished in the last months of the war. It's a miracle I survived Theresienstadt and its horrors. Elsa, the young woman who greeted you, and I escaped shortly before the Russian troops took over the camp. We walked for most of the way to get back to Essen. I was driven by the need to be reunited with my child. I was thankful that you left the note posted by the gate. I knew you had done it for us. I was always thrilled to find your messages letting us know that you and Miriam were safe. Please tell me I may see her."

"May I suggest you come to the cloister school in a few days? Give me a chance to prepare Miriam in some way. I'm not quite sure at this moment what I will say to her. Allow me to pray over this; God would want me to do it the right way. He guided me in every decision I made since the first day I met you, Otto, and your precious child."

Mother Superior rose from her chair and held Rachel's hand. They smiled at each other with tears in their eyes. Rachel spoke. "This is Monday; I don't see patients on Wednesdays. If it is acceptable to you, I would like to see you and Miriam this Wednesday. It's the seventeenth of October. Would you want me to come in the morning or in the afternoon? I realize other children are enjoying their 'Potato Vacation' right now. Does the cloister school adhere to the public-school calendar?"

"As a matter of fact, we do, Rachel. While we folks in the city don't call it by that name, we do offer the students the fall break in October, like all schools in the region. Plan on seeing us at ten o'clock. Breakfast and morning prayers will be done by then. I'll do my best to make this a positive experience for all of us, including the other sisters. I will finally have to own up to my long-standing ploy." She hugged Rachel firmly before she walked smilingly out of the office and hopped on her bike.

Chapter 31

SISTER Maria-Angelika went straight to the little chapel the nuns had created in one of the small rooms left in the remains of the once-proud main building of the cloister school. She knelt, raising her eyes to the small statue of the Holy Mother. "I pray for thy guidance for what I'm about to do. I believe you have long forgiven the sins I committed when I took on the responsibility of raising this child. The time has come for me to set Marika free, allowing her to be reunited with her true mother. Give me the strength to do the right thing; give me the proper words to say all that needs to be said. I do not want to hurt Marika or Rachel." With her rosary beads held in her hands, she made the sign of the cross and rose to her feet.

She carried herself proudly as she walked toward her quarters. She found Miriam sitting by her little desk. She was drawing the figure of a woman. Working intensely, she hadn't even heard the door open. "Marika, please come to me. We need to talk about something. I want you to listen carefully to my words. What I have to tell you will not be easy for either of us. It is very important that you accept my words with an open mind. You've often heard me talk about the need for us to always have an open and accepting mind.

This is one of those moments. Hold my hands and look at me. I want your full attention as I'm speaking to you."

Miriam was all eyes. She realized it was a serious matter Mother Superior wished to discuss with her. "You look sad. Did someone die? I know Sister Ursula-Divina has not been feeling well. She is very old and frail. Did she pass away?"

"No, Marika, no one passed away. But someone has returned to the living, so to speak. It's that someone I want you to meet in a couple of days. I can't say it any better or any easier. You have known for years that I'm a great believer in facing the truth and speaking it. Oh, I've had to fib a few times in my life, even after I took my vows. Holy Mother and God have forgiven my trespasses. The person I'm speaking of is your mother."

Miriam almost stopped breathing and clutched her mouth. Staring at Mother Superior, she spoke. "My mother? You've told me for years that I'm your niece and that your sister, my mother, died shortly after I was born. How can she be alive? Did someone make a mistake or lie about her death?"

"No, Marika. No one made a mistake, but I committed a sin and fibbed to my sisters about you and your parents. First of all, your name isn't Marika. Your name is Miriam Daniella Salm. Your mother's name is Rachel Adina Salm. At the time when you were born, your parents weren't married yet. Your father's name is Otto von Graben. He and your mother were students at a university in Munich and couldn't get married because the laws of the land wouldn't allow it. Your mother is Jewish, and your father is Protestant. Under the Nazis, they were not permitted to get married. The hateful things that were done to Jewish people in those dark days forced your mother to give birth to you in an insane asylum because no other hospital would allow her to have you there."

Mother Superior stopped talking. She needed to reach out to Miriam and hold her. She could read the utter confusion written all over the child's face. Miriam hung on to every sentence the nun had spoken. "Don't stop there. I need to know more."

Sister Maria-Angelika held Miriam close to her as she described the scene when her parents made the decision to leave Miriam in the care of the nuns. "My sister had died in childbirth about the same time you were born. Yes, I lied, and I made up the story of you being my niece. It was a believable story for the other nuns. I asked Holy Mother and God to understand my actions. I always knew the time might come when this nightmare would be over. I knew this very moment of facing you might arrive."

Miriam's face was marked by anger. "How could they do this to me? How could you go along with such a crazy scheme? I don't know who I am any longer. I'm no longer Marika Leander. I'm no longer your niece. I'm not Catholic but part Jewish and part Protestant. I love you like a mother. Now you are telling me I have to learn to love a total stranger and to love her like a mother? I know I'm only eight years old, but you raised me well. I have a brain that can think. I need time to dwell on all of what you just told me. Where does my mother live? When will I have to meet her? You must give me time. Are you telling me that I must leave you and live with this total stranger?"

"Miriam, I want to start calling you by your given name. Your mother is a practicing dentist and lives in our neighborhood. When I was out on my bike earlier this morning, I noticed a new shingle where your father and her offices used to be. I decided to stop and talk with your mother. She was pleased and shocked to see me. We hadn't spoken to each other since the day your parents left you in my care. She is a good woman. Please, don't hate her. Your parents felt they did the right thing by protecting you. You must believe me; while they were not allowed to see you or make contact with you while you were under my care, they were always concerned about your welfare. It's for that reason I always posted notes at the gate. I have invited her to meet you on Wednesday morning. Please, give your mother a chance. I don't expect you to abandon your present home, but I want you to make every effort to get to know your birth mother. You may never know your caring father; he may have been killed during the waning months of the war. Your mother never heard from him after he was sent to the front in April of last year. These were desperate times."

Miriam hid her face in her hands and began to sob. "I don't want to leave you, and I don't want to leave the school. This is my home. I love the sisters and my classmates. This is where I belong. I can't be torn out of here just because the war is over and my mother has returned and wants to take me away." She stomped her feet. "I won't do it. I don't want to talk to my mother. I hate her!"

Mother Superior became concerned. "I've never seen you with a temper tantrum. This is not the time to start that. How can you say you hate someone you haven't even met? Remember what I asked you earlier? Please have an open mind! I know you are quite capable of that. Just think what I must do. I must fess up to my sisters about the lie I have lived for the last eight years. You think that is easy? Put yourself in my shoes; I'm trying very hard to feel what you must be going through." They finally reached out to each other and cried on each other's shoulders.

Sister reached into her habit and showed Miriam the Blue Sapphire amulet. "It's been almost two years since you first saw me wear it. Remember, I told you it was given to me by a very special person. Also, I promised you that someday you would learn the story of the person who entrusted it to me. It was your mother. The amulet has been in your family for generations. It was passed on to your mother by your great-grandmother just before she died. She had been wearing it for many years because your grandmother died when your mother was born. The piece was always passed from mother to first-born daughter. When your parents left you with me, your mother made me the keeper of the precious family heirloom. Like you, she didn't want it to fall into the hands of the Nazis. She had always wanted it to be handed to you when you were of proper age. Now that your mother has been found, I will return it to her because I want her to be the one to pass it on to you."

Miriam reached out. She wanted to touch the jewel. She had always kept her promise to Mother Superior; she never told a soul of its existence. Sometimes in the privacy of their bedroom, she had asked to see and touch it. Something deep in her gut had always drawn her to the forbidden jewel. "I like the way those little stones sparkle." She seemed to be mesmerized by the deep blue of the large blue sapphire. She smiled at Sister. "You mean I'll get to wear that thing someday? Won't it be heavy hanging from my neck? You mean I'll have to wear it day and night?"

"It won't be heavy, Miriam. You'll love wearing it. It's the link to your mother; it's the link to an unbroken chain of wonderful women. You will carry on the tradition of the Salm family that goes back many generations. I will return it to your mother when she comes to speak with you. I'm happy to know that it will be worn by its rightful owner until it is time for you to have that honor." She slid the amulet under her habit and grabbed Miriam's hand. She smiled. "Let's join the others for our midday meal." They walked out of Mother Superior's office hand in hand. Maria-Angelika's eyes turned upward. Her thoughts traveled a long distance. "Thank you for helping me through these last hours!"

At evening vespers, Mother Superior confronted the sisterhood. Sister Irmgard-Dolcinea sat next to her. Maria-Angelika owned up to the whole unbelievable story. She had been praying for most of the afternoon, hoping her sisters would not demand that she step down from her post or even consider leaving the order.

All bowed their heads in prayer. They elected Sister Irmgard-Dolcinea to speak for all of them. "That's a shocking revelation, dear Mother; however, none of us in any way feel violated. You did what needed to be done. You saved Rachel and Otto's child from persecution and provided Miriam with a loving environment. You gave all of us an opportunity to love her and in return discovered her love for us during many hours of trials and tribulations. Miriam often was and is the sunshine in our daily lives. While we pray for her reunification with her mother, we hope she will continue at our school until she is ready to face the world. We pray for guidance when Miriam confronts you and her mother."

Mother Superior looked radiant. "Thank you all for your support. I appreciate your understanding of the predicament that I found myself in all those years ago. I regret my creative fabrication but didn't know how else to deal with accepting a four-week-old infant into our midst. If it hadn't been for your love and support, this could never have worked. It is my belief we had the blessings of Holy Mother and the Almighty. I hope and pray they will guide me through the labyrinth of questions, suggestions, and demands that may arise from this mother-daughter conflict.

Chapter 32

RACHEL thought about asking Elsa to join her when she was getting ready to meet Miriam. She decided against it. She wanted it to be just Sister Maria Angelika, Miriam, and herself. She rang the bell promptly at the appointed hour she was expected at the cloister. Sister Irmgard-Dolcinea greeted her at the gate. "Please, follow me. Mother Superior and Miriam are waiting for you." They climbed all those stony steps leading to the second floor. Irmgard-Dolcinea knocked lightly on the door. She opened it for Rachel to step through.

Rachel's first glance fell on Miriam. Her eyes filled with tears; she couldn't help herself. Her left hand flew up to her mouth. "Oh my God; I can't believe what I'm seeing. Forgive me, Mother Superior, for using the Lord's name in vain." She rushed over to touch Miriam, who stared at her with a blank look. Miriam seemed to be frightened by the whole experience.

Rachel had lost all confidence in herself. She was shaken to the core and all of a sudden frightened to face her child. There was that understated elegance in the simple dress she wore. Her shoulders were covered by a colorful scarf. Her appearance belied how she felt.

She was still guilt ridden as she looked at the child she believed she and Otto had abandoned eight years earlier.

Miriam kept staring at Rachel. What struck her most was her mother's beautiful hair and the way she wore it. She looked closely at the face, searching for any resemblance between her mother and herself. She detected a certain hint of commonality. Her hair was the same color as her mother's, although styled in a typical youthful fashion. She envisioned herself wearing a lovely chignon like her mother's some day.

She stuck out her right hand as she was taught from the time she was old enough to stand on her two feet. Miriam spoke at last. "Hello, Dr. von Graben. Or should I say Dr. Salm? Do you want me to call you Rachel or Rachel Adina? Perhaps you want me to call you Mom, Mutti, or whatever. I'm totally at a loss."

Rachel opened her arms. Tears were flooding her face. "I want to hold you, Miriam. You have no idea how desperately I have longed to do this for years. You are my baby; you are my big and very smart girl. I've missed you for so long. I would love it if you just made it Mutti; that's all I wanted to be called since the day you were born. I want to recapture the loss of eight precious years. Let me make it up to you in any way you would like." In spite of Miriam's standoffish behavior, Rachel caught her in her arms and hugged her fiercely.

"You are hurting me!" screamed Miriam. "You are pressing those bones of yours into mine. That hurts." She nearly pushed Rachel away. Rachel lost her balance but caught herself quickly. She had a vision of landing clumsily on the floor. "Sorry, Miriam Daniella, I didn't intend to hurt you. Forgive me." Miriam liked the sound of her full name. She had to get used to not being called Marika. All of a sudden everything was so different. She had a real mother, and she had a different name to get used to.

Rachel looked toward Mother Superior, who had shrugged her

shoulders. In their hearts, they had known it wouldn't be easy for an eight-year-old child to bridge the gap of all those lost years. It was an unreasonable expectation. Miriam thought there were more important issues to settle than who cried for whom or who cared to be hugged or not hugged.

"What about that blue sapphire amulet you were planning to give back to my mother?" demanded Miriam. Mother Superior and Rachel were left speechless.

Rachel thought, "Leave it to a child to know what's important."

Mother Superior reached for the jewel and removed it from her neck. "Miriam has known about the amulet for some time. She discovered it accidentally a few years ago. She kept her promise and never revealed its existence to anyone; it was our deep, dark secret. However, I only let her know two days ago the name of the rightful owner and the story behind the amulet. Miriam knows that she will be the next one to wear it." Sister Maria-Angelika walked toward Rachel. She slipped it easily over Rachel's crown of hair and made sure it was properly seated around Rachel's neck. Miriam seemed to be running the show.

"Well, aren't you glad we took such good care of that thing? You're lucky we didn't trade it in for food or coal when we were starving and freezing in this place during the war."

Mother Superior frowned. "Miriam, I'm disappointed in you. I thought we taught you better than that. I have never heard or seen you that disrespectful. You are speaking to your mother. She's missed you terribly and suffered immeasurably. Please be kinder in your behavior. This is totally out of character for you."

"I'm confused too. I don't know what's going to happen to me. Where will I live? Will I continue going to school here? My head is full of questions since you first talked to me about meeting my mother." Rachel and Mother Superior grasped the importance of Miriam's concerns.

Rachel spoke up. "Those are good questions you have, Miriam. I would be wondering too if I were in your place. This is all happening so fast. I don't want to force you into doing anything you don't want to do. Where would you like to live? If you want to stay here for a while until you get used to the idea of having me around, I could fully understand that. You can come and visit me after school and spend time with me. We could learn to know each other. Whenever you are ready to be with me, I'll be ready to have you. How does that sound?"

"That sounds OK. What about school? Can I continue my schooling with the sisters? I'm used to the routine, and I'm used to my classmates and friends. We've been together for so long."

Mother Superior thought she needed to jump into the conversation. "I believe your mother has the right idea. I want you to stay at our school. Changing both your home and your school might be too much for you. I like your mother's thoughts on visiting her regularly and not changing your school. You are too accustomed to us to make such drastic changes all at once."

Rachel took a deep breath. She smiled at both Sister Maria-Angelika and Miriam. "I'm glad we had this first meeting. I know it wasn't easy for you, Miriam, to meet your mother after all these years of believing I was someone different and long dead and gone. We need to take baby steps toward finding each other. All I want you to know is that I love you with all that is in me. I have longed for eight long years to hold you in my arms. Know that I will be here for you from this day forward. I am your mother; I gave you life. Please make it possible for me to share your life." She hugged Miriam intensely. Miriam's eyes were brimming with tears as she smiled at her mother. Rachel held Miriam firmly in her arms; at last, she let go of her.

Chapter 33

It was a chilly day in late November. Winter was in the air, and nothing but gray clouds hung deep in the sky. It was a dismal scene. Miriam walked into Mother Superior's office. Her right hand was covering her mouth. Mother Superior got up and walked toward Miriam. "What's wrong with you? Did you hurt yourself? Why are you holding your hand in front of your mouth?" the nun inquired.

"I had an accident in my gymnastics class. I seriously damaged one of my new front teeth. It really hurts."

Please, open your mouth, and let me take a look at you." Mother Superior touched Miriam's face gently. "Can you think of a better reason to see your mother? She is a dental surgeon and specializes in working with children. I'll walk you to her office. Your promised visit to see her is long overdue. I'd expected you to visit her sooner than this."

Sister Maria-Angelika reached for her woolen cloak and helped Miriam into a warm jacket trimmed in rabbit fur. They walked hand in hand down the street. Mother Superior could tell by Miriam's sweaty hand that she was clearly apprehensive about seeing her mother. "We should have worn gloves. Miriam, are you afraid of seeing your mother, or are you afraid of seeing a dentist? You need that tooth repaired. It is one of your new permanent teeth. This should not be put off indefinitely. It will not hurt. I've heard nothing but good things about your mother's professional skills. Either way, there is nothing to be afraid of."

They walked into the office, and Elsa greeted them. When she recognized the visitor, her face became radiant. "Nice to see you again, Sister Maria-Angelika. And you must be Miriam. I'm Elsa. I work with your mother. She will be so glad to see you. She's with another patient. Just have a seat. I'll tell her you are here. Do either of you have need of her professional services?"

Miriam couldn't wait to speak. "Yes, I broke off one of my new front teeth. It hurts badly, but even worse, it looks terrible." She flashed her broken tooth at Elsa with a goofy smile. "You think my mother can fix it? Listening to Mother Superior, there's nothing to it."

Elsa took one look at Miriam's broken tooth. "Looks to me like you will need a crown. You are lucky it didn't break off completely. You will be your mother's next patient. Please have a seat, and relax. No need to be nervous. She'll take good care of you. I just know she'll be so pleased to see you."

Rachel beamed when she spotted Miriam. "That's a nice surprise. You brighten this gloomy day. And I see you didn't come alone. Is anything wrong?" She wanted to give Miriam a quick hug and a kiss on her forehead but just shook her hand. She could sense a certain hesitancy in Miriam.

Mother Superior thought she better explain. "Our young lady had an altercation in her gymnastics class." She couldn't help watching Miriam. "Please stop covering up your damaged tooth and making those funny faces. That's not good for you. Let your mother take a look at you."

Rachel got the message. "May I take a look at your tooth?"

"I suppose, if you must."

"Don't be silly, Miriam. Have you ever heard of a dentist doing a job without looking into someone's mouth?"

"No, I guess you got me there, Dr. von Graben—I mean Mutti."

Rachel touched Miriam's face gently and succeeded in looking at the damaged tooth. She knew right away what needed to be done. "I'll give you a little Novocain. After that, you will hear the drilling. There won't be any pain. You are perfectly safe with me."

Miriam got into the dental chair. She was a regular trooper. The little prick from the Novocain injection was nothing. Rachel put her hand on Miriam's forehead. Not only did she want to reassure Miriam, but she longed to touch her child. "The drilling and grinding down of the tooth sounds bad but really doesn't hurt. The sound is more annoying than anything else. The last thing we have to do today is to take an impression. Again, this doesn't hurt, but the impression material is a sticky mess and leaves an awful taste. Be forewarned."

It tasted unbelievably bad. Once the material set up, Rachel pulled down the impression; Miriam thought the rest of her upper teeth would come out in one single swoop. "No problem, Miriam. All your teeth are still in place. I will send this impression to a lab. We will have your new crown in a week."

"Thanks, Mutti. That really wasn't too bad. I've never had Novocain before. It seems to do strange things. I feel like half of my mouth has gone lame."

"That's what it is supposed to do. You didn't feel any pain, did you?"

"No, I didn't. I've never liked seeing the dentist. You were different. I liked your gentle touches and telling me what was going to happen. It made it a lot easier for me. Thanks again, Mutti." Rachel nearly melted every time Miriam called her Mutti.

She turned to Elsa. "Make sure we have Miriam down for her crown fitting in a week. She's been a very good girl. If she didn't have that temporary, I'd ask you to give her a lollipop. Not today. Maybe next time. Bye, Miriam. Now that you know where I live and work, maybe you will want to come and see me more often. For now, I look forward to seeing you with that beautiful new crown. No one will ever know that you damaged that tooth so badly. How she longed to give her a hug, but she didn't want to push herself on her long-lost child. Miriam's "two mothers" beheld each other and smiled. It was a step in the right direction. "Thanks for bringing Miriam to see me. It was wonderful being so close to her." Miriam quickly curtsied and shook Rachel's hand. She wasn't quite certain about hugging and kissing her mother.

Chapter 34

MIRIAM showed up for her follow-up appointment. She arrived early enough and hoped to spend a bit more time with Rachel. Miriam was beginning to feel like she could ask Rachel some questions she would never have asked Mother Superior. Elsa showed her into the examining room promptly. Rachel walked in. She wasn't wearing her white coat. Miriam's jaw dropped. She noticed right away that Rachel was wearing a maternity frock. "What's with your tummy? Are you having a baby? Who is the father?" the precocious girl inquired. Rachel was caught short. She had to think fast on her feet.

"It was an immaculate conception. The man was a biblical figure. I'm not in a position to tell you anything else. You just have to take my word for it. I'm sure Mother Superior will understand. She'll know what I'm talking about when you share your discovery with her.

"Now let's get this crown seated. First I need to remove the temporary. None of this will hurt. There will be just a bit of pressure when I cement the crown to the prepared post of your tooth. The rest, you will do by biting down firmly for a few minutes. You simply wait until I tell you to do so. Do you understand me, Miriam?"

Miriam kept looking at Rachel's expanded belly and her face.

Her eyes were moving back and forth. She was still in total disbelief. For the moment, Miriam decided not to ask any further questions. Shrugging her shoulders, she realized Rachel would not reveal the name of the father.

"That's one nice-looking crown. No one will ever know you lost a tooth unless you tell them. It's our personal secret."

Miriam just couldn't let it go. "Why can't you tell me the name of the father of your baby? You must know who it is. I know this much; it takes two people to make a baby."

"Miriam, you are too young to understand. Some day when you are older, I will tell you. Then you will discover who the father was. For now, no more questions, please?"

Miriam gave up. She decided she wasn't sharing her news with anyone. Deep down, she had gotten to like her mother.

Before she walked out of the examining room, she kept looking at Rachel. "How long did it take you to grow your hair as long as it must be? When I'm older, I want to wear my hair in a chignon. I really like the way that looks on you. Your hair looks elegant."

"Well, thank you, Miriam. What a nice thing for you to tell your mother. When your hair gets to be long enough, I'll show you how to put it up. I've done it for so many years, I could do it blindfolded."

Miriam blocked her mother's way out of the examining room. "I want a hug, Mutti." Rachel first smiled; then she held Miriam close to her body. There were tears of joy in her eyes. She walked Miriam to the front door. "Don't be a stranger. Come to see me soon. How about on a Sunday afternoon for Kaffeeklatsch? I'd like you to get to know my friends."

Miriam was already running across the street. "I'll let you know. I'll check with Mother Superior. I'm sure she's OK with the idea. Love you, Mutti!"

Rachel slipped on a clean, white coat. "How could I honestly answer that girl's questions? I don't know myself who the father is—certainly not for sure." She was glad when the next patient needed her attention. "How stupid of me not to wear my white coat. She never would have known I'm more than seven months pregnant." Rachel was glad the morning sickness had only lasted for a month or so.

※

Elsa opened the Sunday paper. "Rachel, according to this article, postal services are supposed to resume in early December. You think we should try sending a note to Fritz Unrat? He's probably been wondering what happened to us."

Rachel was thrilled to get the good news. She had been wanting to tell Fritz all that had transpired in the last seven months. She pulled out her writing paper and started to put down some of her thoughts. She elaborated on their journey across Germany and the events that shaped their long walk. She delighted in telling him about her discovery of Miriam and the positive recent developments. Last, she mentioned that she was expecting a baby in February, and was hoping he could be with them for the baby's baptism. She related the conversation she had with Miriam and how she honestly had no idea who the father might be. She was hoping to hear from Fritz. Rachel expressed her and Elsa's eternal gratefulness for the many kindnesses he had shown to them.

Fritz replied promptly. He was pleased to hear from Rachel and Elsa. He was astounded to learn of the impending birth. He was delighted that Rachel and Miriam had discovered one another's existence. Things had quieted in his neck of the woods. He had restored some of his garden and was pleased with things he was able to grow for his personal use. Fritz learned that the government was considering placing some of his farmland into a collective. He had much time on his hands and was planning to accept Rachel's invitation to be with her at the baptism of her child. He was looking forward to hearing from "his girls" again.

Chapter 35

ON February 6, 1946, Rachel's water broke while she was seeing the first patient in the morning. It was a consultation regarding major bridge work. She excused herself. "Elsa, call a cab. I need to go to the Elizabeth Krankenhaus. My water just broke. Please make another appointment for Frau Feinschmecker. I should be back in two weeks." She sat down by the front desk. The cab couldn't get there fast enough. She was counting. Her contractions were five minutes apart. When she touched herself, she could feel the crown of the baby's head. It wouldn't take long for this baby to see the light of the world. Elsa saw to it that Frau Feinschmecker was taken care of. She ran to Rachel's bedroom and grabbed the "emergency bag." It had been ready for at least two weeks. Both women knew how to count to nine.

"You stay at the office. The next two appointments are yours anyway. The clients are scheduled for dental hygiene. When you have a chance, reschedule all my appointments. I'll deal with the cabby. He'll make sure I get to the emergency entrance. They wouldn't dare turn me away this time." A handsome elderly man walked in. "Anyone here call for a cab?"

"Yes, sir." Rachel patted her huge tummy. "I'm about to deliver this baby. Get me to the Elizabeth Krankenhaus as fast as possible, please."

The cabdriver took charge of Rachel. "Take my arm. I'll carry your satchel. We'll be there in short order. You just hang on. Whatever you do, don't push. You don't want me to deliver this child."

He seated Rachel comfortably in the back seat. Comfortable was an oxymoron. She wailed loudly as another contraction passed through her body. The cabby watched her writhing in agony when he looked into his rearview mirror.

Rachel breathed hard. "Step on the gas. I can feel movement."

The old man felt sorry for Rachel. "Yes, ma'am. We are almost there." He pulled up near the emergency door. He limped to the entry and called, "I need a wheelchair—and real quick. I have a baby popping out in the back seat of my cab any second now."

A large nurse responded. "You step out of the way, good man. Let us handle this." She wheeled Rachel as quickly as she could waddle to the delivery room. She was lying on the birthing table within seconds. They hardly had time to place her feet in the stirrups. A midwife and an OB-GYN were on duty. Ten minutes later she heard the baby's first cry. It was strong. She was confident she had given birth to a healthy child, her second child. This one she was going to raise herself.

A young nurse carried the baby to Rachel's room. "Here you are, ma'am. It's a beautiful blond boy. He weighed not quite ten pounds and is longer than most babies. You have a gem of a healthy baby." The nurse placed him in Rachel's arms. She was given another love child. She knew without a doubt Johann was the boy's father. Rachel was overjoyed as she smiled through her tears. He was baptized before she left the Elizabeth Krankenhaus. She named him Jochanaan Jethro Salm von Rondstett.

When Elsa visited her, Rachel discussed with her the plans she mulled over in her mind. "I want Jochanaan to be raised in the Jewish faith. Of course, I could not even begin to consider raising him orthodox."

"Why not?" wondered Elsa.

"Good question. Let's say Otto returns. He wasn't Jewish. What about Miriam? She's a Catholic for all I know. Orthodoxy is out of the question, but I want him exposed to many of our rituals and to have him grow up respecting and honoring certain aspects of his faith. That means he should have a bris."

Elsa reminded Rachel, "The bris will have to be performed on February fourteenth, exactly eight days after the day of birth. If you want to postpone the ceremony for whatever reason until March first, you need to seek special dispensation from the rabbi."

Rachel spoke with Rabbi Weisskopf and received permission to delay the bris by two weeks. "I'm fully aware of the difficulties of communicating at the moment and understand that you want your gentleman friend to be in attendance at the bris. Go ahead and invite the man promptly."

Two days after giving birth to Jochanaan, Rachel wrote to Fritz. She told him about the birth of her baby and that Elsa and she were hoping he could see his way clear to visit them in Essen. "The boy's name is Jochanaan Jethro, and his bris is on March 1. Elsa and I would be delighted if you could be here for the event and possibly spend a little extra time with us."

Fritz responded promptly. He would be arriving on April 26.

Rachel and Elsa met Fritz at the main railway station, such as it was. When they got off tram number eighteen at Breslauerstrasse, Fritz was amazed to see all the damage surrounding their building. He thought they were fortunate it wasn't razed during one of the many bomb attacks. Approaching their home, he couldn't help seeing the shingle:

Otto von Graben, DDS
Rachel Adina Salm von Graben, DDS
Elsa Brand, Dental Hygienist

One of Rachel's patients was a well-known seamstress in Essen. Her atelier had survived the war. She offered to create a dress for the occasion of Jochanaan's bris. It turned out to be a simple but stunning creation in black shantung silk. Rachel was a vision as she stepped out of the cab at the Rabbinerhaus. Her hair, glistening in the sun, was fashioned into her favorite style, a chignon. It was held by the amber clasp Johann had given her to replace the one taken and smashed at the time of her arrest. Her shoulders were hugged by the Varanasi scarf. What stories that piece of adornment could tell were it capable of speaking. She proudly wore the Blue Sapphire Amulet.

Rabbi Adam Weisskopf performed the bris. Rachel was pleased with the service and happy that Fritz, Elsa, and Mother Superior had stood with her and Miriam during the ceremony. In her heart, Fritz had taken on the roles of her male ancestors and that of Johann, the boy's father. Jochanaan made just one little cry when his foreskin was lanced by the rabbi. In the end, it was a much less painful act to endure than Otto, Miriam's father, experienced as an adult male.

All returned to the apartment and were joined by Mimi and friends for the celebration. Mimi was only too happy to rock baby Jochanaan to sleep after Rachel had nursed and burped her little treasure. Miriam, Mimi, and Fritz took turns being in charge of little Jochanaan during the afternoon. At first, Miriam wasn't sure how she would feel about this little half-brother, but she was trying to keep an open mind. Mother Superior had reminded her of the importance of giving things a chance. Miriam was looking forward to spending more time with her mother and getting to know her, as well as the baby. Fritz was thrilled to be part of the celebration. Rachel and Elsa were his family now; he treasured knowing them since their brief but profound serendipitous meeting in May 1945.

Before Mother Superior and Miriam left, Miriam wanted to speak with Rachel. "Mutti, may I try spending more time with you and Jochanaan? How would you feel about my being with you on weekends? I could be here on Fridays after school lets out and leave

Monday mornings for school. I do want to continue my schooling at the cloister school." Rachel kissed her and hugged her. She couldn't believe her good fortune. "I will love having you with us." Mother Superior nodded in agreement.

When all retired, Rachel slipped into the silk kimono Johann had secretly acquired in Dresden during their shopping spree. She loved having her naked body surrounded by the silk garment. Holding Jochanaan to her breasts, feeding him, she tried to recall the day when he was conceived.

Chapter 36

ON Jochanaan's first birthday, Rachel received a small package by registered mail. It was sent to her from a cemetery in Liège, Belgium. She opened the package hesitantly. "I wonder what this is about?" Along with a note written oddly enough in English, was a solid brass vial. She read the note:

Dear Madam,

During an early attempt at plowing his fields, one of our farmers in the region unearthed a badly decomposed body. The skeleton was covered by less than two feet of soil. Still clad in a German uniform, the farmer assumed it to be one of the soldiers killed during the Battle of the Bulge. He contacted us at the cemetery. When we examined your husband's remains, we found his identification tags still suspended from his neck and the enclosed brass vial in his left pant pocket. We were grateful for his foresight to note your address in Essen in his last diary entry. We placed the remains in a body bag and are holding them at our morgue. Please contact us ASAP with your wishes as to the disposition of your husband's remains.

Rachel was stunned. "Elsa, please hold my next appointment.

Wait until I tell you what the mail was all about. You better reschedule my afternoon appointments. I need to make a visit to the Parkfried-hof." She rushed to her bathroom to wash her face. She was a wreck.

Rachel fingered the brass vial. It opened more easily than she expected. Perhaps the people who had accessed it in Liège had made it easier for her to unscrew the lid. The contents fell into her lap. She recognized Otto's distinctive handwriting immediately. Rachel started to shake like Aspen leaves in a fall breeze. She lifted the papers closer to her eyes. The ink in his writings had begun to fade. As she read the pages Otto had secretly written, tears streamed down her face. She clutched her hands. Her knuckles turned white. Perspiration covered her forehead. Her armpits felt damp. Rachel was touched by Otto's words. She always had wondered if she betrayed him. Johann had been right; Otto died in December 1944. She began to read.

August 27, 1944

Dearest Rachel,

If and when you should read this, I might be dead or alive. No one knows that I'm writing; I plan to always keep this journal well hidden on my body. We are stuck near Verdun, France. I almost made it to Paris, but the Americans beat me to it a couple of days ago. We are stuck in these muddy trenches, which are reminiscent of World War One. Our leaders are very young officers. Sometimes I wonder if they know what they are doing. What little food we are getting is pretty lousy. Most nights I lie down to rest with my stomach growling. My uniform reeks from sweating so much; my pants are particularly disgusting. On a few occasions, I have come close to pissing and/or shitting in them. The sergeant tells me to turn my nose up and not think about my odoriferous uniform. It's easy for him to say; he gets a clean outfit every day. You can tell I'm miserable. I miss you terribly and wish I could get in touch with you. Whatever we did, we did not deserve this separation imposed on us. If we survive this nightmare, let's never be separated again. Deal?? I kiss you in my mind and hope you are well.

Much love always, Otto

September 10, 1944

Dearest Rachel,

You probably wonder why I have not written again before this. One of my comrades suspected what I was doing. He told me if he would actually catch me writing, he would report me to the commanding officer. I decided I didn't want to wind up in the brig. Circumspection seems to be the operative word.

We have left France behind us and are hunkering down in the Liège area in Belgium. I have the feeling we are building toward a massive counteroffensive. Don't worry about me. I'm in good hands; the Lord will look after me. I wish I knew what is happening with you. I hope to God the Nazis have left you alone. It's something always on my mind. The horrors of war are constantly with me. I wish I could declare myself a pacifist. If I did, I would be shot on the spot. We wouldn't want that to happen, right?

In closing my notation, let me assure you that I love you deeply and miss you terribly. Consider yourself kissed all over, taken in my arms, and passionately loved.

Always, Otto.

December 6, 1944

My Dearest Rachel Adina,

We have been embroiled in serious battles for days. The ground is soaked in blood. The mutilated bodies of my comrades and those of the Allied forces surround me. I was chosen to assist with the burial of the fallen. We have little time to do so. First, we make sure that we are dealing with corpses. We don't want to bury anyone still alive. The graves we dig are shallow. Sometimes we commit more than a single corpse to a site. It's a gruesome job.

Today is St. Nick's. I remember the joy I experienced on this day in my childhood. Where did all those wonderful years go? Memories! That's what sustains me in this nightmare. I think of our days in Munich. I remember our lovemaking. I try to visualize the face of Miriam and what she might look like today. I wonder if she is still safe in the care of Sister Maria-Angelika. Essen has been subjected to many terrible and devastating bomb attacks since September. I still believe we did the right thing by protecting her. I didn't want you or her sent to some horrible camp. I pray you are still safe. It looks like the war might reach an end in a few months. Things are not as good as we are made to believe. I probably shouldn't even commit such thoughts to paper. By the way, a couple of days ago, I found a solid brass vial with a screw top. It's about eight inches long and one and one-half inches in diameter. I keep it in my left pant pocket. It makes a perfectly safe vessel to store my few diary notes. I have actually written our full names and address on a separate slip. I want to include it with my notes. Should something happen to me, they might send the vial along with my dog tag. Just to make you smile, one of my comrades looked at me kind of funny yesterday. "Are you horny? Looks like you have some hard-on." I cracked up and showed him the brass vial. He almost went in his pants. That's all the funnies for the day. I must return to my ghastly work. I constantly think of you. As I'm writing, I pretend to be holding you in my arms. I embrace you and kiss you gently. Farewell, my dear wife. God bless you.

Always, Otto.

Otto von Graben, DDS
Rachel A. von Graben, DDS
Breslauerstrasse 6
Essen, Deutschland

The pages slipped from her hands. She covered her face with her hands and sobbed. "Otto, Otto, Otto!"

)(

Miriam stored her bike in a convenient spot in the hallway. She walked in. One look at Rachel, and she knew something was wrong. "Mom, what happened? Your eyes are bloodshot." Rachel guided Miriam to her office and asked her to sit down. She handed Miriam the pages. Miriam started to read. Her hands began to shake. She was touching something her father had held in his hands. She grasped the enormity of the moment. "My God, my father wrote these words. I wish I could put my arms around him and thank him for saving my life. I never knew all that you and my father sacrificed to keep me safe."

Rachel held her close. She could feel the heat of Miriam's body radiating toward her own. She was chilled to the bone. "You don't know what it means to have you share this moment with me. He loved both of us deeply."

Miriam cried and grinned at the same time. "Mom, I feel so stupid. But what does 'horny' and a 'hard-on' mean that Dad mentioned in his last note?"

Rachel smiled. "You are too smart for me. For the moment, let's forget about that lesson. Someday, when you are a bit older, we'll revisit your question, and I'll answer it then. After lunch, I would like it if you would go with me to the cemetery."

Rachel and Miriam took a cab to the Parkfriedhof. This was the first time Rachel attempted to locate the grave site of her family. She wasn't even sure it still existed. As she walked up to the Rondell, she spotted the large, black granite marker with the Salm name embossed prominently. The names of her grandparents and parents and their dates of birth and death were shown. The stone could stand a good scrubbing, perhaps even professional cleaning or polishing. The site itself was terribly neglected. She felt ashamed not to have visited her ancestors sooner. She stopped by the cemetery office. Rachel explained the situation to an agent. He assured her they would arrange for the grave site to be restored and have Otto's remains transferred to Essen for interment. Rachel was pleased with the help she received at the cemetery offices.

She held Miriam's hand as they were leaving the place. "Thank you for being with me on this day. You have no idea what it means to me to have you share my life. We've lost your father. Through your presence, he will always remain in our lives."

When they got back to the office, Rachel turned to Elsa. "You'll be pleased to learn, our cemetery plot still exists and will remain in the family in perpetuity. The Parkfriedhof offices will arrange for Otto's remains to be transferred. I will have him buried in the family plot. Barnebeckers are restoring the grave marker and will add Otto's name on the stone.

"I was glad Miriam was with me when I read Otto's pages from his diary. I would like you to read his last words as well." Elsa began to cry as she finished reading Otto's last entry.

Ten days after she first contacted the personnel at the cemetery, Rachel received word that Otto's remains had been received from the cemetery in Liège, Belgium. Rachel arranged for the burial service to take place on February 19. She and Miriam decided a visit to the cloister was in order. When they arrived, Sister Irmgard-Dolcinea responded to the bell.

"How nice to see you. Sister Maria-Angelika will be happy to greet you." Miriam charged ahead and stormed into Mother Superior's office without knocking on the door. She startled her mentor. "What seems to be the hurry, young lady? Have your forgotten your manners?"

"Oh, I'm so sorry, Mother Superior. I was so excited to share our news with you. Actually, I brought Mutti with me. They found my father's body in Belgium. I read the last letter he wrote to my mother. He talked about stuff I didn't understand. But most of it was very sad and made me cry. He must have been a nice man. We are having a funeral and would like it if you could come. Can you?"

With that, Rachel and Sister Irmgard-Dolcinea caught up to Miriam. Mother Superior smiled at Rachel and then gave her a heart-felt hug. She knew what Rachel must be experiencing. "Miriam told me the reason for your visit today. Of course I will be there for Otto's interment. What a sad day for both of you. Miriam told me about the notes Otto left for you. It's all so sad, so very sad. I always include both of you in my prayers. Deep in my inner being, I hoped he would return to you."

"Thank you for wanting to stand by Miriam and me during the service. You played such an important part in all our lives. I am moved that you wish to be with us to honor Otto with your presence. The service will be at eleven on February nineteenth."

"Sister Irmgard-Dolcinea and I will be there. We'll take a cab. Don't worry about picking us up. I am pleased you asked me to attend."

The mourners were few. Rachel bundled up Jochanaan. It was a gray and chilly day befitting the occasion. She, Miriam, Jochanaan, and Elsa rode with Mimi and her friend to the Parkfriedhof. Rachel was touched that Miriam Daniella could witness her father's interment. When the mourners arrived at the family plot, they were pleased that Otto's coffin had already been sunk into the ground. It was Miriam's first time to attend a funeral.

Miriam looked into the large hole and started to cry. "How come the box is already in there?" she asked her mother.

"Miriam, they tried to make it easier on you and me. It's not called a box; it's a coffin. Your father's is made from solid oak and will protect his remains for many years." Miriam knew she shouldn't ask any more silly questions. It was a sad event for all who were present.

The grave marker and the site were restored to pristine beauty. Mother Superior said the Lord's Prayer and recited the twenty-third psalm before she ended her part by gently dusting Otto's coffin with soft soil as she uttered, "Ashes to ashes; dust to dust." Tears were falling down her face as she turned toward the others. Miriam and Rachel followed suit before the remaining mourners said their farewells to Otto. Miriam was pleased to see that her father's name had been added to the Salm grave marker. Otto was finally at rest. There was no celebration after the interment. Rachel found consolation in loving her children. They were her everything; they were all she had. She mourned both Otto and Johann.

Chapter 37

WITHIN weeks of Otto's burial, Rachel petitioned the courts to legally change her and her children's names. Both Miriam and Jochanaan were victims of circumstance. Rachel did not want either of her children to be referred to as bastards. She had seen too much of that sort of ostracizing of classmates when she grew up.

She appeared calmly before the judge who had been assigned to handle the case. Rachel had provided any documentation she had at hand. The judge turned to Rachel. "I have read your petition and studied the documents you made available to the court. I believe everything to be in good order. I, therefore, grant you the right to henceforth call yourself Rachel Adina Salm von Graben von Rondstett. Your daughter shall be known as Miriam Daniella Salm von Graben. Likewise, your son will bear the name Jochanaan Jethro Salm von Rondstett. You will need to sign these documents. That should take care of the matter."

Rachel couldn't wait to share her good news with Miriam, who hadn't come home for the noonday meal that day. When she got off her bike late in the afternoon, Rachel saw her come into the house.

"Why are you all hot and sweaty? You look terribly frustrated. What's wrong with you, Miriam?"

"Mom, there's something terribly wrong with me. When I went to pee at school, all of this blood came rushing out of my bottom. I think I'm dying."

"Come here. Let me hold you and talk to you. You are not dying. Something very natural and normal is happening to your body. You are a bit young for this to occur. Perhaps your development has been affected by the conditions under which you grew up. You are no longer a child; your body is telling you that you are a young woman. This will happen to you once a month from now on. Some women call it a curse, others call it a blessing. If you would do certain things with a boy, you might have a big tummy like I did with Jochanaan. You might have a baby. Maybe the time has come for me to answer those questions you raised just the other day."

Miriam stared at Rachel; her eyes were wide open. Rachel knew the time had arrived for her to have a motherly chat with her daughter. She told her all that was possible as a result of the physical change that had taken place. Miriam wasn't so sure how she would deal with the monthly occurrence of the bleeding but was glad that her mom had explained everything to her. At the moment, that chapter of discussion was closed for her. "You said you had something to tell me, Mutti?"

"You managed to steal my thunder. I wanted to share some special news with you when you came home from school. I wanted to tell you your new name. From now on you are 'Miriam Daniella Salm von Graben.'"

"I like having yours and my father's names. How did that happen?"

"After your dad's service, I decided to have the courts change your, Jochanaan's, and my names to honor the men who fathered you. I didn't want other kids calling you nasty names later in life. Neither you nor Jochanaan could help that your fathers were not allowed to marry me before I had you. Your brother will be known as Jochanaan Jethro Salm von Rondstett for the rest of his life."

Rachel could tell Miriam was trying very hard to process all the news she had just discovered. It was a lot for a girl not quite ten years old. Rachel wasn't sure if she wanted to share more with her precious daughter.

"Why is Jochanaan von Rondstett and I'm von Graben? Wouldn't it be more practical to have just one name? You grownups sure can make things complicated!"

"Miriam, Johann von Rondstett was a man I encountered in the camp at Theresienstadt. He was one of my captors. At first, I hated him for what he did to me. He forced his body on me when I first knew him. Women call that rape. He learned to respect my wishes and left me alone. He always told me that he loved me. I didn't want anything to do with him since I loved your father and thought I was still married to him. I didn't know that your father had died months before that. So you might think I'm a bad woman.

"Another man at the camp hurt me very much and many times. I learned to hate men with a passion. Someday I will tell you what happened to him. Two days before Elsa and I escaped from the camp with Johann von Rondstett, he made love to me. Jochanaan was conceived that night; I mean to say, Johann and I made a baby that night. The major was murdered by some Russian brutes who raped Elsa and me. Johann never had a chance to marry me. On our march from Dresden to Essen, I was violated by a black American officer. All these men could have been the father of the baby I carried when you first discovered that I was pregnant.

"When they laid Jochanaan into my arms, I knew immediately that his father was Johann von Rondstett and not one of the other men who had hurt me. I wanted to make sure the boy had his rightful father's name. I chose to have our names legally recorded to give you and Jochanaan legitimacy."

"That sounds complicated to me. Mother Superior talks about truth being stranger than fiction. Now I understand why you wouldn't or couldn't tell me the name of the father of the unborn child. I'm so happy to have a brother. Complicated or not, I love him, and I love you. I can't imagine all you went through."

Rachel smiled and held Miriam close. She was glad to have unburdened herself to her. "When you are a bit older, we'll talk some more about the things that I experienced while I was in Theresienstadt. I hope you will forgive me. One of these days, you must share with me what happened to you and the sisters during the war."

"Oh, Mutti, that happened so long ago. Mother Superior would call it an eternity. I want to forget those terrible hours in the bunker. The scenes of seeing the church and chapel in flames and eventually smashing to the ground still give me nightmares. There was nothing left of the whole school except the little corner of the building where we hid. The worst happened during that last bomb attack in March. We couldn't stay at the school. That long walk from Essen to Münster was terrible. I thought some of those old nuns were going to die. What would we have done had that happened? Sister Irmgard-Dolcinea was the one who kept us all going. She often was fun with her cheerful singing. She sure knew how to keep the troops moving. I got so tired of that awful soup we were forced to eat. It was nothing but burnt flower, salt, and water. Do we have to talk about this? I will if you really need to hear all of it. I'd rather forget it, Mutti. For now let's be happy, just the three of us, and Elsa too."

Chapter 38

THE year was 1951. Miriam wanted to talk about the subjects she wished to study in high school. During the last four years, she had been exposed to Greek, Latin, French, and English, a smattering of the sciences, German literature, philosophy, history, and geography. "Mutti, why are the sisters making me study the Greek and Latin stuff? It's all so boring and old. Biology and chemistry I could handle for a year. I did it, but I don't want to become a doctor. I love my French and English teachers. It was good they finally hired some new teachers; some of the nuns are getting too old for the job. I wish they would talk about something different than the 1930s and 1940s in my history class; I've too much personal acquaintance with the subject. I want you to visit the cloister school during their next open house. You will love the progress on the new building. The modern classrooms are bright, sunny, and friendly. I am so glad I'm still attending school with the nuns."

"My, my, Miriam. Those are big words. You are beginning to sound like a philosophy professor."

"Sorry, Mutti. I do love my teachers, but as I said, some of the subjects are not what I really want to study. I am intrigued by my geography lecturer. When I have my Abitur, I might consider spending a year in Israel. I'm interested in learning more about the formation of a country for the Jews."

Rachel was taken aback. "Did you say Israel? My God, that is a long way from here. How can you even think about leaving me and going that far away? I've only had the pleasure of being with you for the last six years. And now you are talking about living in Israel. Please don't do this to your mother."

"Mutti, it's all just talk at this point. Who knows what I will want to do in four years? I may have a hard time leaving you and my beautiful brother. I love mothering him. He's such a smart kid. You always said I was precocious. What about Jochanaan? If any kid is way ahead of his years, it's my brother. Where is he anyway?"

Rachel knew where he was at all times. "He's having fun in his room. He loves playing with that toy camera Fritz sent him for his birthday. Speaking of Fritz, I enjoy talking with him on the phone. He has taken such an interest in you and Jochanaan. He just adores that boy. When those two talk on the phone, I have the feeling it's father and son or zayde and grandson chatting."

"What's a zayde?"

"Sorry, Miriam. That's a Yiddish word for grandfather."

"What does Fritz do where he lives? Didn't you tell me that he is all alone."

"Right. His wife, daughter, and two granddaughters were killed during bomb attacks on Dresden. He always tells me how lonely he is in his little house. He putters around in his garden but has next to no close neighbors or friends. He's always happy when I call and tell him the latest in our lives. I'm so glad he finally broke down and got a phone. Sometimes I feel like asking him to consider visiting us more often."

"Wasn't he here when Jochanaan was born, Mutti?"

"Yes, he was here for the bris. That's the last time we saw him. I can't believe five years have gone by."

"Mutti, why don't you call him? I'd love to see him again. There is no problem with having him with us for a while. I'm so glad you decided to get the apartment above us for Elsa when that old man died. You've done a great job of renovating the place. Elsa is so much happier with having her own apartment. Although she doesn't need three bedrooms, it's nice to know that you and she have more space. Jochanaan and I surely are happy to have our own rooms. I love coming home these days."

She hugged and kissed Rachel and said good-night. Miriam wanted to talk to Jochanaan before she hit the books and studied for upcoming exams. Rachel picked up the phone and called Fritz.

"Hello, Fritz. How are you tonight?"

"How nice to hear your voice. Now that I have you on the line, I feel just fine. How are Miriam and Jochanaan?"

"I've just had a delightful conversation with my daughter. She's fourteen and turning into a smart young woman. Some days I have the feeling she is going on forty. The things she says and does rack my brain. Jochanaan loves that toy camera you sent him. It won't be long and he'll want a real one. He's absolutely fascinated with the idea of taking pictures of people and things. His fantasy is boundless when he talks about his imaginary photographic subjects. He's playing in his room as we speak. Tell me, how are things in your life?"

"I love talking with you and hearing all the great news about Miriam and Jochanaan. It's been too long since I've seen you all. Jochanaan must be five going on six by now. How does he like school?"

"He loved kindergarten and will start in first grade in the fall. He's very artistic. He loves listening to classical music and enjoys drawing pictures. Sometimes, he tells me he's drawing his images from photographs stored in his head. I'm always dead serious when he comes up with his tall tales."

"Great to know the children are doing well in school. How about you? What's happening in your life?"

"I keep busy in our dental practice, and Elsa has worked out well as dental hygienist. Other than work, my life is fulfilled by my two children. They are my everyday joy. What about you?"

"The government decided to usurp the rights to most of my land. They believe in big-time farming and have consolidated much of the open land into collectives. That leaves me with taking care of my little hut and the personal garden. I never replaced the animals they stole in 1945. My nights are pretty lonely, especially during the long winter. I walk a lot and do a lot of exercises."

Rachel felt sorry for him. "I have an idea. Since you seem to be free to leave your place, why don't you consider visiting us for the upcoming high holy holidays? Rosh Hashanah is on September fourteenth. You could come even earlier and be with us for Miriam's birthday on September sixth. She'll be delighted to see you again. And you know how much Jochanaan loves to talk to you on the phone. He will be thrilled to have a man around the house. In the last year, he often wondered who his father was. I have shown him the one and only photograph I have of Johann. I've tried to tell him a little about what his father was like. I don't want him to hate the man. At least he has an inkling what his father looked like. He knows nothing of who he really was."

"Hm, hm, how about if get there on September fifth? Will you or Elsa be able to meet me at the train station? I would appreciate having your help with getting to your place. I probably could remember where to catch the tram and where to get off."

"No problem, Fritz. In the meantime, I have learned to drive. I have my own car and get around easily. I'm overjoyed to know that you are considering spending time with us. The children, Elsa, and I will be looking forward to having you with us."

"Thanks for the call, Rachel. And thanks for the invitation. Good-night for now. Sleep well. God bless you."

She hung up the phone quietly.

Ж

Rachel was in the examining room with Frau Feinschmecker, who was being fitted with another crown. Elsa was managing the reception desk. There was a knock on the door.

"Please, come in. How may I help you?" Elsa was momentarily speechless as she looked at the woman who stepped into the office. The resemblance was uncanny.

"I would like to see Rachel Salm. I don't have a lot of time. It's important that I see her immediately. A cabdriver is waiting for my return."

"I'm sorry, Dr. von Graben is with a patient."

"Point me to the examining room. What I have to say will only take a minute or two. And I don't care if I speak to the doctor in front of her patient."

Elsa wasn't quite sure how to handle the intruder; she was beginning to feel that was who she was dealing with. "Let me ask Dr. von Graben if she is agreeable to speak with you. Just a moment, please."

Elsa walked toward the examining room; the woman was right on her heels. "Dr. von Graben, this woman insists on speaking with you this minute. She is in a great hurry and doesn't care if your patient listens to what she has to say."

Rachel looked up and nearly dropped her instruments in Frau Feinschmecker's lap. She was looking at herself. Juliana Salm spoke with vengeance in her voice. "What do you say now, Salm bitch? Surprised? It's me, the long-lost twin sister. I wonder if you were even told about me. I'm not here for idle chitchat, and I don't give a hoot about getting to know you. All I'm here for is what is rightfully mine."

Elsa sensed that this scene could turn ugly. She stepped back to her desk and reached for Fritz's pistol. It was well maintained and loaded. She stuck it quickly into her lab coat and joined the discussion in the examining room. She believed that she needed to shield her friend at all cost if necessary.

"How do I know about that precious amulet you are probably

wearing? I learned it from the women who raised me. Would you like to know who they were? They were both married to your mother's brother, your dear Uncle Avraham. He's the one who abducted me from the crib at the hospital in 1913. They practically raised me in a closet for all those years until the Nazis searched the place on Kristallnacht and arrested and shipped all of us to a concentration camp. Eventually, we wound up in Auschwitz. Both your bastard uncle and his second wife were gassed at Birkenau. The bitch who instigated the kidnapping in 1913 died of consumption in 1919. I don't know why I was left to live.

"The only reason Avraham and Tilly showed up at your grand-mother's funeral in 1937 was to make sure that she was really dead. They didn't have the guts to demand the amulet from you right after the funeral; they were certain you would be wearing it. When they returned from the burial, they told me all about its existence and that I was the rightful heir since I'm the older of the two of us. They made sure I never forgot the value of the damn thing. And I want it!"

Frau Feinschmecker became extremely uncomfortable and attempted to convey her anxiety to Rachel. Rachel was likewise stunned by the intruder and her revelations. Before she could react to her sister's protestations, Juliana stepped right in front of Rachel and affronted her by reaching into her lab coat. She tore off the coat and then ripped Rachel's blouse to shreds, revealing the Blue Sapphire Amulet. "I want it, bitch. Didn't you understand what I said? Do I need to draw you pictures? That fucking thing is mine. I've been dreaming about ripping it off your neck for the last thirteen years, ever since I learned who I was and what I had coming to me should I survive the war. Your bastard uncle and his partner in crime told me the whole fucking story riding on that lousy train to hell. Do I need to rip it off you, or are you handing it over to me?" She reached into her coat pocket and pulled out a revolver.

"Perhaps this will make it clear that I mean business." She

pointed the weapon at Rachel and ripped the amulet from Rachel's neck with her other hand. As she did so, Juliana tripped over the foot pedal of the examining chair. Frau Feinschmecker ducked and screamed, "Help, help, someone help!" Juliana's pistol went off, and the bullet hit the examining light shattering it. There was broken glass everywhere. When she aimed the gun at Rachel's chest again, Elsa fired her pistol and struck Juliana three times in the back. The intruder fell to the floor with the amulet clutched in her left hand. Juliana Daniella Salm was dead. Rachel was bleeding profusely from her neck. The amulet had caught on one of her arteries.

The cabdriver walked in. He coughed and didn't speak a word. His hand flew to his mouth as he began to vomit. He then fled the bloody scene.

Elsa alerted Rachel and Frau Feinschmecker not to move. She handed Rachel a thick towel. "Press this as firmly to your neck as you can. I'll deal with your injury in a second. And don't touch anything." She rushed to the phone and called the police. They could hear the sirens within minutes. Three officers arrived ten minutes after the last shot had been fired. They took photographs of the scene and then began their interrogation. They took closeups of Juliana's hands, the right holding the revolver, the left still clinging firmly to the amulet.

"Who made the phone call?"

"I did! And before you ask any more questions, I want to call our attorney. My name is Elsa Brand. That's all I'm obliged to tell you without the presence of legal counsel."

Elsa walked over to her phone and called Aaron Finkelstein. His secretary answered the phone.

"Finkelstein and Finkelstein, Attorneys at Law; this is Erika Schutz speaking. How may I direct your call?"

"Hi, Elsa Brand calling for Dr. von Graben. There has been a shooting in our clinic, and Dr. von Graben and I need Dr. Finkelstein to represent us. The police are on the scene, wishing to interrogate us. Is there any chance that Dr. Finkelstein could see his way clear and meet us at the police station in Holsterhausen?"

"He is in his office. Let me check his calendar. I believe he might be able to be there, but let me check with him."

Frau Schutz knocked firmly on Aaron Finkelstein's office. "It's Rachel von Graben and her hygienist who have a serious issue. Apparently, a shooting took place in the clinic. Dr. von Graben's associate, Elsa Brand, is asking for you to meet them at the Holster-hausen police precinct. What may I tell her?"

"Tell her I'm on my way and not to say a word other than giving their names." She conveyed the message to Elsa and could hear the sighs of relief.

Elsa faced the officer in charge. "I'm sure you want to speak with me further at the precinct. Our attorney, Dr. Aaron Finkelstein, is on his way to meet us there."

The officer in charge addressed Rachel. "Dr. von Graben, you and your patient may move now. We've taken plenty of photos of you and the deceased. Her body will be removed after we've done more photographs of her. We will interrogate all parties involved at precinct thirty-seven. We'll make sure an officer will stay on the premises while you are away. Do you have any questions?"

"I would like to speak to my neighbor, Miss Mimi. My five-year-old-son and my daughter will be coming home from school in a while. I don't want them to see this scene and wonder where we are."

"Allow me to go with you to see your neighbor."

"You don't have to worry; I won't run away. I haven't done anything wrong."

"I advise you not to say another word pertaining to the shooting." Rachel was glad he was decent enough to warn her.

Rachel knocked on Mimi's apartment door and told her quickly that she and Elsa needed to meet Dr. Finkelstein at the police precinct and that she appreciated her taking care of Jochanaan and Miriam when they came home from school. "I can tell you are distraught. Of course I'll leave my door open so that I hear when they come in."

Elsa realized Rachel needed serious attention to the wound she had sustained. She turned to the police officer in charge. "As you can see, Dr. von Graben has been wounded. May I at least tend to her injury before we proceed?"

"Yes, of course, but then we must get to the police station at once."

Rachel, Elsa, and Frau Feinschmecker were escorted to the police car. Aaron Finkelstein was waiting for them when they arrived at the police station. He conferred with the three women in private and learned what had transpired at the dental clinic. Aaron knew Rachel and Elsa outside the clinic and was just as shocked to learn of Juliana Salm's appearance. The officer in charge took down all the information Elsa and the two witnesses provided within the guidelines spelled out by their attorney. When questioned about the possession of the weapon, Elsa advised the police of its origin. "Eventually, I obtained the proper permit and participated in target shooting practice on my days off."

The testimony of Frau Feinschmecker clearly supported Elsa's position of having fired her pistol to save the life of Rachel. Upon Aaron's recommendation to plead not guilty before the presiding magistrate, Aaron posted bail for Elsa, and they were dismissed. The trial would take place in one month or so. All were advised not to leave town until the trial was over.

When they walked out of the police station, Aaron drove Rachel to her doctor's office and then drove Frau Feinschmecker home. By the time he called and checked in with his office and got back to Rachel, she had received the necessary injections, and the wound was sutured. He then took Elsa and Rachel back to their clinic.

Juliana Salm's body had been removed from the dental suite, and the floor was cleaned. However, the clinic was still viewed as a crime scene. Elsa's first job was to cancel all patients for at least a week.

Rachel needed to face Jochanaan and Miriam and come up with acceptable answers for her children. "What happened, Mommy? Aunt Mimi couldn't or wouldn't tell us," Jochanaan shared.

Miriam stared at her mother in total disbelief. "That's quite a bandage you have on your neck, Mutti. Are you feeling OK? Did you lose a lot of blood?" She walked over and hugged her mom. "When I walked in, that woman was still on the floor and clutching your amulet. I didn't ask any questions, and the policeman told me to beat it. As I was leaving, I kept looking at the amulet, and the officer removed it from her hand, saying he had to take it for evidence."

Rachel finally found her voice. "Children, that woman was a visitor of mine and was badly hurt in the examining room. Because of the seriousness of the case, the police are involved. Neither I nor Aunt Elsa did anything wrong. Let's go to our apartment, and I'll make you your favorite hot chocolate. That will do all of us some good." Aaron Finkelstein took her aside. "Did you have any idea Juliana Daniella Salm existed?"

"Yes and no, Aaron. My grandmother informed me on her deathbed in 1937 that I was a twin and that my older sister had vanished from the earth right after we were born in 1913. My grandparents and the police gave up searching for her after seven years. The rest you know from what Juliana spit out before Elsa shot her. I'm still shaking in my boots. I would have given her the amulet if that was all she wanted, but she didn't give me a chance before she threatened my life with that pistol of hers. I didn't even know Elsa had a weapon and that she knew how to use it. Thank God she did. That nutty woman would have probably made my two children orphans if it hadn't been for Elsa." Aaron just kept shaking his head. He couldn't believe what he was hearing.

"As soon as the court date is confirmed, I'll let you know."

"Thanks, Aaron, for being there for us."

The door closed quickly behind Aaron. Elsa dialed Fritz's number.

She related what had transpired that day. Fritz was all ears. "I'm glad I'll be able to leave right away. Keep up your chin. In the meantime, you girls can handle this, especially with Aaron Finkelstein's help. I'll be on the train tomorrow."

Chapter 39

FRITZ had no difficulty securing the necessary permission to leave East Germany for the West. He got on an early train and arrived in Essen six hours later. He wore one of his newer suits in a light color. He was so tired of always wearing dark suits and dull ties. Fritz Unrat wasn't ready to be laid out in a coffin. His dark hair wasn't as full as it had been when he married Erna. At least he wasn't bald yet. Significant hints of gray gave him that distinctive look. He wore a sporty hat. "Not too bad looking for fifty-five" he thought as he stepped off the train.

"Hello, Fritz. I'm down here." Rachel waved at him. She wore a fashionable black and white polka-dotted dress and high heels. The stand-up collar hid the large bandage partially. She still had a very attractive figure. Rachel never appeared robust and certainly not slovenly. She could hold her own at thirty-eight. They met on the platform. He set down his suitcase and hugged her. He gave her a kiss. It wasn't kissing like many do in Europe—friendly and quick, touching both cheeks. "I see the bandage on your neck. Are you feeling OK? What a terrible thing for you to experience. Have you heard anything more from the police?"

"No, and I doubt that we will. We will learn more during the trial."

"How are you two holding up?"

"Elsa isn't worrying one bit; I've learned to be less optimistic. However, the testimony of the patient and the evidence of the scene ought to bring a ruling in her favor."

"I'm glad I insisted on Elsa taking that pistol of mine when you left for your walk six years ago."

"So is she, and so am I. I probably wouldn't be here to tell the tale. Juliana was totally out of control and enraged. She probably would have killed me had it not been for Elsa."

Fritz realized Rachel needed him. He kissed her lightly. She looked into his shiny eyes and smiled. "Let's get you to my car. Jochanaan is anxiously waiting for you as are Miriam and Elsa. You don't look a day older. Perhaps a little grayer around the edges when you lifted your hat in greeting. It's that professorial, distinguished look." She winked at him. He reciprocated. They walked arm in arm to her Mercedes parked at the railway station garage. "I'm so glad you were willing to come sooner. Both Elsa and I cannot thank you enough for wanting to be there for us."

Rachel tucked his suitcase in the trunk. He helped her into the car. As she backed out of her parking spot, he couldn't help complimenting her on her driving skills. He hadn't driven a car in years. No way did he ever want to try it in Essen's city traffic. They arrived at Breslauerstrasse in twenty minutes. Jochanaan came running out of the house. He couldn't wait to shake hands with Fritz. "Come and look at my newest toy. Mom bought me a nice camera; it's a used Leica! I loved pretending taking photos with the toy camera you sent me two years ago. Now I don't have to fake it anymore. I can take some real photos. I think what they can do is amazing. To catch a person's picture and save it for as long as you want is a wonderful thing, don't you think so, Uncle Fritz? May I call you that?"

"You certainly may. I'm honored. I've never been an uncle. I didn't have any brothers and sisters. You are correct about the wonder of photographs. Your mom told me about you looking at one of your father. Just think, if that photo hadn't been taken, you would have no idea who he was and what he looked like. I totally agree with you. They are a marvelous invention. I often look at photos of my wife, daughter, and my grandchildren. If it wasn't for those photographs, I would have to rely completely on my memories. I hate to tell you, but after so many years, they fade. Pictures help a lot and are great."

"Maybe we can take walks while you are here. You could help me decide what and who to photograph. You could be my teacher. You look like you have experienced eyes." This brought a chuckle from Fritz. He was only too willing to spend time with Jochanaan. At the moment, Fritz was thankful that Jochanaan's interest in photography was a good detractor from what had happened the day before. It was fortunate that the crime scene had been cleared by the time the boy had returned from school. He probably would have wanted to test his photographic skills.

Rachel shivered, just thinking what might have happened. At the moment, she wanted to change the subject. "How about a glass of wine—red or white, or would you prefer a beer? We have both. Or perhaps something else?"

"I'll have a glass of red wine. I'm told it's good for me. I might have a beer with the meal."

Rachel poured them each a glass of red wine and sat down with Fritz in her living room. Except for different fabric covering her comfortable chairs, the room was still pretty much the same.

Fritz lifted his glass toward Rachel. "Here's to happier days. I like the new fabric you chose for the upholstered furniture; it gives the room a soft and warm glow. Very nice, Rachel. What are the plans for tonight? May I take you and the children out to dinner at a nice place nearby?"

"Under the circumstances, I'd just as soon make it a family dinner at home. It will be good for all of us to stay here and talk. I haven't told Miriam all the details about the woman who tried to lay claim to the amulet. Jochanaan will be perfectly happy to talk with you about photography, and it will give me time to share yesterday's events with Miriam without being constantly questioned by my precocious son."

Rachel continued. "Miriam is very anxious to see you. She's grown a lot. Miriam is not a kid any longer. Wearing her hair like mine makes her look more mature. Of course, that's what she wants. I don't know if there are any boys in the picture. Sometimes it worries me. She matured in many ways at too young an age. She wasn't even ten when she started having periods. That was much too early. Of course, there was nothing I could do about that. I tried to explain to her the consequences of this fluke of nature. So far, so good. Like I said, I don't believe she is seeing any boys, certainly not boys who might get her pregnant."

"I didn't see Elsa. Did she go out for the evening?"

"No, no. You'll see her later. She decided to hibernate in her apartment for the time being. Elsa is eager to see you again. She loves having her own apartment right above us. She thought it would be nice for us to have some time to talk. Five years is a long time. So much has happened; so much has changed. The children are growing up much too fast. And now this added concern."

"Does Miriam still like to be at the cloister school?"

"Oh, absolutely. She wouldn't want to attend any other school. She's a very sensible girl, and the nuns absolutely adore her. Miriam and I have become very close. I love having her live with me. In so many ways, other than her looks, she reminds me of Otto. Now and then, I see some sibling rivalry but nothing that disturbs me. Being nine years older than Jochanaan, Miriam likes to mother him at times. You can imagine that doesn't go over too big with him."

"Sounds to me like you are happy and fulfilled."

"I am, and I'm not. I still miss Otto. I hadn't envisioned myself as a widow at age thirty-one. But it is what it is. Let's talk after

Miriam retires for the night. Jochanaan has school tomorrow and needs to go to bed early."

"I'm pleased to learn that working with Elsa has been a positive experience. Did she ever consider moving back to Bavaria?"

"No, Fritz. She likes living in a large city much better than being stuck in the little town where she grew up. Her parents are gone, and she doesn't have any other relatives. The children and I are her family. We've become good friends. The kids love Aunt Elsa."

"Does Elsa assist you, or does she work independently?"

"She has become a skilled dental hygienist, and her patients love her. Elsa is a secular Jew and doesn't recognize any of the Jewish holidays. It's for that reason that she will see patients when I'm not in the practice for the next ten days. She will see some of her patients as soon as the clinic can reopen. I have none booked between Rosh Hashanah and Yom Kippur. My Jewish patients wouldn't show up. Christian patients know why I'm closed for the holidays. In an emergency, I would see them except on Yom Kippur. If need be, I can always refer them to colleagues." Fritz was pleased knowing they would have time alone later in the evening.

"We'll have an early dinner and just a snack in the evening if that's OK with you, Fritz?"

"By all means. I'd rather not go to bed with a full stomach. I've been watching it for a few years. It seems harder and harder to keep that belly of mine trim and taut. Whatever you girls are cooking smells awfully good. I don't cook very much for myself these days. I often head for the village and grab a bite at one of the little inns. A home-cooked meal will be a real treat."

Miriam walked into the living room. Fritz was shocked by her beauty. She looked a lot like a younger Rachel. Fritz found his voice. "You look wonderful, Miriam. Allow me to give you a hug." Rachel was right; Miriam wasn't a kid any longer. She was tall and slender and had an excellent figure.

"Great seeing you again, Fritz. It's been too long. So glad you can be with us for my fourteenth birthday. I know Jochanaan will love having you here. He's so tired of always having just women around him. He needs that male companionship. I missed knowing my father too, but it's different for boys; they need their fathers more than their mothers. Mutti does a great job of keeping us happy. Education is important for both of us. I still love my school; Jochanaan enjoys the teachers at the institution he attends too. I'm so glad you came. Mom really needs you right now. I'm still all puzzled by what happened with this woman and who she was. None of us had any idea she existed."

"Time for dinner, everyone," called Rachel. Elsa was glad to be included and that the sad chapter was momentarily closed. The five of them sat around the dining room table. Dinner smelled divine as far as Fritz was concerned. "Let's hold hands. I would like to say a prayer," said Fritz. "Dear Lord, bless this gathering, bless our thoughts, and guide us in all our future decisions. Bless all our loved ones, wherever they might be. Bless this abundant food prepared for us and always fit us for thy service. In the name of the Almighty, Amen." None commented; they appreciated his sincere expression for their well-being.

"Mom, I hate to eat and run. My friend from school, Melissa, asked me to see a movie with her. Her parents didn't want her to go out alone. I should be home no later than nine o'clock. We are taking in the early show of *Forever Amber* at the Lichtburg. They are finally showing it with a German soundtrack."

"That's fine, Miriam, as long as I know where and with whom you spend time."

"Thanks for dinner, Mom. You and Fritz have a pleasant evening. Bye. See you all tomorrow." She was out the door in a flash, heading for the number eighteen tram stop.

After the evening vesper, Elsa decided to retreat to her quarters as soon as the dishes were done. She shook Fritz's hand. "Thanks, good friend, for all you've done for us." Rarely given to emotional outbursts, she kissed Fritz on the cheek.

Rachel thought she would take Fritz for a spin. She wanted him to see where the cloister school was located that sheltered Miriam for all those lost years. "This whole complex was completely destroyed by the end of the war. It was a miracle the remaining nuns and the seven children survived the last attack. I'm astonished by the progress they are making in rebuilding it." Fritz was amazed by what he saw. When he was in Dresden a few weeks earlier, there was hardly any evidence of rebuilding the city. The differences between the East and West were unbelievable.

Fritz and Jochanaan talked about taking pictures with the Leica. The visitor was more than delighted to spend time with Jochanaan and teach him how to get the most out of his newest toy. It wasn't really a toy. Jochanaan was serious about taking photographs.

Finally, it was just Rachel and Fritz. Both of them took deep breaths and looked at each other. "Would you care for a cognac or another beer? I feel like having a little something," offered Rachel.

"A cognac will be nice. Haven't had one of those in years. I'm not much of a drinking man. Why don't you come and sit a little closer to me? I'm not going to hurt you. You are much too precious to me. I just would like to have you near me. I do have feelings for you. Ever since we last talked on the phone, I can't get you off my mind. Just thinking of you gets this fifty-five-year-old man aroused. I hadn't experienced these feelings for many years. You got under my skin. I feel like we need each other. Never mind our age difference. If you are worried about what other people will think, don't. It's strictly our business and none of theirs. To use a nasty expression, I don't give a damn any longer what other people think." He drew her closer to him and kissed her gently on her lips.

She didn't reciprocate. "I want you as a friend, Fritz, and not as a sex partner."

"This may come as a shock to you, Rachel. I want to marry you. I want to be a father and grandfather to your children and children's children. I need you, and I need to be connected to a family. Being alone for all these years has done things to my mind. You having reached out to me has given me a new lease on life. I would be a liar if I didn't tell you how I've fantasized about my physical needs being met by you. Yes, I desire you. It has been too many years without a woman. I love you and want to love you. I hope I can please you. Let us share the remaining years we may have together on this earth. I'm sure both Otto and Johann would want you to have a life after their deaths all those years ago. It's time for both of us to rejoin the living."

Rachel was totally caught off guard by Fritz's proposal. "Fritz, I don't want to hurt your feelings, but I am not ready to get married again. Your proposal flatters me. Please, do not be angered by my hesitation. It's not our age difference, but I'm just not ready to commit myself to marriage." She could tell he was hurt. Rachel got up from the sofa and poured herself another glass of wine. She decided to sit in one of the chairs rather than next to Fritz on the sofa. Her body language underscored her spoken message; she was not interested in a serious relationship with Fritz.

"Let me show you to the guest bedroom. Make yourself comfortable. I know it's not what you had in mind. I'm just not ready to be something other than a good friend to you." Fritz retrieved his suitcase and followed her to the designated room. She kissed him on his left cheek and wished him a good night.

"You sleep well too. I'm not giving up, Rachel. I can wait."

Chapter 40

FRITZ had been with Rachel and her family for more than six weeks. As much as she treasured the time she spent with him, she wasn't quite ready to commit herself to marriage. Rachel felt extremely self-conscious in front of her children, especially Miriam. "How long is he staying? Will he be living with us for good? Is he going to marry you? Are you ready and wanting to have another man in your life? I know I was the one who encouraged you to call him and invite him to visit us. I didn't realize he was that interested in you."

"I'm glad you asked all your questions while Fritz is practicing photographic tricks with your brother at the Gruga. They won't be home for a couple of hours. I do want to respond to your concerns. I feel I can do this with you. You are a young woman. Have you been with any of the boys at school?"

"Mom, I will be honest with you. A couple of the guys have tried to kiss me. And yes, I have experienced what Dad referred to in his note to you. But that is it. No one has violated my virginity to date. I can tell Fritz really likes you. He seems to be a gentle sort of man. I don't think he would ever hurt you. Do you have any feelings for him? I know he likes kids. He's nuts about Jochanaan, and I believe he likes me a lot. That isn't important. Does he like you enough for you to consider marrying him? If and when I get married someday, I want a man I can talk to about all sorts of things. He must enjoy many of the things I like to experience and actively pursue. My man will have to be a romantic and not just wanting to make babies day and night."

"You amaze me at your age. Where did you learn about romance and having fun making babies? Is that the sort of thing your teachers talk about? I can't believe that is the case."

"Some of us girls exchange romance novels. Some of the characters are famous women. Have you ever read *Madame Bovary,* or do you know the stories about the famous French Queen, Marie Antoinette? It's all available in our library. Did you expect the nuns to hide that kind of literature from us?"

"I get the picture. Fritz asked to marry me the night he arrived. I enjoyed having him with us and believe we could be compatible. He would like me to cut back on my professional activities, allowing us to travel and enjoy ourselves more freely. Of course, that's completely out of the question. Fritz is not a well-to-do man. We have to live on the funds that Elsa and I generate in the dental practice. To be frank with you, your and Jochanaan's needs are far more important to me than getting into bed with another man.

"If anyone would listen to this conversation, they might believe I'm out of my mind discussing such matters with my fourteen-year-old daughter. They don't know you. No one realizes your maturity. I know what you've been through and what life has taught you. You may have been sheltered by Mother Superior, but you are smart well beyond your age. I'm proud of you, and I'm proud of the relationship we have learned to appreciate. To put an end to your questions, I like Fritz a lot; I'm not sure if I love him. If I marry again, I want to be able to say that I did it for love. Did I answer your questions, my dear Miriam?"

"Yes, Mom. That's all I needed to know.

They heard the front door open. Jochanaan came charging into the apartment. "Mom, Mom, I can't wait until I get these photos back from the lab. Someday, I would like to have my own photo lab. Fritz told me he would help with the process of developing film. Won't that be fun?"

Fritz sat down across from Rachel. "That depends on whether I will be living here."

"I'm afraid that won't happen, Fritz. As much as the children and I liked having you here and enjoyed your company, I believe it is time for you to think about heading home."

Rachel could tell he was upset with her sudden announcement. Jochanaan and Miriam understood what was being discussed in their presence. Jochanaan started to cry and clung to Fritz.

"There is a train tomorrow morning at eleven o'clock. Would you mind taking me to the station, Rachel?"

"No need for you to take off in such a hurry. But if this is what you want to do, that's fine with me. I do believe both of us need to get our thoughts in order before we jump into something we might regret. I like you very much, Fritz. I'm sure my children would like you to help me with completing a family circle. Neither of them has ever had a father figure in their lives. It would be wonderful if it worked out that way. At the moment, I need more time to con-template our future together should it come to that. Please don't be hurt. I just need more time."

"I'll give you all the time you need to make the decision. Just know that I love you very much and will miss you terribly once I'm back in that hut of mine. I'll be out of here in the morning." He kissed Jochanaan and Miriam good-night before he reached for Rachel. His kiss was not reciprocated. She smiled at him as he headed for his room.

A few days after Fritz left for Dresden, Aaron Finkelstein called.

"Hi Rachel, I've heard from the court. The trial date has been set for November twelfth. The official notifications for you, Elsa, and Frau Feinschmecker will be in the mail in the next couple of days. I thought it best to let you know ASAP in terms of scheduling patient appointments."

"Thanks, Aaron. That was very thoughtful of you. I believe it will be more convenient if Elsa and I drive ourselves rather than having you pick us up. See you in court."

X

Rachel and Frau Feinschmecker were seated with Elsa's attorney; Aaron Finkelstein made his opening statement. "Birth and police records indeed confirmed the existence of Juliana Daniella Salm, the older twin sister to Rachel Adina Salm born in 1913. There is no documentation that the deceased ever attended any schools in Essen. She was next registered under that name when she entered Sachsenhausen KZ in 1938. She was transferred to Auschwitz in 1941. The identification number tattooed on the inside wrist of the deceased's left arm was the number 147379. She was last identified as a displaced person after she was freed from Auschwitz. There is no further record of her existence after 1946."

The prosecutor presented a brief summary of the defendant. "The person on trial, Elsa Brand, was born to Jewish parents in 1915 in Dachelhofen, Bavaria. Elsa had only a basic education and was eventually apprenticed to a local dentist. The skills she acquired allowed her later to become a certified dental hygienist. She and her parents were incarcerated in 1942 and were sent to Theresienstadt. It was here that Elsa Brand became acquainted with Dr. Rachel von Graben. Ms. Brand's parents did not survive the camp. Ms. Brand and Dr. Rachel von Graben fled Theresienstadt on May fifth, 1945. They sought shelter with a Mr. Frederick Fritz Unrat after being sodomized and raped by several Russian and Polish soldiers along their flight path. It was Mr. Unrat who provided the pistol in question to the accused prior to their departure for their long walk from outside Dresden to Essen in 1945."

Judge Birnbaum called Elsa to the stand. She was questioned by the prosecutor.

"Did you know Juliana Daniella Salm before she appeared at Dr. von Graben's dental practice?"

"No, I had never seen or heard of her before that morning."

"What made you resort to using the pistol you kept in your desk?"

"Ms. Juliana Salm, apparently the twin sister of Dr. von Graben, was clearly threatening the life of my employer. Ms. Salm aimed her revolver at Dr. von Graben. The first shot she fired didn't strike Dr. von Graben because Ms. Salm tripped on the foot pedal of the dental chair. The bullet struck the examining light above the patient, Frau Feinschmecker. When Ms. Salm pointed the gun a second time at her sister, I fired my weapon to save my employer's life. I have nothing further to add to my testimony." Aaron Finkelstein had no questions for Elsa. She was excused and asked to take a seat.

After listening to the testimony by Rachel and Frau Feinschmecker, both prosecution and defense rested. Judge Birnbaum retired to his office and conferred with both attorneys. All rose when the judge emerged from his chambers. Once they were seated again, Judge Birnbaum asked Elsa to stand before reading his ruling. Aaron Finkelstein stood proudly next to Elsa. "Based on the testimony of the accused and the witnesses, I find Elsa Brand innocent of any charges brought against her. Ms. Brand, you are free to go." He ordered the police department to return the Blue Sapphire Amulet to its owner, Rachel Adina Salm von Graben von Rondstett. Elsa breathed a sigh of relief when she heard Judge Birnbaum's final words. "Case closed. Court is adjourned." Aaron Finkelstein and his entourage emerged from the courthouse all smiles.

Chapter 41

RACHEL got into the habit of calling Fritz at least twice a month, the exception being the night after Elsa's trial. She knew Fritz would be anxious to learn what happened. He answered the phone on the second ring. "Fritz Unrat speaking."

"Hello, Fritz. It's Rachel. I thought you would like to know that we survived the trial."

"Tell me what happened. I presume Elsa was found innocent of all charges?"

"Yes. It wasn't a very lengthy procedure. Thank God Frau Feinschmecker was a reliable witness. The judge might have viewed my statements as biased. Aaron Finkelstein handled the whole affair very well. We are all thankful to have this behind us. Miriam and the three of us who were involved still have a hard time forgetting the scene of Juliana lying dead on the floor in the examining room with the amulet clutched in her left hand and the revolver in her right. I keep dreaming about it. But it's over. I can't believe or fathom that I was attacked and almost killed by a twin sister I never knew. But let's change the subject."

"I'm pleased all went so well for you and Elsa. Don't become a stranger. Remember, I always look forward to hearing from you.

Maybe one of these years, you will find it in your heart to love me. I'll say good night, Rachel." He hung up the phone before Rachel had a chance to respond.

Three years passed. Rachel still enjoyed her bimonthly telephone conversations with Fritz. He learned to accept his fate of being the jilted lover. His first question would always be, "How are the children?"

"Jochanaan looks more and more like his father. He's become such a handsome boy. He loves school and has many friends. When he isn't studying, he continues to love his cameras and taking photographs. He told me he prefers to call them photographs rather than pictures. He can be a little smartass. I told you he has three different cameras by now. He's talking about buying lenses with the money he has saved."

"That's wonderful. It's a great hobby for a boy. Is Miriam still enjoying school? Has she any idea what she might want to study after she finishes her Abitur next year? As smart as she is, I presume Sister Maria-Angelika and you are encouraging her to attend a university. With all of her interests, she would be good at almost anything."

"Oh yes, we have talked many a night about her future. She still keeps bringing up this bit about Israel. I'm not so sure I want her to be there. It's still a country with so many problems and unrest. I want her to travel but to places that are more accessible and established. I know why Israel is of interest to her. It's because of my heritage and what happened to my family and so many of our friends. She's told me that she feels guilty to have had the privilege of being protected by the nuns when so many Jewish children were murdered. She's become a very introspective young lady. Yes, I do want her to study, but I'm not pushing any of my ideas on her."

"I think that's smart. Would you want me to have a chat with her? I don't want her to dwell on that guilt issue. She shouldn't feel that way. Miriam deserves to be happy."

"Speaking of happy—that's what Miriam wants very much for me. One of her friends at school lost her mother last year to cancer. Miriam has been trying to fix me up with the father. He's Jewish. His name is Aaron. Miriam thinks he would be a real catch for me. Of course, I totally disagreed with her. He called me the other day wanting to take me out for a nice dinner. Reluctantly, I accepted his invitation. I'm supposed to see him next Sunday. I'll let you know how it went."

"I'm glad you let me know. I felt guilty not telling you about my situation. I met a widow at one of the little inns where I eat now and then. We were always sitting at separate tables and wondering what the other was all about. Three months ago I got up enough nerve. I asked her if she minded if I sat with her. We could talk over our humble meals. That's how it started. Before you get the wrong picture, I'm not into her underwear yet. I don't believe it will ever happen. She's a nice-looking lady. I guess close to my age. Her husband was killed in the war. We've lots of sob stories to exchange over a bowl of soup or whatever. It's good to be talking to someone. That's all both of us are looking for. She made it quite clear at our second meeting, she wasn't interested in having any kind of intimate relationship with me. That's OK. I'm still dreaming of being with you someday."

"Well, that's how I feel. Don't worry about this Aaron fellow. It will be nice to have an adult conversation over a nice meal in a pleasant setting. I do need to make an effort and make some new friends. Don't get me wrong; I love my children and am heavily involved in all they do. I appreciate my close working relationship with Elsa and my friendship with Mimi. But, now and then, it would be nice to be around a man, a man who will treat me like a lady. Is that asking too much?"

"You deserve to be treated like a lady. I'd love to be the one doing it. I don't want to invite myself, but I have every intention of being there for Miriam's graduation next year. I'm hoping this Aaron fellow hasn't usurped any territory by then."

"Never fear. That won't happen. I'm pleased to know you want to be here for Miriam's big day. She's got lots of studying to do before that. I'm not really concerned. She's very bright and an excellent student. Her grades are exceptional. Her dedication to her studies shows. She did tell me that she is dating one of her classmates. She and this friend of hers, Melissa, have gone out on double dates. Actually, I like that idea. Much less chance of sexual experimentation. There is safety in numbers. Both girls love to dance; apparently the boys do too. I get the biggest kick out of them when they are practicing to that hopping American music. I believe they call it jitterbug or jive or something like that. They have a ball doing it. It's too fast for my taste. I used to love doing the foxtrot and waltz with Otto. Well, my friend. It's time to get some sleep. Talk to you again down the road. Good night, now."

"Good night, Rachel. Thanks for calling. I always enjoy catching up with you." The connection was gone.

Chapter 42

IT was a beautiful, sunny day when Miriam stepped off the stage holding her diploma in hand. Mother Superior had done the honors of chairing the graduation ceremony for the class of 1955. She looked upon her graduates with extreme pride. She loved and cared for each one of her students. But Miriam was special. She couldn't hide her feelings as she placed the diploma in her hands. She bent down and whispered into Miriam's ear. "I'm so proud of you, my Marika. I will always love you. My prayers are with you every day. Forgive me for calling you Marika. I loved you then, and I love you now. Do well, my child." She touched Miriam's shoulder and gently prodded her to move on. She couldn't hold up the other graduates. Mother Superior reached into her habit. She needed to wipe away her tears.

Rachel, Fritz, Jochanaan, Elsa, Mimi, and her friend Helena were sitting in the second row of the auditorium watching the whole procedure. They were privy to the touching scene between Miriam and Sister Maria-Angelika. All but Fritz and Jochanaan were wiping their eyes.

Miriam was seated with her graduating classmates. Her friend, Melissa, was seated next to her. The boys were sitting in the row directly behind the girls. Rachel recognized one of the young men.

His name was Lance. Rachel had never heard anyone called that name in Germany. He was tall and very blond. When Miriam reclaimed her seat, he touched her shoulder. He leaned over and kissed her on the neck. Rachel could feel goosebumps under the silk of her sleeves. She hadn't realized the extent of Miriam's involvement with this Lance. "My daughter and I need to talk" ran through her mind.

Fritz turned to Rachel. "I've been meaning to ask you. Whatever happened to your dates with Aaron? Is he here today? Isn't his daughter one of the graduates?"

Rachel looked at Fritz. "If you look over your left shoulder, it's the fellow with the head full of gray, curly hair, wearing the French blue suit. He's good looking but not my type. We called it a day after our second dinner date. He was nice enough. A bit too aggressive for my taste. When he tried reaching up my skirt in the Ritter the second and last time I saw him, I told him I wasn't interested in pursuing the relationship. He accepted my refusal gracefully. We needed to be civil for the sake of our children. I haven't seen another man since. You are safe, my buddy." She nudged him gently with her elbow.

Rachel had made a reservation for eight at the Ritter. She was pleased that Sister Maria-Angelika had accepted the invitation to join them for the celebratory meal. When they were all seated at the elegantly arranged table, Rachel observed that Lance and his family were seated in an adjacent room of the well-known restaurant. She couldn't fail to notice his constant smiling and winking in the direction of their table. His demonstrations of interest were obviously aimed at Miriam. After a while, Rachel became annoyed. But she was smart enough not to say anything to Miriam or the others at the table.

The conversation went along just fine. They were talking about possible universities for Miriam's consideration and the pleasures Jochanaan was having with his photography. Miriam decided this was as good a time as any to lay her cards on the table. "Mom, I don't want you to be shocked. I've totally different ideas about what I want to do with my life right now. I loved my school, and I loved what I studied. Perhaps I've been studying too much. I need a break. At this very moment, I don't care if I ever face another textbook. I loved the time we've had with one another during the last few years. I need a total change of scenery. Melissa has asked me if I would be interested in sharing her studio apartment in her parents' home in Bredeney. We've spent a lot of our social life together in the last couple of years. We like the young men we are dating. I want to stay in Essen rather than in a distant town where I don't know a soul."

Rachel was shocked. "Are you sure about this? Are you that involved with the young man who's been sending messages to you since we sat down at this table? Are you sleeping with him?"

"Yes, Mother. I'm certain about wanting to move in with Melissa. No, I'm not that involved with Lance, and I'm not sleeping with him. Believe you me, he would love nothing better than having me. He's tried. But Mother Superior and you have done a wonderful job of teaching me. I intend to be a virgin until I sleep with my husband. Is that good enough for you?"

Rachel touched Miriam's hand under the table and squeezed it hard. "I love you and only want the best for you. I want you to find happiness and contentment in life. I want you to be as happy as your father and I were when we were young. You were conceived in love."

Other than Miriam's shocking revelation, the dinner party was a great success. Fritz called a cab for Mother Superior. She was delighted to have been included in the celebration of Miriam's milestone. Mimi, Helena, and Elsa joined Fritz for a nightcap at Rachel's home. Jochanaan was looking forward to the next day. Fritz had talked to him about the possibility of creating a photo lab for him. He had some definite ideas he wanted to discuss with Rachel.

Miriam put her arms around her mother. "I'll see you no later than ten o'clock. Lance and his buddy Karl want to take Melissa and me dancing at the Weinstuben. Just a little celebrating among us young folk. You don't mind, do you, Mutti?"

"No, not at all. Remember, I was young, too, a long, long time ago. Have a great time. Just don't have Lance dislodge one of your arms with all those gyrations I've seen you perform. Love you. See you a little later. I intend to be up when you get home." She smiled as she saw Lance putting his arm around Miriam. They were walking down Kettwigerstrasse toward the Weinstuben.

Fritz felt there was need to be attentive to Jochanaan. He had played second fiddle for most of the day. It had clearly been all Miriam's celebration. Elsa had invited Mimi and Helena to join her for a drink upstairs.

Mimi sometimes wished they could find a man for Elsa. She was turning into a regular spinster aunt. Mimi knew what that was like. She was perfectly happy in that role. Apparently, Elsa shared the feeling. Mimi sometimes wondered if something had happened to Elsa in Theresienstadt that completely turned her off men. It was too delicate a point for her to discuss. Mimi thought she knew her problem; she believed she was too fat to attract any man.

X

Fritz walked with Rachel into the examining room Elsa was using for her dental hygiene patients these days. "I've had my eye on this large storage room for some time. Are you using that space for anything?"

"No, not really. There are just a few empty boxes in it. Nothing I couldn't live without."

"It would be very easy for me to access it from the hallway. I could close off that door from the examining room, cut a new door, and actually just move the door to the new location. It would take me a couple days to do the job. I'm sure, John, who bricked in all your windows after the bomb attacks, would be more than willing to let me use some of his tools. What do you think of that idea, young man?" Jochanaan was grinning from ear to ear.

"Really, Fritz? Would you do that for me? I'd love it. How about regular lights and a red light and all that stuff I will need to make it a real lab?"

"There's no problem with getting electricity in there. Getting water for the wet lab is a bit more challenging. I might access it from the pipes for the adjacent bathroom. I'll need to talk to John about it. I bet he has some good information for me. You'll have your lab before I leave if I can help it." He hugged Jochanaan's shoulder and touched the top of his beautiful hair lovingly.

"It's time for you to get under those feathers. You've got school tomorrow." Rachel gave him a quick pat on his rear end. She thought it was so cute. She didn't dare tell him that. Jochanaan was very self-conscious about his body. Lately, he wanted to take his showers unobserved by his mother. He was aware of his developing physique. Like his older sister, he appeared to be maturing sexually much earlier than was the norm. Fritz walked Jochanaan to his room. He didn't mind putting his pjs on in front of Fritz, who tucked him into his bed and kissed him good-night on his forehead. "We'll have fun tomorrow." He closed the door softly behind him.

Fritz and Rachel were still talking when Miriam walked in. She was radiant but couldn't wait to shed some of her clothes. It was evident, dancing had clearly been a workout. "I'm surprised to see you two still up. Is anything wrong?"

"No, nothing is wrong. Fritz is all excited about building a dark room for your brother. They have been planning and designing it all night. He just tucked him into bed. The others went upstairs to Elsa's place for a nightcap. We've just been sitting here talking."

"Talking about what?"

"Not what you think. We were actually talking about you and your planned departures from all that I had envisioned for you. I accept your rationale. For one thing, I'm glad you have forgotten about that stint in Israel. Bredeney is a totally different story. I don't have a problem with that. I remember graduating from school and wanting to get out from under my grandmother's feet. Even not wanting to start at a university right away I can understand. I just don't want you to think about getting married and making babies. I want you to enjoy single life for a few years. Jumping into bed with your first boyfriend isn't the best idea. I was pleased with what you told me."

"Mom, I assure you again. Nothing like that will happen. We had a great time dancing, and I liked my good-night kiss from Lance, but that was all. He's gotten the message. If he ever tried getting too close to me, he'd be very sorry. Melissa and I have taken self-defense classes. Lance wouldn't want to become acquainted too closely with the swiftness of my right-knee hook. He would expose himself to that weapon just once."

"Now I'm really proud of you. There is one other matter I wish to tend to on this auspicious day. That's the reason I have not retired yet." Rachel reached up to her neck and removed the Blue Sapphire Amulet. "It is rightfully yours as of this moment." She smiled at Miriam. She slipped the chain over Miriam's crown of beautiful, dark hair and arranged the jewel lovingly around her neck. She kissed and hugged Miriam firmly. "Wear it with strength and pride, and always remember those who have worn it before you. You are now the link to the past and the future. I hope I live to see the day when you know who the next recipient will be." Mother and daughter clung firmly to each other; their tears melted on their faces. Fritz couldn't help himself; there were tears of joy in his eyes.

Chapter 43

RACHEL'S clinic was a beehive of activities. Elsa had canceled a couple of non-emergency appointments and rescheduled them. Neighbor John and Fritz had the place torn apart. The building of the dark room was well on its way. Fritz was right in his assumption of accessing water from the adjacent bathroom. The two men worked well together, being of roughly the same vintage.

John was happy to help Fritz. "Jochanaan is a lucky kid. I'd do almost anything for him. Lord knows, I've known him since the day Rachel brought him home. Well, let's stick to the job. I like what you did with the placement of the door. Let me see what I can do to finish the plumbing. Would you mind plastering the wall where we removed the door?"

"No, not at all. That's more in my area of expertise than plumbing.

Early in the afternoon, they could admire their handwork. "I know Jochanaan can't wait to get in here with his rolls of film. And Rachel and Elsa are anxious to have this place back in operation for the patients who are scheduled for tomorrow. I think we did a great job. We can be proud of our achievement. How about a beer, Fritz? I believe we've earned it."

Fritz went to the kitchen and pulled a couple of brews from the fridge. He popped the caps and handed one to John. "Here's to a job well done! I know Jochanaan will be one happy trooper. I'll be heading out in a couple of days. Hope to see you around one of these years."

After school Jochanaan burst onto the scene. He had thrown his bicycle carelessly against the wall in the hallway. He couldn't wait to see the progress on his dark room. "Is it done, is it done?" he wanted to know. Neither Fritz nor John answered.

Jochanaan opened the new door Fritz had talked about. He switched the bright light on and couldn't believe what he saw. The work table was just right and the wet lab small but perfectly functional for what he wanted to try. The wires for drying were strung at just the correct height. For the higher ones, he could use a little footstool. He turned off the bright lights and flicked on the red light. "Perfect, perfect, perfect!" No one heard his exclamations of pure joy.

He wanted to thank Fritz and John. Perhaps John was taking a nap in his own place after working with Fritz for most of the day? Jochanaan ran from room to room looking for Fritz. He wanted to thank him for the wonderful job he and John had done. He kept blabbering, "I love you Fritz and John. I love you!" He was obviously in seventh heaven. Rachel and Elsa were with patients and couldn't hear him.

Suddenly, Jochanaan began to panic. He wondered if Fritz left without saying good-bye. Perhaps something happened to Fritz? The door to his mother's bathroom was closed. He didn't think to knock. He was afraid what he might see once he opened the door. He had turned as white as a sheet. He ripped open the door. There was Fritz standing and relieving himself. "Can't I even take a leak in peace and quiet?"

"Sorry, Fritz. I looked for you everywhere. I was scared when I saw the door closed. I thought something had happened to you. Thank you for my wonderful dark room. I checked it out; everything is perfect. I can't wait to get working in it. Are you staying for a while to help me get started?"

Fritz walked to the sink and washed his hands. He pulled Jochanaan close to him. "Yes, I'll stay for a couple more days. I want you to get started in your lab. I also might want to help Miriam with moving whatever she wants to take to Melissa's apartment. But then, I'm out of here. I need to get back east. There are a few things that need tending to. I will be back. I just don't know yet when. Just know that I love you very much."

Jochanaan looked at him with his big blue eyes, tears running down his face. "I love you too. You are the father I never had. Thank you for everything." He reached out to Fritz, wishing to be held. Fritz finally turned away from the boy. He didn't want him to see how distraught and sad he was.

Chapter 44

MIRIAM had met Melissa Holder's parents at several school functions. It was Melissa who had planted the seed encouraging Miriam to make a break with her home environment. Miriam was totally content living with her mother. While she loved Jochanaan intensely, the age difference between her and her brother was significant. Miriam had reached an age where having a nine-year-old little brother in tow was not to the liking of her contemporaries. Jochanaan had similar feelings toward his older sister. Having Miriam enter his circle of friends was viewed as being mothered. Rachel needed to move on with her own life. Miriam didn't view leaving her mother as something bad; it might give Rachel breathing room and a chance to broaden her own social life. Obviously, Aaron had not been the answer to Miriam's wishes for her mother.

Miriam made a call to the Holder house in Bredeney. Mrs. Holder answered the phone. She was delighted to hear Miriam's voice.

"Oh, hi, Miriam, lovely to hear from you. My husband and I are very pleased that you decided to share Melissa's apartment."

"Thank you, Mrs. Holder. I'm very excited about it!"

"I'm sure you are, and I know you get along well and have similar interests. You will be good company for our daughter, Miriam; she isn't at her best making new friends."

"Well, I think we'll continue to be great friends!" replied Miriam.

"Indeed, I hope so. You'll find the neighborhood very quiet and pleasant, and we had the apartment completely modernized just a year ago."

"It sounds great, and again, thank you so much."

"You're welcome my dear, but you no doubt wish to speak with Melissa and not have me going on! I'll get her for you, and it's been good talking with you, Miriam. I'm looking forward to having you here."

"Thanks, Mrs. Holder." Miriam waited a few moments before Melissa came on the line.

"Hi, Miriam. Have you decided when to make the big move?"

"How about in the next couple of days? My mother's friend, Fritz Unrat, is still here. He came for the graduation. I'm sure he would love to give me a hand in getting settled before he takes off for the East Zone."

"That shouldn't be too difficult. Aren't you planning to just bring mostly your clothes and your writing stuff?"

"Right. That's all I had decided to take. There's quite a bit of storage at my mother's place. And besides that, I'll always have my room waiting for me there."

"Whatever you do, don't bring any furniture. There's plenty of it here. We might even want to get rid of some of my pieces. I had little input regarding the selection of the furnishings of the apartment. It was mostly my mother's doing. But it's OK; I'm sure you'll agree. Why don't you plan on dropping your things off tomorrow after three o'clock? I should be back from my job interview."

"Where are you applying for a job, if I may ask?"

"They were looking for a junior secretary at the Handelshof. I figured with my shorthand and typing skills, I might land the job. It could be a great way of meeting some interesting people. All sorts of celebrities stay at that hotel. It's also easy to get to. I like the central location. It's a straight shot down there on the number three tram."

"That's wonderful. I put in an application at Josef Bloom's Department Store. You know me and silk; it's in my genes. I'm meeting with personnel on Thursday. Wish me luck. Same back to you. See you tomorrow at three."

Miriam replaced the receiver. "Mom, I just got off the phone with Melissa. She's having a job interview in the morning but wants me to drop off my things after three o'clock. You think that's OK with Fritz? He offered to help."

"You realize I'll have to come along. He doesn't want to drive in the city."

"I don't mind. That way you'll know where I'll be living. Would you help me with picking out what I should take? I'd really appreciate it. Besides, it'll give us a chance to talk."

"I'd love to help. I'll be right there. Get started."

Rachel went looking for Fritz. He was sitting in the parlor reading the paper. "Sorry to bother you. I saw the paper drooping to the floor. You look like you were ready to take a nap. I'm on a mission for Miriam. "Would you mind getting two or three suitcases from the storage room in the attic? I'll be in Miriam's room. She asked me to help her with packing her things to take over to Melissa's house tomorrow."

"I'll be happy to do it."

"Thanks, Fritz."

She walked into Miriam's room and saw all sorts of clothes piled on the bed. "If it was me, I wouldn't bother to take any of the winter clothes. They certainly wouldn't be in anyone's way in your wardrobe. I don't know how much room there is at Melissa's place. Have you seen it?"

"That's a brilliant suggestion. No, I haven't seen the apartment yet. Leaving my winter clothes and boots here would be a big help."

Fritz appeared in the door. "Oh, thanks, Fritz, for getting my suitcases. This will make things a lot easier for me. You are a big help. I appreciate your willingness to move my stuff."

Miriam looked around her room. "I do want to take my typewriter. You know me, how I hate writing by hand. It just takes so much longer."

Rachel couldn't help commenting. "I'm glad you are just taking clothes and a few personal things. That will make it really easy. There isn't that much room in that cabriolet." An hour later they were packed.

The next afternoon, Rachel drove to Bredeney. Rachel was glad she had convinced Miriam not to take all of her clothes; they barely managed to get everything in the small car. As they arrived Rachel couldn't help commenting. "I like the location of the house. The neighborhood is well preserved and obviously was largely spared by the war." Mrs. Holder greeted them. Melissa's father was running errands.

"Hallo, Dr. von Graben and Herr Unrat. How nice to see you again. Wasn't the graduation a lovely event? We thought Mother Superior did a splendid job of saying farewell to our girls. Please come in. Let me take you upstairs."

Fritz and Rachel were slightly out of breath when they reached the top floor of the house. Frau Holder opened Melissa's apartment and let them step in. "Oh, what a lovely sunny place," said Rachel. Fritz concurred.

Frau Holder walked in and pointed to the bedroom. "I think between the two large wardrobes the girls will have no difficulty keeping their shared quarters neat. If they find the living room too crowded, we can always store some of the small tables in our cellar."

Miriam and Melissa had noticed how Fritz and Rachel were huffing and puffing walking up to the third floor of the house, so they took charge of carrying the suitcases upstairs. An hour later most of Miriam's things had found a place in Melissa's apartment.

She looked at Fritz who had carried up the typewriter. "Are you feeling OK? You are as white as a ghost."

"I'm fine. I'm just not used to walking as many steps as there are in this house. I'm glad it's you and Melissa who will have the daily exercise routine and not me."

They walked downstairs. Rachel thanked Frau Holder for allowing Miriam to share the apartment with Melissa. "That is very kind of you."

Rachel still had many questions about the arrangement but did not want to say anything in front of Melissa's mother. She shook Mrs. Holder's hand. "Good-bye for now. I look forward to having you visit my home in the near future."

"The pleasure is ours. We look forward to having both girls under our roof. They seem to enjoy each other's company. Really nice to see you again. Come any time if you are in the neighborhood." Miriam thanked Mrs. Holder as well. "I'll join Melissa tomorrow night. I would like to spend the evening with my mother and Herr Unrat since he is leaving us soon. Good-bye, for now."

They made the return trip to Breslauerstrasse essentially in silence. Miriam wasn't quite sure what was bothering her mother. As soon as they walked into Rachel's apartment, Miriam suggested they sit down together and have a glass of wine. They needed to relax a bit after all the excitement during the last few days. Fritz poured Rachel a glass of her favorite red wine and an apple fizz for Miriam. He got himself a brew from the fridge.

Rachel became pensive. She still had not completely accepted the fact that Miriam was leaving. "Do you need any money? I know you've saved up quite a lot from your pocket money and gifts people gave you. Have you agreed with Melissa as to how much you want to pay her for staying at her parents' home?"

"Mother, I'm paying Melissa's folks fifty marks a month. That's pretty cheap rent. It will pay for some of the utilities. That's all they expect. Frau Holder is thrilled to have me stay with Melissa. You know she's very shy. Her mother is hoping that I'll have a good influence on her. The two of us get along just fine; we are polar opposites. Karl is good for her too. I'm so glad both he and Lance love to dance. We do have a lot of fun when we go out together."

Miriam could tell her mother was still in a funk. "What's the matter, Mother? Just think, I could be heading on a plane to Tel Aviv. Isn't this a lot better?" Rachel just nodded in agreement; she had a hard time separating herself from the child that had grown into a beautiful young woman. In her heart, she mourned the lost years but treasured the last ten that had brought them together.

"Mutti, snap out of it. It upsets me when you look like you have lost your last best friend. Let's change the subject. What gives with you two?"

Rachel thought she wasn't hearing correctly. "Why did you have to bring up my relationship to Fritz? I have told you before, I am not interested in getting married again. I believe I have made myself perfectly clear on the subject. It's not that I do not like Fritz; I'm just not in love with him." She walked out of the room and was seething with anger. Rachel wished Miriam wasn't so gosh darn blunt.

Fritz was left speechless. At last he spoke. "Guess you got your answer, Miriam. I'll be leaving in a couple of days, as soon as I've got your brother started in his dark room. I was so happy to do that for my dear boy. He's very special to me. He's the kid or grandson I never had. I loved my daughter, but I always wanted to have a boy. Jochanaan has filled that void. And he knows it. He has told me as much." Fritz had tears in his eyes. Miriam reached out to him. "I want you to know I love you very much. I'm at my wit's end with my dear mother."

Fritz was on the train east two days later. He took Rachel's latest pronouncement to heart. As much as he loved her, he was ready to give up on her. Just for a moment, he actually began to dislike her.

Chapter 45

MIRIAM was grateful for the friendship with Melissa and her parents. They had all gotten to know each other at a number of events at school. It didn't take Miriam very long to like her new digs. The two girls got along famously. When Melissa and she were finally alone, Melissa spoke up. "I'm interested in taking some night classes. What about you, Miriam? How would you feel about taking a class in modern dance?"

"That intrigues me," replied Miriam. "Let's check it out. Also, I've gotten that job I applied for in the silk department at Josef Bloom's Department Store. I liked the buyer, Fräulein Salm. I wonder if she's related to us? She has Salm in her name. Strange!"

X

Miriam loved her job working with silks. She could spend hours just running her hands through the delectable fabric. As soon as she had a chance to save some money, she planned to buy beautiful floral silks and have a seamstress design a couple of dresses for her. Miriam was the new star in the silk department.

She and Melissa enjoyed the dance classes. Toward the end of their first course in modern dance, the teacher introduced Miriam to a friend, Harley Andreas. Miriam looked him up and down. He was wearing an expensive suit and tie. His shoes were highly polished. His hair was dark with graying temples. Harley had steely and mesmerizing eyes. He sported a dark mustache, which was neatly trimmed. He was of average height. Miriam was tempted to ask him how old he was. By the looks of the graying temples and lines around his eyes, she thought he might be in his mid forties. Harley Andreas operated nightclubs in the inner city as well as in Rüttenscheid.

Mr. Andreas had his eye on Miriam. "Young lady, you have a talent for dancing. How would you like a real job in the evening? You could make a lot of money with those gorgeous legs. As a matter of fact, the whole package is gorgeous. If you work for me, I'll pay you one hundred marks for each performance. You'd be worth every mark."

Miriam's jaw dropped. That was an unheard amount to be paid for dancing or any job she might have landed in 1955. "He must be making money hand over fist," whispered Miriam.

"Think about my offer. I'll stop by to speak with Frankie, your teacher, in a couple of days. There are other good students but none like you. I really would like you to be in my lineup. I can just hear it. 'Here is the Gypsy Rose Lee of Essen.' The guys will fall over you."

"Would you mind telling me who this Gypsy Rose Lee is? I've never heard that name."

"She was the queen of burlesque in the United States for many years. As a matter of fact, she's still dancing today. I saw her when I was visiting New York years ago. She was a real class act. Gypsy could tease and excite but never revealed anything she didn't want to be seen by leering men. She was the goddess of ostrich feathers and fans."

When she walked with Melissa to the tram, she confessed. "That job and that Gypsy Rose Lee thing sounds pretty exciting. Would you be upset if I tried for it?"

"I wouldn't; I wish he'd asked us to appear as a duo. What we need to watch out for are my parents. They are not exactly avant garde. You might negotiate with Mr. Andreas for a limited engagement. Instead of dancing in his club every night, ask for Thursday through Saturday nights. What do you have to lose by asking? If he really wants you, he might agree to it. Those are the nights that we usually go out anyway. Coming home late at night wouldn't be anything new."

"That's a great idea. I'll talk to Mr. Andreas about it when he shows up. Making three hundred marks in three nights isn't such a bad deal."

The next night Harley Andreas reappeared. He walked up to Miriam and stood right in front of her. He laid his right hand around her left hip—too low for dancing, she thought. Miriam felt he was a bit too close for comfort. "Well, my dear, what's your decision?" He thought he had a malleable young thing in his trusted hands.

"The job appeals to me. My problem is I couldn't do it seven nights a week. I would be willing to fake this Gypsy Rose Lee thing Thursday through Saturday nights in the eight o'clock spot. If that is acceptable to you, I'm in."

He thought for a moment. He was ready to reject her proposal. His inner voice told him he was making a big mistake. "Miriam, you got yourself a deal. How about starting two weeks from Saturday night? That will give you time to work up a routine. Our choreographer will be able to give you some hints. What you have are the basics and a gorgeous body. The house in Rüttenscheid is usually packed on Saturday evenings. I'd like you to meet me after work on Friday at the club. I'll introduce you to the other performers and the staff. You may want to check out the props you'd be using during your appearances. Thanks for giving me a whirl."

As asked by Harley, she ventured out on her own and went to the place on Friday night right after store closing. The bartenders and the other "entertainers" were considerably older than she. Miriam thought she could handle it. The fans and ostrich feathers looked a bit shabby. "If you want me to act like this fancy lady, you better invest in some new and clean props. I wouldn't hide behind those shop-worn things for all the tea in China," Miriam advised Harley, who realized he hadn't hired a dummy.

"You'll have all new feathers and fans by the time you start working for me. Here are some records for you to listen to. They'll give you an idea what the music you dance to will be like."

Melissa and she listened to the records. It was pretty bumpy music. They did like the beat. For the next two weeks, they worked on Miriam's act. It got better with every performance. "Can you imagine me stepping out on stage stark naked with nothing but twirling fans and ostrich feathers?"

They hit their stride, keeping the bumpy music low. "My parents won't hear a thing. They've gone to bed long ago. My dad snores terribly. It's a great masker. My mother doesn't hear too well. So, go for it. Let's see what you can do, Gypsy Nose Lee."

"It's Gypsy *Rose* Lee. She doesn't do it with her nose but with her legs and her hips. And a big smile. Harley showed me photos of her. She's quite beautiful. She's in her forties by now and still very attractive. I wish I could see her do it in person or have her as my teacher. Too bad she is so far away."

They had worked every night for the last ten evenings. Melissa had been watching every practice session. "You've come a long way, Miriam. You are quite convincing with your props. I love the quickness in your performance. It's almost like watching a juggler or a magician. You'll be absolutely great when you step out on that stage. I'm jealous. Those guys are gonna go crazy. I just know it."

Melissa rode with Miriam to the nightclub. "Relax, relax, relax— and have fun. You know the routine well. Our practice sessions will pay off!" With that she gave Miriam a gentle push out of the cab.

Miriam Daniella's appearance was at eight o'clock. The place was packed. She was assigned her own dressing room. She didn't feel right about undressing completely in front of total strangers. "What about dancing naked in front of a bunch of howling men? After all, I was raised in a convent," thought Miriam as she was getting ready for her first performance. She had bathed, creamed, and powdered every body part that might be revealed to her rowdy audience. A touch of Chanel No. 5 and she felt ready.

There was a hefty knock on her dressing room door. She was being paged by her stage name. "Miss Leander, they are ready for you. Come on. We only summon you once to the stage." She stepped out hesitantly, with a huge fan covering her breasts. Ostrich feathers flirted in front of her. When she twirled, the feathers would shield her derrière. That could work for her. The bumpy music was blaring as she stepped on the stage; that is, she just peeked out from behind the curtain right of center stage. She gave them a big smile. The audience of mostly men yelled, "More, show us more!" Miriam kept smiling while projecting her beautiful gams one at a time, teasing her baudy audience.

They went silent at first as she twirled onto the stage, never revealing any more than her stunning legs, beautiful face, gorgeous hair, and smooth shoulders. She was a class act, just like Gypsy Rose Lee. As she exited the stage on the left, she pulled the curtain around herself and blew them kisses. The crowd went wild. Harley Andreas knew he had discovered a winner.

He was waiting for her off stage. He enfolded her in his arms. He was ready to let her have a taste of his body. She took one look at him. Miriam had never seen a man's penis before. She kneed him with vigor. He found himself rolling on the floor. He stuck his right fist in his mouth stifling his screams as he grabbed his insulted dick with his left. "I opted for the Gypsy Rose Lee thing; I hadn't bargained to be raped by you, even if you offered me two hundred marks per performance. Do you get my message?" She stepped over his shaking body and walked to her dressing room, holding her head high. She might have been raised in a convent; she wasn't born yesterday.

Melissa had opted not to attend Miriam's first performance. She wanted Miriam to feel totally at ease and believing she was only performing for a bunch of horny strange men. When she got home, it was after ten o'clock. Melissa had waited up for her. "How did it go? Were you nervous? Did the guys go wild? I was glad you opted for that stage name. No one would recognize you by the name Leander."

"That's why I did it. I was glad Harley didn't alert the press to his new attraction. Can you imagine my mother seeing me in that outfit in the press? Can you even call it an outfit? It's an outfit in absentia. Melissa, we did it. If we hadn't practiced that routine as often as we did, I would have exposed my whole body and probably tripped all over my props. It went just as smoothly last night as it did in practice. I really did feel at ease. And you know what? I loved doing it. I had Gypsy doing it in my vivid imagination; she always was just one step ahead of me with her routine."

"I'd like to come to the show next Saturday. I'll just stand in the back and have a glass of wine. I wouldn't want to sit among all those ribald men. You know how I would handle that kind of scenario. Would you mind?"

"Of course not. Remember, you were the one who got us into the dance class to begin with. You are my personal choreographer and have every right to watch my act. I'll make sure you won't have to pay the admission fee. I can see how Harley can afford to pay me one hundred marks a night. He's hauling in the dough big time. I'm his star attraction; that is, in more ways than one. He tried to seduce me as I came off stage. I gave him a good taste of my right knee; he's probably still soaking his Glockenspiel in cooling waters."

"I'm proud of you, Miriam. Aren't you glad we took that class?"

Miriam's wheels were turning. "Under no circumstances do I want my mother, her friends, and certainly not your parents to know about this little night show. I'll open up a savings account under my stage name. No one will be the wiser, unless I get screwed up by the press. I hope and pray that won't happen. I need to get some sleep. I'm so glad I'm only doing this on three nights. I'm worth three hundred marks for three performances. I pull in thousands on the nights I'm there. And he better not have any more surprises for me backstage." Miriam jumped into the shower and then hit the sheets. She was in dreamland within seconds. She saw Gypsy Rose Lee being applauded after a stunning performance; she didn't want the dream to end.

Rachel telephoned after breakfast on Sunday morning. It would become a routine. "How was your first week with Fräulein Salm? I have no idea who she is. I've never heard of her before. It's quite possible that we are distantly related. Is she a nice-looking woman?"

"Mother, she must be some relative. When I look at her, I picture you in your seventies, perhaps midseventies. Her hair is clearly dyed. It's a good dye job, and she wears it just like you and I, swept up in a stylish chignon. She is quite stately and completely in control of every situation. She has these beautiful high cheek bones and piercing dark eyes. I would call her extremely attractive. She must have been stunning in her younger days. I like the job. It's wonderful being in touch with all the different silks. When I get my first paycheck, I'll buy enough yardage for a dress. I'll have that seamstress of yours make me a new outfit. I want it to be something that will show off the amulet."

"That's a wonderful idea. How would you feel about meeting me for lunch next Wednesday? I love having a free day in the middle of the week. How about noon at the Weinstuben? It's practically across the street from the Josef Bloom Department Store."

"Love to, Mutti. It will be great catching up on things. I can't believe I haven't seen you in a month. I want to hear all about Jochanaan and what's new in your and his life. Talk to you later. See you Wednesday at noon. I miss you!"

Miriam confided in Melissa. "Mom wants to have lunch with me on Wednesday. I hope none of the waiters at the Weinstuben stray into the nightclub. Wouldn't that be the pits if someone would recognize me in public? Oh God, what would I do, Melissa?"

"That is a distinct possibility. Let's just wait and see and not lose any sleep over it. If worse comes to worse, you have to own up to what you are doing and enjoying. At least you are not working as a hooker. I can't imagine what Mother Superior would think."

Miriam confessed, "She'd be absolutely shocked. Although, I always told her I could never make it as a nun. I just wasn't cut out for that calling."

When Miriam walked into the Weinstuben, the headwaiter recognized her. Not from the nightclub but from having danced there on several occasions with her friends. "I believe your mother is waiting for you. You look so much like the lady I just seated. She told me she was waiting for her daughter. Your resemblance is striking. Let me help you with your chair." Miriam hugged her mother quickly and gave her a friendly kiss. The headwaiter kept holding her chair until she was seated. "He thought we looked a lot alike. We've gotten that often lately. Must have something to do with the way we wear our hair. We do have that Salm look about us."

The waiter came and took their orders. Soon they were alone again. "I like the new dress you are wearing, Mom. Is it something you had tailored for you?"

"Yes. I saw the fabric in Wenzel's window and bought it. My seamstress suggested the pattern. I think it turned out well. Now I just have to find excuses for wearing it. And don't come up with another date for me. I'm tired of being checked out like a prized show horse at an auction."

"Sorry, Mom. I thought I was acting in your best interest. I won't try to match make again. Hopefully, one of these days you'll see the light at the end of this very long and dark tunnel of celibacy. You are too young to be living alone."

"Let's enjoy this food; it looks delectable. It smells divine. Glad you could join me. Let's do this more often. How's Melissa's job going at the Handelshof?"

"Mom, you are changing the subject!"

"Did I now? But tell me about Melissa."

"She adores the man with whom she works. Melissa loves all the celebrities who stay at the place. It's a fun job from what she tells me. And, before you ask, we are getting along just fine. The apartment is very comfortable. We are still enjoying our dancing, but we are doing it now on Sunday nights. Lance got a nighttime job during the week." She looked in a heavenly direction a la Mother Superior and mouthed an aside, "Holy Mother, forgive my blatant fib."

Rachel hugged her daughter before she got into her car. "Let's do this again. I loved being with you and hearing of all your adventures." Miriam couldn't help wondering what her mother might think were she to discover her sideline.

Chapter 46

RACHEL'S days were filled with her work in the practice. Elsa and she had found their profession to be rewarding. Jochanaan loved school and enjoyed most of the subjects. His early adventures into the sciences weren't particularly exciting, although he did like math. His favorites were music and all the visual arts. He couldn't wait for weekends, when he spent all hours in his dark room. His cameras went with him everywhere. Often, he even snuck one into his backpack for school. As young a photographer as he was, some of his teachers recognized his talent and encouraged him to go further.

While she phoned Miriam every Sunday morning, Rachel liked speaking with Fritz most Sunday evenings. She hesitated asking him how he enjoyed his weekends. She knew that there was little joy in his life. He liked hearing what Jochanaan and Miriam were doing.

His phone rang, and he rushed, knowing it would be Rachel. "I was pretty certain it would be you. No one else calls me on Sunday nights. What's new in your life?" was his opening question.

"I saw Miriam for lunch on Wednesday. She still likes that job at the silk store. My son I hardly see other than at the dinner table. He does enjoy eating with me. We don't talk a lot. The exception is when Elsa joins us for a meal. Then he makes polite table talk. When he isn't doing his homework, I can always find him in the dark room. You couldn't have done anything more pleasing for him. What did you do today? Is there anything exciting happening in your life?"

"I'm not sure if I would call it exciting. I spent most of the day weeding my vegetable garden. It was high time! It's a backbreaking job for me these days. The old bones aren't what they used to be."

"Have you talked to your doctor about that shortness of breath you experienced when you climbed those steps at Melissa's apartment? I know I was puffing too, but nothing like you did. That loss of color in your face scared both Miriam and me."

"As a matter of fact, I did since it concerned me as well. Dr. Haas gave me a thorough checkup and told me not to worry about a thing. He did suggest that I do something for my health every day. He has me walking six kilometers every morning. He wants me to work toward doing it in less than thirty minutes. I've gotten started and am beginning to enjoy my morning walks. I like being out in the fresh air. Just wish I had someone doing it with me. I might even consider getting myself a dog."

"That's a really good idea. I'm happy to learn that you are doing something other than sitting in the house and moping. I need to get involved and doing some form of exercise myself. I'm getting varicose veins on my legs. Probably from all that standing. I had dinner with one of my patients last week. He was a nice enough man, but just like the other dates, I had nothing in common with him. Miriam keeps pushing me, but I just cannot bring myself to a serious relationship with any man."

"I'm sorry to hear that. I'm still hoping you'll change your mind someday. I would like to be part of your and the children's lives. I better hang up before I start complaining about my life and crying on your shoulder. Let me say good night. Sleep well." He hung up before she could say another word.

Chapter 47

MIRIAM held her day and night jobs for three years. She loved working in Fräulein Salm's Department of Silks. But she had gained fame and notoriety as a dancer in Harley Andreas's nightclub. She was fortunate that almost exclusively young males were her greatest admirers. No one she knew, other than Melissa, was aware of her nightclub act and her dalliances for which she was generously rewarded. Not only was she well paid by Harley, but eventually many of the attending men sent paper airplanes made from hundred-mark bills in her direction. Some of her admirers tried meeting her at the stage door, perhaps hoping to collect some sort of a reward for their generous ovations. She never became entangled with any patrons of the nightclub and would rush off into the night.

Miriam became skilled at picking up the enticements during her routine, never skipping a beat. She only revealed what she found respectable. Harley didn't make another attempt at seducing her after her dancing. He learned his lesson well. She locked her dressing room while changing; the other dancers had warned her, not that she needed further warnings about that bastard.

On a Thursday night during her last month at the club, a young man waited for her by the stage door. He flashed her a big smile. "Hi! I'm Josh Bernstein. I love what you are doing. You do it in such good taste. I was sorry to learn that you are leaving in a couple of weeks. Has the engagement run its course?"

She looked at him with open eyes and thought, "Not another one of those reward seekers." She stared at him before she finally answered his question. "No, it was my decision. I believe I'm ready to continue my education. I always was a good student. My work here has allowed me to save a bit of money. I'm ready to investigate universities that feature my disciplines of interest." When she stopped speaking, she thought, "Why am I telling this guy all that I revealed about myself? He's a total stranger."

Josh Bernstein saw an opening. "Without appearing nosy, which disciplines might that be? I'm a student myself. I study at LMU in Munich. I'm a freshman."

Against her better judgment, she responded, "I'm interested in philosophy, logic, and languages. I know, those are very diverse fields of study." Somehow this guy was different and getting to her. She could be a very cool customer, especially after her encounter with Harley Andreas.

"That's interesting. I'm pursuing philosophy and languages. Logic isn't my thing. You want to share a glass of wine and talk? I would love to know more about you, Miss Leander."

"I'm sure you would, but I'm not certain whether I'm interested in prolonging this chat." She could tell she had totally deflated his trial balloon but realized immediately he was different from Lance. Lance was fun to dance with but lacked totally in ambition. He was doing odd jobs for his very wealthy father, who owned a Mercedes dealership. Lance liked showing up in some snazzy little number trying to impress her with his latest toy. He had little to talk about. She was ready to dump him.

The Weintraube was an intimate little café not far from the Kasanova. They found a quiet table for two in the back. "Which do you prefer, red or white wine?"

"I'd rather not have any wine. A glass of cold lemonade would suit me just fine. If they don't serve lemonade, ask the waiter to bring me apple juice with a dash of soda water. I'm always really thirsty after dancing in that smoky den of iniquities."

"I hear you. I understand why you are thirsty. That place does get pretty smoky with all those guys puffing away on their cigarettes and cigars. And I certainly wasn't trying to get you drunk. All I want to do is talk. Can't really do that in the place where you work."

Miriam listened closely to his spiel. "Actually, I don't work there. I just entertain three times a week for a few fleeting moments. I love putting on my little act and enjoy the applause. I have a full-time day job."

Josh was all ears. "I will say this; you fooled a lot of guys with that act of yours. Most of them would not believe what you just told me. Have you considered studying acting? I believe you would do really well."

"I'm not acting. I'm telling you the truth, although I don't know why I do. I've just met you and know very little about you other than what you like to study at that fancy university in Munich. Are you Jewish?"

"Yes, I was raised in the Jewish faith. My parents are not orthodox but keep to certain traditions."

"I'm half Jewish. My mother came from a family of successful business people. Today, she is a prominent dental surgeon and operates a dental practice here in Essen. Most of my family were murdered by the Nazis. My father was killed in the waning months of the war."

Josh wanted to know more. "Where do you live? Where did you grow up? Why are you dancing in the club?"

"Boy, you are full of questions. I don't know if I want to tell you my life history. Isn't that a bit much to ask after meeting me less than an hour ago?"

"Sorry, I was just curious."

There was something about the encounter she found refreshing. She liked talking with him. She didn't know why. "I was raised by Catholic nuns and attended Catholic school until completion of my Abitur. I left the cloister school three years ago. I live now with one of my classmates. Melissa and I became good friends. We are sharing an apartment in her parents' house. During the week, I sell silks at a department store in the inner city. I only perform at the club Thursday through Saturday at the eight o'clock show.

"My dance routine was Harley Andreas's idea; he's the owner of the nightclub. He met me where Melissa and I were studying modern dance. He came up with that Gypsy Rose Lee approach to my dance routine. I had never heard of her before I met him. It suited me just fine. I couldn't have done what some of the other dancers do. I'm not that free with my body. I learned to love what I did; I did it with class. Harley Andreas was a real prick. He tried having me the first day we met. When he welcomed me after my perfor-mance the first night, he greeted me off-stage with his dick aimed at me. I kneed him so hard, he never touched me again. The word got around. I haven't really dated other men. I have a sort-of steady boy-friend. We were friends since our high school days. We love to dance. The liaison has run its course. If you are interested in an easy lay, you picked the wrong girl. I have no interest in getting screwed. I'm looking for a serious relationship. Tell me something about yourself. I've been fully revealing myself to you in more ways than one. What makes you tick, Mr. Bernstein?"

"My mother came from a wealthy family in the banking business. My father studied medicine and became a well-known surgeon. I was born in Munich in 1935. My parents were smart enough to see the writing on those ugly Munich walls. They got the hell out of Germany in 1938. They escaped with some of their money to Casablanca. Eventually, they wound up in Switzerland, where they remained throughout the war. All of us survived. My family again lives in Munich. My father teaches at LMU. My mother is living a life of luxury. She is the ultimate social butterfly. From her I inherited my love for classical music, especially opera. We have season tickets for the Bayerische Staatsoper. I want to be a university professor teaching philosophy. My linguistic interests are French and Italian. I love playing the piano. That just about does it. Did I answer all your questions correctly, Fräulein Leander?"

"Don't be such a smartass. Am I supposed to be impressed with your litany of familial facts? By the way, stop calling me Fräulein Leander. That's my stage name. My name is Miriam Daniella Salm von Graben. Got that, buster? I'm not about to genuflect just because you're a couple years older than I. And I prefer to be called Miriam. This whole seduction scene has been lovely, but I've had a full day on my feet and want to get home. Let's call it a night. I wouldn't mind talking to you again."

Josh got off his duff and helped Miriam get out of her chair and into her jacket. "May I accompany you on your way home?"

"You've got to be kidding. Why would I want you to do that? I don't need a man to see me home. If you haven't learned anything from what I alluded to relative to my experiences with my boss, the nightclub owner, then let me set you straight. I don't need you or any guy to protect me. I can handle myself perfectly fine. Thanks for the drink. I enjoyed talking to you—most of the time. Give me a knock on my dressing room door if you care to see me again."

Miriam ran out of the café with a flourish; she practically jumped on the last coach of the number three tram as it was pulling away from the curb. Josh's feet were anchored to the floor of the café. Stunned, he just stood there with his mouth wide open as his eyes followed Miriam. All he could say was, "I'll be damned!"

Chapter 48

THE following Thursday, Miriam walked off the stage and headed straight for her dressing room. As usual, she locked the door tightly. She was in the process of removing her stage makeup when she detected a harmless knock on her door. "Who is it?"

"It's me." She didn't recognize the voice.

"Who the hell is me? Don't you have a name? Preferably one I know? I don't open this door for just any yokel."

"Sorry, it's Josh Bernstein. We talked last Saturday after your breathtaking performance."

She got off her stool still wearing cold cream all over her face and cracked the door open. She looked into his eyes. He acted like he was pleased to see her. He carried a single, long-stemmed red rose in his left hand. He stuck out his right, wanting to greet her in typical German fashion. Miriam backed away from Josh. "So what's this all about? Are you trying a different kind of seduction scene? I would've thought you got the hint last week."

"OK, Miss von Graben. I thought you might like my floral peace offering after you took off rather abruptly last Saturday night. You are mean. Did I treat you that badly last week? I realize you have every right to be gunshy of men."

"I'm not scared of men. I've just learned to be cautious. I don't like to be rushed into relationships."

He moved closer to Miriam. His hand was shaking as he tried handing her the rose. Reluctantly, she snatched it from his hand. She walked back to her makeup table. There was a smirk on her face when she tossed his rose on her dressing table. The bloom looked like it had broken off. Miriam grabbed a washcloth and wiped the ugly white cream off her face. She looked in the mirror and reached for her powder puff. She dusted her face lightly. Last, she applied just a touch of rouge and lipstick. She looked stunning.

"Turn around while I slip into something more suitable for stepping out. I'm not used to having an audience when I come offstage. I fear rear or frontal attacks. Harley did that to me three years ago. I never forgot. I'm always on my guard when I deal with strange men. Don't take it personally. So what's with the flower?"

Josh finally had enough courage to respond. "In spite of everything you said and did on Saturday, I thought you liked me. I wanted to see you again and continue our conversation at the Weintraube. You, yourself, suggested another get-together. Why are you treating me like shit? Didn't you like the little café? Was it not fancy enough for your sophisticated taste? I liked the intimate setting."

"Come, come now. Do I strike you as a snob? There is nothing wrong with the little café. I just felt you were too damn nosy. I don't know what possessed me to share as much of my life with you as I did during our first encounter."

"Can we start all over again? I really like you, Miriam. I'm not a snot-nosed kid. Treat me like a man, who is very much smitten with you. You probably will think me to be a total jerk; I was going to get down on bended knee and ask you to marry me already when we first met."

"You are not a jerk, but you are out of your mind. I've heard of fast work before, but this is just a bit too fast for my taste. You are a student. How the hell do you expect to support a wife and perhaps even a mother and child, were I to become pregnant right away? Stranger things than that happen all the time. Get real. You can't marry me. I wouldn't be one of those wives who expects to be kept in a certain style to which she became accustomed. Nevertheless, we wouldn't have a pot to piss in. I couldn't live that way. We'd be at each other's throats from day one."

"Can we get out of here? I want to talk some sense into you. What kind of a *shmok* do you believe I am? I wouldn't ask you to marry me if I were just a poor student. Before I go on, let me buy you a glass of wine at the Weintraube." He reached for her hand and helped her into her jacket.

"Save your money buying wine. I'm not too keen on alcohol. Didn't you listen? I told you, I prefer lemonade or apple juice."

They walked over to the table where they sat before. "Lemonade it is. I'll try it myself. On second thought, I'll have a brew. So, why the cold shoulder? Why are you treating me like the scum of the earth?"

She grinned at him. "Just testing your mettle. I thought you were a bit cocky cornering me that way as I was leaving the nightclub. That was pretty gutsy. I'm glad you showed some backbone and didn't just piss in your pants. That's exactly what you looked like standing in my dressing room shifting from one leg to the other while I was letting you have it."

"You were a mean bitch but still a very beautiful one at that. I forgive you this once. And you were right; I almost did wet my pants. Speaking of which, excuse me, but I do have to use the men's room."

She looked up and winked at him. "Don't take too long."

When he returned to the table, Josh decided to set Miriam straight. "Miriam, I'm an only and very-much-indulged son. I hate sounding like a bragger. My tuition and board at LMU are free. My father has a substantial income, and my mother is well off in her own right. I have a pretty healthy monthly income from a trust my maternal grandparents established for me six years ago. The money is well invested and grows every year. There are no financial concerns were you to consider marrying me. Does that make me sound less jerky?"

"I still believe you are moving too fast. We need to know more about each other—our likes and dislikes, our aspirations in life. Who wants to have children and who doesn't. How many children might I want, and what about you? Only children often don't want any kids themselves. They are so used to indulgence. Were we to get married, would we get married in a church or in temple? Remember, I was raised and educated by Catholic nuns. Doesn't that bother you being a Jew?"

"Boy, you really can put on the squeeze. I have no problem discussing with you all that concerns you. They are all sound points. Right now, all I want to tell you is that I love you. I fell in love with you the first time you stepped on that stage. It wasn't your well-disguised and hidden body parts that caught my eye but the glowing smile on your beautiful face. I fell in love with the elegant lady who gracefully captured the imaginations of hundreds of men in that auditorium. I could see right through that wonderful act you presented."

"You know how to lay it on really thick. But I like it. I'm beginning to feel flattered. No, that's not what I wanted to say. I believe you are being sincere. How would you expect this whole scenario to play out were I of a mind to accept your proposal of marriage? Why are you in Essen frequenting nightclubs and dance halls when you are telling me you are a student at LMU?"

"My favorite uncle and aunt live here. They have always doted on me. They are kind of like second parents to me. I believe Christians call them godparents. I need to get back to my studies in Munich. Semester break is almost over. I presume you have a phone in your apartment. May I have the number and call you tomorrow afternoon? By then, you will have had time to think about all this, whatever all this is!"

She wrote down Melissa's phone number. "Just walk me to the tram station. It's only a block from here. There is no need for you to waste your money on an extra tram ride. That's silly. I'm used to riding that thing late at night. I feel perfectly safe. Give me a quick kiss and call it a night. I loved our talk."

"Talk is cheap. Not so fast, young lady. I don't give a rat's ass about spending a couple of marks on a tram ride. As long as you have me around, I won't have you ride home alone. You think you are safe? You have no idea what goes on in the shadows of night. With the kind of money Harley pays you, you should take a cab home. It sure would make me feel a lot better knowing that you are not endangering yourself. The other evening, you got away from me just a bit too fast. I would have told you then what I think of you riding the tram alone at night."

"Looks like I have found myself a father protector. Let's blow this pop stand. I need to get some rest. Tomorrow is Friday. I'm working at the store from nine to five. I'll be in feathers and fans parading across Harley's stage at eight o'clock. Pretty busy schedule. But I'm young, and I love what I'm doing."

They didn't wait long for the tram. He followed her onto the platform. No one else but the conductor was on the streetcar. Josh didn't care what the guy saw or thought. He took Miriam in his arms and kissed her deeply. She almost swooned. He caught her. They both sat down. The tram stopped at Wiedfeldtstraße. He got off with her and walked her right to the front door. He held her in his arms, kissing her good-night. Josh became aroused but didn't push his luck. He remembered what she had done to Harley. He had waited for the right girl too long. No way was he going to spoil things on their second date. "I'll call you tomorrow." He whistled a familiar tune as he walked to catch the last tram back to Rüttenscheid.

Chapter 49

WHEN Miriam twirled onto the stage, she spotted Josh. She gave him a quick wink. He realized he was seen. Miriam did her usual routine to rousing applause. Most guys knew Saturday would be her last night. Harley was assured of a packed house for her final performance. He decided to surprise Miriam with an extra bonus.

Josh was standing by the stage door. He held another single red long-stemmed rose in his hand. "Here's to the star of the show. You were wonderful. I reserved the little table in the back of the Weintraube. I hope that's OK with you?"

"Of course. Love it. Thanks for your thoughtfulness. The rose is lovely. I'd use it in my last routine tomorrow night if I didn't have to hold a fan in one hand and those giant ostrich feathers in the other. I suppose holding it between my teeth might work. On second thought, I won't be able to smile clutching a rose between my teeth. It was a good thought while it lasted."

"I have another little surprise for you. I really love this Gypsy Rose Lee. She's terrific. I wish she would dance right into my bed when she retires from the stage tomorrow. I would love to teach her a few new routines. None for public consumption. Perhaps I should first ask her to make the entry to my bedroom legal by marrying me.

He reached into his pant pocket, pulled out a little red box from a jewelry store, and placed it in Miriam's hands. She popped it open. It held a gorgeous blue sapphire surrounded by diamonds. "It was my grandmother's. I've worn it most of the time on my left pinky after she gave it to me for my bar mitzvah. I had it sized for you at Deiter's." Miriam gasped. He slid the ring on her finger as he went down on bended knee. "Will you do me the honor of marrying me, Miriam Daniella Salm von Graben?"

There was a wicked twinkle in her eyes. "Should I, Josh Samuel Bernstein? Well, since you asked me so nicely, I'll accept your proposal." She pulled Josh close to her face and kissed him.

"I want you to meet my mom before you return to Munich. We should fill her in on our future plans. I don't want her to miss out on anything that concerns my life. She missed too much already. I'll call her tomorrow. I'm sure she would like us to join her for dinner on Sunday. You better get me home. I have a full day tomorrow. You will be at my last performance, right?"

"Wouldn't miss it for the world! Let me put you in a cab." He put two fingers between his teeth summoning a cab. He stuck a twenty-mark bill in the guy's hand giving him Miriam's address. Before he tucked her into the cab, he gave her a lingering kiss. "Goodnight. Sleep tight."

Josh walked back to the nightclub. He went straight for the public phone. Dr. von Rondstett's phone was listed. He dialed the number. He was nervous. How shocking should he make his request? How would Miriam's mother feel when he revealed her secrets?

The phone rang. Rachel picked it up on the second ring. She wasn't used to getting phone calls after ten o'clock at night. "Von Rondstett Dental Services. How may we help you?"

"Hello, are you Dr. von Rondstett?"

"Speaking. How may I be of service?"

"My name is Josh Bernstein. I just asked your daughter to marry me."

Rachel gulped and then sputtered. "I beg your pardon. Did you say marrying my daughter? How did you get into the picture? I've never even heard of you. My daughter doesn't keep secrets."

"I know this will come as a total surprise. Miriam and I met at the Kasanova nightclub where she has been dancing for the last three years. She is fabulous. Tomorrow night is her last performance at eight o'clock."

"Just wait a minute. My daughter isn't a dancer and certainly not one who dances in a nightclub. You must have the wrong girl. How did you get my name and my telephone number? This is all a mistake."

"No, it's all true. I'm not a scam artist. I know about her upbringing and where she went to school. You must believe me."

"What did you say your name is?"

"It's Josh Bernstein. Would you do me the honor of sitting at my front-row table tomorrow night? I want Miriam to be totally surprised. You have no idea what a star entertainer she is in this city. Who would expect it from a girl who spent most of her life in a nunnery? I would love nothing better than to ask Sister Maria-Angelika to be there as well. Of course, that would be pushing it!"

Rachel was shocked. "You are kidding me, young man. You are not talking about my daughter, Miriam. She's been working at Josef Bloom's Department Store and not at some nightclub. You must be talking about someone else." Her mind was racing. How would he have known my name or be aware of Sister Maria-Angelika? He must have met Miriam somewhere. Dancing in a nightclub? "You've got me thoroughly rattled. My God, Mother Superior would have a stroke. Mr. Bernstein, you left me speechless and breathless. Did you say you were marrying my nightclub dancing, convent-raised daughter, Miriam Daniella Salm von Graben? Is there something wrong with my ears or my brain? Did you by any chance get her pregnant?"

"Make it Josh; and no, I didn't have that pleasure yet. There is nothing wrong with your mental faculties. I'd feel the same were I in your shoes. I'm pleading with you to consider being there tomorrow night. She is planning to call you tomorrow. She wants you to meet me before I return to LMU in Munich next week. I have to be back for the start of the fall semester. I'll fill you in on the rest on Sunday. Please promise to meet me tomorrow night. Don't say anything to Miriam. I want to see the expression on her face when she recognizes us sitting together."

"I don't know if I should thank you for telling me this unbelievable story concerning my daughter. But thank you, Josh, for wanting to include me on this very special occasion in Miriam's life. As you probably know by now, I've missed too much already. Thanks again for being so thoughtful. I like you already, sight unseen. I look forward to meeting my future son-in-law. Good-night." The connection was gone. She couldn't wait to share her news. She ran up the steps to Elsa's apartment.

"Sorry to bother you at this hour. I just needed to talk to someone. I just had a phone call from a young man called Josh Bernstein. He informed me that he is marrying Miriam in the very near future. If that wasn't shocking enough, he shared with me that my Miriam has been dancing three nights a week at the Kasanova nightclub, otherwise known as a strip joint. She's been at this for the last three years. Apparently, every horny male in the region is familiar with her act. She is considered the prima donna of nightclub dancers. We are talking about my daughter who was raised and educated by Catholic nuns. I almost lost it. Are you as shocked as I am?"

There was dead silence. "I can't believe what you're telling me. But coming from you with a straight face, it must be true. I suppose it could've been worse. Just think, she might have been a hooker."

Elsa was still totally perplexed. When Rachel mentioned the name of the club where Miriam had been strutting about, Elsa became curious and concerned. "Did you say she danced at the Kasanova nightclub? You can't be serious. Do you know what kind of a place that is? Our cloister-raised girl is dancing in a strip joint? Where did Mother Superior go wrong? I thought she was working at Bloom's. Was she fibbing?"

"No, not that. That is her daytime work. She did the dancing only three nights a week. Now you have me curious as to what kind of dancing this involves. I can't imagine my girl parading stark naked in front of a bunch of horny guys. This brings up another matter. What do you think I should wear going to the Kasanova tomorrow night? Josh, my prospective son-in-law, wants me to sit with him at his front-row table and surprise Miriam with my presence. It's her last night to perform. You got any bright ideas?"

"Wear that elegant black number and your Varanasi scarf. That ought to make a good impression all around. I think you should look your best meeting Mr. Bernstein."

"Good idea, Elsa. Too bad the young man cannot be with us for the high holy days. I had planned on a special dinner for Rosh Hashanah. It's a week later this year than the year Miriam was born. The new year starts on September fourteenth, eight days after Miriam's birthday. I was wondering if I should invite Fritz? He seems to be so lost and lonely in that little nest. I might just give him a call tomorrow. Jochanaan loves Fritz; it's good for him to have some adult male modeling. Having neither a father, grandfather, or any uncles, he's just been around us women. He is such a good boy and becoming more handsome every day. He will eventually look exactly like his father. But right now I've got to concentrate on my little girl."

"Little girl? Remember, she is the star attraction in a strip joint. Would you think me to be presumptuous if I asked if I could come along tomorrow night? I would really like to see what this is all about."

"Why not? I can always tell Josh I invited you for moral support. If you don't like what you see, you can always take a cab home."

Elsa had one more comment. "One more thing. It's too late for this Sunday. But will you start thinking about replacing that chandelier in the dining room?"

"My problem is that I keep seeing the one that was there. It was our big splurge. Otto loved it. The chandelier was imported from Bohemia. It was a gorgeous piece. Whoever stole it knew it's value. Maybe I should get over my sentimentality and buy a new light fixture. And you are right; it won't happen before Sunday."

Chapter 50

IT was with some nervousness and trepidation that Josh called his mother to tell her the news. He fumbled for the coins in his pocket, and his finger trembled slightly as he dialed the number. He almost hoped she'd be out, but she answered on the second ring. After the usual small talk of how they each were, Josh took a deep breath.

"I've got some exciting news for you. I met a wonderful girl."

"Oh really?"

"Yes, Mom, and I have asked her to marry me!"

"What? I only spoke to you two weeks ago and you said nothing then."

"Well....it's been sort of a whirlwind, but we kind of fell in love at first sight. And....err....I gave her Grandma's sapphire ring last night."

"But we know nothing about her, Josh! Are you sure you're not behaving like teenagers?"

"No, Mom, absolutely not! I think you will really like Miriam."

"Well, I hope so. Where did you meet?"

Josh gulped and wondered if he should tell the real story later but then decided his mother could take it.

"You probably won't believe this either, but I met her at this nightclub. She is the star entertainer. When she dances, she wears nothing but a fan and ostrich feathers. It's absolutely amazing what she can do, but no one ever sees anything!"

"I give up! I can't wait to meet her. For now, I am hoping we will play a role in this wedding."

"Mom, I have asked Miriam's mom to join me at my front-row table for the last performance tomorrow night. She had absolutely no clue what Miriam did in her spare time. Seeing her mother at my table will be a total surprise for Miriam. On Sunday, I'm invited for dinner. Miriam wants me to meet her mother and some of her friends before I return to Munich. I imagine the wedding will be the major topic of the evening. I'll phone you when I get home to Uncle and Aunt's place. Have a great weekend. See you real soon. Smile! It's all good! Love you, Mom."

"Love you too!"

Punctually at eight o'clock came the announcement. "Gentlemen and ladies, for the very last time, here is the incomparable Marika Leander as Gypsy Rose Lee."

Thunderous applause greeted Miriam as her face peeked around the curtain stage right. The biggest smile flashed across her face as she opened her classic routine. She worked her way across the platform. Only then did she see Elsa and Rachel seated at Josh's table. She hesitated just for a split second but continued her performance flawlessly. She couldn't help it. She almost laughed out loud but caught herself. The audience went wild at the conclusion of Miriam's final performance.

She stood stage left draped in the bright red satin curtain. The audience was on their feet clapping and shouting, "More, more, more...." Miriam decided earlier there would be no encores. Miriam stared at the vacant front-row table. Rachel, Elsa, and Josh had left their seats. She assumed they were coming backstage to wish her well. As she took the thirteenth curtain call, two arms enfolded her. The right hand held some kind of an envelope; the left grasped her naked breast. "This is my farewell offering, my dear," whispered Harley into her ear as he tried to force himself on her. He had no idea Miriam's entourage had come backstage. They were all standing behind him taking in the whole scene. Miriam was shocked; she could feel his nakedness behind her. Still smiling at her admirers, she gained distance from him by backing her right elbow forcefully into his chest. She dropped the curtain, stepping away from its protective fabric. Miriam landed a single karate chop to Harley's larynx. He fell backward, hitting the floor hard. Her eyes wandered from Harley to the faces of her loved ones gasping in disbelief. In the auditorium, the applause continued. Miriam took no further curtain calls. Harley didn't move. He was dead.

The backstage onlookers realized what had happened and called one of the stage hands. The police were summoned. There was no doubt what transpired. Harley's body was taken to the morgue. The oldest-appearing of the officers on the scene grabbed Miriam by her exposed shoulder. She was stark naked. The fan and ostrich feathers had hit the floor when she defended herself against Harley. The old geezer gaped at her gorgeous body. "Ms. Marika Leander, you are under arrest!"

"That isn't my legal name. When I'm not on stage, my name is Miriam Daniella Salm von Graben." She said it with pride. Rachel handed her a wrap.

The old grouch turned to one of the younger officers. "Get the names of all these folks congregated back here. They are all potential witnesses. As he listened to Rachel, Elsa, and Josh stating their full names, he winced, making an off-handed remark. "Sounds like a bunch of kikes."

Josh overheard what the man said. He was pissed and getting hot under the collar.

"Did you just call us a bunch of kikes? And what's your name, while we are speaking of names?"

"You heard correctly, you young whippersnapper. You are nothing but a bunch of Jids. And for your information, I'm Sergeant Teufelshund. I've been on the force since 1934."

Josh just about lost it. "Sounds to me like the name fits; you are a dog of the devil. If I were in your profession, I'd have changed my name long ago."

"I'm proud of my name, Bernstein. How come you haven't left for Jerusalem yet? I suppose your tribe didn't benefit from the gratis treatments at Auschwitz-Birkenau."

Josh raised his fists. He was ready to haul off at officer Teufelshund. The SOB obviously was a Nazi in a new uniform. Josh turned to Rachel. "Dr. von Rondstett, I presume you have an attorney? I would advise you to secure his or her services at once. There's a directory by the coin phone over there. Here's some change you might need." He fished in his pant pockets and retrieved several *Twenty-Pfennig* coins and handed them to Rachel.

Josh put his arms around Miriam. "Don't say a word until your attorney is with you and advises you what to say. This jerk didn't even state your rights, citing paragraph 136, which he is required to do according to the laws of the land. You've given him your name; that's all you needed to do. Please keep your mouth shut until your attorney is by your side." He held her close to him and whispered into her ear. "If this asshole of a man asks you one more question, just ignore him and look away. By the way, I'll make damn sure this will be his last day on the force. People like him ought to be locked up. We don't have to live with scum like that bastard any longer. We are free at last."

Miriam returned his hug. There were tears in her eyes when she smiled at Josh. "Thank you for being here, Josh. I know I've found the man I've been looking for. I love you!" It was the first time Josh heard her say those words. He gave her one more reassuring squeeze.

Chapter 51

JOSH walked Rachel and Elsa back to Rachel's car. "Dr. von Rond-stett, I hope you don't mind. I would like to ride with you to the police station. Officer Teufelshund instructed me to be on hand to give my witness account when Miriam will be seen before a judge. I didn't know they had magistrates available at this hour of the night."

"No problem, Josh. You may want to sit with me up front. Those long legs of yours might be a bit cramped in the backseat of this car. Miss Brand doesn't mind, right, Elsa?"

"Got that right; my short legs handle the back seat just fine. You better step on the gas, Rachel, if you want to keep up with the police cars."

Rachel did just that and arrived within seconds of the law-and-order people at the police headquarters. They watched as Officer Teufelshund manhandled Miriam into the station. Josh rushed to hold the door open for Rachel and Elsa. "You just wait until I get into that judge's office. I'll love nothing better than giving this brute what he deserves." His face was as red as a beet.

Rachel was relieved to be greeted by Dr. Aaron Finkelstein, her attorney. "Thanks, Aaron, for meeting us here. I apologize for the timing, but Miriam needs your help. The whole thing seemed so obvious to all of us who witnessed what transpired backstage at the Kasanova nightclub."

"Why was Miriam at the Kasanova nightclub? Isn't that the strip joint on Karstrasse? And what were you doing there?"

"I didn't know of the existence of the place. Never mind my daughter having been the star attraction for the last three years. Yes, my cloister-educated, beautiful Miriam has been dancing at the club three nights a week. She's very much loved by many clients in the region. I would like you to meet Josh, my future son-in-law."

"Did you say future son-in-law?"

"Yes, Aaron. Josh saw Miriam at the club a few times and fell head over heels in love with her. It was he who coaxed Elsa and me to attend her final performance tonight. I didn't just get to see the Gypsy Rose Lee of Essen for a first and last time as a performer but made Josh's acquaintance as well."

Aaron took Rachel aside. "Is there a particular reason why they are rushing into this marriage? You know very little about this man. I'd advise a little prudence if I were you or Miriam."

"I better let you go to work. I can see Miriam desperately looking for your rescue efforts. She is in that examining room with the large window. That officer with her is absolutely obnoxious."

Josh sidled up to Dr. Finkelstein. "Sir, when we get done with this deal and Miriam is free to go, I want you to speak to the judge about the totally unacceptable behavior of Officer Teufelshund. It's obvious he still lives in the world of the 1930s and '40s. He detests Jews. I want him gone from the police force. People like us do not deserve to be treated the way this man conducted himself in our presence; all of us have lived through encounters with his ilk. He needs to be fired, perhaps even put in jail. Lord knows what he did during the Nazi regime."

"Thanks, Josh. I'll fix his wagon." Aaron Finkelstein knocked on the examining room and walked right over to Miriam. He towered her by at least a good foot. In his fashionable suit and tie, he made quite a striking figure. He wasn't the least bit impressed by Officer Teufelshund. He gave him a cursory look and concurred with Josh that the name fit the man. He shook Miriam's hand, turning to the officer. "I would like to consult with my client in private. I'll call you back in when I have need to speak with you."

Miriam told Aaron the whole story from her first encounter with Harley Andreas until the moment of his death. "I believe he's still clutching some large envelope in his hand. I noticed it when they put him in the body bag and took him to the morgue."

"You said your mother, Elsa Brand, and Josh Bernstein witnessed the whole final moments before Harley hit the floor?"

"They saw the whole thing unfold. I didn't intend to kill him, but my training gave me the power to protect myself. The man was ready and willing to attack me. And remember, I was totally nude coming off that stage."

"I believe I have all the facts I need to handle this case. Josh will be the most likely witness. Your mother and Elsa, being family so to speak, wouldn't have to testify. Let's call Officer Teufelshund back. I've a feeling his days on the police force are numbered, if Josh and I have our say."

Aaron Finkelstein opened the door and gestured to Teufelshund to join him and Miriam.

"Who's the magistrate on duty tonight?"

"It's judge Walter Braun, not exactly one of my favorites. I suppose you get along with him. He can be so arrogant."

"You should talk. My client and I have nothing to say to you. There's no need for her to be further interrogated. I've got all the facts and wish to address the court immediately and directly. I expect my client to be absolved of all charges before we leave the judge's offices."

"Please follow me. I'll take you directly to Judge Braun's night courtroom."

The judge smiled when Aaron and his client entered the room.

Josh, Rachel, and Elsa sat down in the observers' area. The only person present, other than the judge, was a young female recorder.

Aaron stood close to Miriam. He made her feel there was nothing to fear. He presented his case to Judge Braun in great detail, including Miriam's act of self-defense. Officer Teufelshund believed he held a smoking gun. "I removed this sealed envelope from the hand of the dead man. If I hadn't done so, it might have disappeared at the morgue in the event his body was viewed by the accused and her attorney. I believe Mr. Andreas, the deceased, intended to give it to Ms. Salm von Graben before she murdered him."

"Your statement is totally out of line. I warn you to refrain from using such judgmental language in my courtroom. Hand me the envelope!"

Teufelshund was seething with anger as he handed the envelope to Judge Braun, muttering further derogatives. The judge opened the envelope. A check made out to Miriam under the name of Marika Leander in the amount of DM 1,000 fell on top of his bench. There was a note as well. "Here's your reward for allowing me to fuck you on the evening of your last appearance in my establishment." It was signed: Rejected once too often, Harley Andreas.

Judge Braun raised an eyebrow after he read the note. "I believe this case is closed. Miriam Daniella Salm von Graben, you are absolved of all charges. You are free to go home with your mother. I believe you are entitled to have this check." He handed it to Miriam. She took it and tore it in four pieces, handing it back to the judge. "I think you may want to keep this in the evidence file. I do not want any part of it." Teufelshund nearly barfed when he saw her tear the check into pieces.

Aaron Finkelstein looked up at the judge. "There is one other important matter I would like you to address. This officer is not fit to serve in this jurisdiction. His conduct toward my client and all witnesses is not in keeping with post World War Two statutes. None of my people should be subjected to the insults of this Nazi.

His comments and behavior toward all present in this courtroom are beyond the pale of dignity. I want him removed from the police force." He closed his folder with a finality that underscored his stipulation.

Judge Braun responded. "I will take your request under advisement, investigate, and act upon it in due time. Thank you for bringing this matter to my attention. Court is adjourned."

Rachel walked out of the courtroom with a straight back, hand-in-hand with Miriam and Josh. She was proud of the next generation. Elsa and Aaron Finkelstein watched them as they walked away from the judge's domain. Everyone smiled. Teufelshund made his last mistake. He tried spitting in their faces as they passed him. "Fucking Jews!"

It was unfortunate for him that Judge Braun still had excellent vision and hearing. His shout echoed through the empty courtroom. "Now you've done it, Teufelshund. I'll see to it that this was the last day you served on the police force." He tore off his robe as he slammed the office door shut behind him.

Chapter 52

RACHEL'S apartment was atwitter with happy voices. Josh had popped the first champagne cork with aplomb. Everyone was still talking about Miriam's final act at the Kasanova nightclub and the events that ensued the night before.

Rachel still couldn't believe that her little girl had killed a man in self-defense. "We loved your performance on stage. I can see why the men in the audience appreciated your act. You did it with such grace. I heard about this Gypsy Rose Lee many years ago. My doctoral advisor, Professor Weiss, at LMU spoke about her in glowing terms. He saw her perform while he lived in New York in the 1930s."

Rachel continued to speak. "The 'afterglow' was something else. I was thankful that we were able to witness what that scum was trying to do and that Aaron was available. His services were invaluable. I was so proud of what you did with that lousy check in the courtroom. I can still see the expression on officer Teufelshund's face as you tore the check to pieces. I'm sure Harley Andreas had not expected the payoff he received. Neither did Officer Teufelshund. Good riddance to such scum. Well, let's move on to new shores."

Rachel turned to face Miriam and Josh. She lifted her glass, as did the others. "Here is to your happiness and a wonderful life together. I'm sorry you won't be here for Miriam's birthday or Rosh Hashanah. It always was cause for much celebration in my home as I grew up. There will be other years. Tell us a bit about your family. We hope to get to meet your parents really soon."

They sat down in comfortable chairs. All eyes were on Josh and Miriam. He was holding her left hand. No one could miss the reflections of light bouncing off that stunning sapphire ring Josh had given Miriam a few days earlier.

Rachel kept her eyes on Miriam. She could tell that her daughter was not fully in the present. Rachel realized that Miriam was reliving the events of the very recent past. She decided to rescue her troubled child. "Josh, I will let you share your family's experiences during the Nazi era with our dear friends. You all need to excuse me and Miriam for a few minutes. My daughter and I need to talk in private."

As Josh told the story how he and Miriam met, Rachel took Miriam's hand and walked with her into one of the examining rooms. "You don't need to sit in a dental chair. Come sit next to me on this comfortable divan. You and I need to have a chat."

"Why are you doing this to me? I'm perfectly OK. There's just so much to think about and plan."

"True, very true. But that isn't what's troubling you. You can fool the others, but you cannot fool your mother. I know what's on your mind. You are wondering how a good girl like you could murder a man. You didn't murder him; you killed him in self-defense. I watched you doing it."

"But I didn't want to kill him; I just wanted to hurt him. I'm thankful that the evidence presented allowed me to go free. If it wasn't for the witnesses and Harley's despicable note, I might have wound up in jail. Just the thought of it gives me the shivers."

"I'm going to share something with you that no one but Elsa knows about. It's an event that is buried deep in my psyche. I have not thought about it in over thirteen years. I want to confess to you and hope that my story will set you free of any guilt."

Rachel reached for Miriam's hands and looked into her beautiful eyes. "When I was at Theresienstadt, the commandant of the camp singled me out. He was Johann von Rondstett's superior and a vicious man. He murdered many people ruthlessly. His name was Klemens Rost. This man raped and whipped me mercilessly every week. No one knew about it, at least I didn't think so. The day before Elsa and I intended to flee from the camp with Johann, Rost came to von Rondstett's apartment for the purpose of raping and whipping me just one more time."

Miriam looked at her mother in disbelief. She began to cry. Rachel needed to tell all. "The man was stupid enough to set his holster on a table when he undressed himself completely. What saved me was that he needed to use the WC. I had an opportunity to reach for his pistol. I knew how to use one since your father had taught me to do so while we were living in Munich. When Rost emerged from the bedroom, he was facing me holding his gun. I gave him three seconds to make the sign of the cross before I killed him with his own pistol in cold blood. I've never regretted doing it because he might have killed me. He certainly had almost succeeded in killing my spirit."

Miriam thought she would lose control. "Mother, you didn't?"

"Yes, I did. Elsa helped me dispose of him. We wrapped his body like a mummy and dragged him down many steps. Elsa took him on his last journey in a wheelbarrow and dumped him in one of the mass graves. He joined the many victims for whom he was responsible. Johann's place was completely restored when he came home. Elsa and I had done a great job of concealing the evidence. But we forgot about getting rid of the weapon. That's how Johann learned what had happened. He took the secret to his grave.

"Do I suffer from recrimination? No! No! No! Rost got exactly what he deserved. Just like Harley got what he deserved. We are both survivors. I want you to forget the whole bloody event and go on with your life. Have no regrets. Know that I love you very much and will always be on your side. What I regret most in life are the eight years of not being there for you." She couldn't help showing her deep sadness as she hugged Miriam fiercely. "Let's wash our eyes before we face the others."

Josh was ready to open another bottle of the bubbly. All were eyes and ears as he shared some of his and his family's background. Rachel felt the need for changing the topic. "Have you two given any thought as to when you wish to get married? Or have you been too euphoric to even think about that?"

"Miriam and I would like to be together as soon as possible. On the other hand, I believe we want to respect your as well as my parents' wishes. I believe a phone call from you, Dr. von Rondstett, to my parents should be the first order of business. I'll be glad when I may call you anything but Dr. von Rondstett."

"You may call me Mom or Rachel, whichever you find comfortable."

"I believe I'll stick with Mom. That works for me."

Rachel couldn't hide a smile. How long she had waited to be called Mom or Mutti. That secret wish was fulfilled when Miriam called her Mutti and Jochanaan started calling her Mommy. They had finally filled that space in her heart that was left barren when she entrusted Miriam with Sister Maria-Angelika at the cloister so many years ago. Sometimes she couldn't fathom all that had happened to her. At the moment, she was thrilled to be called Mom by Miriam, Josh, and Jochanaan, who seemingly was twelve going on twenty-two years of age. He was a joy in her life and a challenge at times. He was terribly bright and precocious.

"Let's enjoy our dinner. I had a lot of help from Elsa and our friends. They all contributed to this feast on such short notice. Impromptu happenings have always been my favorite events in life. Nothing beats spontaneity." She lifted her glass for another toast. "Here's to my children, to my new son-in-law, and to my friends. Here is to all who can no longer be with us." For a split second she envisioned Otto and Johann gracing her table. They were deprived of so much joy that finally was hers.

All enjoyed the dinner conversation and getting acquainted. There were hugs and kisses as Josh made his good-byes. He took Miriam by cab to her apartment in Bredeney. He kissed her lovingly and hugged her firmly before taking his leave. They would be spending much time on telephones in the days to come. Much planning was in the offing. Elsa and Mimi retired, and Helena walked the couple of blocks to her home on Kupferstrasse. Rachel had kissed Jochanaan goodnight. All had thoroughly enjoyed meeting Josh. So much had happened in their lives during the last week. Rachel picked up the phone and called Fritz.

"Hi, Fritz, glad I caught you. I wasn't sure you'd be home. When last we spoke, you mentioned something about thinking of joining a bowling club that met on Sunday nights. Did you do that?"

"Nice to hear your voice, Rachel. As a matter of fact, I did try it a couple of Sundays. I gave up on it. The guys that were there could talk about nothing but the wonders of Communism and drink beer until they passed out. That's just not my thing. I'm done with that."

"Oh, shucks; here I thought you finally found something fun to do on Sunday nights."

"How's my boy doing with his photography?"

"He still loves it. Jochanaan has acquired quite the collection of cameras and uses them all. He's becoming more introspective these days. I often wish you were around him. He worships the ground you walk on."

"What's Miriam up to? Is she by any chance still dating that skinny kid, Lance? He was a regular beanpole. I did like him, though. I presume Miriam is still sharing the apartment with Melissa. It was great that those girls liked their jobs."

Rachel told Fritz all about the Gypsy Rose Lee affair and the dancing star, Marika Leander, as well as Miriam's encounter with Harley Andreas. By the time she got to the final performance and the aftermath, Fritz almost dropped the phone.

315

"Now I've heard it all. Miriam, your cloister-raised daughter, a nude dancer in a nightclub?" Fritz laughed out loud. She could picture him slapping his knee with a vengeance. "I can't believe what you are telling me. And she is getting married? When is this supposed to happen?"

"None of the details have been worked out. Josh has to get back to Munich. His next semester at LMU starts in a few days. They are both anxious to be together. Not to sound opinionated, I agree with Josh that she has become a gorgeous-looking creature. He's a very handsome, but most importantly, an extremely caring and loving person. I wish them well. I'll miss Miriam when they marry and, more likely than not, live in Munich. He likes LMU, and Miriam is thinking of matriculating after they are married.

"This place will be pretty lonesome. When the last patients are taken care of for the day, it will be just Jochanaan and myself. And of course, he isn't much company for me. We talk about school and daily events at the dinner table. He's hardly done eating and puts down his fork and knife when he jumps up to get into that paradise you have created for him. John can't believe how that kid can get himself so involved with his hobby.

"Elsa is glad that she has her own place upstairs. It's a convenient arrangement for all. She's learned to cook for herself and only eats with us on special occasions. She's still a reliable partner in the practice but rarely does anything socially with me."

Fritz saw an opportunity. "You don't sound too happy. As a matter of fact, you sound almost as lonesome as I am. I've given up on finding a new mate. I'm getting too old. And besides that, I have never discovered another woman I really like to be with other than you. Erna was a good wife. She was good company. When I lost her thirteen years ago, I thought my life was over. And then I met you that fateful May day. I've told you on many occasions that I love you. I wish you could find it in your heart to love me."

Rachel had been listening to Fritz intently. She could hear his sadness, sincerity, and his love for her in what he just said. "Would you consider a visit to be with me at Miriam and Josh's wedding?"

"I thought you would never ask. Of course, I would like to be with you and especially would like to meet Miriam's future husband. My God, I might become a grandpa after all. I'll be damned."

Rachel's face was flushed red. She was glad he couldn't see that school-girl look on her visage. It couldn't be menopause. She had gotten over that phenomenon a few years ago. Her child-bearing days were over. She would have lied had she told him she was no longer desiring male companionship.

She decided the ball was in her court since she was certain how Fritz felt about her.

"It's been some time since you were with us for the high holy holidays and Miriam's birthday. I wouldn't be surprised if Josh would show up for the event. Her birthday would be as good an excuse as any for him to get away from his studies and spend time with her and us. They are very much in love. Come a few days earlier. Jochanaan will be thrilled to have a man around the house—especially when it's you."

"Thanks for inviting me. I can't wait to see you and the children. I look forward to meeting Josh. How would you feel about my getting there on September first? I gather you are still driving? There's a train that gets me to Essen Hauptbahnhof about three in the afternoon."

"I'll be there to fetch you. Have a good trip. Give me a call if you change your mind." She hung up.

Chapter 53

THE train from Dresden arrived with German punctuality at three o'clock. Rachel was anxiously waiting for him on the platform. She saw him get off the train. He hadn't changed much since his last visit. He was still in pretty good shape. His new suit flattered him. She liked the French blue he had chosen to wear. His suitcase was a little larger than when he came to visit the previous times. She was wondering if he anticipated an extended stay. He didn't walk toward her like a sixty-two-year-old man.

She greeted him with a broad smile. "Good to see you, Fritz. How was the train trip?"

"I like the new coaches. The electric ones seem to run so much more quietly."

He walked right up to her and sat his suitcase down. Fritz took her in his arms. He wasn't going to hold back. He kissed her fiercely and passionately right there on that platform. "You don't know how often I have fantasized about this moment. I'm not going away empty-handed this time. As a matter of fact, I'm not planning to go away. I need you and want you. I cannot live without you any longer. It's been far too long to be away from you. I've loved you for thirteen years; I won't be rejected this time."

"Phew! That was some greeting. You practically knocked me off my feet." Rachel caught her breath. Fritz was holding her closely. There was another deep kiss before he picked up his suitcase.

"Let's find that car of yours. I can't wait to get home and kiss you some more."

Rachel decided to enlighten him. "Jochanaan won't be there for a couple of days. His school is having a retreat at the youth hostel in Langenberg. Miriam plans to spend the evening with Melissa. They are discussing matters pertaining to the wedding. We'll have the place to ourselves." She smiled at him. "You may play that seduction scene in your mind all the way home."

When they walked in, Fritz noticed right away the dining room table was attractively set for two. Silver, linens, and crystal made for a pretty picture. He liked the candles on the table. He envisioned looking into her beautiful eyes. He was intoxicated by the touch of Chanel No. 5 as she stood close to him. For a moment, he felt like he was forty years younger. He couldn't hold back. He set the suitcase down and reached for Rachel's hands.

"I want to marry you, and I want to love you the way you ought to be loved. We've deprived ourselves for far too many years. I'm hungry, but not for the wonderful food you have prepared and will serve us later. I'm hungry for you; I'm hungry for your touch. I've often dreamt of making love to you in the late afternoon. I will see your eyes and your beautiful body in the most flattering light of day."

After they made love, Fritz whispered into her ear. "I love you, Rachel." She had tears in her eyes when she finally said the words he had longed to hear for thirteen years. "I love you too, Fritz, my Frederick the Great."

"Thank you, Rachel, for saying those words. They mean the world to me. You have no idea how much I have wanted you in my life. There were times when I was ready to kill myself. I felt so rejected when you sent me packing the last time I was here. Sometimes I thought maybe I wasn't smart enough for you. Perhaps not attractive enough as a man. Perhaps it bothered you that I wasn't Jewish. Perhaps it bothered you that my manhood wasn't circumcised. I thought about Otto and contemplated having myself fixed— so to speak. None of that matters now. I finally had the feeling you like me just the way I am. Tell me I'm right."

"Oh my God, Fritz. I didn't realize I put you through this much torture. That was selfish of me. I needed you and wanted you too, I just wasn't sure I wanted to get married again. My first love was Otto. My relationship with Johann was anything but love, certainly to begin with. He, like you, always told me he loved me. I didn't reciprocate that love until long after he was murdered. I felt that love when they laid Jochanaan into my arms. I knew from the first moment I held that beautiful boy that he would be a blessing to me. Raising Jochanaan made me realize the profound sacrifice Otto and I had to make when we handed Miriam over to Sister Maria-Angelika. I could never have done that a second time. Perhaps it was selfish of me to deny you marrying me for all these years. We might have had a chance at having a child together. That can't happen now. It will always be just you and I."

Fritz held her gently in his strong arms. "There, there. No more weeping. Let's enjoy the years that lie ahead of us." He kissed her until they fell asleep holding onto each other.

Rachel served an elegant late dinner. He loved looking at her with candlelight flickering in her dark eyes. It was an evening he couldn't have imagined in his wildest dreams. Rachel was his at last.

✗

"After we have our breakfast, I must call Josh's parents in Munich. I can't put this off any longer. Miriam wants me to be the one who speaks first with the Bernsteins. After that disastrous ending of her dancing career, she feels scared to death of dealing with them. She's ashamed of what she did. Personally, I believe she did the right thing defending herself. She just didn't realize how deadly her actions could be when she struck that monster of a man. I think she'll be just fine once this wedding is behind them and she and Josh can be together and get to know her in-laws. From what Josh says about his folks, they are pretty open-minded." Rachel dialed the number in Munich.

"Bernsteins, Esther speaking."

"Hello, Mrs. Bernstein, it's Rachel Salm von Rondstett."

"Please, call me Esther. You mind if I call you Rachel?"

"Not at all."

Esther kept talking. "You sound like my kind of person. I guess you and I have been designated wedding planners by both of our children. They want to get married but not have a big to-do wedding. It seems we have two children who are madly in love. Can't really blame them."

"I agree, Esther. You don't have a problem with having the wedding in Essen, do you?"

"Absolutely not. We'll plan some kind of party for the kids with the many people we know in Munich. It will be fun for Josh and us and a good way to introduce Miriam to our friends."

"Miriam and I spoke with Josh by phone. The young folks agreed with my suggestion of having the wedding at the end of the semester. It would mean minimum disruption of Josh's studying. How would you feel about the twelfth of December? That's a Friday."

"It certainly would work for us. Samuel will be done with finals a couple of days before."

"Are you sure about my planning the wedding itself in Essen? Miriam is my only daughter, and I would like her to have a church or church-type wedding. I'm sure Josh has filled you in on Miriam's education and being raised by Augustiner nuns. I have already spoken with Rabbi Weisskopf, who performed the bris for my son, Jochanaan. I am raising him in our faith. He said he would be agreeable to a dual service; that is, our children would be married by representatives of both faiths—Jewish and Catholic. Rabbi Weisskopf is willing to perform the ceremony along with Mother Superior, Sister Maria-Angelika, who raised and primarily educated Miriam before, during, and after the war. She became Miriam's mother while I couldn't be there for her."

"That sounds challenging, but I see your point. I'm glad you are arranging that part. By comparison, the party we are planning will be a cinch."

"I discussed my ideas briefly with Miriam and Josh before he left for Munich. They seemed to be OK with the plan. I wish Miriam wouldn't be so upset about that fiasco after she quit being a night-club dancer. I can just imagine what you thought when your dear Josh revealed what kind of a girl he planned to marry."

Esther spoke. "He was trying to be diplomatic with me. He can be a cool customer."

Rachel came back to the wedding plans now that the little discussion regarding Miriam's extraordinary career was no longer a bone of contention. "Neither Miriam nor Josh want a big wedding by today's standards. Basically, only the immediate family and very close friends will be invited.

"There is one other fly in the ointment. I met a wonderful man thirteen years ago when we were trying to avoid Russian occupation forces and escaped from Theresienstadt. Elsa, my dental hygienist and associate, and I walked all the way from Dresden to Essen. Fritz was our very first Good Samaritan. He helped us on our way. We have stayed in touch since then. He's seventeen years older than I. I have accepted his marriage proposal and do want to marry him. I've talked to Miriam; she thinks it's a great idea to have a double wedding. She's known Fritz since she was eight years old. Would you or your husband have any objections to that?"

"That sounds terribly romantic, Rachel. More power to you. If you feel this is the right man, you go for it. I would hate living alone. If something were to happen to Samuel, I wouldn't wait thirteen years if a good man came along. I just can't stand sleeping alone in that big bed. Sounds like we have done OK raising our kids. Glad they have practical heads on their shoulders. I can say this now, I was initially shocked about the dancing career of Miriam's. When you stop and think about it, that girl has chutzpah. I'm thrilled they found each other."

"I am too. Thanks for going along with the idea of a double wedding."

"Rachel, you proceed with the plans in Essen. We'll chat with Josh and ask him if it would be OK for us to plan some kind of party for him and his bride that includes our closest friends from Munich and Switzerland. I'll make a note in our calendar for December twelfth. Obviously, Samuel and I will be in Essen for the festivities. I can't wait to meet all of you, especially Miriam and Mother Superior. She sounds like a winner too. It's wonderful to know that there were people who went out on a limb to help us fend against a mad world. We are all lucky to have survived hell on earth. I need to run. Goodbye."

"Thanks, Esther. You are making this easier for me than I had imagined. Talk with you soon. Good-bye."

She hung up the phone and let out all the air she had inside her. "Phew! Guess what? We may be husband and wife in a few weeks. We'll have a little time to practice prior to the honeymoon." She giggled. He took her in his arms.

Chapter 54

JOSH and Miriam were totally taken by their wedding planner. "Mom, you have done wonders, just a fantastic job of getting everything lined up. Josh's closest friend, Harry, has agreed to be his best man. The guys will leave on the early-morning train the day after they finish their final exams. Josh's parents plan to arrive two days before the wedding."

"I will book reservations at the Hotel Handelshof for Josh's folks. They will find the location across from the Hauptbahnhof convenient. I'm sure they'll like it." Rachel continued. "Fritz would like to walk you down the aisle. He and I will have our little ceremony after you and Josh are pronounced husband and wife. He doesn't mind doing double duty. I was pleased that Esther and Samuel offered to be our witnesses."

"That makes me happy, Mom. I can't wait to meet them. Tell me again who all will be invited to the dinner party at the Ritter.

"I've made the reservation for a table of twenty. That includes our families, my closest friends, the Rabbi Weisskopf, Sisters Maria-Angelika and Irmgard-Dolcinea, Josh's best man and his date, as well as Melissa and her boyfriend. That leaves us with three extra places at the table. You may want to include Melissa's parents. What about

Fräulein Salm? If you can think of any other close friends, just let me know. There's absolutely no problem with any number. I'm just trying to act upon your and Josh's wishes not to turn this into a circus.

"I'm very pleased that you and Josh have agreed to the dual service to be conducted by Rabbi Weisskopf and Sister Maria-Angelika. I love the intimacy of the new chapel at the cloister."

"Mom, thank you, thank you for all you have done. I'm thrilled about you and Fritz getting married but especially that we'll share our wedding day. To tell you the truth, after Fritz's last visit, I had given up on you. I thought you'd let that wonderful man slip right through your hands. I often prayed for you, hoping you'd see the light. He's such a great guy. And what love he has for you and Jochanaan and me!"

"By the way, Esther called me this morning. They have booked the first-class Pullman sleeper arrangements for you as well as the hotel reservations in Venice. The train leaves in the evening on December thirteenth. You are booked for twelve days at the Hotel Gritti. Your return trip to Munich is scheduled for second Christmas day. By that point, you'll be ready to get settled in Munich."

"Did Josh's mom say anything about the party in Munich?"

"She wasn't quite certain. Samuel thought Saint Patrick's Day might be a possibility. As soon as we know, I'll book the train trip and hotel reservations in Munich for the three of us. I just assume that Jochanaan will come along. Of course, Elsa may have to do some juggling with my patients. They'll all understand."

Fritz walked into the room. He caught the last of Rachel's sentences. "Miriam and I are doing a great job of finalizing their wedding plans. What about our wedding plans? I've never planned a wedding for myself. Where would you like to take me on our honeymoon, Fritz? I never had one with either of my previous men. Only one, my first, eventually did become my husband. Remember, Johann never had a chance."

Fritz reached for Rachel's hand. "I would love to take you some-place warm. A place with secluded beaches. I picture us frolicking on a warm, sandy strand."

"I picked up these brochures at the travel agency. I'll see if I can find a train that will take us to Cannes and the Cote d'Azur. We'll leave the same day as Miriam and Josh. I don't think I'll have any trouble getting hotel reservations."

"Sounds wonderful, love. It will be a good change for both of us." Fritz and Rachel smiled at each other. She knew for sure she had finally made the right decision.

𝄪

On the morning of December 12, 1958, the two happy couples and their witnesses went to the *Standesamt* (registry office) at the Gildehof on Hollestrasse 3 in Essen. They participated in the civil ceremony of marriage, a requirement under German law. When they emerged on that bright sunny morning, both couples were legally married. The celebrations at the cloister's chapel were a personal option.

Miriam was a beautiful bride. She used almost no makeup on her flawless skin. She wore her hair in the usual style held by an amber clasp, a gift from Fritz. Her dress was a Dior vision of satin and lace with a neckline that allowed showing off the piece de resistance. She had to wear the family heirloom, the Blue Sapphire Amulet. She was stunningly veiled as Fritz Unrat walked her down the aisle. All males in the wedding party, including Jochanaan, wore classic black tuxedos and white neck wear. Sister Irmgard-Dolcinea agreed to be the organist. As she started to play the music from *Lohengrin*, all rose to greet the bride.

Esther nudged Rachel. They decided to sit together. "Rachel, I brought extra handkerchiefs. I'm about to cry myself. I'm so glad you arranged for the intimate weddings in this beautiful chapel. You and Miriam have so much history here. I'm so glad you shared some of those events with me. What a wonderful idea of joining the two faiths in which our kids were raised. I don't really care what they do, as long as they believe in a higher being. After all, we believe in just one God no matter what he might be called from one religion to the next." Esther Bernstein had taken a great liking to Miriam's mother. One could tell by the fleeting smiles crossing her face as she spoke.

Rachel nodded in agreement. She was happy when Fritz had safely delivered Miriam to the altar. He sat down and held her hand. He had tears in his eyes. In that very moment, he was the happiest man on earth. He had mourned Erna and their daughter, Trudi, and her children for many years. Fritz was ready to share his life with Rachel and her family. He loved them all. At last, he could start a new life.

Rabbi Weisskopf had insisted on Miriam and Josh fasting before the wedding day and Miriam wearing a veil. When he spoke the seven blessings, Esther and Rachel were moved to tears. The Jewish part of the ceremony concluded with the breaking of the glass. All shouted, Mazel tov!

Mother Superior did a splendid job of co-officiating. As she swung the censer over Miriam and Josh as they were kneeling, she spoke the words from Corinthians 1:13. "Love is patient, love is kind. It does not envy, it does not boast, it is not proud. It does not dishonor others, it is not self-seeking, it is not easily angered, it keeps no record of wrongs. Love does not delight in evil but rejoices with the truth. It always protects, always trusts, always hopes, always perseveres." She proceeded with the exchange of rings and ended her service by reminding both Miriam and Josh "to have and to hold, from this day forward, for better or for worse, for richer or for poorer, in sickness and in health, to love and to cherish until death do us part." The fragrance of the incense floated throughout the chapel.

Their respective recitations brought tears and smiles to all faces.

At last, Mendelssohn's march from *A Midsummer Night's Dream* had the newlyweds marching to the back of the chapel. They were spared the pelting with rice or whatever. They sat down in a pew, wanting to witness the simple wedding of Rachel and Fritz. Rachel looked resplendent in a pale blue dress of Shantung silk. Her shoulders were graced by the Varanasi scarf. Her still-beautiful dark hair was held by the amber clasp she had received from Johann. Her beautician suggested a rinse; it had enhanced the color and sheen. She and Fritz made an elegant pair as they walked to the front of the chapel to receive their blessings in both faiths from Rabbi Weisskopf and Sister Maria-Angelika. There was neither Wagnerian nor Mendelssohnian fanfare. They didn't need it. They just wanted to be legal in the eyes of man and God. Fritz promised Rachel she didn't have to get a new shingle for her dental practice.

Rabbi Weisskopf, Sister Maria-Angelika, and Sister Irmgard-Dolcinea were the last of the wedding party leaving the chapel. Suddenly, the rabbi started to cough. He turned to Mother Superior. "Do you smell smoke? That's what's making me cough!" They turned back toward the altar and gulped.

Mother Superior screamed "Fire, fire!" as she rushed toward the box for the fire alarm. One of the large altar candles had dropped out of the stick and set the altar cloth and the hardwood flooring on fire. By the time they heard the fire trucks arrive, the altar and chancel stood in flames. Mother Superior and Sister Irmgard-Dolcinea were in hysterics and shock. They were utterly distraught.

The wedding party stood helpless and shaken on the lawn of the campus. Rachel saw a public phone not far from the cloister school gate. "Does anyone have change? I have none in my little purse. I need to phone the Ritter and tell them what happened."

Samuel reached in his pocket and handed Rachel all the coins she might need. He could tell she was shaken. Miriam felt totally useless in her fancy wedding gown. Josh took over. He looked up the telephone number for the Ritter in the book hanging from a hook in the booth. Rachel handed him the coins, appreciating Josh's concern.

"Hotel and Restaurant Ritter, Kurt Braun speaking. How may we be of assistance?"

"Hallo Herr Braun, Josh Bernstein speaking. My bride and I and our wedding party are supposed to arrive at your hotel for dinner at one thirty. The chapel at the cloister school where we were just married went up in flames. The fire department just arrived. I've conferred with Dr. von Rondstett, mother of the bride, under whose name the reservations were made. If at all possible, may we please reschedule the dinner party to five o'clock? Of course, my bride and I will stay with you tonight as previously planned."

"Sorry to hear of the unplanned event. Of course, we have no difficulty accommodating you under the circumstances. The tables were set in a private dining room. I see no conflict with any later bookings. Thank you for calling us right away. Extend my concerns to Dr. von Rondstett; she is a regular patron of ours, and we shall do anything to still make this a memorable day for all."

Josh stepped out of the phone booth. "Everyone relax, if that is possible. We are all set at the Ritter. Herr Braun was more than willing to move dinner to five o'clock, and we are still staying there tonight." Rachel breathed a sigh of relief.

Samuel walked over to speak with Rabbi Weisskopf and Mother Superior. "I trust the damages are covered by insurance. It is practically a new building."

"Oh yes. The documents are in my office. All of our facilities have to be insured. It just makes me so sad to be dealing with another destruction so close after rebuilding. But we shall survive."

"That's good. Had that not been the case, we would have liked to help in any way we could."

Fritz took charge. "Why don't you young folks head down to your hotel and make yourselves more comfortable? All the wedding photos were taken before the service. The rest of us will gather at

Rachel's for a light snack and a drink. I surely could use one myself. Dear Sisters and Rabbi Weisskopf, my wife and I hope you will still be able to join us for dinner later. The damage is done; it will be good for us all to dwell on the joy of this day rather than being sad."

Rachel looked at Fritz with pride. "Good idea, Fritz. Let's do as my husband suggested." She turned to Mother Superior. "I'm so sorry for what happened. Fritz and I hope that you and the sister will come to the dinner later. It looks like the firemen have things under control. As Fritz said, the damage is done. It can all be replaced. At least no one was hurt."

Mother Superior smiled for the first time. "You are right, at least no one was hurt. Things can be replaced. And yes, Sister Irmgard-Dolcinea and I will see you later at the dinner party. We need to be there for Miriam." She hugged Rachel and Miriam before she turned toward her quarters.

✗

Josh and Miriam spent the night at the Hotel Ritter. When they were finally alone as husband and wife, Miriam wasn't so sure of herself. She was nervous. It was one thing to strut naked in front of total strangers, hiding behind fans and feathers. It was another thing to be undressed by Josh and undressing him.

"Come here, let me hold you." Josh was looking at Miriam's beautiful body. He loved touching her soft skin. She reminded him of alabaster statues he had seen in museums. He drew Miriam close and kissed her. "Boy, talk about starting off with a bang. I wasn't so sure at first how our wedding day would end. I think everyone had a great time at the dinner. But let's concentrate on us. I want to make love to you and make you forget the world. I know you want to make a baby. I'm with you on that. We know a few people who can't wait to hold in their arms what we might create during the next few

330

days and nights." He grinned from ear to ear. "It will be my distinct pleasure to fulfill their dreams."

Miriam led him over to the bed that had been turned down by the maid. Josh lifted her easily and placed her gently on the soft sheets. He lay beside her. "Don't be afraid. I won't hurt you. I know this is all new for you. She turned her face up to him, wanting his soft kisses. He willingly obliged and began to caress her with his hands and his languid tongue.

"I love what you are doing to me. I've often wondered what it would be like to lie naked with a man." Seeking each other's pleasure was foremost on their minds.

Miriam enjoyed Josh's gentle touches and the sweet nothings he was whispering into her ear as he straddled her body. She began to moan. When he finally entered her quickly, the sharp pain surged through her body only momentarily. Miriam looked into his eyes. "You think we made a baby?"

He laughed out loud. "You are really anxious to do this, aren't you?"

"I am. I don't know how long Fritz will be around. I want him to have the experience of holding another grandchild in his arms. I'm thrilled that he and Mom found each other. They seem to be very happy."

"Wait a minute. What about me holding my first child in my arms? I'm fond of your and my folks, but right now, all I'm thinking of is making us happy and enjoying the moment. You probably won't believe this, but when I came just now, I was envisioning creating a baby that would look just like you. Most guys want to have a boy. They want an heir. I don't care about that. I would love nothing better than making a baby girl with you, a little Miriam. I could see her develop and grow up to be as beautiful as her mommy."

Chapter 55

JOSH and Miriam's train pulled into the Hauptbahnhof in Essen on time. They found their sleeper car with ease. "It ain't the Orient Express, but I think we'll have a comfortable ride all the way to Venice! This mattress feels pretty good."

Miriam smirked at her new husband. "What do you mean by comfortable ride? I had something else in mind. How about some more work on getting this baby started?"

"What do you mean by 'work'? I was under the impression it was all pleasure. At least that's the way I see it. Looks to me like my friend is ready, willing, and able to show up for work." Josh slammed the door shut with one quick motion of his heel. Miriam had already started to help Josh out of his clothes. He was giving her a helping hand with shedding her travel attire.

There was no question about Josh and Miriam enjoying their bodies. As much as Josh would have liked to have oral sex for a change, Miriam informed him otherwise. "Sorry buddy, that won't work with this girl. Doing it that way will not result in babies. I might be a novice at this and raised in a cloister, but I did pay attention when the nuns taught us something about anatomical functions.

Now, if you are successful at getting me pregnant, your dream of oral sex might become reality. I might consider pleasuring you when I'm eight or nine months pregnant with your child. Got that? Now, hop to it and make me a baby!"

Josh cracked up. He hadn't realized how entertaining his wife could be. "I still haven't quite grasped the reality of being married, never mind being married to you, someone I picked up strutting in feathers and fans across a stage."

"It was fun, but I'm glad you rescued me. I love being Mrs. Joshua Samuel Bernstein. It has a nice ring to it. Now, come on top of me; I want to hear your bells ringing."

"Boy, first it's a prick, now you're calling my dick a Glockenspiel. I don't know about you and that cloistered upbringing. Sometimes I wonder what went on in those hallowed halls with Sister Maria-Angelika and Sister Irmgard-Dolcinea. She is the one that might have paved your path to promiscuity."

"Oh, stop that fancy talk. Promiscuity, my foot. All I did was walk around concealing my nudity with feathers and fans, pretending to be some elegant, famous American burlesque queen called Gypsy Rose Lee. I often wanted to meet her in person. She did intrigue me."

"Well, you were good at it. You did a great imitation of her. And further, you sent a lot of guys home with new ideas. Perhaps not always ideas their prim and proper wives were willing to make reality. Speaking of reality, my friend is ready for overtime."

When they pulled into the Venice station, they were both sound asleep. The porter had to knock several times on their door to get their attention. "Last stop, Venice!" he kept yelling.

Josh finally responded and got rid of the talking alarm clock. "I loved all the rides you gave me. The sleeper was a great idea. Otherwise, we couldn't have worked on the baby project as diligently. However, sleeper is an oxymoron. Neither one of us got much sleep. We have twelve days here to catch up. Let's get off this thing. We can pretend we are emerging from the Orient Express. It takes a certain way of walking and holding your head up high to convey that air and snootiness. Of course, there is no sign of pretense on your part. People will stare at you no matter where you walk or what you wear. I like that pale-blue bouclé suit you chose to wear this morning. Its neckline really shows off your amulet."

Josh got the attention of a cabdriver using his two-fingered whistle. He helped Miriam into the cab. "Hotel Gritti, *per favore*," Josh tried his Italian. They were on their way. "*Eccoti qui.*" (Here we are.) They had arrived at the Gritti. They were overwhelmed by the opulence. Miriam knew what it cost. She thought to herself, "It better be opulent at those prices. But we are worth it."

Their suite was the height of elegance. The furnishings, the art, the oriental rugs all spoke of old money and class. Miriam couldn't stop talking. "Personally, I could have handled a bit more modernity and a more reasonable price tag."

Josh looked around. "My mom likes all these wonderful antiques. I decided to humor her rather than contradict. When we start furnishing our home in Munich, I would like things much more streamlined."

Miriam agreed with Josh. "The dusting will be a lot kinder to my timetable once I pursue my studies at LMU."

"Let's not worry about studying, dusting, and cleaning house in Munich. You are in Venice, my dear. And at one of the fanciest hotels in the world at that. I'd like to check out the springs of this opulent canopy contraption before we venture into the city. Could you imagine making love in a gondola? The gondolier probably would drop into the Grande Canale."

Josh yanked the elegant bedspread to the floor. He went to the bathroom and took a quick shower. When he strutted back into the room, he got the shock of his life. Miriam had bedded herself on the magnificent bed. All she was wearing was the sapphire amulet. She had positioned herself like Goya's *Nude Maja*. She looked stunning.

"I'm impressed. I could be only half tempted not to disturb this vision. But then, we do have 'work' to do."

He removed the amulet carefully from Miriam's neck. "As much as I admire it, I don't want it hitting my face when you get on top of me and give me the ride I so desire."

Finally, catching their breath after having reached exalted heights of pleasure, Miriam felt it was time for a shower, getting dressed, and exploring the wonders of Venice.

They strolled to San Marco and admired the Doge's Palace. The Basilica di San Marco with its many wonderful turrets was a must. They ate pizza under the Rialto Bridge. Miriam loved the mystique of the carnival masks on display everywhere. The gondolier serenaded them on their ride to Murano. She was tempted to reach for Josh when the gondolier wasn't looking. She decided to be a good girl and save it for his next rendezvous with the *Nude Maja*. The sun made her hair glisten. Some of the Italian men couldn't help touching Miriam's derrière, whispering in her ears, "*Bellissima.*" Josh was ready to kick them in their nuts. He restrained himself physically but yelled, "*Giù le mani!*" (Hands off!)

Venice was all they could've wished for. It was sheer romanticism and total debauchery in one. Their days were filled with exciting adventures, exploring the sites, the enjoyment of countless culinary treats, the wonders of every kind of music from jazz to opera, and their searches for souvenirs and sexy underwear. All was available in great abundance. Their nights were filled with sexual explorations one could only imagine. The honeymoon was a complete success.

They boarded the train to Munich on December 26. It was still Christmas in Germany. Esther and Samuel met them at the train station. "Welcome to Munich. How was Venice? Did you enjoy the Gritti? It's one of my favorite hotels."

"Mom, it was a total disaster. The beds were so bad, we had to make love on the floor. It's too bad someone spent all that money.

We were glad they weren't our shekels that paid for that dump!" He winked at his dad.

"Josh, you are joking. Don't do that to me. You can be terrible. They are teaching you bad things at the university. Is that what you learn in your smartass philosophy lectures? I have to check on that professor. You are a naughty boy!"

"Mom, it was wonderful, and Miriam and I did enjoy making love in that fancy canopy bed until we shook the rafters. The neighbors on occasion told us to keep it down. Miriam always wanted more. She was determined to return pregnant from our honeymoon. All my 'hard work' was for your and Dad's benefit. And, of course, to read smiles on her mother's and Fritz's faces."

"There you go again. I don't know what I'm going to do with you. A nice Catholic Jew like Miriam wouldn't say such things."

"Could've fooled me!" Josh had to have the last word.

Samuel wanted to talk to his son. It could be a challenge getting a word in edgewise when Esther had the floor. "I look forward to having both of you attending LMU. It's a great institution, as you have discovered during your first year. You and Miriam will enjoy taking in some of the same lectures. The philosophy department is home to several well-known profs. How long do you think it will take for both of you to be finished with your doctorates?"

"For me, it will be another six or seven; for Miriam, probably seven or eight years."

"Are you planning to have children while you are still studying?"

"If Miriam has her way, she wants to have at least two kids right away. She is funny. I don't know how often she cracked me up while we were making love. She's quite the humorist."

Samuel thought back to his early days with Esther. "I'm happy to hear that both of you have a good sense of humor. Mom and I will do anything to help you get started with everything: Your house, your studies, and with having a family. We'll be more than happy to play grandma and grandpa when the time comes."

)(

Josh was thrilled to learn that he would be a father. He couldn't resist telling Miriam, "I told you good workers are hard to find. I believe you hired the best!"

Chapter 56

RACHEL and Fritz enjoyed their sleeper accommodations on the train to Cannes. Perhaps not quite the way Josh and Miriam did on their ride to Venice. They had their moments of mutual enjoyment. Their explorations were somewhat less acrobatic. They were comfortable with their bodies and with each other. Positional adventures were clearly for younger folks.

Fritz beheld his beautiful bride. "We are doing OK for a couple of geezers."

"Speak for yourself. I don't consider myself a 'geezer' at age forty-five. And neither are you. You still know how to pleasure a woman. Don't shortchange yourself. I have thoroughly enjoyed you and your body since the first time we tried it. You've made a world of difference in my life. I never thought there would be love again after I watched Johann being murdered. You've brought joy into my heart. And, you are a wonderful father to Jochanaan. He adores you. That means so much to me."

The hotel in Cannes was an excellent choice. The bed was large and comfortable, clearly suitable to them. "It's a nice day. Let's unpack later. I want to walk on the beach, OK?"

"That's fine with me, husband of mine." They walked down to the strand. There were few visitors to be seen. Most beach baskets were vacant. It was a sunny day but rather breezy and cool. Rachel thought it was downright cold. "You won't catch me in a bathing suit. You can forget about making love on the beach." He gave her a big smile. She turned back to the hotel.

"Let's unpack. I always feel better when it's done. Then one can relax until it's time to head home. I've always been a very organized person." It didn't take all that long. The job was done. There were plenty of drawers to accommodate his and her things. It was early in the afternoon. Fritz decided it was time for him to enjoy Rachel. He wasn't all that comfortable having her on the train. Often, they heard conductors and passengers walking by their compartment door. It made Fritz less at ease with himself. People might be listening to what they were doing.

Fritz got Rachel's attention. "When we walked back from the beach, did you notice that charming little bistro? I took a quick glance at their menu, and it looked intriguing. How about checking out the place? Let me spoil you."

They walked hand-in-hand into the little place. Some of the seated guests looked up and smiled. Anyone who beheld Rachel and Fritz knew they were very much in love. He helped her with her chair. Before he could seat himself, an attentive waiter helped Fritz with his chair. "May I offer you an apéritif? Would you care for champagne or a glass of wine?"

Fritz looked up, enjoying the French accent. "May we see your wine list?"

"Of course, of course, I'll be right back." Fritz looked it over and ordered a bottle of Cabernet that would be to Rachel's liking. She had preferred red wine for as long as he had known her.

"What do you think of the place?"

"It's charming. I love the atmosphere. That waiter sounds so cute with his wonderful accent. It's so French. They surely know how to live. I believe they work to live. We seem to live to work. We need to learn a lesson from them."

"You are so right, Rachel." He reached across the table and touched both of her hands. She pretended to send him a kiss across the table. The waiter had opened the wine and offered Fritz a chance to approve of his selection. Fritz held the glass up to the source of light to check its color; he swirled the sample and checked for its legs. Then he took a deep breath through his nose seeking the intensity of the wine's aroma. At last, he took a healthy sip, wanting to sample the taste. He was satisfied and indicated to the waiter to pour a glass for Rachel. Fritz lifted his glass toward her. They liked the sound of crystal when their glasses touched. "Here's to a wonderful honeymoon; here's to many happy years together. I love you with all my being." He rose from his chair. He bent down to kiss her. Rachel felt tears falling from her eyes.

They ordered nothing but seafood. It was freshly caught and prepared to perfection. "I loved the escargot and the oysters Rockefeller. That sea bass was absolutely superb. I don't care for dessert, but a digestif would be just what the doctor ordered."

Fritz had to agree. "The wind has died down. It's rather pleasant right now. Shall we walk to the hotel? It's only a five-minute stroll. I don't know how you feel, but I could use a constitutional."

"By all means, I enjoy walking. I love the fragrance of jasmine in the air." She reached for Fritz's hand and turned toward the hotel.

Approaching the main entrance, they noticed several police cars with flashing lights. Fritz looked worried. "I wonder what that's all about?" No one stopped them as they walked into the lobby. They took the elevator to the fifth floor. As they emerged, they became concerned. They could see policemen entering their room.

They were stopped by one of the officers. He addressed them in French. Rachel understood what the man was asking Fritz. "What's your name? Is this your room?"

"We are Mr. and Mrs. Unrat from Essen, Germany. And yes, this is our room. We arrived today by train. We are on our honeymoon."

"I'm sorry. I have bad news for you; you have been robbed. Our initial search did not turn up anything of value. If you had any jewelry or money outside the safe, it's gone. Whoever broke into your room and ransacked it took anything of value. Please come inside, and we'll complete an official report."

Rachel and Fritz stepped inside their room. It looked like bedlam. Everything in the wardrobe and drawers had been dumped on the floor. The bed was stripped of all linens, and the mattress had been removed from the bed. Obviously, someone had done a very thorough search for valuables. Fritz smiled at Rachel. "Aren't you glad I left all your jewelry and money with the concierge?"

Rachel nodded. "Looks to me like they took nothing. They just made a terrible mess of our room." The officer interrupted them.

"You cannot stay in this room. It is a crime scene even if nothing of value was taken. The hotel staff will move you to another accommodation. You may take your toiletries and nightclothes. The rest must stay until we have finished our investigation."

"That's OK," said Fritz. "We have no intention of going out again tonight." They were given the bridal suite as a consolation prize. Rachel was pleased that Fritz had left nothing worth stealing in their room.

Fritz couldn't help laughing. "I thought setting the chapel on fire was bad enough. Getting robbed during our honeymoon adds insult to injury. No harm done; it will give us something interesting to talk about when we get back. We've certainly started out with a bang!"

The investigation showed that there was no sign of forced entry; the break-in was staged by a couple of new employees. The following day Fritz and Rachel's belongings were neatly transferred to their new room.

After an exciting beginning, Fritz and Rachel treasured their time alone in Cannes. It had indeed turned out to be a honeymoon to be remembered. Nevertheless, both were ready to return to their home and be with Jochanaan. Rachel was anxious to see her patients. Fritz had to give thought about what to do with his place in the East. They were wanting to learn when the festivities were taking place in Munich. Rachel was even more interested in learning how Miriam and Josh fared on their honeymoon. She didn't care how they did it; all she truly wanted to know was whether Miriam achieved her goal.

Chapter 57

ELSA picked up the phone on the first ring. "Dr. von Rondstett's office, Elsa Brand speaking."

Miriam was pleased to hear her voice. "Hi, Elsa. How are you?"

"Just fine. Your mother was hoping you would call today. You didn't forget. It's Jochanaan's thirteenth birthday."

"Did you really think I would forget his birthday? How's he doing in Hebrew shul in preparation for his bar mitzvah? Both Josh and I are planning to be there for the event. Is Mom in this morning? I need to speak with her."

"Yes, she is. I'll get her for you."

"Thanks, Elsa. Have fun at Jochanaan's birthday party."

"Thanks, I will. Bye, Miriam. Here's your mom. She's just finished with Sister Maria-Angelika. She needed a crown."

"Hello, Miriam. How nice of you to call today. Jochanaan will love hearing your voice. He's missed you terribly since you moved away. He loved having you around—most of the time. You just have to come visit us often. Fritz and I are wondering how you and Josh are getting along."

"Actually, we are doing well. Both of us like our profs and our lectures. We are slowly getting the house furnished. Josh's parents are exceptionally good to us. I had to work on them. They initially wanted me to call them Esther and Samuel; I prefer to call them Mom and Dad. They seem to like my choice."

Rachel nodded in agreement. "I'm so pleased that you have a good relationship with Esther and Samuel. That's not always the case. What else is new in your lives?" The answer she was looking for she didn't get.

"We are working on a special room in the house. I believe you and Fritz will like it when you visit for the bash the Bernsteins are planning on St. Patrick's Day. It's on a Tuesday. Maybe you could come for a long weekend. I'm sure it wouldn't be a problem for Elsa to rearrange your patient schedule a bit. Also, on another matter, why don't you discuss with Rabbi Weisskopf April seventeenth for Jochanaan's bar mitzvah? We would be on semester break and could stay for Passover. How does that sound?"

"That sounds great, Miriam. It will be one party after another. Fritz is doing very well. He's been good for me. What's even more pleasing is the relationship he has with Jochanaan. He accompanies him to shul for his lessons and then works with him at home. He's become quite good at Yiddish and Hebrew. And, of course, when they are not occupied with matters pertaining to shul, I always know I can find them in the dark room. Fritz hit the jackpot when he built that darkroom for him. He's a real joy in our lives.

"In a couple of weeks, Fritz wants to take a trip east. The traveling between zones isn't too bad right now. He wants to see what he can do about his little farm. He'd like to sell it but isn't sure the authorities will allow it with that 'collective deal' that's going on now. We shall see."

"Glad everything is going so well there. Tell Fritz we wish him a safe trip and good luck with disposing of his farm."

"Thanks, I will."

Rachel knew she was pushing it. "Any news on the baby front?

Are you and Josh still working on it? Sure hope so. I would love to hold my first grandchild in my arms real soon."

"Be patient, Mom. We are happy with our busy lives."

Rachel continued to relate to Miriam what really bothered her these days. "I'm beginning to wonder whether Jochanaan ever plans to get married and have children. He's got this strange notion he would like to become a monk. I have no clue where that comes from. You'll need to have a chat with him. He's a perfectly normal thirteen-year-old boy. He's seeing some girls, and Fritz has caught him masturbating. We thought he was sleeping when Fritz went to check on him. He told Fritz it felt great when he ejaculated. Fritz had to agree. It's perfectly normal. I just don't know where he got this idea about becoming a monk. Try talking some sense into your brother. Oh, oh. Sorry, I have to run. My next patient is here. I'll let Elsa put you through to Jochanaan's room. Love you. Here's Elsa."

"Hold on, Miriam—I'll find the birthday boy for you.

"Thanks, Elsa."

"Here he is. Bye again."

"Happy Birthday, Jochanaan. I hope our package got there in time. Did you like the special lenses Josh selected for your Leica?

"They're fantastic. Tell Josh I'm thrilled with them, especially the close-up one. That must have set him back a few marks. I really like the snazzy scarf you sent too. The silk and merino wool feels fantastic around my neck. And you know how susceptible I am to colds."

"What are the plans for today?"

"We'll have a nice party since this is my big birthday. According to our faith, I'm a man as of today. I have to watch what I'm doing. Fritz caught me jerking off one night. I had another long birds-and-the-bees lecture from him. Don't get me wrong. I love the man. He's to me the father I never knew. He understands me very well. I love him for taking me to shul and practicing my Yiddish and Hebrew with me. He's becoming really good at it. What's new in your life?"

"You are coming to see us with Mom and Fritz over St. Patrick's Day when the Bernsteins are throwing that big party for us, right? Josh and I are tentatively planning to be in Essen during our semester break. I asked Mom to check with Rabbi Weisskopf to see if you can have your bar mitzvah on April seventeenth. We could stay for Passover. How does that sound?"

"Awesome. I'll have Mom get on it right away."

"What's this bit about becoming a monk? Where on earth did you ever get that idea? You are out of your mind. You are a healthy, good-looking Jewish boy. You are not equipped or meant to be a monk. Forget about that idea. You and I will have a serious talk when I see you in March. You just wait until I tell Josh. He'll be on the phone setting you straight in a minute. Have to run. I'm due for my next lecture. Love you, little brother. You're not so little anymore. Enjoy your manhood. Talk to you again real soon. Bye."

Walking away from the phone booth, Miriam was shaking her head. "Monk! Now I've heard it all!"

Chapter 58

"Welcome, welcome to Munich. We are so delighted to have you with us. There is no need for you and Fritz to stay at a hotel. Jochanaan can stay in Josh's former room. He'll be very comfortable by himself. Let me show you two around."

Rachel assumed Jochanaan must be unpacking or checking out his room. The trio continued walking from room to room. "I like the large windows looking out on the gardens. These high ceilings are very attractive. It's fun seeing some of your beautiful antiques. The eclectic feel between old and new you have achieved is great. The warm colors are pleasant to my eyes. This is a lovely home. How did you ever find it, Esther?"

"We owned the land. When we returned from our confinement in Switzerland, we gained some special privileges from the new government. Once Samuel accepted his full professorship at LMU, we were able to build on our property. We were lucky. If it hadn't been for my parents, we never would have had the means of getting out of Germany and certainly not in time to escape being sent to a KZ. We probably would have wound up in Dachau. Miriam has shared some of your tragic life with me. What a horror to witness Johann being sodomized, killed, and cremated in front of your eyes. How can you ever forget those scenes? You must have nightmares from time to time."

"You are absolutely right. No matter how happy I am these days, there are many nights when I am haunted by what I experienced at Theresienstadt."

Esther gave Rachel a hug. "Make yourself comfortable. You and Fritz join us for cocktails downstairs. The children want us all to go to their house for dinner. It's not as elegant as this place. They love all that modern stuff. It's not as warm as our or your home. They have to live with it. I believe you will like what they have done with their little place. It's a good starter home for a young couple. With their full-time commitments to studying, it's plenty big and livable. You'll see. The kids are doing OK. Neither has to pay tuition, partly because of government support and partly because of Samuel's position with the school. They will be just fine. Before my parents passed away, they created a substantial trust for Josh. He's taken care of for life. Just come down when you two are ready."

"We will. I'm still wondering where Jochanaan disappeared to."

"Don't worry about it, Rachel. I'm sure he's in his room and all right."

Esther got Samuel's ear. "I hope they'll all have a good time with us. Fritz seemed awfully quiet when we walked through the house. I really want this to be a happy time for them. The party ought to be fun for everyone. I enjoyed planning it. Can't wait until they see the kids. I played down the appearance of their home. I want them to be totally surprised. Don't you spoil it now. You hear me, Samuel?"

"Yes, dear. I got the message loud and clear. You never leave any doubt."

Samuel greeted them. "Come in, Fritz. Hello, Rachel. Good to have you here. What may I get you from the bar? I believe we have a good assortment on hand."

Rachel looked at Samuel. "I would love a glass of red wine. That's always been my preference."

"If you don't mind, I'll have that cognac you are showing. I've developed a taste for it since being with Rachel. I keep forgetting how miserable people are who live in the East Zone. Being there just recently gave me the creeps. For now, I'm not budging from Rachel or Jochanaan's side. I love my new family."

Samuel and Esther smiled and lifted their glasses. "Here's to new families; here's to the future. After cocktails, we'll drive over to see the kids. They're expecting us by six thirty."

They left the house shortly after six o'clock. It took them about twenty minutes driving to the kids' house. Josh opened the door. He hugged both his mother and Rachel. The men shook hands. "Good to have you here. Now you'll be able to picture us better where and how we live. Miriam will be right down. She wanted to change her attire after being all over campus today. Drinks anyone? Or did Dr. Samuel sufficiently anesthetize you?"

Miriam hugged her mom, Fritz, and Jochanaan. She almost curtsied to Samuel but hugged Josh's mom. They had become very close. Esther admired her spunky daughter-in-law. Josh and Jochanaan shook hands. "Thanks, Josh, for my birthday presents. You couldn't have thought of anything better."

"Don't thank him. Who do you think gave him the idea?" Miriam put in her two cents.

Jochanaan wanted to stay downstairs with Samuel and Josh; he needed some man-to-man talk. "Josh, I see you have the same Bordeaux your dad was serving earlier. My mom really seemed to like it. May I have a glass? I am thirteen and considered an adult, right?"

"You sure are, young man. Here is your drink." Josh swept his glass toward Jochanaan. "L'chaim! For life!" They toasted each other and partook of their libation. Esther sat by a window. She was looking at the invitation to this evening's party. It was most attractive.

Miriam was pleased to see how well Jochanaan got along with her husband and his father. "I see Josh has offered everyone refreshments. Would you care to have a tour of the house before dinner? I love showing it off. I never dreamed of having my own house so soon." She let Rachel and Fritz go ahead to the upper floor.

Josh and his folks were pinching themselves. They had succeeded in not spilling any beans. They couldn't help listening to the "tour guide."

Miriam was in her glory. "This is our bedroom and bath. The next room is one of our guest bedrooms. Not as big as Mom's but comfortable. You two ought to try it on one of your next visits. And this is our special room. It is a room in waiting. Waiting for tiny little feet pitter-pattering around." She caught Rachel and Fritz's eyes as they stared at her waistline.

"No, Mom and Fritz, I'm not that far along. It must have happened on that train ride to Venice. I'm finally over the morning surprises. I'm glad for that."

Both reached out to Miriam and enfolded her in their arms. There were tears of joy all around. Fritz looked into Miriam's eyes. "Thank you for making it possible for us to hold a grandchild in our arms. You have no idea how your mother and I have longed for this moment. I toast and welcome the next generation. Let's head downstairs. Jochanaan, Josh, and his parents deserve to share in our unending happiness. This is a day for celebrating, a good day for looking to the future."

Chapter 59

ALL but Esther and Samuel arrived at the synagogue by six o'clock. The edifice had been restored after the war. It was the cultural center for the Jewish community. Esther had no difficulty arranging the reception for Josh and Miriam for Tuesday, March 17. There were no conflicts with activities at the temple.

Esther and Samuel were greeting the guests at the entrance to the celebration hall. She was wearing one of her designer silk brocade, full-length gowns in shades of red, orange, and purple with touches of gold. Samuel donned a dark blue tuxedo. The hosts were all glamor. Esther had outdone herself with the decorations. Round tables for ten were set with the finest of linens, china, and silver. Raised epergnes holding tasteful arrangements of roses in various shades of pink graced the center of each table. Floating clouds of ivy and miniature lights vaulted the hall. A ten-piece band played dance music of the thirties, forties, and fifties.

"You've outdone yourselves, Esther and Samuel. What a spectacular way of celebrating our children's union. They do seem to be very happy with their lives. Miriam looks well and says she feels wonderful. There is a certain glow about her. We share in the joy they seem to have found in each other."

Esther smiled at Rachel. "I'm so glad you chose to wear your wedding outfit. That dress and the Varanasi scarf look stunning on you. Did Fritz have anything to do with your choice? He is such a thoughtful man."

"How did you guess? I was ready to go out and treat myself to a new outfit. He can be terribly frugal. When he suggested I wear my 'wedding dress,' I had to agree. I'm comfortable wearing it. The scarf is special to me; it always reminds me of my very dear grandfather. He loved me very much. I never knew my parents. My grandparents were everything to me. I hated leaving them when Otto and I studied here in the 1930s. On the other hand, the choice of attire was easy for Fritz. All he had to pack for this gathering was his 'uniform.' That's what he calls his tuxedo. He's right. It's a lot easier for men to go formal. I like Samuel's choice of tuxedo. It's a nice change."

Esther commented, "I talked him into getting it. He has so many occasions to wear a tux. He finally agreed to get this one. I like it too; it's different. Here come our children. Josh always looks great in a tux with that youthful figure of his. And Miriam is again a vision in blue and purple. She is so proud of wearing the sapphire amulet. I told Josh he needs to get insurance for that piece. It must be worth a fortune."

"It's funny you say that. I don't believe it has ever been insured as long as it's been in my family. Pretty trusting, don't you think?"

Esther agreed. "When you stop and think about its journey, it's amazing that it has survived the ups and downs in the history of your family. And here we are. In six months, give or take a day, you shall know if the next recipient has been born. Samuel is hoping it will be a girl. He always wanted to have another child, especially a little girl. It wasn't meant to be."

Esther's eyes swept across the room. "Just look at this crowd. It's exactly what I wanted, an elegant party for our closest friends. Most of them saw our Josh grow into manhood. He was bar mitzvahed in this temple. Samuel and I are so happy that Josh discovered Miriam.

Isn't serendipity wonderful? Had he not heard about that 'famous dancer,' he probably would have never gone to that nightclub. Like I always say, timing is everything. How about getting out on the dance floor? The band is doing a great job." They talked, laughed, cried, and danced into the wee hours of the morning.

Chapter 60

THE Munich contingent of the family arrived in Essen on April 15, two days prior to Jochanaan's bar mitzvah. Miriam was showing signs of her pregnancy. She was feeling wonderfully healthy and looking forward to being with Rachel, Fritz, and Jochanaan. Jochanaan was pleased Fritz was willing to become acquainted with Yiddish and the Hebrew language. He listened for hours as Jochanaan was trying to perfect his pronunciations in Hebrew when he was preparing to read from the Torah at his bar mitzvah. Hours in the darkroom were always the reward for his intense studies.

"Have you given any thought to what you might like for gifts from family and friends?" inquired Fritz after one of the lengthy study sessions.

"As far as my friends are concerned, I'll let myself be surprised. When Miriam asked me, I let her know that I would appreciate money from them and Josh's parents rather than a bunch of stuff I really don't care about. You and Mom know already how I feel. I still am seriously considering entering a religious order after I have my Abitur at age eighteen. I'll have five years to change my mind and pursue something different."

Fritz couldn't help himself. "Would you mind sharing with me how you came up with the idea of becoming a monk? Why are you going through the process of growing into manhood in the Jewish faith if you want to become a Catholic monk in five years? What's your fascination with Catholicism?"

"Fritz, it has nothing to do with faith. I believe ultimately I will be more comfortable in a world that primarily involves men. I would be able to realize my academic aspirations in an environment that would preclude having to deal with women. I'm afraid of women. I have no interest in being with them. I'm much closer to you or any other man than I am to women. It's something I discovered several years ago. I have tried to overcome these feelings, but I can't. Please don't share this with anyone. I know what I am. But I'm not ready to tell everyone that I am gay."

Fritz almost fell off his chair. He had expected anything but what Jochanaan confessed. "You can't be serious? You are a normal boy with normal sexual drives. You love your mother and your sister. You are fond of Elsa, Aunt Mimi, and Helena. You love Esther. Don't tell me you don't like women. What makes you believe you are a homosexual? What makes you think you dislike women?"

"Perhaps I didn't make myself clear. I didn't mean to say that I dislike or hate women. I like and love the women in my life very much. The difference is, you are physically very much attracted to my mother. I'm not physically attracted to any girls or women."

"Jochanaan, I'm not an expert in such matters. Would you consider discussing your feelings with Samuel? He's a medical doctor. Or would you rather have a talk with your mother? She was so happy when I came into your lives last year. She was relieved that she didn't have to discuss your sprouting sexuality with you. She liked having me around to assume that responsibility. We've had our share of talks along those lines. I never felt that you were uncomfortable during our man-to-man talks. I leave it up to you. Samuel might be a good man in whom to confide. I won't say a word to anyone unless you ask me to."

"Thanks, Fritz. Let me think about discussing this with Samuel. First, let me get done with the bar mitzvah. We'll take it from there. Sorry to lay this on you. You have been very good to me. I felt I could share my innermost feelings with you."

All gathered at the Rabbinerhaus with Rabbi Weisskopf officiating. They were familiar with the man. Sister Maria-Angelika was absent. This was strictly a Jewish event. Having completed his introductions into the Hebrew faith, Jochanaan was pronounced a man. He would assume the responsibilities of an adult male Jew and was allowed to participate in all adult aspects of his religion. Jochanaan understood the concepts related to his coming of age. He wasn't sure if he was indeed ready to fully commit at his tender age of thirteen. The reception at the synagogue was anticlimactic. The party in Munich had been far more enjoyable.

The family met for an intimate gathering at Rachel and Fritz's place. A few non-Jewish friends joined them for the postevent celebrations. Rachel could tell Fritz was clearly distracted. At times, he would just stare out the window. That was possible again after bricks were replaced with plate glass. She walked over to him. Everyone had a drink in their hand about to toast Jochanaan. "Would you like a glass of my wine, or would you rather I fetch you a cognac?"

"I'll have your Bordeaux. I need to keep a level head." He winked at her and smiled. She didn't have a clue what transpired between Fritz and the celebrant earlier in the day.

After the evening meal, Jochanaan gathered enough chutzpah to confront Samuel. "Dr. Bernstein, may I have a word with you in private?"

"Jochanaan, you are a man as of today. I'm family. You may call me Samuel. What's this all about a talk in private? Did you say you wanted to speak to me in your mother's examining room? Then let's go before people begin to wonder."

No one saw them leave the party. Jochanaan closed the door to the examining room quietly behind them. "Samuel, I have a problem with my sexuality. I believe you might call me 'schwul' or a '*Hundert-fünfundsiebziger*', gay, queer, or whatever. No one knows about my feelings aside from you and Fritz. I had a long talk with him earlier today. It was he who suggested I speak with you because of your medical background."

"What makes you think you are gay? Don't you like girls?"

"As I told Fritz, I like girls, but they don't turn me on. Is there anything that could be done to me to change my feelings?"

"I'm not a psychiatrist. From what I have observed in my professional life, there is nothing that will change your feelings. You have to accept what and who you are and live with it. I wish I could tell you otherwise. Being gay doesn't make you a bad person. Many famous and not-so-famous people in this world have shared your orientation and have lived a secret and also a successful life. I hope humanity will become more accepting and tolerant of people like you. I wish I could have been of more help. I view our discussion as privileged information. I will share this with no one. I won't discuss it with Fritz either. It's between you and me. If you want to tell Fritz about our discussion and what I told you, that's for you to decide."

They walked out of the room together. Fritz saw them but acted as if he hadn't seen anything unusual. He was glad Jochanaan had discussed his concerns with Samuel. The bar mitzvah event had turned into something far more reaching than Jochanaan and Fritz had ever imagined.

Chapter 61

THE world greeted Madeline Rachel Esther Bernstein early in the morning of October 3, 1959. She opened her eyes to her mother's greeting. "Mazel tov, happy New Year." Another generation was born on Rosh Hashanah. Josh and his parents were delighted. Zayde Samuel smiled broadly as his first grandchild was laid into his arms. He loved having a grandchild; he loved even more that it was a girl. Josh and Miriam looked on with satisfaction spelled all over their faces. They had delivered on their promise. They would call her Maddie. She was a good-sized baby. Maddie weighed in at just under nine pounds and was of average length. The delivery had been natural and without complications.

Maddie began to cry. "It's time for you to nurse her. She's looking for nourishment." Esther picked her up and put her near Miriam's left breast. Josh stood directly behind his wife and baby, looking proud. Samuel thought he was beholding the nativity scene. As soon as Maddie began sucking on her mom's nipple, her beautiful little hands reached for and touched her breast. Maddie serendipitously made contact with the Blue Sapphire Amulet. At her insistence, Esther had placed it back around Miriam's neck after giving birth to Madeline. Miriam didn't want to be without it for any longer than she had to. Esther took in the whole scene. "That's my girl. You know what's coming to you. You'll just have to wait for a few years." Miriam and Rachel had shared the history of the amulet with her.

Samuel dialed the number in Essen. "Dr. von Rondstett's office, Elsa Brand speaking."

"Hello, Elsa. It's Samuel Bernstein calling. We have good news for all of you. We have a little granddaughter. She was born early this morning. Might I be able to speak with Rachel or Fritz?"

"Sure thing. I'll get them on the phone right away. Here they are. Congratulations, Grandpa!"

"Thanks, Elsa. You're talking to one happy zayde."

Rachel picked up the phone. "Hello, Samuel. What's the good news? Are we grandparents yet?"

"Sure are. Miriam gave birth to Madeline Rachel Esther Bernstein early this morning. Mazel tov, mazel tov, mazel tov! Happy New Year to us all. We are thrilled. She is perfect in every way. We watched her being nursed by Miriam as soon as she came out of delivery. The 'holy family' was a sight to behold. And guess what? While Miriam was nursing her, the little dickens touched the crown jewel accidentally. Esther got a kick watching Maddie and Miriam. She laughed and winked at Miriam. She whispered to Maddie, 'It will be yours in years to come.' More importantly, how soon may we expect you in Munich? I presume Jochanaan is still in school and won't be coming with you?"

Fritz wanted to speak for Rachel. She was speechless. She reached out to him, wanting to be held. "Can you believe it? We are grandparents. I never thought I would live to see this day. My little girl, all grown up and now a mother herself."

She took the receiver from Fritz. "I love the name the kids chose for our first grandchild. I'm so happy they chose to call her Maddie. How soon can we leave, Fritz? I must hold our little bundle of joy in my own arms. Samuel, I heard you ask about Jochanaan. It went right over my head when you talked about Maddie. Talk about tuning things out you don't want to deal with. You are right; he won't be coming with us to Munich. Elsa will look after him. He pretty much takes care of himself these days. After all, he is a man and frequently reminds us of the fact.

"Dear Sam, thank you so much for calling us with the wonderful news. Fritz and I will be there tomorrow afternoon. We'll take a cab to the hospital and meet you there. Can't wait to see and hold our granddaughter. Our love to Esther and Josh. Hugs and kisses to Miriam and Maddie from all of us." Rachel was crying. She handed the phone back to Fritz. He smacked his lips close to the receiver several times, pretending to send kisses. The connection was gone.

Rachel was still in disbelief. "I'm a grandmother; I'm really a grandmother. Can you believe that?" she questioned Fritz and Elsa. Suddenly she felt chilled. "Fritz, would you mind fixing me a hot drink? I need something to settle my stomach. I feel like I'm having sympathy labor pains. Elsa, please cancel all my appointments through Tuesday, October thirteenth. We aren't planning to stay that long in Munich, but I want the flexibility of doing so if we are needed. I may never have another chance of welcoming a new grandchild. I wasn't there for my daughter; I want to be there for my granddaughter. Fritz, let's start packing. Elsa, please check on the train schedule to Munich." She grabbed a clean coat before she saw her next patient. She had dribbled all over her white lab coat. "I need a new box of tissues in the examining room." She still couldn't believe her good fortune. She was thrilled that the next recipient of the Blue Sapphire Amulet was born.

Their train arrived at the Munich Hauptbahnhof at three o'clock in the afternoon. Rachel held Madeline in her arms an hour later. She was laughing and crying at the same time. Rachel kept looking into Maddie's beautiful eyes. She counted all toes and fingers and touched her cute little nose. Rachel hugged Maddie firmly against her breast; she could feel the warmth radiating from the baby. When it was Fritz's turn to hold her, she placed Maddie gently in his arms.

She was crying tears of pure joy. Fritz, too, had tears running down his face. "Thank you, Miriam and Josh. You made us the happiest people on earth. We never thought this would happen. After your mother's and my losses during the war, you have given us a light to brighten the rest of our days."

The time in Munich flew by all too quickly. Rachel felt badly that they didn't live nearer to Miriam and Josh. But there was always the chance they might move closer once she and Josh had completed their doctorates.

Chapter 62

LIFE in Essen, as well as in Munich, was kind to the Unrat and the Bernstein clans. Three years passed without the experience of tragic events. Telephone calls and periodic train trips kept both families in close touch. Madeline was the joy of her parents and grandparents. Josh and Miriam accelerated their studies and had begun work on their doctoral dissertations.

It was 1962. Miriam called Rachel and Fritz. "Hello, Mom. I just felt like talking. We got good news from our advisors today. We have tested out of some of our lectures and have advanced significantly on our timetable. Josh was told he could have his doctorate in two years, and I will earn mine in three. Isn't that great news?"

"Congratulations to both of you. That's wonderful! You deserve these rewards for all your diligent studying. How is our little girl? Last you said, she was talking up a storm. When I spoke with Sam the other day, he told me she is a walking encyclopedia. He said Maddie is an expert on every subject. She is carrying on some serious conversations with her zayde. He loves it when she calls him Zayde. A few days ago, supposedly she asked him how much he spent on his latest Mercedes. Sam thought Maddie would be an economist at the rate she is going. Can this be true? After all, she is only three years old."

"It's true, Mom. She is so smart, she scares both of us. We are not sure how she will handle a little competition."

"What competition? Are you trying to tell me you are expecting again? Please say yes."

"Yes, Mom. We are having another child in February. All are hoping for a boy. It would be nice for Josh and Samuel. Personally, I'd be just as happy with another healthy girl. They will be not quite four years apart. Guess we just have to wait. I thought you and Fritz could use some good news. How is Jochanaan doing?

"He's doing very well in school."

"I know that. Josh and I are concerned about his continuing interest in becoming a monk. Do you know of anyone who might have planted the seed? Is this all his idea? We just cannot understand any of this. Did you ever have an inkling that he wasn't happy with your decision to raise him in the Jewish tradition? Did he ever express an interest in switching schools? Maybe even attend the cloister school?"

"I really don't believe it has anything to do with being Jewish. He seems to have difficulty relating to other kids in school; both with boys and girls. He's become a real loner. He doesn't want to participate in any sports other than swimming and tennis. He's becoming a regular recluse. I wish he wouldn't spend that much time in the darkroom. He's almost obsessed with that place. But at least I know where to find him. Some of the boys bully him, and he has lost all interest in interacting with girls in his class."

"That's really weird, Mom. I wish I had an answer for you. He seemed such a normal boy."

"A few months ago, Martha was cleaning his room. She found a flashlight and a metal box under his bed. It was locked. I confronted him and wanted to know what it was all about. He finally told me it was none of my business. He was a man, an adult, and he could have anything he chooses to have under his bed. He asked me to get rid of Martha. She had no right to question his personal property. I have an idea the box contained some pornographic material. The labeling on the outside was all in French."

"Mom, Jochanaan is sixteen years old going on seventeen. You and Martha should respect his privacy. Whatever you do, don't push this thing any further. If he really is set on becoming a monk, for whatever reason, so be it. There are worse things than being a monk. They are some of the smartest men in the Catholic church. Most of them make fantastic teachers. I might have become a nun; I discovered it wasn't a life for me. I wanted a man, and I wanted to have children. Now that I have both, I have no regrets. I made the decision on my own; no one tried to influence me. Mom, I don't know the answer. All I can say is, don't push him away. Try to listen to him."

"I guess you are right. He is such a handsome boy; becoming a monk is a waste of a good man as far as I'm concerned. His father will probably spin around in his grave. There were no such aspirations in his makeup. He never would have made it as a monk."

"How is Fritz doing health-wise and otherwise?'

"He's doing just fine. He helps me a lot around the house. One of the things I have learned to truly appreciate is his interest in cooking. Most nights, he has the table set for the three of us. His culinary adventures have been surprising. It's nice not to have to go out for dinner every night. I didn't ask him to do it. He just started experimenting on his own. He's doing a fantastic job running the kitchen. Dusting and cleaning are not his forte. He says those jobs are in Martha's domain. He certainly wouldn't want me to fire her.

"It was good chatting with you. Call more often. Let me know if there is anything I can do for you from afar. Please let me know when you want us to come to Munich. Sister Maria-Angelika was in the other day. She asked me to send you greetings. She's happy that the chapel is completely restored. She's having some issues with arthritis in her shoulders. The dampness in the cloister is getting to her. Enough of this idle chitchat. Best to Josh, my beautiful Maddie, Esther, and Zayde Samuel. We love you."

After she hung up, Rachel walked into the kitchen and spoke to Fritz. He had just put a cake in the oven. "I just heard from Miriam. She and Josh are having another baby in February. Doesn't that make your grandfatherly heart skip a beat? Things are going well for them in school. Maddie is so smart, it blows their minds. I mentioned some of our problems with Jochanaan. My daughter told me to mind my own business. She reminded me that he is almost a seventeen-year-old man and entitled to his privacy. I had no business snooping around in boxes he keeps under his bed. I guess I was told."

"That's wonderful news about the baby on the way. I had hoped for one; getting another does make my heart skip a beat indeed. As far as Jochanaan and his secret treasures are concerned, I concur with Miriam. You might be opening Pandora's box. If and when he decides to go through with joining a monastery, you may learn of his reasoning. At age eighteen, he should be allowed to do anything he wants of his own free will. That's how we've tried to raise him; that's the way he wants to live his life. I have to respect that. I have his full trust. He has shared some of his very personal feelings with me. As much as I love you, I'm not privy to share them with you. He has asked me not to do so!"

Rachel was flabbergasted. She decided not to push the issue. It was obvious to her that Fritz had fostered a special relationship with her son. She knew she had nothing to fear from him.

Chapter 63

THE phone rang in Essen. "Hello, Rachel. Sam here. We have another grandchild."

"Oh, that's wonderful news! A girl or a boy? Are they all right?" gushed Rachel, her heart pounding. She wanted to listen to hear Sam's news but couldn't wait to ask more questions.

Sam could tell by Rachel's response how pleased she was. "Jethro Samuel Otto was born shortly after midnight. He is a healthy-looking boy. Esther thinks he looks like Otto and me. Those kids got their timing just right. Isn't it great that Jethro will be sharing his birthdays with Jochanaan? What do you say now? We are both overjoyed to be blessed with a second grandchild. Why don't you put Fritz on the phone? Let me tell him about Jethro's arrival. I know he'll be tickled to get the good news."

"Just a minute, I want to hear more. I'm not just tickled pink. I'm overwhelmed. How is my girl? Did she have an easy time of delivering Jethro? Was she in labor for a long time? If she's anything like me, she probably barely made it to the hospital. Those kids will have their hands full with their studies and two children under four."

"Rachel, they are young and healthy and motivated. And don't forget, we are here to help. Esther has become a regular bubbe. The kids adore her. She'll talk to the rabbi. We'll let you know about the bris as soon as we know. You asked about Miriam's health. She's as strong as an ox from all that running and exercising the kids do. I'm glad they are so health conscious. Miriam had no problem with the delivery. Jethro popped out relatively easily and fast. Must be in the genes."

"Thanks for the wonderful news, Sam. Here's Fritz."

Sam loved talking with Fritz. They teased each other mercilessly. "Hello, young man. How does it feel to become Grandpa for the second time at age sixty-five?"

"Hi Sam, thanks for the fantastic news. I was thrilled when Maddie arrived; having a boy is icing on the cake. It's good the Bernstein name will be carried on. I'm happy for Rachel that the kids chose to include Otto in the boy's name. That's a nice testimonial to Miriam's father, whom she never knew. But he was the man who had the foresight to shield her from all evil. Nice touch. I admire that girl so much. I guess at twenty-six I should call her a woman. We'll be there for the bris. Make it a great day."

When Fritz got off the phone, he rapped on Jochanaan's bedroom door. "Wake up, buddy. You are an uncle for the second time. You have a new nephew. Jethro Samuel Otto was born shortly after midnight. We'll be celebrating his birth and your seventeenth birthday later today. What do you say now?"

"Boy, that's quite a name. I suppose you expect me to go with you to Munich to watch that prick-cutting session. I think it's barbaric. It was a good thing they did it to me when I was a newborn. I would have never stood for it like Miriam's father. Can you imagine getting your dick mutilated at age twenty-four?"

"Jochanaan, I'm disappointed in you. That's sacrilegious. You studied the history and aspects of your religion just four years ago. You are a smart man and should understand the rationale behind the ritual."

"Listen, I wash my dick every day when I shower. I don't need to be circumcised to avoid walking around with a smelly prick in my pants. That's old-fashioned hogwash. I can't understand why modern people submit to all of this shit. None of it is meaningful in the twentieth century."

"OK, OK. We'll talk about it later. Happy birthday anyway. I love you, ornery or not. You are turning into a very confrontational young man. You never used to talk this way to me."

Rachel, Fritz, and Jochanaan were on the train to Munich on February thirteenth. Jethro's bris was to be conducted in accordance with Hebrew law eight days after his birth. They were seated at the synagogue on Reichenbachstrasse in time for the ceremony. "Maddie, come sit on Grandpa's lap." She was only too happy to cuddle up to Zayde Samuel. They had become a team. He worshiped his first grandchild. Fritz was seated next to them. The two grandfathers took turns holding her. Maddie liked Opa Fritz as well, but she adored her zayde. He was always there for her. She saw him almost every day of her young life. Her papa was often too deep into his books, and Mommy wasn't much better. Zayde and Bubbe were always on hand.

The rabbi was about to cut Jethro's foreskin. Jochanaan turned his head. He couldn't stand to watch it. When little Jethro began screaming, Jochanaan couldn't help himself; he yelled, "Barbarians!" He tore out of his seat and left the temple. He touched his own prick, almost feeling sympathy pains. He would not have sons; if he did, legitimate or otherwise, they would never be subjected to such an inhumane act of torture.

Samuel and Fritz caught up with Jochanaan leaving the temple. Sam lit into him. "How could you do that? It's part of our and your religion. All Jewish men are subjected to the ceremony. It only hurts for a few seconds; then it's all over. It's always done on the eighth day, even if that day falls on our highest and most solemn day—Yom Kippur. We do it to a newborn who doesn't have a developed sense of pain. It's the same when dogs and cats, even bulls, are castrated or have their tails cut off. The procedures are done at a very young age most of the time."

"Spoken like a surgeon. The dif is, the animals are anesthetized, we little boys and our little pricks are not. Ouch! Just the thought of it."

"You are right in that respect. But you are a man and no longer a kid. We expected you to be just a bit more mature about the whole thing. It's done. The rabbi has heard the reaction before, I'm sure. Let's change the subject as long as we men are by ourselves. What have you decided about continuing your education? Are you still set on joining forces with a religious order? We know you'll get a good education, but what do you see yourself doing ten years from now? Are you envisioning any sort of profession or career?"

"Too many questions already. Yes, I have every intention of joining a monastery after finishing my Abitur next year. I'll be eighteen and able to do anything I choose.

I had a preliminary interview with Father Frederick Emanuel at the abbey at Maria Laach a couple of weeks ago. The Benedictine monks there took a particular interest in Jewish people who were persecuted by the Nazis. I feel a certain connection to this order. We talked for about two hours. It was a most informative and productive session. I came away with the decision to join the brothers next year. Father Frederick Emanuel and I felt a certain kinship when we shook hands. You can always tell the character of a person by the way they shake your hand. The press of his fingers in the palm of my right hand told me a lot about my future advisor and mentor."

Fritz wanted to know how he managed to go to Maria Laach, and what was so special about the handshake of Father Frederick Emanuel.

"I took a day off from school and took the train. Mom wouldn't let me drive her car. Father's handshake conveyed to me that we share similar feelings."

Samuel and Fritz exchanged questioning glances as they shrugged their shoulders. "Let's head for the Tabu. They have a wonderful lunch set for us to celebrate little Jethro's bris." It was Jethro's day, but Maddie was the star of the show.

No one paid particular attention to Jochanaan; he was beginning to feel like a pariah within his family. He realized he had no one to blame for their behavior but himself. He knew in his heart he was different from any man in the room.

Chapter 64

IN the spring of 1964, Jochanaan graduated and finished his Abitur with highest honors. The event was celebrated in the circle of family and friends. Esther, Miriam, and the children surprised Rachel with their attendance. Miriam couldn't miss seeing her brother prior to his entry into the monastery. Josh and Samuel stayed behind in Munich. Samuel had too many professional commitments; Josh was in the final throes of his dissertation. Jochanaan could understand and accepted their decisions to skip the event.

Rachel spoke to the visitors. "I am terribly disappointed. Fritz and I were so looking forward to having everyone here for Jochanaan's graduation. But we are thankful for having you, Esther; our sweet Miriam; and the children with us. I can't believe Maddie is five and will be starting kindergarten. And look at you, Jethro, trying to walk still holding onto furniture. And he's even trying to say a few words. How fast they are growing! Lord knows what they will be up to when we see you in Munich the next time."

Miriam took Jochanaan in her arms and kissed his face. "Be well, little brother. I hope this is really what you want. I never thought my brother would seek the priesthood."

Only Rachel and Fritz drove Jochanaan to Maria Laach. They

liked the abbey and the monks they met. His housing was less than humble. Jochanaan didn't mind. He was seeking physical punishment and deprivation. Lately, he had developed almost masochistic tendencies. He had this need to suffer for things that were done to his people.

He discussed these feelings with Fritz while they walked in the gardens of the abbey. Rachel was unpacking his things in his cell. "I want to be abused by men. Ever since I saw the photo of my father in his 'glorious' SS uniform and learned who he was, I wondered who I am? Before he met my mother, he fucked every skirt he could get his hands on in Paris and Theresienstadt. He was the right hand of the man who ran the camp. I imagine he sent many a Jew to the gas chambers and the crematoria in Auschwitz-Birkenau. Have you ever seen pictures of those places? Have you ever read about the horrible things these pigs visited on my people? Did Mom ever tell you what they made her and Elsa do to those poor inmates? I shudder to think that prick of a Nazi fathered me by inflicting his semen into my mother's womb."

"I feel sorry for you and your suffering this kind of guilt. Johann, your father, was kind to your mother and loved her. It was his love for her that shielded her from a worse fate. What he did before your mother met him, we don't know. All I know is that he did everything in his power to protect her. If he was ever overheard how he felt about the camp, the leader, and the leadership of the country, he probably would have been shot as a traitor. You cannot make this your responsibility just because Johann was your father. If this is what drove you to the monastery, I believe you are sadly mistaken in the choices you are making. But you are a man indeed, and you must make your own decisions. Once you are established in the monastery, don't become a stranger to your family. Know we all love you very much."

"Mother told me not too long ago how my father was abused by Russian and Polish soldiers outside of Dresden. She described how seven men sodomized him and eventually killed him by firing their guns into his rectum and back until he finally was lying dead on the ground. His Mercedes became his funeral pyre. What Johann von Rondstett suffered, I seek to suffer now."

"That is crazy talk, Jochanaan. You didn't do anything to deserve what you are wishing upon yourself. You are a handsome, intelligent young man with a bright future ahead of you. You have no reason to feel this kind of guilt. I hope you will come to your senses and abandon these way-out ideas. You are no flesh and blood of mine, but I couldn't love you more if you were. I met your mother within hours after she conceived you. I feel like I am your father, although I had absolutely nothing to do with your conception."

"You are the father I never had. I always felt loved in your arms. I knew you loved me deeply from the time I was old enough to realize the part you played in Mom's life and mine. I never thought I couldn't trust you. You are the only person other than Samuel to whom I confessed my sexual orientation. I have taken your and Samuel's advice. I am what I am, and I can accept that now. It's not what I wanted to be, but I have no choice in the matter. It's not something I can be cured of; I just need to live with it. May God forgive me."

"Remember, we have a grace-filled God, not a vengeful one. Come here, let me kiss you good-bye. Pretend that I'm Wotan." With that he kissed Jochanaan on his forehead and his closed eyelids.

Jochanaan stopped walking and got Fritz's attention. "I should tell you that I love Father Frederick Emanuel. I believe he will be a good teacher. He fully accepts and is willing to meet my personal needs." Fritz understood what Jochanaan was trying to tell him.

They walked back to Jochanaan's cell. One of the monks was ready to help Jochanaan out of his clothes and dress him in a light-weight dark-brown tunic with a hood. He walked them out to the car, wearing his monastic garb. Rachel looked at him solemnly and with love.

"Son, there will come times when you wish you weren't a monk. It's only human. These are human feelings and human needs. I hated your father after he raped me on the day I arrived at Theresienstadt. I made a pact with him that I would pretend to the outside world that I was his whore as long as he would never touch me again. He shielded and protected me from the evil that surrounded us. He always told me he loved me. I didn't believe him and succeeded to keep him at bay. I succumbed to human needs the day before we fled Theresienstadt. Let me assure you, you were conceived in love, not in a hateful act. Johann would have cherished having you as a son. Let me kiss you farewell. Please come and see us whenever you have the need to be loved by us."

She kissed him on his forehead and then on the eyes he had closed. They shared their tears as they held each other tightly. Jochanaan knew how much his mother loved him. Fritz just shook his hand; they had said their farewell in the garden of the abbey.

Rachel and Fritz were grateful to have Esther, Miriam, and the children waiting for them when they returned home. Taking Jochanaan to the monastery had been challenging for both. The day following Jochanaan's departure for Maria Laach, Rachel asked Miriam to accompany her to the Parkfriedhof. She had this need to stand in front of her ancestors and Otto's grave site. "Miriam, I would like you and Maddie to accompany me to the cemetery. I don't know why, but it's almost like an inner voice asking me to visit your father's grave with you and the granddaughter he never knew. Would you mind?"

"Not at all, Mom. It's so long since I was last there."

"Maddie might be too young to understand what we are talking about, although she is a pretty smart girl for her age. Esther tells me Maddie is fascinated with books, the letters of the alphabet, and now she even enjoys sounding out words."

Holding Bubbe Rachel's hand, Maddie was looking at all the

beautiful flowers at the shops just outside the cemetery. "Bubbe, can we buy a few fresh flowers to put on the graves?"

"Yes, we will put them in the vases I keep at the grave site. These tulips are colorful and will look cheery. Let's get two or three dozen, and we'll divide them among the two vases."

With their bouquet of parrot tulips in hand, they walked under the archway of the large burial complex with its endlessly long hallway and many tiny cubicles where the dead were laid out. "What's this building?" asked Maddie.

Grandma Rachel answered the child. "When people die, other than Jews, they are brought here to be viewed by family and friends for three days. Usually, they hold a service in the chapel down that way. Afterward, the dead person is taken to be buried. Often, six men carry the coffin to the site. When Jews die, they are buried in a wooden box or coffin before the next sunset. Someday, you will learn about all these different customs." Rachel decided not to take it any further. Why clutter the child's mind? There were more important things to learn and know about.

"Grandma, why do some people come to this place even if there is no funeral?"

"Well, my dear, the Parkfriedhof is a lovely park. I don't come as often as I should. Most of our relatives are buried here. These are the resting places of yours, mine, and your mommy's ancestors, plus that of your grandfather, Otto von Graben. We just have to walk down this beautiful pathway through the rhododendron, and we will be at the grave. Maddie kept looking at everything they passed, taking in the scene with her eager young eyes. They walked by the fishpond, and then they were there. Since Otto was taken to his final rest, the grave was well kept; blue and yellow pansies, as well as cheery daffodils, were nodding rhythmically in a light breeze. Maddie stood next to her grandmother. She was trying to decipher the writing on the large stone.

Maddie studied the letters *S-A-L-M* and sounded out the word. "That's right, Maddie. Adam Jethro Salm was your great-great-grandfather and your great-great-grandmother was Adina Daniella Salm. They were my grandparents."

"They must have lived a long time ago; they sound so old!"

"You are a smart girl, Maddie. They were born almost one hundred years ago. They've been at rest at this site for many years."

"Who is O-t-t-o v-o-n G-r-a-b-e-n?"

"He was married to me, your bubbe Rachel, and was your mommy's father. He died during the war. He would have been your zayde Otto. When his body was returned to us many years after the war, I wanted him buried here."

"May I get the vase from behind the stone, Bubbe?"

"Yes, you may; but be careful where you step. It looks like the caretakers have just been here. Everything looks very neat and freshly raked." Miriam was just watching and listening to the conversation between her mother and Maddie. She was such an inquisitive child.

Maddie tiptoed along the side to retrieve the vases with the sharp points, making it easy to push into the soil of the grave. She had seen the water spigot just around the corner and, without much ado, decided to go ahead and fill the vases with water. Bubbe Rachel and Mommy were on another planet. When Maddie returned, her elders snapped out of their respective thoughts. "Oh, there you are, Maddie; thanks for getting the water. These tulips will look lovely with the other flowers in bloom."

After she placed the bright flowers on the graves, Rachel bent down to hug her grandchild. She was so thankful for the harmonious relationship she enjoyed with her children and grandchildren.

Walking back to the car, they passed hundreds of gigantic rhododendron in every imaginable color. Maddie spotted row after row of identical gravestones that appeared to be nothing but concrete forms. "What are these Grandma? They all look the same. Can we stop for a moment?"

"Of course, Maddie, these are graves of people who died during the bomb attacks on the city in World War Two. The simple graves were small. The stones are more than fifty years old and thus covered with green moss and discolored from air pollution."

Maddie went down on her knees. She started to decipher the inscription on the first marker. "*U-n-b-e-k-a-n-n-t.*" She thought that was a strange name. She moved on to the next stone and discovered that that person's name also was "*U-n-b-e-k-a-n-n-t.*" When the results of her serious efforts at the third, fourth, and fifth concrete markers were the same, she got up from her knees and faced her mom and Bubbe Rachel. "Isn't that weird? They all have the same name. If they came from the same family, why didn't they just put one marker on the big grave site?"

"No, no Maddie, these are all individual graves." They could tell by the child's puzzled expression this revelation gave Maddie much to think about. "Someday, when you are older, Maddie, you will study about these things in history. For now, let's not dwell on the ghosts of the past. I have a great idea. Let's stop at Kikas and order the biggest dishes of ice cream they offer. We'll be bad with you. Mom and I will order ours with whipped cream as well. Let's just not tell Grandpa Fritz where we stopped. He'd be really jealous having missed out on the ice cream."

"OK, Grandma, but would you mind if I first ordered some French fries with lots of ketchup?"

"No, not at all, as long as you don't get sick to your stomach." And with that pact on their lips, they passed under the archway of the great hall of the dead and headed for Bubbe Rachel's car.

They were seated at Kikas, enjoying their ice cream with gusto. Rachel noticed that Maddie was still looking pensive. "Don't you like your ice cream, Maddie? Did we order the wrong thing? Maybe having all those French fries first wasn't such a good idea; what do you think?"

"No, no, Bubbe. I'm fine; I'm still thinking about all those gravestones with the same name,

'U-n-b-e-k-a-n-n-t.' What a strange family."

"Oh no, child. It's not a family name. More likely than not, none of these people knew each other in life. Worse yet, no one knew who they were when they were buried. That is why each of the markers simply says 'Unknown' and the year they were buried." Miriam looked at her mother and smiled. They remembered those times of war.

Chapter 65

ON the morning of October 17, 1965, Rachel's phone rang. Elsa picked up the receiver.

"Von Rondstett and Associates, Dental Care, Elsa Brand speaking. How may I help you?"

"It's Esther calling." Elsa immediately realized that Esther was crying.

"What's wrong Esther? I can tell by your voice something terrible has happened."

"Josh was in a serious accident. We don't know if he will live."

"Oy Gevalt; that cannot be. Let me get Rachel on the phone. She'll be devastated." Elsa resorted to her megaphone voice. "Rachel, Rachel, come quick to the phone. It's Esther. Josh was in a terrible accident." Rachel picked up the phone. She instantly felt the pain Esther must be suffering.

"Esther, Esther, tell me what happened. Will Josh be all right? Those poor children and poor you, and poor Samuel."

"He was riding his bicycle home from school and was struck by a streetcar. No one seems to know exactly what happened. All we know so far is that both of his femurs and his pelvis were crushed. They are not certain if he sustained any spinal injuries. Please pray for us that he will recover. Samuel is with Miriam at the hospital. I've got Maddie and Jethro with me. Maddie knows that her daddy was hurt, but she doesn't know the extent of the injuries."

"Fritz and I will be on the next available train. We'll stay with Miriam rather than at a hotel. I'm sure she would want us to be close to her. Know that we love you and keep all of you in our prayers."

Rachel went looking for Fritz. Passing by Elsa's desk, she stopped. "What devastating news! Please, cancel all my appointments and refer any emergencies to Dr. Bierbaum. He'll understand. Then please book us on the next train to Munich. We've got to get to them as quickly as we can." When she finally found Fritz sitting on the stool, she spoke. Her voice broke relating the sad events. They were on the express train to Munich in less than two hours.

They took a cab to Miriam's house from the Munich Hauptbahnhof and dropped off their luggage. Samuel was waiting for them. "I'll take you to the hospital. Miriam is anxious to see you. Josh is still heavily sedated; his lower extremities are in a full body cast. The initial examinations and tests do not sound promising. Josh may be in a wheelchair for the rest of his life."

Rachel and Fritz were in shock.

"Oh no, no, no—this cannot be." Rachel tried to suppress her outbursts of sorrow. "Sam, once the healing of his legs and pelvic area take place, you must have him evaluated again. You know yourself, a second opinion is clearly indicated.

"I absolutely agree with you, Rachel."

"Would it be possible for us to leave right away? Josh and Miriam have to be utterly distraught, and we so need to be with them."

"We certainly understand. Let's go."

Rushing down the endless corridors of the hospital, surrounded by everything white and glaring, Rachel felt she had entered a morgue. Her mind was racing. "What would Miriam's life be like if Josh was paralyzed for the rest of his days? Even worse, if he were to die?" She couldn't imagine him unable to play with his children or to even hold them. She barely spoke a word to Fritz; she was so deeply in thought and envisioning the worst.

When they walked into Josh's private room, they faced the severity of the injuries. Miriam rushed to hold Rachel and Fritz. "Thank you, thank you, Mom and Fritz. I knew you would want to be with me. I still can't believe this happened. We were so close to a better life with our professional goals fulfilled. I'm still hoping the doctors are wrong about Josh's spinal injuries. Please keep praying for us for a positive outcome." Mother and daughter cried on each other's shoulders, trying to comfort each other. Fritz quietly talked with Samuel outside the room.

All were glad to know that Esther was there to take care of her grandchildren. Maddie kept asking about her daddy. "Please tell me what happened to Daddy. Will he die? I want to see him before he dies." Esther made sure Maddie went to see her ailing father as soon that was possible. Maddie was fascinated by the cast on his lower body. "I have heard of people writing on casts. Can I do that?" The nurse brought in a special marker. Maddie wrote: "I love you, Daddy. Get well real soon."

$$\text{X}$$

Two months later, Josh was discharged from the hospital. After the casts were removed, the attending specialists had Josh attempt to wiggle his toes on command. The result was positive and hopeful. Post-traumatic rehabilitative training was clearly indicated. Josh and all in the family began to be encouraged by the daily progress he was making. Eventually, Josh got around campus in a wheelchair and pursued the completion of his doctoral studies. But every opportunity he had, he invested in exercises leading to the use of his legs. Watching him work, Miriam and Josh's family began to have faith in his mantra: "I can do it! I will do it! I will walk again!"

Josh received his doctorate a year later. At commencement, he walked with a cane to the podium to receive his diploma under thunderous applause from classmates, faculty, and his family. He knew he was well on his way to a full recovery. It would be only a question of time before he and Miriam would be running again together.

Miriam was happy to finish her degree a year later in 1966. There was a family reunion coinciding with the event. It was Fritz's seventieth birthday. All were present but Jochanaan. As much as he wanted to be there, he could not undertake a trip for such a family event. He was only allowed to leave the abbey in the event of death or serious illness of members in his immediate family.

Rachel and Fritz traveled by train. Maddie and Jethro were the sunshine in their lives. The children were close to all their grandparents. "Opa Fritz, will you read me some stories? Bubbe Rachel is playing with Jethro. She loves listening to his cute phrases. Did I ever say those kinds of things?"

Miriam and Esther couldn't help overhearing Maddie's last question. Miriam answered. "Yes, you did, and a lot more. By the time you were Jethro's age, you were talking like a waterfall. Your daddy and I loved listening to you. Now that you are almost seven years old, you often sound like an adult. The things you say and ask at times blow our minds."

"Mom, it's being around you and Daddy and that school you make me attend. Nobody ever talks like some of the kids I play with. Sometimes I hear words I'm not supposed to use."

"Words like what?"

"One of the boys in my class uses words like 'asshole' and 'shit' a lot. That's what he calls Mr. Dibbel, our teacher. When we get our home assignments, he says that is nothing but 'shit' that 'asshole' makes us write."

Esther got into the act. "You are correct; we do not want you to use such words. That's not ladylike, and you are quickly becoming a young lady. Your zayde would be shocked if he ever heard you using such bad language.

"Your father and zayde will be home from the office very soon. You can tell them what a great time you had today with Bubbe Rachel and Opa Fritz. When we go out to dinner tonight, you children will come along. I know you will be on your best behavior. That makes me so happy. Your mom will be here as well. She has her last meeting with her advisor today. Then she will be all finished. She is so looking forward to spending more time with you. Won't that be nice?"

"You mean Mom will stay home?"

"Well, she'll work only three days a week away from home. The other days she'll be spending with you."

"Yippee! That's the best news ever, Bubbe. I love you and Zayde, but I'm glad to see my mom and dad more now that they are done with going to school. I don't think I ever want to be a doctor. That's too much school for me. I like shopping and playing better."

"You just wait and see. You'll change your mind in good time. There are some wonderful schools you may attend. I see Zayde and your dad pulling up to the curb. We better get you two dressed for the dinner party. Your mom should be here any minute now. It's wonderful seeing your father getting around with just a cane."

Maddie added, "Every night when I pray, I say thank you to God for making my daddy all better." Rachel and Esther hugged her fiercely.

"Rachel, come upstairs. We can talk while we are getting the kids into more appropriate clothes. This is always fun, especially with Jethro. He has a mind of his own."

Rachel needed to say it. "You have been wonderful, always being willing and able to help Miriam and Josh. She couldn't have kept up her studies without your help. I don't know what they would have done without you during the last year."

"That's what bubbes and zaydes are for. Glad to do it. It was too bad you couldn't do it for Miriam during all those years. When I stop and think about the sacrifices you and Otto had to make! And all for that darn war and their crazy ideas of annihilating our race! Thanks to the Almighty, we survived it. So happy that you and Miriam finally found each other.

"Well, it's time to join the others. Let's have a drink before we head out."

The chateaubriand was prepared to perfection, and the children's menu was to Maddie and Jethro's liking. The grand finale, *Schwarzwälder Kirschtorte*, was a big hit for all. Most of the conversation centered on Josh's and Miriam's academic futures.

Sam spoke up. "We are most thankful to the Almighty for having spared our Josh. He's made remarkable strides. As hard as he works at building up his body, I believe he'll be back to near-normal capacity before too long. There might always be a slight limp, but it's something he and all of us can accept and live with. He's happy and enjoys his appointment as assistant professor in the philosophy department. His profs liked him so well, they offered him a position. Miriam's part-time job is great for now. When both kids are in school, she might consider teaching full time. It's a good thing Esther is always available, and I, of course, love being Zayde on weekends."

It was Fritz's turn. "Rachel and I envy both of you for living so close to the kids and grand-kids. It gets pretty quiet around our place with Jochanaan being gone. We miss him very much."

Deep down in her heart, Rachel always hoped he would leave the monastery after a short stint and come to his senses. She wanted grandchildren from him and Johann's memory kept alive. Rachel had tears in her eyes as she spoke. "Where did I go wrong with that boy? What could I or we have done to prevent him from seeking solace in a monastery?" she muttered, mostly to herself.

Samuel believed he needed to speak. "Rachel, neither you nor Fritz did anything wrong. Being homosexual is not something we learn. It's something we are born with. It's in his system. He can't help himself. He is what he is. It sounds to me like he has accepted the fact and will live by his decision. All of us need to respect it. Being gay doesn't make him a bad person. He has a brilliant mind, as have many gay men and women of the past, present, and future. In time, he will make his contributions to society. All we need to do now is not shun him but love him. Let's not act like the Nazis who tried to erase these men and women as much as they tried to eliminate us."

Rachel shuddered.

Maddie added levity to the change in the celebratory atmosphere. "What's a homosexual?"

"That's for you to discover when you are much older, child. Just remember, they are good people, like your uncle Jochanaan."

Sam knew he had blown it. Rachel never knew of Jochannaan's sexual orientation. "Let's head home. I could use a stiff drink or two. What about you, Josh and Fritz? I know we could have that here, but I don't want to chauffeur any of you when I'm under the influence." Pandora's box had been opened. The party was over. All had to live with it. They were speaking in hushed voices with each other as they left the restaurant.

The return trip to Essen was uneventful. Rachel continued brooding about what she learned the night before. "If you knew about it, why didn't you tell me?" Rachel confronted Fritz.

"My silence was dictated by Jochanaan's pleading with me not to let you know. I respected that request. I gave him my word. I was proud he loved me enough to share his feelings and thoughts. When we took him to Maria Laach, he told me he loved me like the father he never knew. It meant a lot to me. Rachel, Jochanaan being gay is not your fault. Just like it isn't his fault that you had him with Johann."

"I couldn't figure out what you were talking about for that length of time. I was wondering what was going on between the two of you. I was hoping you talked sense into him, making him forget about joining the order. Guess I was wrong."

"This probably will add to your distress. Jochanaan let me know in a subtle manner that he and Father Frederick Emanuel are lovers.

He believes he is in good hands. We have to accept and respect his wishes."

Rachel went to the WC on the rapidly moving train. When she returned to her seat across from Fritz, her face was as white as chalk. He held her hands; neither said another word until the train pulled into the Hauptbahnhof in Essen.

When they finally got home, she walked through the dining room and looked up. She never had replaced the stolen chandelier. Romantic candlelight dinners with Fritz and her friends had made her completely forget about the missing object. Looking at the massive hook mounted in the heavy beam of the ceiling, strange thoughts crossed her mind as she got ready for bed, and her body suddenly convulsed as she slid beneath the covers.

Chapter 66

RACHEL awoke at seven o'clock. Fritz was an early riser. She was surprised to see him still lying next to her on his usual side of the bed. She touched his head. Hesitatingly, her hand moved to his chest. She knew he was dead. She ran to her apartment door and yelled as loudly as she could. "Elsa, Elsa, I need you!" All neighbors in the building probably heard her. Rachel had thrown on a wrap. She was bent over Fritz's dead body. Her eyes filled with tears. When Elsa rushed in, she knew what she was facing.

She walked over and hugged her friend who was unwilling to be consoled. It was the third love she'd lost. How much more could she take? She'd hoped for at least ten more years with Fritz. It was not meant to be.

Elsa took charge. She got on the phone. "Hello, Esther, it's Elsa. I have very sad news. Fritz died during the night. It's an apparent heart attack."

"Oh, what terrible news! I'm absolutely stunned."

"Fritz's body has been taken to the Parkfriedhof. He'll be buried Friday, three days from now. I'm hoping for Rachel's sake all of you can see your way clear to attend the services."

"I'll get in touch with everyone in the family right away."

"Esther, I already put in a call to Jochanaan. He wasn't sure if he could make it. He said he would try his best to receive permission to be there. Please call me as soon as you know who is coming, and I'll make the necessary arrangements for all of you."

"We would appreciate that. How is Rachel doing?"

"She's still in shock and isn't ready to speak to anyone. My next job is to call and cancel all her appointments for the rest of the week. I'm so sorry to be the bearer of such sad news. I'll be waiting to hear from you."

"Thank you, Elsa. I'll get back to you as soon as possible."

Josh, Miriam, the children, and Josh's parents all came. Rachel decided to have Fritz interred in the family plot. Several weeks earlier, without telling anyone, she had the stonemason add Johann's name to the gravestone. She felt he was part of her life; she wanted him recognized as the husband he would have become had he not been murdered. In time, her full name would be added to those of her three husbands.

The funeral was small. Although Fritz was Protestant, Rachel had Rabbi Weisskopf conduct the service. Outside the family, only Mimi and Helena were in attendance. Josh wanted to honor Fritz with a few words. He held onto Miriam as he walked up to the grave using his cane. Miriam took a scoop of the soft earth and placed Josh's free hand above her own. As they committed the soil to the top of Fritz's coffin, Josh spoke. "Farewell, dear friend. You were good to us; I know you loved us like a father."

Rabbi Weisskopf was about to conclude his service when Rachel looked back to face the other mourners. She saw a lone monk standing in the rear of the small group. Jochanaan realized his mother needed him badly. He walked up to the grave site. His hair was cropped very short; it was slightly covered by the hood of his dark tunic. He was wearing a large crucifix on his chest. Brother Jochanaan was a presence in his monasterial garb.

He held a small Bible in his hands. Jochanaan opened it and began to read the twenty-third psalm. He spoke in his dark and vibrant voice: "The LORD is my shepherd; I shall not want. He maketh me to lie down in green pastures: he leadeth me beside the still waters. He restoreth my soul: he leadeth me in the paths of righteousness for his name's sake. Yea, though I walk through the valley of the shadow of death, I will fear no evil: for thou art with me; thy rod and thy staff they comfort me. Thou preparest a table before me in the presence of mine enemies: thou anointest my head with oil; my cup runneth over. Surely goodness and mercy shall follow me all the days of my life; and I will dwell in the house of the LORD forever." All present spoke softly in concert with Jochanaan.

His eyes connected with Rachel's. He looked back at the open grave. "Thank you for being my father, for being my trusted friend. I loved you as you loved me. I will remember you in my daily prayers for the rest of my days as I have done so for many years. You were my staff and my support in turbulent times. You were my soul mate while I lived my days with you. Thank you, Fritz. Jochanaan's tunic became splotchy from the tears falling from his eyes, and he could barely speak. He whispered, "Farewell, my friend. I love you." He picked up the shovel. Keeping with tradition, he spread soil on Fritz's coffin. The hollow sound gave him goosebumps.

He walked over to his mother and hugged her intensely. Looking over her shoulder, he couldn't help seeing the gravestone. He sobbed as he read: Otto von Graben, Johann von Rondstett, and Frederick Fritz Unrat. His father had finally found a dignified resting place. His body wasn't there. His burned corpse had long decomposed in an unmarked grave on some remote farm outside of Dresden, but he was remembered with love.

Chapter 67

IN late summer of 1973, Rachel began complaining about severe pains invading her abdomen. She had a high pain tolerance. "Elsa, I really don't need to consult with a physician. It will all go away soon. Just don't cancel any more of my patients' appointments. I can handle it."

When the pain did become intolerable, she finally agreed to see her doctor. That same day, she was seen by an oncologist. The final diagnosis was pancreatic cancer. At best, she was given eight weeks to live. At first she was devastated. Then she accepted her fate. What did she have to live for? She had outlived three loves. Her daughter, Miriam Daniella, and grandchildren lived happily near her husband's family miles away in Munich. Her one and only son lived in a distant monastery. Was that all there was for her? She began to make final arrangements. Rachel even went to the stonemason. She knew exactly what she wanted on the Salm grave marker. "I want you to place my full name under the names of my three husbands, whom I will join in the not-so-distant future. All you have to add when the time comes are the dates. That should be simple enough; 1913 – 1973. I have only weeks to live. The inscription is long: Rachel Adina Salm von Graben von Rondstett Unrat. Please take care of it right away, and send me the bill."

Rachel placed a call to the monastery. At first, she was turned away. She then begged to speak to Father Frederick Emanuel. "Father, I truly need to speak to Brother Jochanaan, my son. I am deathly ill. I wish to see him one more time before I die." Within seconds, Jochanaan was on the phone. "Is it true what Father Frederick Emanuel tells me?"

"Yes, Jochanaan. I have been diagnosed with pancreatic cancer. I've been given only weeks to live, perhaps only days. It is my dying wish to hold you and see you one more time. I cannot believe that you will not be granted permission to honor my request."

There was a pause. "I spoke to Father Frederick Emanuel; I will be on my way within the hour. I'm very sad. I love you, Mom."

"I love you too, Jochanaan. She hung up.

She then glanced at the calendar as she was dialing Miriam's number. It was September 24.·

"I hope I didn't call too early, but it is urgent I speak with you. How are my darlings, Maddie and Jethro? I miss them so much. I wish all of you and your brother lived closer to me."

"Mom, sometimes I wish that as well. What was the urgency of your call? You don't sound right at all. Are you ill?"

"Miriam, I'm saddened to tell you this. I am indeed very ill, and the doctors have given me very little time to live. Perhaps a few weeks; perhaps a few days. It's pancreatic cancer. I'm in great pain. I'm told it will get far worse. Pain meds help only minimally. It is my wish to see all my family one more time. I cannot travel. This time you must come to me. I would like all of us to be together just this once. Please do not disappoint me."

"Oh no, Mom. That cannot be. Have you spoken with Jochanaan?" Rachel could sense that Miriam was crying.

"Yes. I just spoke with him minutes ago; he is leaving Maria Laach this morning."

"Mom, let me call Josh and his parents. I'll get back to you right away. If no one else, the children and I will be on the train later this morning. I love you so much. I can't believe this is happening. I wish I could hold you this very instant." Rachel felt Miriam's love in what she said.

The phone rang twenty minutes later. "Mom, it's Miriam. All of us will be on the train at eleven. We should be arriving at five o'clock or so. I've called the Handelshof and made reservations for Mom and Dad. My troops will be staying there as well. It's all taken care of. Sam called a car rental. We're all set. I presume Jochanaan is staying with you?"

"Yes, Miriam. I asked him to do so. Thanks for making the arrangements at the Handelshof. I was going to do that as soon as I knew who was coming. Thanks; it's one thing less for me to tend to. There is no problem feeding people here; there's just not enough space to house everyone. I suppose Esther and Sam could have stayed upstairs with Elsa. Well, you took care of everything. Thanks, Love. I can't wait to hold you and Maddie and Jethro. I miss Fritz. I'm also glad he didn't have to see me suffering like this. Here are hugs and kisses over the wires. Thank God I'll be able to do it for real in a few hours." They hung up.

Jochanaan pulled up in the rental car shortly after one o'clock. Elsa greeted him when he walked in. He bent down to give her a quick hug. "Where is Mom? How is she feeling?" She could tell by his bloodshot eyes that he had been crying.

"She had John move one of the comfortable chairs from the living room. She wants to sit by the large window in the dining room. Your mother loves to watch the birds at the feeder. You'll see. She's in an awful lot of pain. Her face shows it. Don't be shocked when you first see her. Go in. She's been waiting for you."

Rachel looked up at her beautiful son. He had pushed the hood off his head. His hair still was cropped very short. She thought he looked manly although very thin and gaunt. Rachel managed to flash him a big, tearful smile. "Come let me hold you, my love. You can kiss me, Jochanaan. I'm not contagious."

He rushed to his mother and put his arms around Rachel's frail body. His kisses touched her all over her face as his tears fell on her countenance. Jochanaan was bawling. "I've missed you so much. I know you have hated the way I live. I'm sorry, but I cannot help the way I am. I was sad to learn of your illness, but I was touched that you wanted me to be with you. Thank you for loving me."

"Jochanaan, I have always loved you; I never hated you. I hated what Mother Nature chose you to be. One of the last things Fritz succeeded in doing was to teach me that what and who you are is not anything you choose to be. You can't help yourself. I love you just the way you are. You are a very handsome, loving man with a big heart. Come sit by me. Miriam and the entire family will be here later this afternoon. As much as I hurt, my heart is filled with joy."

The entire Munich family arrived at dinner time. Miriam could tell immediately that her mother was in unbelievable pain. She was shocked to see her mother was a mere shadow of her former self. Her eyes were marked by deep, dark circles. Her once-striking cheek bones almost gave her a hard look. Death was written all over Rachel's face. As she held her mother in her arms, she couldn't restrain herself any longer. She poured out her sorrow. "Mom, why didn't you let us know sooner? How long have you been suffering like this? Why didn't Elsa call us?"

"Now, now, my dear child. I've only known my diagnosis for a few weeks. I finally listened to Elsa and saw my doctor. I thought it would all go away. I forbade Elsa to call you. Please don't be harsh with her. She's been a good and true friend for many, many years. Where are my little angels? I want to hold and hug them."

"We are all here. The kids, Josh, and Mom and Dad are with Jochanaan. He was in his room crying his heart out. He concerns us. He seems to be devastated by your illness. Jochanaan has a hard time dealing with himself and what you might think of him and his lifestyle."

"Miriam, I've told him that I love him just the way God made him, and I truly do." As Rachel tried to push herself up, she said, "I have to get out of this chair. You all must be hungry. Did you all have something to eat on the train?"

"Mom, I wish you wouldn't fuss over us and our comforts. It is much more important for you to rest and not wait on us." Jochanaan and the others walked into the dining room at the moment Rachel fell back into her chair. She had no strength left. She spotted Maddie and Jethro and reached out to them. "Come give your grandma a hug and kiss. I've missed you so much. My, my, how both of you have grown. Maddie, you are almost a young lady. And what a healthy boy my Jethro has become." Maddie and Jethro hugged and kissed Rachel tenuously. Her frailty scared them. Her appearance had drastically changed since they last saw her.

Finally, Josh, Esther, and Samuel greeted her. All knew instantly that Rachel's sojourn on earth was about to end. Esther and Rachel beheld each other; their tearful smiles said it all. Rachel reached out to Josh. "You made me so happy, my other son. How are you managing the residual pain? I'm glad to see you using your cane. If that makes it easier for you to get around, do it. There's nothing to be ashamed of. Our hearts are filled with joy knowing that you are still with us. Give me a hug and kiss; I've missed you so much."

"Thanks for calling me son. I love you too, Mom. I'm doing OK with the pain. I'm glad to be here for Miriam and the children. Is there anything Dad or I can do to make you more comfortable?"

Rachel at last consented to let the family care for her. Elsa made sure there was plenty of food on hand, particularly snacks and goodies for the children. Maddie was fourteen and Jethro ten. They had good and healthy appetites. Between Esther, Elsa, and Miriam, the children and the men were well taken care of. When Rachel was sufficiently medicated, she could enjoy being with her family. The visit turned into a celebration of her life. Miriam asked Sister Maria-Angelika to be with them. She was delighted to meet Miriam's family but was devastated when she saw Rachel. What the cancer had done to her was beyond belief.

Elsa arranged for a feast to be served in the apartment on the evening of September 26. Some ate in the dining room and others in the adjacent parlor. Rachel was seated in the comfortable plush chair. She was thrilled to be surrounded by all who mattered to her. It was a convivial evening of recalling happier days and memories. She was thankful for Samuel's attention to her medicinal needs. He tried to make her as comfortable as possible. At last they all retired. Miriam held her mother as tightly as she dared and kissed her good-night. Jochanaan was the last one to wish her a good night.

Rachel slowly made her way over to her desk. She started to write a note to Miriam and Jochanaan.

Rosh Hashanah Eve, 1973

My Dearest Children,

I'm writing this note with a heavy heart. I thank you for being with me during these last days. It meant the world to me to have you nearby. I tried to be brave, but the pain I am suffering is nearly unbearable. I feel I have hurt enough. I'm pleading with God to release me from my suffering and take me home.

You have been worth all the trials and tribulations I suffered in my life. I'm sad about the loss of both your fathers. Fritz came into my life when I needed him the most, and I do not just mean as a man. He was my friend and advisor; more importantly, he was father, grandfather, and friend to you and your loved ones. He helped me through some of the saddest days in my entire life. When I suddenly lost him seven years ago, my life came to a complete standstill.

I feel secure in the knowledge that both of you have found your way in life. I am at peace with you, dear children. I regret the years you lived with Sister Maria-Angelika, Miriam Daniella. At the same time, I believe your father and I made the right decision under the cir-

cumstances. Shielding you from the evil visited upon us was worth the sacrifice we made. I am overjoyed to have had the time together that we were allotted by the Almighty since the end of the war.

I look back on the happiest years I was allowed to spend with you, Jochanaan. Later, we didn't always see eye to eye about what you desired, but I'm grateful Fritz taught me to love you for the person you are, not the person I wanted you to be. I'm at last at peace.

I'm not sure if I shall survive this night. I feel my end is near. I look forward to my release. Kiss and hug my little angels, Maddie and Jethro. Tell them that I loved them very much. Hug all for whom I cared. I'm ready to meet my maker.

> *With all my love,*
> *Mom, Rachel Adina, Bubbe Rachel*

Rachel set the note on the credenza and slowly crept back to the plush chair. Every step was torture; she wasn't certain she would make it without collapsing to the floor. At last, she sat and closed her eyes. She almost felt like she was in a trance. Her entire life flashed in front of her eyes; it was a parade of events of pleasures and pain. Once more, she beheld the faces of her loving grandparents. There were the days of pleasure with Otto during their time in Munich; she remembered the night of ecstasy that gave them Miriam Daniella and the hateful actions by the Nazis. She felt the heartbreak of giving up Miriam into the loving hands of Sister Maria-Angelika. How could she forget the horrors of Theresienstadt and the pain inflicted by Klemens Rost and the pleasure of her final revenge? Or the rape and the love linked to Johann that gave her Jochanaan? The memory of Johann's murder passed her eyes. The friendship with Elsa who shared in her joys and pains since their meeting in Theresienstadt. Rachel recalled their first meeting with Frederick Fritz Unrat and the endless walk from Dresden to Essen. There was the reunion with Miriam and the joyful years that followed. How could she forget the encounter with the twin sister, Juliana Daniella, a total stranger until she threatened her life? She was thankful for the years she was allowed to experience with Fritz. Perhaps her greatest joys as she grew older were Maddie and Jethro, her grandchildren.

Rachel did not live to greet the new year.

Jochanaan was the first to be up. He went to kiss Rachel good morning. He knocked on his mother's bedroom door. There was no answer. After repeated attempts at getting a response, he opened the door. Her bed was untouched. He walked all through the apartment. His heart began to beat faster. His brow was covered with perspiration. His tunic became soaked from the perspiration escaping his body. He felt dirty. The last room he approached was the dining room. The door was locked. He called for Elsa.

Neither of them wanted to attempt to break down the dining room door. Elsa called Miriam and Josh. Samuel got on the phone. "Don't do anything until we are there. It may be twenty minutes by the time we get the car out of the parking structure. Don't fear the worst yet. She might have just sat in the comfortable chair she used all through the meal yesterday. She might be heavily medicated. I have to hang up. They are all ready to get into the car. See you real soon."

They arrived in less than the expected twenty minutes. Samuel tried the locked door and pounded on it with both his fists. There was no response. With one hard push of his right shoulder against the door, he dislodged the lock. The door popped open. The adults were in shock. Esther took the children and walked them into another part of the apartment. Miriam and Jochanaan hugged each other and sobbed. Rachel sat in the plush chair. Her head slumped down. She had been dead for hours. Rachel clutched the Varanasi scarf in her hands.

Miriam found Rachel's letter on the credenza. Samuel Bernstein, MD, called a medical colleague. Rachel had died of natural causes in her sleep. Her body was prepared for burial before sunset. Her remains were placed in a simple pine coffin. She was shrouded in the Varanasi scarf.

It was Rosh Hashanah 1973. Thirty-six years had passed since Rachel's grandmother died on the eve of Rosh Hashanah in 1937, the night she had bestowed the Blue Sapphire Amulet on Rachel. Her daughter, Miriam Daniella, would have the honor of giving the precious jewel to her first-born, Madeline Rachel Esther Bernstein, in a mere seven years. The chain of honored recipients would remain unbroken.

Miriam called Sister Maria-Angelika; she needed her to be at Rachel's funeral. Samuel agreed to drive the aging nun to the cemetery. Rabbi Weisskopf conducted the final rites for Rachel. The only mourners not decked out in stark black were Jochanaan and Sister Maria-Angelika. Her flowing cream-colored habit with touches of black gave her an almost angelic countenance as she walked up to the Salm cemetery plot. The huge grave marker bearing prominently the name of Salm could be seen from a considerable distance. It was one of the largest at the Rondell. Only her family and the very closest of friends came to bid goodbye to Rachel. Rabbi Weisskopf spoke the Mourner's Kaddish. All stepped up close to commit the traditional shovel of dirt.

Jochanaan was one of the last. His face looked solemn. He removed his only adornment from his chest, holding it in his right hand. He made the sign of the cross over Rachel's coffin. His eyes were flooded in tears. He could hardly speak. Placing the cross back on his chest, he bent down to grasp a handful of the soft earth. He whispered, "I loved you. Thank you for giving me life. Farewell, my gentle and courageous protector." He softly let the soil drift from his hand onto Rachel's shrine, saying, "Ashes to ashes; dust to dust." He turned to face Miriam and her family. He walked away.

Miriam, Madeline, and Sister Maria-Angelika were at last

standing close to Rachel's grave. Miriam took off the Blue Sapphire Amulet. She made the sign of the cross holding the amulet over Rachel's coffin. She gave it to Sister Maria-Angelika to hold for a moment. Mother Superior handed it back to Miriam. "It's yours now to pass on." She smiled with tears in her loving eyes. Miriam let Madeline touch the amulet before she placed it again around her own neck. She quietly repeated the Mourner's Kaddish. As a final act of kindness, the last three mourners took a handful of soil and placed it on Rachel's coffin. Miriam Daniella hugged her child as she spoke her final words to her mother. "Thank you for all you gave; your love for me was immeasurable." She glanced at the Salm grave marker and smiled through her tears at Maddie. She was pleased to see the latest engraving by the stonemason. She spoke lovingly to her beautiful daughter. "There's one thing for certain, dear Maddie, Bubbe Rachel will never be remembered as 'U-N-B-E-K-A-N-N-T.'"

Acknowledgment

THE author wishes to express his sincere gratitude to Graham Schofield for his invaluable critical support and suggestions during the editorial process of this work. Expressions of great appreciation are extended to the staff of Wheatmark Publishing Services for their efforts in bringing this first novel to fruition. Many thanks are due those who have encouraged the author to write, in particular the members of the Green Valley Writers' Forum and family and friends. Last but not least, the author wishes to recognize his wife Lynne with heartfelt thankfulness for her endless hours of reading and providing critical editorial commentary.

CPSIA information can be obtained
at www.ICGtesting.com
Printed in the USA
LVHW09s2321260918
591534LV00002B/175/P